The Dreamcatcher

Maggie Christensen

For another bookshop owner - Annie of *Annie's Books on Peregian*
with gratitude for all of her support

One

It was a typical spring day in Florence, Oregon. A fine mist covered the river, a sharp breeze was blowing up, and rain wasn't far away. The line of buildings opposite the river had been erected some years back and were now home to several shopkeepers. The old-fashioned wooden frontages lent a sense of history to the Old Town, which was an area loved by tourists and locals alike. The overnight rain had left several puddles on the roadway where a family of three jays were competing for the available water.

Ellen Williams stood outside her bookshop, *The Reading Nook*, and examined the window display with a critical eye. Since she'd moved into the premises a few years earlier and set it up as a bookshop, she'd worked hard to make it what it was today. Now, tourists to the area headed there, eager to sample her wide selection of local and Native American offerings, while the locals enjoyed her skills in sourcing hard-to-find books as well as the provision of new releases by their favorite authors.

Weak sunlight sparkled on the cobweb-fine threads and feathers in the dreamcatcher hanging from the top of the window. She'd made it the focus of the display for the Native American fantasy books, much loved by the local youths. Ellen sighed, and fingered her long plait of black hair streaked with grey as a gust of wind blew the tails of her shirt. Gazing at the dreamcatcher, she wished she could catch her good dreams and dismiss the recent nightmares. The display would have to do. She didn't have time to tweak it any further this morning.

Turning away, she became conscious of a dark cloud obscuring the sun and shivered with a sense of foreboding.

Signs and portents weren't unusual to Ellen. Since childhood she'd been able to see things others couldn't. Usually they helped her to see the future for others, enabling her to assist them through difficult times. This was something different. It was as if she could smell trouble brewing, but without her usual innate sense of what it referred to. It seemed she had no option but to wait for something to happen, something momentous perhaps, something over which she would have no control.

Back inside, Ellen lit the scented candle she always kept behind the counter, breathed in the calming aroma of bergamot and geranium, and set to unpacking and sorting a carton of books which had arrived the previous day. She'd hoped to lure the author featured in her display to a book signing, but his publisher had replied that Peter Travers wasn't doing any signings in the foreseeable future. Ellen was in the process of setting up the inside display, when she heard the familiar jangle of bell above the door.

"You Ellen?"

Ellen nodded. Accustomed to meeting most men's eyes, she had to raise her head to meet his steely blue ones. Tall and broad shouldered, wearing a soft dun colored, fringed suede jacket, the man's faded blonde hair was tied back in a shoulder-length ponytail. A scruffy goatee and unkempt moustache completed the picture. He slouched in the entrance, filling the doorway. His neck was festooned with the turquoise jewelry usually only worn by members of the Native American community, but his Nordic looks indicated he didn't belong to one of the local tribes. *His* ancestry hailed from much farther away. All of this must have passed through her mind in an instant, because the man was speaking.

"Ron's sister?" he asked.

Ellen nodded again, warily. Coming so closely on her presentiment of disaster, she had a strong sense that his arrival and her premonition were somehow linked. *What had her brother been up to now? And who on earth was this guy pretending to be a Native American? Could he be the source of her fears?* She'd come across a few wannabes in her life and had no time for them. They had no understanding of the profound history of her people. They were an insult to all she held dear.

"It's Ron." He seemed to be fumbling for words. "Maybe you'd better sit down." He looked around. There were a number of chairs in the shop, but none by the door. They were all hidden in secret corners designed to enable readers to curl up and lose themselves in a book.

"Spit it out!" Ellen's stomach churned, her anxiety leading her to speak more sharply than usual. Her hands curled into fists, and her quickened breathing sounded loud in her ears. Since being invalided out of the forces after Vietnam, her older brother, Ron, had shunned finding gainful employment and spent his days jawing about his experiences with a group of old comrades down by the lake. He'd returned a broken man, in body and spirit, and to the despair of his family, was content to spend his time with those guys, rehashing what he saw as the highlight of his life. But he was still her brother, the brother she loved, irritating though he might be.

"What's up with Ron? Did he send you here?" she asked, beginning to suspect her visitor's motives. "And who are you, anyway?" She looked him up and down as dismissively as she could. One of Ron's old Vietnam cronies, no doubt – another layabout.

"Travis, Travis Petersen," he smiled, a wide smile showing a mouthful of perfect teeth.

Travis, he *would* be a Travis, Ellen thought. All the Travises she'd ever met meant trouble. "So?" Ellen folded her arms to still her trembling. *Was there really something the matter with Ron?* She tapped her foot impatiently, her earlier sense of foreboding in the forefront of her mind. *Was this what she'd been warned about?*

"Ron's in trouble." The man stretched his arm up and leant against the doorframe as he spoke. Clearly he wasn't going anywhere soon.

"Tell me something new."

"No, really." He removed his arm from the doorway and straightened up. "He caught his arm on a boat hook. He needs you to drive him to hospital. Can't manage it himself, and I couldn't take him on the bike," he shrugged, a bashful grin flashing across his face.

Ellen burst into movement, picking up her keys and purse in one swoop, and throwing a pashmina over her shoulders. "Why didn't you say so right away? I'll just leave a note on the door," she said, writing one quickly.

The man followed Ellen out of the shop, hesitating on the sidewalk to point to his Harley. "Would you…"

Ellen shook her head, looking at the customised Harley complete with riser bars, reminiscent of *Easy Rider*. Come to think of it, the fellow did have a look of Dennis Hopper – Dennis Hopper with blonde hair and a beard. "I'll drive. Be better that way."

She climbed into her car, which was parked nearby, wondering how long it had been since she rode on the back of a motorbike. She shook her head. Not since she and Ron were teenagers together and… no, she wouldn't go down that track. Those days were long gone. She was a respectable shopkeeper, spinster of the parish, and set to remain that way. She drove carefully along the street and out of town toward the lake, unsurprised when Travis roared past her on the bike.

When Ellen arrived at the lake, Ron and Travis were sitting on the grass talking and laughing as if they hadn't a care in the world. She stomped out of her car ready to do battle, her plait flying. Usually even-tempered, Ellen's brother had the ability to provoke her to anger with his laidback attitude to life. Using his battle scars, mental and physical, as an excuse, he'd holed up in his cabin at Yachats and managed to avoid any family responsibility, leaving it all to Ellen. Now here he was, having dragged her away from work, casually chatting and laughing with this wastrel.

"So here you are," Ellen said and walked towards him smiling. Then she noted the blood-soaked towel wrapped around Ron's forearm. Her relief might be short-lived. He might be more seriously injured than he appeared. "Well, let's get you to hospital."

*

"Want a coffee?" Travis' voice broke the silence.

Ellen looked at her brother's friend, seated beside her on the hard blue chairs in the Emergency Department, along with numerous other injured folk and their relatives. The place was not conducive to conversation, even if she had anything to say to her companion. Ron was being treated in a cubicle somewhere, and Ellen had been trying to ignore the figure sitting beside her for the past half hour. She was about to refuse, but a coffee would be good, and she didn't want to move in case Ron, or the doctor, appeared.

"Okay. Black, no sugar."

"Yeah, I took you for one of those. Sweet enough, huh?" Travis walked off before she could reply, giving her time to calm down. She guessed the guy was only trying to be helpful.

Ellen sighed, trying to work out how she'd break the news to Mom and Dad. They'd had enough to deal with in the past year, with her cousin from Australia appearing out of the blue. That had really upset the applecart, bringing back memories of an uncle Ellen hadn't known existed. Ellen had been overjoyed to discover her new cousin, and the two had got on famously. And now, although initially returning to Australia to open her own bookshop, Jenny was back in Oregon and was staying with her partner, Mike, up at Seal Rock.

Lost in thought, Ellen was surprised when a large hand bearing a paper cup full of coffee appeared in front of her.

"This do?"

"Thanks." She took a sip of the warm liquid and raised her eyes to look at the man beside her. Maybe he wasn't so bad. After all, he *had* informed her of Ron's predicament, though she wasn't sure why he hadn't driven Ron to the hospital himself. "Don't you drive?" she asked bluntly, voicing her thoughts as she wrapped both hands around the cup, the warmth preferable to drinking the weak liquid that passed for coffee.

"No, only the bike." His reply was equally blunt and brooked no further discussion.

Ellen decided to try another tack. "How do you know Ron? You're not from around here, are you?"

"You're right there." Travis leaned back, crossing his right leg over the left knee and revealing a few inches of tanned skin. "Hail from further south – California. Small place called Carpinteria. Near Santa Barbara, but not so socially pretentious. Met Ron in Vietnam. Back then we were good mates. Lost touch. Found him on Facebook." He tugged on his beard reflectively. "Who'd have thought it? And who'd have thought he'd have a sister like you?"

Ellen felt her blood rise. If he thought he could charm her with his compliments, he was mightily mistaken. "Are you here on vacation?"

she asked, refusing to rise to the bait.

"Vacation? See how I like it here. May stay on. Bunking down with Ron at the mo' – waiting to figure out how the land lies."

And what does that mean? Another of Ron's lame ducks, though this one looks pretty hale and hearty. No obvious signs of war wounds. But Ellen knew that not all war wounds showed on the surface. Her brother bore testament to that. She decided not to interrogate him any further.

*

Travis stole a glance at his companion. She sure looked riled. What had he said? This sister of Ron's took some getting used to. Tall for a woman, with a round, open face like her brother. Despite her obvious impatience with him, she emanated a sense of peace. Her all-seeing deep brown eyes and melodious voice had a calming influence, making Travis feel he could curl up in her and find comfort. She was quite a woman, but it seemed he'd been putting his big foot in it ever since he walked into her shop. And what a shop it was! He'd dearly like to spend some time browsing around the shelves, sure he'd pick up some gems, and he was intrigued by the display she'd been working on. But Ron was his first priority.

When they'd come across each other on the 'net he couldn't believe it. He thought he'd left Ron for dead in 'Nam, but there he was, large as life and twice as ugly. Then, when things had gotten bad down home, Ron's invitation to visit had come like a gift from the gods. He'd only been here a week and liked what he'd seen so far. Places like Yachats and Florence were about the right fit for him these days. Travis was tired of California, the glitz that seemed to spill over from places like LA and San Francisco. He was ready to settle down in a small town, and the Oregon Coast seemed to have everything he needed. He couldn't sponge off Ron for much longer, though. Best to find something for himself.

"Good thing you were with Ron." Ellen's voice broke into his thoughts. "He'll need someone to help him for a time. At least it was his left hand…"

"Sure thing. Might stay around a bit." Travis could see Ellen was itching to ask more about him and was glad she didn't pursue it. "Here's the main man," he added, seeing Ron walking down the corridor.

"They patched you up, then?" he enquired, as his friend held up a heavily bandaged arm for their inspection.

Ellen rose quickly to hug Ron. Travis watched the elegant woman move towards her brother – a movement that could almost be described as a glide. He shook his head, baffled yet again that his old army buddy could have been hiding this sister of his, with her regal bearing.

"You can go home then, Ron?" Ellen's lilting voice was music to Travis's ears. A man could drown and go to heaven in that voice.

"Right as rain. Or will be in a few weeks. You'll see me through till then, bud?"

"Sure." Travis clapped Ron on the shoulder. "We'd better get you home, then. See you there." He walked out to his bike whistling and left the other two to make their own way to Ellen's car. As he rode up the highway, Travis cautioned himself. Ellen was his buddy's sister, as good as family. It didn't do to mess with family, and given his recent history that was all he was good for. Now he'd caught up with his old buddy again, he didn't want to shit on him – and messing with his little sister would be exactly that. Still…

*

"Thanks, sis," Ron eased himself into Ellen's car and closed the door.

"You okay?" Ellen checked, before driving off and heading northwards. Although she hadn't planned on this interruption to her day, she was glad to be able to help her brother.

"I'll live. Bit of a bitch, though." Ron leant back in his seat, and Ellen felt his eyes on her. "You didn't fancy a bike ride?"

"No, I remember yours too well." There was a smile in her voice, and both were silent remembering their teenage years.

"Those were the days," Ron said, "before…" His unspoken words hung between them. The war had changed her brother. The cheerful and outgoing boy had become a silent and morose man, preferring his own company or even that of fellow veterans to his family.

"This Travis…" Ellen began, not sure what she wanted to ask.

"Knew him in 'Nam," Ron said, clearly unwilling to expand on those few words.

"Mmm."

They drove on in silence, before Ellen tried again, "The folks... do you want me to...?"

"Tell them? Suppose you could."

"Don't you think they should know? They'll be worried about you."

"Don't tell them, then. I'll stay away till it's mended."

Ellen bit her lip to stem her retort. She'd tell them. She knew her parents would worry if Ron stayed away for the time it'd take his arm to mend, and she didn't want to burden them any more than necessary. "That's not a good idea. You know how Mom becomes anxious when you don't drop in, thinks something's happened to you. You're there seldom enough as it is. Best she knows."

"Your call," Ron said, as the car drew to a halt outside his house where Travis' bike was already parked. "See you, sis," he called as he struggled out and slammed the car door behind him.

*

Ellen hurried back to *The Reading Nook* and removed the *Back Later* sign from the door. The whole episode with Ron had taken much longer than she'd anticipated. A wasted day! And she'd had to make polite conversation with that waste of space called Travis. Though it would be useful to have him there with Ron for a while – save her having to drive up to Yachats to check he was okay. She'd drop in on Mom and Dad tonight to let them know the news. Meanwhile, there was just time to put the finishing touches to the display she'd been starting on when she was interrupted.

Ellen had placed the last book in position and was standing back to admire her work when she caught sight of the photo on the back of the book. Picking it up, she gave it a closer look. There was something familiar about the face, but she couldn't quite... At that moment, she heard a roll of thunder, and at the same time, the phone rang. She shook herself and grabbed the phone, "Yes?"

"Ellen?"

"Jenny, good to hear your voice. How's everything? You got back okay, then?"

"Yesterday, yes. I wanted to ring you first thing, but by the time we'd caught up with Maddy and Ben's welcoming committee, jet lag caught up with *us*. But we're feeling more refreshed today, and I want to see you. There's so much to tell."

"I'd love to see you too, but…"

"Is something wrong?"

"No… sorry… yes. That brother of mine has gone and gotten a boat hook through his arm, and I have to go round to tell Mom and Dad. I don't know how they're going to take it. It's been quite a year." Ellen sighed.

"Sorry to hear that, and I guess *I* didn't help with your mom and dad. But it's not like you to be in the dumps. You're the one who kept me going last year when I was in such a mess."

"You're right. I'm not my usual self. I had this strange premonition today and have been having these dreadful nightmares… But, yes, love to catch up. Drop over tomorrow, why don't you?" For the first time that day, Ellen's customary sense of calm reasserted itself. Jenny was back, and this time it might be her turn to provide a sympathetic ear.

Two

The door closed, and the two men heard Ellen's car start up. "So that's your sister? You might have told me."

"Told you what? It's just Ellen, my little sister."

"So you say." Travis sucked on his cheek. "Sure you're okay with me here a tad longer?"

"Look at me," Ron gestured with his bum arm. "I should be thanking you for staying on. Just one thing… my car. It's still out there at the lake."

"Don't look at me." Travis slumped into an old armchair and picked up a toothpick. "You know…"

"And you haven't driven since?"

"No. Find it hard even to sit in one."

"Hmm." Ron seemed about to add something, then pointed to the fridge. "Love a brew. And help yourself."

The pair were soon sitting either side of the wrought iron table on Ron's veranda, looking over the ocean. They sat in silence for a while, Ron sipping his beer while Travis nursed a Coke.

"She married? Kids?" Travis downed the remains of his drink and squashed the can in one hand, tossing it down onto the wooden deck. He leaned back in his chair and looked up at the sky.

"No kids, never married. There was someone…" Ron hesitated, as if wondering how much to say. "She's not been lucky with her men. Hell, I can't talk. Relationships aren't my thing either. Guess we've both disappointed the folks in that regard." He took another gulp of beer. "Interested?"

"Not me!" Travis was quick to deny. "But I seem to have put my foot in it with her. Not sure what I said out of turn."

"Another?" Ron held up his now empty bottle and gestured to his companion, then rose to walk back into the house.

"Sure," Travis stretched his legs and rested his feet on the veranda rail. He had the impression Ron's sister was out of bounds, but couldn't let it go. He waited till Ron returned with a fresh bottle of beer under one arm and a can in the other hand.

"Thanks." He was wondering how to continue the conversation, when Ron spoke.

"You started to tell me about your travels, back there at the lake. Seems you rode the length and breadth of the west coast."

Travis dropped his feet, and holding his drink in both hands, leant his elbows on his knees. "Sure did. For close to two years. From California up through Canada, back down through Mexico then back home. Hiked through the National Parks, too – Yosemite, Crater Lake, Yellowstone, Lassen. You name it, I've been there." He sighed and gazed off into the distance. "Didn't make a blind bit of difference. I couldn't shake it."

He looked up to see Ron nod in agreement, and rolled the can of drink between his hands. "Going back home wasn't the answer. It was waiting for me – waiting for me there. I had to get away, make a fresh start." Travis gestured to the ocean in front of them. "It's peaceful here. No memories. Maybe …" his voice broke.

"It's okay, pal. You're among friends. We all feel that way sometimes. No shame in it."

"But there is!" Travis snapped. "There is shame. It was all my fault! I don't deny that, I can't. And I can't forget either." He finished his drink in one gulp. "Mind if I rest awhile? I'm not good company like this."

*

"Mom, I'm here!" Ellen pushed open the door and walked through the familiar old house. Her mother bustled out of the kitchen, wiping her hands on an apron.

"Thank goodness," she said, hugging Ellen fervently. "I didn't know what to do. Your dad…"

"What about me?" Dick Williams came out of the kitchen. "Ellen, what brings you here on a week night?"

Unsure what was going on, Ellen looked from one to the other, then, pulling herself together, chose to ignore her mother's concerns. "It's Ron," she began.

"What's the lad done now?" Ellen's father's voice held the impatient tone he tended to use when his son was mentioned.

"Dad! I've been to the hospital with him. No, Mom he's okay," Ellen reassured her mother, seeing her begin to wring her hands. "He had an altercation with a boat hook and came out the worse for it. But they've bandaged him up, and he's home now."

"But how will he manage?" Rita Williams started to remove her apron, then seemed to remember something and gave her husband a worried look.

"Sit down, Mom." Ellen led her parents into the lounge room and waited till both were seated, her father slouched in his armchair, while her mother sat on the edge of hers. "As I said, he's okay. It's his left hand, so he can still manage to do things for himself, and he has an old army buddy staying with him at the moment."

"Oh?" Rita sounded surprised.

"Travis something. Up from Carpinteria." Ellen looked at the pair, hoping for some sign of recognition.

"Haven't heard of that one," her father said. "But then, we don't know all of Ron's old buddies, do we, Rita? Keeps that side of his life to himself."

"Well, he's here now, and he's bunking down with Ron for a few days, so that'll see him right. No need to rush up there."

Rita visibly relaxed and rose, signaling Ellen to join her.

"I'll just see to dinner. You'll be staying, Ellen?"

"Yes, Mom. Anything I can do to help?"

The two women left Dick picking up his paper. Closing the kitchen door behind her, Ellen rounded on her mother. "Now what's this about Dad? He seems perfectly all right to me, but you sounded concerned on the phone."

"He is now." Rita picked up a knife then put it down again on the chopping board beside some potatoes. "He was real strange earlier. We were sitting right here." She pointed to the kitchen table. "We were talking about the newspaper delivery, and he was laying down the law in his usual fashion when… when he stopped."

"He stopped talking – is that all?"

"He stopped in the middle of what he was saying and stared into space. It was weird… as if he'd been turned to stone…, then a few minutes later, he continued with what he'd been saying. As if nothing had happened."

"Did you ask…?"

"He acted as if it was me that was mad. You know what your dad's like."

"Often wrong, never in doubt." Ellen laughed, then sobered up. "But it's no laughing matter, Mom. Is this the first time it's happened?"

"Ye…es, but…"

"But what?"

"He's becoming a tad forgetful. Nothing specific, and I forget things too. It's all part of getting older, I suppose. Oh, I'm probably worrying about nothing." Rita picked up the knife again and began slicing the potatoes. "Forget it, dear. Nothing for you to worry about."

"It was enough for you to ring me."

"But you were coming over anyway. So that's all right. It's over and done with. It might not happen again. It just gave me a turn."

Ellen hugged her mother. "Let me know if it does, you hear me? I'm not far away. I can drop in anytime." As she said it, Ellen realized this was one more thing she had to cope with. Aware her parents weren't getting any younger, it was only a matter of time before they'd need more care. And Ron certainly wouldn't be there to take his share of what could become a burden, albeit a pleasant one. It would all be up to her. Forcing down the resentment threatening to boil up, she hugged her mother tighter.

Extricating herself from Ellen's hug, Rita wiped her eyes with her knuckles. "You're a dear. But it'll be all right. I don't know what we'd do without you."

Ellen bit her lip, aware she didn't spend as much time with her parents as she might. She lived in the same town and managed to get home for dinner most weekends, but apart from that… She vowed there and then to change, to drop round more frequently – and to prevail upon Ron to do the same, once he was mobile again.

"Now, leave me to it. You go through and keep the old man company. We don't see nearly enough of you."

Ellen followed her mother's instruction.

"Finished your secret woman's business?" Dick lowered his paper.

"It's not like that, Dad. Mom wanted to talk with me. Nothing secret about it."

"Hmph," Dick muttered to himself. He folded his paper and fixed Ellen with a steely glare. "Who's this Travis staying with Ron? Haven't heard Ron mention him."

"Well, you wouldn't, would you? Ron keeps things pretty much to himself. But Travis, he didn't impress me. Another of Ron's lame ducks, wearing a swatch of Navajo jewelry, as if he had a right to it." Ellen's voice rose, remembering how Travis had slouched in her shop doorway as if he had a right to be there, too. The heat rose to her face as she remembered his broad shoulders and careless compliments.

"Don't be too harsh on the lad."

Ellen gazed at her father in surprise. Maybe he really was sick. It wasn't like him to defend one of her brother's layabout friends.

"He'll be one he knows from Vietnam, I'll be bound. We'll never understand what those guys were up against, so it's not for us to judge. And what makes you so sure he doesn't have some of our blood in him?"

"His appearance, for one; blonde, blue eyed, sharp features – high cheek bones, aquiline nose…" Ellen would have continued, but her father interrupted,

"Seems you took a good look at him, hmm?"

Ellen blushed, realizing she *had* noticed a lot about this man she purported to despise. She could fool herself, but not her dad. He'd always had a way of seeing right through any subterfuge. She had no idea why Travis had engendered such a strong reaction in her. It wasn't anything he'd said or done. It was simply that he was there, that he existed, and had barged into her world. Something about him spelled danger. Arriving as he did, so soon after the portent of disaster, her subconscious had linked the two, that was all. *Was she jumping to an unwarranted conclusion? Could Travis be harmless? Or did his arrival herald the catastrophe she'd sensed?*

Three

Jenny bounced into *The Reading Nook*, the doorbell jangling behind her. "It's good to be back!" she exclaimed. "We've tried to create the same atmosphere back home, but I guess it *is* on the other side of the world."

"So it's different," Ellen laughed. "And I bet it bears your unique style."

"And Rosa's," added Jenny, referring to the friend who'd joined her in the new enterprise. "Without her I couldn't be here. I need a partner to hold the fort."

"Bet Mike's happy about that too. And how *is* your significant other? That's the term, I believe."

Jenny blushed. "He's good. You were right – there *were* good things in store for me. But what's been happening here while I've been gone? Emails don't tell the whole story."

"True," Ellen said, hugging her cousin, "and you've stopped by at a good time. I was about to fetch a coffee. Why don't I close for a bit, and we go across the road to catch up?"

"I was hoping you'd say that. Gosh, I've missed this place," she added, as the two women crossed to the coffee shop on the river, where they'd shared many confidences the previous year.

Ellen ordered the coffees while Jenny sat gazing at the river, lost in a reverie. She started when Ellen pulled out the chair beside her.

"Now tell me all about it," Ellen said. She listened without interrupting, sipping her coffee, while Jenny regaled her with her news.

She told of her excitement in starting her bookshop, discovering her friend Rosa wanted to join her in the enterprise and Mike's surprise arrival in Australia.

"But it wasn't a surprise to *you*, was it?" Jenny asked finally. "You knew," she accused her companion.

Ellen smiled, her secret smile. "Well, I did have an inkling…"

"All that talk of challenges and things working out. You really had me spooked. I didn't believe a word of it."

"No?"

"Not really. But…"

"Aha, so you did feel there was something?"

"Maybe," said Jenny. "Now what about you? What's this about premonitions and nightmares? Doesn't sound like the calm lady I came to know and love last year. What's been going on?" She cupped her drink with both hands and raised her eyebrows.

Ellen sighed and lowered her eyes, working out how much to tell Jenny. Her cousin was beaming and full of the joys of life, so different from the worried woman she'd first met. *Was it fair to burden her with her own troubles?*

"Come on," Jenny insisted, "spill."

Ellen pushed her now empty mug to one side and clasped her hands on the table. She gazed out at the peaceful river, then back to the woman sitting opposite. The tables had turned. This time it was Jenny who was at peace with herself, while Ellen was filled with confusion.

"It started a few weeks ago," she began. "The nightmares. Strange, I'm not sure who they refer to. I can't…" she paused, drew breath, then began again. "I don't usually see myself in events but…" She shook her head as if to untangle her thoughts. "This time it's not clear. It's as if I'm there, but not there. Oh, I'm not making any sense." Ellen waved her hands about in an attempt to dismiss her words.

"No, go on." Jenny was listening intently, leaning on the table with both elbows. "I'm interested. You can't stop now."

"There's a car. I seem to be in it, yet not in it. There's a huge bang and a child…" Ellen's eyes began to water as she spoke. "The child…" her voice petered away.

"And that's it?"

"That, and a strange premonition I had yesterday. I was standing looking at the shop window when a dark cloud passed over and…" Ellen began to shiver uncontrollably. "There, it happened again just thinking of it. Then this friend of Ron's appeared out of the blue," she added.

"And you think all those events are related?"

"I don't know what to think."

"Mmm."

Ellen sat back, relieved to have put her misgivings into words. Somehow sharing them with Jenny had taken away the feeling of dread which had been stalking her. Picking up her purse, she began to rise. "I'd better be getting back. I do have a shop to run."

"When are we going to see you up at Seal Rock? Mike and I would love to have you to dinner and I'm sure Maddy would like to see you again too," Jenny said, referring to her godmother.

"Soon, yes. Mom and Dad…" Ellen paused. This was one more thing to cause her concern. "It's Dad. Mom's worried about him, so I plan to visit them more often, and Ron's cut up his arm – on a boat hook of all things so…"

"Kill two birds, then. Why not come up to see us when you visit Ron? I presume you *will* be visiting him?"

"Ye…es." Ellen's voice wavered. Seeing Ron probably meant seeing Travis, and the thought of seeing *him* again was not something she wanted to contemplate. "Sure, can I let you know?"

"Well don't take too long about it."

By this time, the two women had reached the door of the bookshop, and they hugged before parting.

"Take care, now," Jenny admonished, before stepping into her car, but Ellen was already opening the door, and the rest of her words were lost as the bell made its unique sound.

Fortified by the coffee and the long chat with Jenny, Ellen went to her office at the rear of the store and began the tedious task of sorting out her invoices. She was engrossed in her paperwork when the sound of the doorbell interrupted her, and she heard a familiar voice.

"Ellen, where are you? Have you heard?" Coralie's voice was laden with doom as the owner of the hairdressing salon next door came closer. Finally she was standing outside Ellen's small office, her forehead wrinkled, and her usually immaculate hair looking as if she had been continuously running her fingers through it.

"Heard what?" Ellen' heart was booming.

"They're going to tear us down!"

Ellen stood up and walked slowly over towards the distraught woman. "Steady on. What do you mean, tear us down? Who's going to do that?"

"The developers. It's in today's paper. They're planning to buy out our line of shops and build a row of condos with some hideous thing they call a retail precinct underneath. Just like they've done at the other end of the river." The words flew out of Coralie's mouth. She took a deep breath, clearly preparing to continue.

"Slow down," Ellen took Coralie by the arms, propelled her back to the main part of the shop and sat her down into a well stuffed armchair. Coralie began panting heavily, seemingly having difficulty in breathing. "Now, take your time. You're having a panic attack. Let me…" Ellen adroitly whipped one of her brown paper bags – usually used for packing books – from behind the counter and placed it over Coralie's mouth. "Now breathe… slowly… that's it." Ellen held the bag there for a few seconds.

Slowly the younger woman began to breathe normally and pushed away the bag. "Sorry, I don't know what came over me. You heard what I said, didn't you? What are we going to do?"

"The local paper, you say? A news item?" Ellen decided that to be brisk with her neighbor was the only way she'd get any sense out of her.

"I don't know," Coralie wailed. "There's a picture too, an artist's impression or some such thing. Looks real ugly, all modern-like. My last client was reading it. I saw it over her shoulder when I was drying her hair. I had to wait till she left, to tell you."

"So you don't have the paper?" Ellen was fast losing patience, but she had an inkling that maybe this was for real. There was the presentiment of doom she'd had, but none of this tied in with her nightmares – or with Travis Petersen. She shook her head. She'd wait till closing time and buy a paper on the way home. Maybe there was nothing in it, but it wasn't like Coralie to panic.

"No," Coralie pushed herself up in the chair and ran her fingers over her hair in an attempt to bring it back to its usual casual froth of blonde curls. "I'd better be getting back."

"Anyone home?" The loud male drawl broke into their conversation, causing Ellen to turn with a start, and Coralie to rise preening.

"Wa...al, who have we here?" Panic forgotten, Coralie sashayed towards the intruder, hips swaying in her workaday black leggings, her loose flowered top clinging to her ample bosom. "New in town?" she intoned, in what she obviously took for a sexy twang.

"What brings *you* back?" Ellen couldn't believe her eyes. "This is Travis, a friend of Ron's," she threw the words at Coralie, noticing as she did so, that this Travis looked a lot more presentable than the one she'd seen the day before.

"Howdy to you too. Ron's car," he said, dangling a set of car keys from his fingers as if daring Ellen to come closer to take them.

Ellen stepped past Coralie, who was gazing up at Travis, now sporting a trimmed beard, neat moustache and chin length hair. "Put them on the counter," she said brusquely, wondering yet again why this man irked her so much. He hadn't said anything inflammatory, yet his arrival so soon after the sign of disaster she'd experienced had set alarm bells ringing. "What does Ron expect me to do with them?" she asked.

"He'd like to have his car up there. Feels a bit lost without it, but he can't drive so..."

"So he'd like me to pick it up for him, I suppose. And how does he expect me to get out to the lake then back down to Florence?"

Travis looked pointedly out of the window to where his Harley was sitting by the kerb.

"No! I'm not going to ride on that thing, not with you, not ever!"

"I could..." Coralie looked from one to the other as if trying to judge who would best suit her purposes.

"Thanks, Coralie. I'll work something out." Ellen faced Travis. "Tell Ron I'll let him know." As an afterthought, and as Travis was turning to leave she asked, "Why didn't he call?"

Travis shuffled and looked at his feet. "We... he... he thought..."

"I get it. He thought I'd refuse. My brother knows me pretty well." She paused, then added, "Or was it your idea to come down here without calling first."

Travis had the grace to look shamed. "No... it wasn't like that..." He shuffled his feet again – an awkward look for such a tall well-built man – then met Ellen's eyes with such an intense stare she couldn't look away. "Had to come down anyway… get myself fixed up," he stroked his now neat beard. "Thought I'd see you again." He took a long breath and looked sideways towards Ellen's author display. "Wanted to check this out too." He pointed to the books set out to their advantage, and the large author picture depicting Peter Travers leaning over some Native American artefacts.

"Sure you did!"

Coralie, as if realizing there was something going on here that she didn't understand or have a part in, began sidling around Travis, who was still standing in the doorway and filling it with his bulk. "Gotta go. My next appointment's due. Maybe I'll see you later?" She treated Travis to a flirtatious smile as she slid past and out the door.

"Bye, Coralie. I'll check that…" but Ellen's words were lost as Travis moved forward, and the door swung closed behind him.

"Really," Travis said, adding, "knew a boy who was fond of those books." He picked up a copy and stroked the spine, his large tanned fingers touching it reverently. It was then Ellen noticed a hint of deep sadness about the man. Her breath caught in her throat making it impossible for her to speak. This man was troubled. He had experienced a profound tragedy and was still held in its thrall, but she couldn't work out exactly what had happened. Any semblance of anger faded as she attempted to come to grips with this new insight.

In an attempt to break her mood she asked, "Fond of the Native American way?" and indicated his jewelry. Today it was resting on a pressed white shirt which he wore under the same fringed jacket as the previous day.

"Actually, yes. May not look it, but among the various Danish, Scottish and Irish there are a few Native Americans among my ancestors. Yes, quite a few – Cherokee. It's always been an interest of mine."

Ellen was stunned. She'd been wrong. She'd maligned this man on at least two counts, but she still couldn't dismiss this odd sense of something about him – something that… He spoke again.

"Suppose a coffee is out of the question?" The poor man looked as if he didn't know what to do with his hands. Ellen surmised that if he'd had a hat, he'd be twirling it.

"Sorry, I've just had one."

Travis' face fell.

Surely the guy couldn't really want to spend time with her? What on earth would they talk about?

"I have masses of paperwork to do too." Ellen gestured to her office as if to convey how busy she was, in the hope that he'd leave.

"Right… well… guess I should go." He turned on his heel and left. Ellen closed the door behind him and leant against it, breathing deeply. Her whole body was shaking. She had no idea why Travis' presence disturbed her so much. She shivered remembering the presentiment she'd experienced just before he came on the scene. Was he a threat to her? To Ron? She couldn't believe her brother was in any danger. They were two of a kind. But herself? She decided to keep out of his way.

Four

"Glad to be back?" Mike Halliday wrapped his arms around Jenny as she stood at the kitchen sink. She'd been lost in thought, gazing out at the trees, but turned into his arms and leant against him with a sigh.

"I am, though it feels strange to be here rather than down the track at Maddy's." The pair stood for a time in silence, only broken by the chirping of birds from outside and the snuffling sound of Ben, Mike's Labrador, around their feet. "Ben's glad to see us again too. Maddy and Marylou looked after him well, but it's not the same as having his master with him."

On hearing his name, Ben gave a short bark and ambled closer to Mike's feet, licking his bare toes. "He's going to have to get used to you being around too, now. Not just the two of us anymore, old fellow." Mike released Jenny to bend down and give his old friend a scratch behind his ear. The dog began to lick Jenny's feet too as if understanding the new order.

"Oow, he tickles!" Jenny leapt back, trying to remove her feet from Ben's ministrations. "Must be time for my shower."

When she returned to the kitchen, Mike was sitting at the table with *The Oregonian* spread out in front of him. A coffee mug in his right hand was making a ring on the paper. Jenny dropped a kiss on his head, and was rewarded by a hand reaching up to encircle her waist. "Anything interesting?"

"Same old, same old. We may have been on the other side of the world for five months, but nothing much has changed here. What did you have in mind for today?" Mike swung round to face Jenny.

"Oh, I don't know. Maybe another trip to Florence?" she suggested. "When I was in Ellen's shop the other day, I noticed a book display – something about Native American Myths and Legends, I think. I'd like to have a closer look."

"Do you need me with you?" Mike said, attempting to return to his paper.

"You're the expert on these things. I'd like your advice before I buy anything."

"Surely Ellen…" he began, then as Jenny looked downcast, relented, "Okay, I'll get dressed, then. After all, that's why we're here – to be together, not for me to hide out while you go gallivanting."

Jenny smiled at him, her eyes lighting up at his willingness to spend time with her. When they'd met, she'd been widowed for over twenty years, and never expected any more romance in her life. Mike had put paid to that idea, and they'd gradually felt their way into their relationship.

*

"Ellen's certainly gone to town on this one," Mike exclaimed, as he and Jenny stood outside *The Reading Nook* admiring the window display. "Looks very authentic, but then if Ellen can't set up a Native American display, who can?"

"Let's go in," Jenny nudged her companion and grabbed his hand. "Ellen'll think we're mad if she sees us peering in like this." Mike gave her hand a squeeze and grinned, before pushing open the shop door.

"Anyone home?" Jenny called, seeing the shop apparently deserted.

A voice from the back office called "Won't be a sec," and Ellen emerged to greet her friends with warm hugs. "Didn't expect to see you two today."

"Jenny wanted to check out some display of yours," Mike explained, "and your window is looking pretty spectacular."

"Why, thank you. You like my dreamcatcher theme, then?"

"Love it! Did you make it yourself?"

"I wish. No, that's a commercial one, though I do have one I made when I was younger – it's at home, in my bedroom."

"But it's not doing its job catching those nightmares?" Jenny said. "Are you still having them?"

"Not for the past couple of nights, thank goodness. I have other things to worry about." Ellen sat down with a thump and Jenny was concerned to note the lines below her friend's eyes.

"Haven't you been sleeping?" Jenny asked, sitting down beside Ellen and taking her hand. "Women's talk," she whispered to Mike, who sauntered off to browse the shelves at the back of the shop.

"You haven't heard? Didn't you see the paper? They want to tear us down!"

"What? Mike, come here!" Jenny called to her partner, who hurried to join the two women.

"What's up?"

"Listen to this." Jenny turned to Ellen and held her friend's hands in hers. "Now tell Mike," she instructed.

Jenny and Mike listened in disbelief, while Ellen reported what she'd read in the newspaper.

"It was exactly as Coralie said," she finished. "They want to revamp this part of Old Town and turn it into some sort of modern monstrosity with no place for a shop like this." Ellen gestured toward the interior of the bookshop, which was her pride and joy.

"Steady on," Mike spoke calmly as always. "I think I read that article. Didn't realize it was this part of town they were referring to. But my recollection is that it's still at the proposal stage. There are a lot of hoops for the developers to jump through before anything definite happens." He looked around. "I can't imagine the Chamber of Commerce approving anything that'd harm the tourist trade down here. It'll be up to the Florence Building Department to have the final say, and you'll all have a chance to put your views across." Mike pulled on his beard, as if thinking it through. "Yes, I expect you won't be the only one to object to the loss of these historic buildings."

"So what can we do?" Ellen's face brightened at Mike's words, and Jenny patted her hands.

"Leave it to Mike. He's a wealth of information," she said. "Now, on another topic, how's your brother?"

"Oh," Ellen paused, looked down and withdrew her hands from

Jenny's grasp. "I haven't seen him again. But that friend of his, Travis –
he appeared the other day with Ron's car keys."

Jenny raised her eyebrows. "But what…?"

"Exactly! Seems the pair of them expected me to ride on the bum's
bike up to the lake to fetch it. Then God knows how I was to get back
down here again."

"The same way, probably." Jenny stifled a laugh. "Is he actually all
that bad?"

"Probably not, but he really bugs me. Not sure why. So I don't intend
to see him again if I can help it. But about the car… I don't know…"

"Couldn't they have put the bike in the back of Ron's pickup?" Jenny
enquired, wondering why the other two started to smile.

"No, honey," Mike explained. "You'd need a ramp to get a bike on
one of those. And I guess it's a pretty heavy machine, isn't it?" he said
to Ellen.

"A customised Harley complete with riser bars," Ellen nodded.

"I know," Jenny turned to Mike with a pleading smile, "we could do
it, couldn't we, Mike?"

Ellen appeared puzzled.

"We could go back to Seal Rock via the lake and Ron's place. There
are two of us. We have a car, and one of us can drive Ron's car. It's not
such a big detour. What do you say?"

Both women looked at Mike beseechingly.

"We…el, I suppose…"

"Good, that's settled," Jenny squeezed Mike's arm gratefully. "Now,
there's the display I wanted to check out." She led Mike over to the
table display and picked up one of the books, opening it at a random
page and holding it up to him.

"Hold on," Mike took the book from her, closed it and turned to
the back cover. "Hmm. Peter Travers, I've heard of him. Writes fiction,
but based on pretty realistic stuff. Does his research. You'd be okay
with one of these."

"Good. It's not for me… well, only partly. I guess I'll read it first, but
I wanted something for the boys, my grandsons, even though they're
too young for these books just yet. Something to fill in their Native
American heritage," she added, with a smile in Ellen's direction.

After some further conversation between Jenny and Ellen, during which Mike continued to peruse the books on display, studying the back of each carefully, Ellen reached behind the counter.

"Here are Ron's car keys… if you're sure…"

"We are." Mike took them from her. "It'll be no bother. Be good to see Ron again… and to meet this Travis guy."

"Yes, I want to see the man that's spooked you so," Jenny chimed in. "He must be quite something." She raised her eyebrows and gave Ellen a knowing look.

"No, not that," Ellen clearly understood the implication of Jenny's look and was quick to deny it. "Definitely not that."

Mike seemed puzzled, but continued out the door with Jenny following, turning only to hug her cousin. "You're still invited to dinner," she reminded Ellen. "Maybe at the weekend?"

"Maybe," Ellen agreed, as she closed the door behind them.

*

The two pickups drew up outside the beach cabin and Jenny hopped out of one, while Mike drove the other into the driveway. Jenny stood still for a moment enjoying the silence. She'd thought Seal Rock quiet, but this was something else. Built right on the ocean, Ron Williams' home took her breath away. It was old, wooden and a bit rundown, more like a mobile home. The house had a covered front porch and a wide set of steps leading up to the front door, but the location… She'd bet there were uninterrupted ocean views from the back.

As soon as Mike slammed the door to Ron's pickup, the door at the top of the steps opened. As the pair climbed the steps, they were met by the scent of the ocean and a stiff breeze which threatened to blow them away.

"Ellen said you'd be here," greeted the tall, slim man who stood in the doorway. He was clean-shaven and his thick grey hair was tied back from his face – a round face not unlike his sister's. "Good to see you again, Mike. And you too, Jenny." He shook hands with Mike and gave Jenny a quick hug. "Come on in. Thanks for bringing up the car."

Jenny felt a little shy with Ron. She'd only met him a couple of times before, and he wasn't an easy man to get to know – a bit of a recluse.

"You'll need these." Mike handed him the car keys.

"Thanks." Ron led them into an open living area, furnished sparingly with an overstuffed sofa, a couple of chairs and a square dining table. The only concession to modernity was a forty inch television set, facing the sofa and surrounded by bookcases.

"It's not much," Ron apologized, "but I don't need much. There's just me."

"Ellen said you had a friend staying," Jenny looked around, trying to figure out where Travis might be hiding.

"Yeah, needed some help," he grimaced, holding up his arm covered in a thick greyish-white bandage. It stretched from his elbow over his knuckles leaving only his thumb and fingertips sticking out. "Once I get this off, we'll be back to normal. Travis is out for a ride. Gets cabin fever in here all day," he added. "Would you guys like a beer? Least I can do."

Jenny and Mike looked at each other. Jenny was keen to get back on the road, but felt it would be churlish to refuse Ron's offer of hospitality. She'd learnt on her visit last year that someone like Ron, who was a bit of a hermit, might take their refusal as an insult. She sighed, looked at Mike and gave an imperceptible nod.

"Sure."

"If you can give me a hand…" Ron indicated his arm, ruefully. "Maybe you'd like to sit out back?" He gestured to Jenny and indicated the glass door leading to a wooden deck which faced the ocean.

Jenny walked out and leant over the edge of the balustrade, the wood aged and bleached from years of sun, sand and rain. She ran her fingers over its smooth surface. Although the day itself wasn't hot, the wood had soaked up warmth from the sun. She gazed out at the wild ocean, so typical of the Oregon Coast. Today the wind had whipped the sea into a frenzy, and the beach was deserted, save for the large pieces of driftwood the sea had thrown up. The deck itself was sheltered from the strong breeze they'd experienced out front, so she relaxed as she took a seat, closed her eyes and enjoyed the weak sunlight on her face.

Jenny was so relaxed she was startled when the two men returned. She accepted the beer Mike proffered with raised eyebrows. Beer wasn't her usual tipple.

"Thought you'd prefer this to Coke."

"Afraid my range is somewhat limited. Not used to entertaining," Ron apologized.

"That's okay, thanks."

"Not used to having ladies up here." Ron took a pull on his beer before sitting down.

"It's a beautiful spot," Jenny complimented Ron. "How long have you lived here?"

"A few years now," Ron said reflectively, holding his beer up to the light. "Bought it when I got out of the forces. Couldn't afford anything up here these days. Prices have gone through the roof."

"I can imagine." Jenny sipped her beer, and the three sat in silence admiring the view. Looking around she noticed a pile of white driftwood lying in the backyard below the deck.

"What do you do with that?" she enquired, pointing to the bleached timber.

"Oh," Ron scratched his head with the fingertips protruding from the bandage. "Pick it up on the beach, comes in useful…"

"Is that your work?" Mike pointed to a roughly-hewn head sitting on a high shelf inside the home.

"Yeah, fills the time," Ron muttered.

"But it's beautiful!" Jenny rose and went back inside to examine the sculpture more closely. The two men followed her in.

"It's nothing much." Ron shrugged and changed the subject: "So you two have really gotten together."

"We sure have." Mike wrapped his arms around Jenny from behind, while she wriggled in embarrassment. Disentangling herself, Jenny walked across to the window and turned.

"What about Ellen? Isn't it time she found herself a nice guy, too?" As she spoke, Jenny wondered if Ron would mention his friend Travis. She was surprised at his reply:

"At one time I thought she and my pal Paul might make a go of it, but Ellen didn't seem interested. No, I think my little sister's like me – destined to live out our lives alone." Ron sucked on his cheek as he said this.

Mike checked his watch. "We'd better be going if we want to make it back before dark," he said, and he and Jenny prepared to take their leave.

Jenny and Mike were sitting in the pickup about to leave, when a large silver bike roared past them, turning right in front of them. It stopped in the driveway with a final roar, before the driver killed the engine.

"What the…"

"That must be Travis," Jenny reached her hand over to touch Mike's arm in a half-hearted attempt to prevent him from starting up the vehicle, but he shook it away, his foot already on the accelerator. As they drove off, the man dismounted and waved. He wore a fringed beige jacket and had a black and red bandana tied around his hair. Jenny turned and peered out of the back window, noticing his height, his broad shoulders and the trim blonde goatee and moustache, before the details of the figure were lost in the distance. So this was the man who was proving to be such an annoyance to her cousin.

"He wasn't wearing a crash helmet," Jenny said in surprise, turning back to Mike.

"It's not compulsory over here," he returned. "Not like Australia." He grinned. "Some of the bikers fought for their right to dress as they please – even if it kills them. And it often does."

Jenny turned again, catching a last glimpse of Travis climbing up to the cabin. He was a bit of a hunk, and certainly unconventional enough for her cousin. Maybe this annoyance Ellen felt had more substance than she imagined.

Five

"See you got your car back," Travis grabbed a can of Coke from the fridge and joined Ron on the deck, pulling a chair out with his foot.

"Yeah, my Australian cousin brought it back. You just missed her; her and her fella."

"He Australian too?" Travis took a swig from the can and propped a foot up on the railing, tipping his chair up on its back legs. He threw his head back enjoying the feel of the cool liquid trickling down his throat.

"No," Ron leant back in his chair. "He's from around here, Seal Rock. Leastways, he is now. Hailed from California before that, some big dude at the university, so I've heard. Mike – Mike Halliday – came up here full of this research he wanted to do on our Community. Knew a bit too – not one of these white geezers poking their noses where they don't belong."

Travis dropped his leg and chair in a thump. "Mike Halliday you say?"

Ron's mouth fell open in surprise: "Know him, do you?"

Travis quickly regained control of himself. "Heard of him," he muttered. "Came from California, did he?"

"That's right," Ron paused. "San Francisco, I think. Wasn't that where…?"

"Yeah." Travis didn't elaborate. He'd put that part of his life behind him, intent on making a new start. "How come you have an Australian cousin?" he asked, to change the subject. "One of your family go down there?" He finished his Coke in a large gulp and crushed the can in one hand.

"Funny thing that." Ron gazed out at the ocean. "We only found out last year. Jenny came here to stay with her godmother up at Seal Rock. That's where she and Mike got together. Seems her dad was an uncle of mine – one I'd never heard of, and she was adopted out as a baby. Grew up down in Australia. We never knew." Ron scratched his head. 'It all came out. Caused quite a stink in the family. Dad still hasn't got over it. Took it hard. Her father was his little brother it seems, but no one ever talked about him. Can't imagine anyone not talking about our Ellen if she died."

He fell silent, then checked his watch. "Must be about time." He walked inside and turned the television on. Travis heard the raucous noise heralding the start of the ball game – not his viewing choice. He followed Ron in.

"Might disappear for a bit," he said, moving toward his room, but Ron was oblivious, already lost in the game.

Once in the bedroom, Travis flung himself down on the bed. This was the worst time – when he was alone. That's when it all came back. He closed his eyes in an attempt to shut out the memories but they kept coming.

10 years earlier

"Daddy," the little voice calls from the yard, "can you help me?" The blonde seven-year old is wrestling with several pieces of wood, which he's trying to fashion into some sort of a wagon.

"Sure thing." The father, who shares his son's blonde looks and blue eyes, crouches down to the boy's height, and finding some nails, joins the two pieces together. "How's that, Ricky? Should be strong enough to hold you now." Ricky jumps into the wagon to test his father's words and, sure enough, it holds.

"Push me!" he says, and the father pushes the wagon down the driveway with the boy yelling in his excitement.

The pair play happily together till they hear a voice call, "Dinner – or is no one hungry around here? Shall I give the meatballs to the neighbor's dog?"

"Yum, meatballs." The boy dashes inside leaving the wagon on the driveway.

The father shakes his head, smiling, and puts the little wagon into the garage before entering the house to greet the tall dark-haired woman with a warm hug. They stand together arms linked, watching their son climb up to the table and pick up his knife and fork.

"Where's dinner?" he yells.

The couple share a secret smile before all three sit down to eat.

Sometime later the boy sits up in bed. "Read me a story, Dad. One of your special ones, the ones you make up just for me." He snuggles down under the covers as his father sits on the bed, propped up by the pillow, and opens the book. He reads and reads to the eager little fellow. He reads until the little eyes droop, and he knows his son's asleep. Then he goes downstairs to where his wife has dinner waiting.

"He wanted a long one tonight?" she asks, smiling. He wraps his arms around her and kisses her on the top of her dark curls, silently giving thanks once again for his life. After Vietnam he'd been damaged goods. He'd never believed anyone would take him on, but Allie had, and now there's Ricky, and he's beginning to make a name for himself with his writing. It won't be long before they'll be able to move out of their rented condo and buy a home of their own — one with a bigger yard, one where Ricky can have the dog he craves.

Travis opened his eyes and brushed away the tears. These were the happy memories — ones he could almost cope with. It was when he was asleep, in the dead of night; that's when the unbearable ones came. He blinked to blot out even the thought of them and swung his feet off the bed. He sat still, his hands hanging limp between his legs, a cloud of despair threatening to overwhelm him. He needed to do something. The inertia was killing him. He needed to write again, but not what he had been writing before. He couldn't bring himself to continue in that vein. He needed fresh inspiration.

Travis opened his laptop and fired it up. He typed *Chapter One* and paused, looking at the blank screen. For a few minutes there was nothing. The only sounds were his own breathing and the roar of the ocean from outside the window. What if his muse had gone completely and there was nothing left? Then, amazingly, the ideas began to flow. He wrote and wrote. Three hours passed before he finally stopped typing and stretched his arms above his head. He looked around in surprise.

It had grown dark. Ron's game must be finished by now. Closing down the computer, Travis wandered through into the other room where, as he'd anticipated, Ron was reading the paper, the television newscast blaring in the background.

"Hey!"

Ron looked up. "Hey! Had a nap?"

"Yes," Travis said brusquely to avoid further enquiries. "How'd the game go?"

"Bloody *Ducks* lost again!"

"Need a better team, mate." He sat down on the sofa, elbows on his knees. "Tell me about your family. Is it just you and Ellen?"

"Yeah, big disappointment to the folks. They'd expected grandkids by now. We've both let them down on that score."

Travis' stomach contracted with a jolt. He took a deep breath before replying, hoping Ron hadn't noticed, but he had.

"Sorry, bud. Insensitive of me. Didn't think." Ron rubbed his good hand across his forehead. "That's me all over. Don't think, put my big foot in it. Better to keep my mouth shut altogether."

"Hey, it's okay." Travis punched Ron's shoulder gently. "Don't mind me. Can't have everyone walking on eggshells around me. Got to talk about it sometime." As he spoke, Travis realized it was true. He'd kept it all bottled up for the past two years, soon it would be three. Scared to talk about it, terrified to think about it. And what had been the result? Nightmares. Nightmares so horrific he woke up in a sweat most nights, then couldn't get back to sleep again.

Travis clenched his fists and began to speak in a low voice. "It was bad. When I got out of hospital and went back to the house, it was so empty. I walked from room to room. Silence. Like a ghost house. Couldn't bear it. I had to get away. That's when I bought the bike." He raised his head and looked off into the distance, his eyes glazing over. "I found freedom – or so it seemed. I could go anywhere, be anyone. No one knew me out there. Grew my hair, the moustache, the beard. I became a different person. The old Travis Petersen was gone. Dead. The new one didn't give a damn, took women like I used to drink beer, a new one every night. Didn't even know their names half the time."

Ron made a sound and Travis looked round, but his companion appeared to have nothing to say, so he continued, "But I didn't drink.

Haven't had a drink for almost three years now. Can't trust myself." He looked down again. "So that's my sorry story. Saw some great places, met a lot of strange and interesting people, people on the road like myself. Heard their stories – but didn't tell mine. So that's why I'd be no good for your sister, even if she'd look at me, which doesn't ever seem likely."

"Don't sell yourself short. Ellen… well, she's Ellen. Keeps herself pretty buttoned up. She hasn't been lucky with her menfolk. That's most likely why she seems so ornery with you. But she's not a bad girl." Ron rubbed his chin reflectively. "Maybe if…"

"Nah! Leave it. It's fine as it is. She has every right to be distrustful of me."

The two men sat, contemplating the vagaries of women, then Ron pushed himself up. "Dinner? How about we saunter downtown for a bite to eat? *Drift Inn's* not bad. Should be music too, if you're up for it."

"Goodo," Travis said, spurred by the thought of music, which would preclude any further discussion of his past or of Ron's sister. He wished he'd never brought the subject up. What was he thinking? But the tall regal woman with her easy smile – though not for him – had stuck in his mind. She wasn't his usual fare. She was what he'd call a real woman, the first real woman he'd come across in years.

The men walked down the road in silence, each lost in his thoughts, until they reached the wooden-framed building, yellow with green trim, and the sign *The Drift Inn* hanging from a bracket. When they entered, the pair slid into a booth.

"Old place, is it?" Travis looked around.

"Been like this since around 2000," Ron grinned. "Before that it was owned by an old guy called Lester. Bit of a boys' club in those days. An old smoky bar. Quite a character, Lester was."

"Coffee, sir?" The waitress poured them coffee and handed them some menus.

When she left, Ron continued, "The present owners took over to save the place before Lester died. Did a complete remodel – weren't without their critics either, but managed to keep the old place going. Caters to families now," Ron swept his arm around to encompass the myriad customers.

"Seems popular," Travis muttered, picking up the menu. He ordered the warm beef salad to be washed down with a root beer, and Ron the chicken pot pie with a Corona.

Suddenly there was a loud squeal, and Travis looked around with a start, the sweat instantly breaking out on his forehead.

"It's only the mike," Ron reassured him. "Music's about to start. Looks like it's one of the local country and western groups tonight." He leant back, clearly prepared to enjoy his favorite genre.

It took Travis a few minutes to regain his equilibrium. He silently cursed himself for his initial alarm. He thought he'd gotten over that. He took a few deep breaths. In-out, in-out, in-out. That was it – back to normal. He looked around at the clientele. People were chatting and laughing, heedless of the three musicians playing and singing for their entertainment, unlike Ron who was lost in a world of his own.

Travis' attention was taken by a family seated to their left, father, mother and two children – a boy and a girl. The boy must have been around ten and the girl a few years younger. He was busy instructing his little sister on the correct way to hold her fork, and typically, she was resisting his directions. The boy had blonde floppy hair, just like… He looked away. He'd been fine for weeks, ever since he landed in Oregon. What had brought these memories back to him, today of all days? He rose. "Be back," he said to his oblivious companion and made his way to the back of the inn where he'd seen the sign for the restrooms. Once there he leant over the sink and dowsed his face in cold water, then let the water drip from his chin. He felt better, able to face people again. He vowed to keep his gaze firmly fixed on his food and Ron, in that order. No more gawking at people playing happy families.

When he returned to their booth, the meals were already on the table, and Ron was tucking in with his free hand, the other held close to his chest.

"Good stuff, this," he said, before shoveling another mouthful.

"Mmm," Travis mumbled as he tucked into his own meal. The two ate in silence, punctuated by the music, which to Travis' delight, had been toned down and was now only a background hum.

To Travis' surprise and, not a little consternation, Ron reverted to the subject of his sister. The normally taciturn Ron became quite voluble on the subject.

"Our Ellen's a character, a great kid, but a strange one," he began. "Sometimes even *I'm* not sure where she's coming from. A bit fey, always has been, but it doesn't seem to help her where men are concerned." He coughed, as if in embarrassment. "There was a guy for a time, divorced. There was a son, I think." He gazed off into the distance. "Kept him pretty much to herself. Met him once as I recollect, nice dude, pretty straight, if you know what I mean. One of those literary types," he grimaced, and Travis smiled to himself.

"But it ended like all the rest," Ron concluded. "Last I heard he'd gone up to Canada to be closer to his son, ex-wife too, I suspect. Ellen didn't seem to feel she could go." Ron rubbed his chin. "Shop kept her here, I expect, the old folks too. I haven't been much help to her in that regard. Upset her for a while, but she seems to have gotten over it now." He gave Travis what the other took to be a meaningful look. "If you have inclinations in that direction, don't know what to advise."

Travis almost choked. Here was Ron practically handing him his sister on a plate, a sister who was quite capable of making up her own mind and seemed to have done that already where Travis was concerned. And he wasn't interested anyway, was he?

"Right," was all he could think of to say.

As the two men ambled back to Ron's place, the conversation, led by Ron, focused on their meal, the music, and the possibility of eating there again in the near future. Travis found it easier to agree with his friend, while keeping his thoughts to himself. He only hoped this would be a night free of nightmares, that he would sleep through till morning and that the horrors would stay away.

But as Travis turned out his beside light, his last waking thought wasn't of the old happy memories or the worry of a nightmare. The image which swam behind his closed eyelids was the smiling face of Ellen Williams.

Six

Ellen was lost in thought as she drove up to Seal Rock. She was finally making good her promise to visit Jenny and Mike. Having closed the shop early this Sunday, she planned to call in on Ron at Yachats, then spend as much time as possible with Jenny and Mike. It was strange to think of them as an established couple. Ellen pressed *start* on the CD and let the sounds of Vivaldi's *Four Seasons* soothe her as she drove along. In the back of her mind she clung to the hope she'd find Ron alone, but as she powered up the highway the sun was shining, and she put any thoughts of Travis in the too-hard basket for now.

She'd almost reached Ron's home when a flash of silver rushed past her with a roar. The rider wore a fringed beige jacket and had a black and red bandana tied around his head. It had to be Travis. Ellen breathed a sigh of relief. She'd be able to visit with her brother on his own, without his pesky housemate.

"Hey, Ellen," Ron greeted her, as she pushed open the door. "Didn't expect to see you today. You just missed…"

"Travis, I know," she smiled. "Thought that was him I saw ride off. Seemed to be in a tearing hurry."

"Oh, that's just him. Riding like a mad thing to drive away his demons. Doesn't work." Ron shook his head. "Takes more than that." For a moment he appeared lost in thought, then seemed to pull himself together, and gave Ellen a one-armed hug. "Good to see you, little sister. What brings you up this way? You didn't come all the way to visit with me?"

"Did, too," Ellen said, adding, "I'm on my way up to Seal Rock to have dinner with Jenny and Mike. Thought I might as well stop off here on the way, but if I'm not wanted…" She made as if to leave, only to have her brother take her by the arm and guide her to the sofa.

"Now just sit yourself down. I'd offer you a coffee but…" he looked helplessly at his arm.

"I'll do it." Ellen went to the kitchen and started putting the coffee makings together. "How *is* your arm?" she asked, as Ron followed her in.

"So, so. Be glad to get this stuff off." He held it up in disgust. "Can't do a darn thing with it. Go back in next week," he added.

"Do you need a ride?" Ellen offered, "or…"

"Nah, Travis'll see me right. Good bloke." Ron accepted the mug of coffee from Ellen, and the pair moved out to the deck. "Been practically living out here the past week," he said, as they sat down to admire the view. "Beats other spots I've lived, but it's pretty tough not being able to get down to the boat."

"Couldn't…" Ellen began, then thought better of it, but Ron anticipated her query.

"Yeah, Travis offered to give me a ride down there, but wouldn't be any good. Couldn't take the damn thing out. Be just sitting looking at it. Might as well sit here."

"Right. And how about Travis? How's that working out?"

"Pretty good. He's a handy dude. Good to have around. Just gets a bit of cabin fever from time to time, and has to get out. He'll be gone an hour or so, I fancy."

"What's his story?" Ellen was curious. There seemed to be more to this Travis character than met the eye. "You knew him in Vietnam?"

"Yeah, lost touch. He's had a lot to cope with since then. Some guys have it tough." He shook his head and took a gulp of his coffee, before gazing off into space.

"Mmm?" Ellen wanted to hear more, but hesitated to show any interest.

"Not my story to tell." Ron clammed up. The pair sat in silence staring at the view again. The ocean was rough today, and from their sheltered spot, they could see a few hardy individuals collecting driftwood and throwing it into their pickups, which were parked close to the edge of the beach.

Ellen was surprised therefore, when Ron began to speak again. "He's a good dude, as I said. Asked a bit about you too." He looked at his sister reflectively. "Pity he's out. Maybe you two…"

"Don't go there!" Ellen's dander was up. "You tried to set me up with Paul, and look what happened there."

"No need to get shitty with me," Ron put his mug down and wiped his mouth. "Paul's an okay guy, too. You're too picky. Good guys aren't hanging from trees, you know. Missed your chance there."

"I don't need a guy, good or otherwise. And Paul!" Ellen was almost shouting. "The casino was his idea of a romantic night out. And he's not my type anyway," she said, calming down. "Though he's probably a nice guy," she admitted. "Just not for me. I'm happy the way I am. I like my life. I have my home, my bookshop, and there are the parents…"

Ron drew his fingers across his brow. "I know I haven't been much help there," he said, "but…"

"How can you do anything stuck up here? But it's been your choice – this hermit existence. You only come up for air to take your boat out and jawbone with your old mates."

Ron had the grace to look ashamed. He opened his mouth to reply, but Ellen said, "It's okay. I don't mind being the one who's there for them. I do live nearby after all. But keep out of my personal life. I don't need your help, thank you very much." Incensed, she drank the remains of her coffee down in one gulp and set the mug on the deck at her feet. "Well, now that I've seen you, and you've had your say about my non-existent love life, while ignoring the fact that your own is in the same pitiful state, I'll be off."

Ellen's anger continued till she was on the road again, then, as suddenly as it had erupted, it dissipated. There was no point being angry at Ron. He wasn't the cause of her unease. It was his mate, Travis – or was it? Hadn't her presentiment of disaster appeared even before Travis had walked into shop? But he had appeared soon afterwards, she argued with herself, *ipso facto*… No, even to her tired out brain, it didn't compute. Her insecurity had nothing to do with him. He was an annoyance all by himself. And he wasn't involved with the proposed development, was he? Now that really would be something to latch onto.

*

"Ellen, it's so good to see you," Jenny's welcome hug dismissed all the negative thoughts from Ellen's mind.

"Good to be here." Ellen looked around. Although she'd visited Jenny's godmother in her house down the track, she'd never ventured up as far as Mike's cabin. "So this is home, now?" As she spoke, a large black creature came loping out to sniff her ankles, and a wet tongue left its impression on her shoes.

"Ben!" Jenny remonstrated, and the Labrador dropped its head and returned to Mike's side.

"Hi Ellen," Mike came to join them. "Glad you made it up here. Maddy's going to be with us for dinner. A drink before then?"

"Love one." Ellen allowed herself to be guided into the house and, once she had commented admiringly on the layout and décor, plonked herself down on one of two cane chairs in the living area. "So," she began.

"So," Jenny twinkled back at her. "This is one of our homes. The other is still in Australia. We plan to spend part of the year here and the other part down there. That way, I can keep an eye on the shop and keep track of the kids and grandkids."

"Of course, I tend to forget you have family of your own. But it's good to have you here. Thanks, Mike." Ellen accepted the glass of red wine and took a sip. "Mmm nice drop."

"Now," Jenny began, "Mike's been doing some research for you on this development business. Thought we could get it out of the way before Maddy arrives. Tell her, Mike."

Mike settled himself comfortably in an old armchair, and Ben took up what was clearly his favorite spot at his master's feet. "Yes," he began, "I looked into it, checked the council webpage, looked up the developers to get a bit of background."

"And…?" Ellen leaned forward, holding her glass in both hands.

"Well," Mike paused, and took a mouthful of his Jack Daniels, "the article in the paper was correct in one respect, there is to be a development application. But it's yet to be filed. Seems as though the article was a way of testing local opinion. It's not even clear whether or not a purchase has actually gone through."

"Does that mean it won't go ahead?" Ellen asked eagerly, her face lighting up.

"It's not that simple. You see, now that it's out there, so to speak, the die is cast, and they'll go ahead with submitting their application."

"Oh!" Ellen slumped back in her seat and took another gulp of her drink. "So what can we do?"

"I'm coming to that. There are a few things you can do – you and the others who feel the same way as you do. As I said, I looked up the developers, and they have quite a track record."

"What do you mean?"

"They have a history of going from state to state, knocking down heritage buildings to put up their modern monstrosities. They argue that they provide low cost housing, but there's nothing low cost about their buildings. Of course, by the time they're built and on the market, it's too late for anyone to do anything about it."

"So, when can we do something?" Ellen asked. "And what can we do?"

"I expect the application will go in soon," Mike responded. "There's not really much we can do till then. But once it's in, there will be an opportunity for those who oppose the development to respond, and time for you to gather your troops."

"Sounds more like a war – not my scene at all," Ellen's voice was despondent. "But you said 'we'. Does that mean you plan to help us?"

Mike dragged his fingers through his faded reddish hair and pulled on his greying beard. "Seems so," he said briefly. He took another sip of his drink, and appeared to be considering carefully before adding: "Depends what we can find. This company I mentioned, Balcombs. They pull down old properties, but if we can find anything really special about your line of shops, then…"

"You mean if Ellen's shop has some special historical significance… something that we could use to prevent its demolition?" Jenny broke in.

"Right on."

"Hmm," Ellen held up her glass and contemplated the rosy hue of the liquid, "don't know how we do that."

"Well, it's something to think about."

"Hello, anyone home?" A cheery voice called from the. "I'll let myself in, shall I?" Maddy's elegant frame appeared in the room, and the three immediately rose to greet her.

"Come and sit here," Jenny instructed, after hugging her godmother, while Mike patted her on the shoulder, and Ellen waited her turn to hug the older woman.

"It's been too long," Maddy addressed Ellen, before taking a seat and bending to pat Ben, who went padding over to greet her. "Hello, Ben. Happy to have your people back? We loved having him," Maddy looked up at Mike, "but he did pine a bit at first. We miss the patter of little paws around. Marylou is talking of getting a dog for us, a pup."

"Really? Maybe I can help you out there," Mike tugged on his beard again. "I can check with my breeder friend down south. That's if you want a lab like Ben."

"You couldn't do better, Maddy," Jenny beamed. "It would be company for you too, when Marylou goes to work."

"Company, yes," Maddy smiled, then turned to Ellen. "That was a brilliant idea of yours, to suggest I have a companion, a paying guest. Marylou has been wonderful. We keep to ourselves much of the time, but just to know she's there. It's a comfort."

"For me too," Jenny put in. "I don't know how I could have gone back to Australia and left you all alone up here, after that fall you had…"

"There was always Mike," Maddy gave him a fond look, "on the other end of the phone."

"Yes, but you're both so damned independent. You could go for days without seeing each other and what if you'd fallen and couldn't reach the phone? No, I feel much happier knowing you have someone actually in the house with you. And thanks to Ellen, you have." She smiled across at her cousin.

"And here we all are!" Maddy looked around at the trio. "My family. And to think this time last year we didn't know Ellen, and Jenny and Mike were at daggers drawn. What a difference." She smiled smugly and folded her hands on her lap. "Now what about you, Ellen?"

"Me? What *about* me?"

"Now we have these two settled, it's your turn. When are you going to find yourself a man?"

Ellen, who had been taking a sip of her wine, spluttered. Only someone of Maddy's advanced years could get away with asking such a blunt question. Wiping her mouth with the back of her hand, she was quick to respond. "Not for me! I'm quite happy on my own. You should appreciate that, if anyone can, Maddy. You've lived up her alone for as long as…"

"Yes, but I knew love." Maddy's eyes glazed over as she appeared to be remembering her lover killed in the war, the man whose photo still held pride of place on her wall. They all sat in silence, then Maddy seemed to pull herself together. "But I don't think you have. I don't think a great love has touched you. No," she said, clearly seeing Ellen about to interrupt, "I know about that one who went off to Canada. But if… if he'd been the one, you wouldn't have let him get away so easily."

Ellen couldn't believe her ears. This was the first time Maddy had ever suggested such a thing to her. She opened and closed her mouth unable to think of a suitable reply. It was Jenny who replied for her.

"Maddy!" Jenny reproved. "Now you have Mike and me settled, you don't need to turn to Ellen. I never took you for a matchmaker. Maybe you need to concentrate on Marylou?"

"Poof!" Maddy waved her hands in the air to dismiss the idea. "Marylou is still young. She's at the experimenting stage, a new man every week. Whereas Ellen here…"

"Enough!" Mike interjected. "Remember that I'm here. I don't really think this is suitable conversation for one of my tender years – or Ben's either," he added jocularly.

"Okay, enough," Jenny rose. "Now, who's for dinner?"

At dinner the conversation moved from Australia, to the development, to Ron's accident, with the latter prompting Jenny to ask, "How is Ron's arm, Ellen? Is Travis still with him?"

"Seems to be on the mend. I called in on my way here, and he hopes to have the bandage off next week sometime. That'll be a boon for him. Let him get back to normal."

"And Travis?" Jenny raised her eyebrows.

"Haven't seen him, thank goodness." Ellen felt her hackles rise at the very mention of the man, but Maddy picked up on the name immediately.

"Travis, who's he?" Maddy looked from Jenny to Ellen and back again.

"A friend of Ron's. He's been staying with him – helping out – till he has full use of his arm again. He's..."

"Another of Ron's lame ducks," Ellen butted in. "They met in Vietnam." Her tone spoke volumes, but Maddy wasn't one to let it go.

"What's he like, this Travis? You've met him?" This last was directed at Jenny, who grimaced at Mike across the table before replying.

"Not exactly, but we saw him arrive at Ron's just as we were leaving. He looked..."

"Like a regular biker – a wastrel," Ellen interrupted again.

"That wasn't what I was going to say," Jenny hesitated. "We only saw him from a distance. We were in the car," she explained. "But he looked pretty much of a hunk to me, though maybe a bit of an aging hippie. What did you think, Mike?" She turned to her partner.

"Don't look at me." Mike held up his hands as if to defend himself. "I barely saw the guy. You women! You'll have him cut up and served for dinner as soon as look at him."

"Now that's not fair," Maddy was quick to remonstrate with Mike. "We're interested in him, Jenny and I. After all, if he's a friend of Ron's, then Ellen's bound to come in contact with him, and we were only just saying..."

"Oh, not you too!"

Maddy's eyes widened. Ellen realized that neither Maddy nor Jenny had seen her in this state before. She hastened to attempt an explanation.

"Sorry, but when I called in on Ron, he was full of the guy and how he'd been asking about me. My brother, who could never hold down a relationship himself, trying to give me advice! Now you're starting. It's all too much. I'm single. I like being single. I intend to stay single. So put that in your pipe and smoke it!" Ellen's face had been becoming redder and redder as she spoke, and now that her anger was subsiding, she looked somewhat shamefaced.

"Well," Maddy was first to speak. "What brought that on? All the time I've known you, I'd have taken bets on the fact you were the calmest person I knew. I've never seen you so riled."

"Sorry," Ellen repeated, now feeling calmer. "There's something about the guy. I don't know what it is but..."

"He sure rubs you up the wrong way," Maddy finished for her.

"Yeah," Ellen agreed.

"But surely," Jenny began. "I mean, you were so ready to predict my future, can't you see what it is about him…?"

"No, I'm never able to see anything to do with myself, only others. Anyway, what would there be to see? He's a friend of Ron's, period. I expect he'll be leaving soon, as soon as Ron's arm's mended. And that'll be that."

"Methinks the lady doth protest too much." Mike, who had kept silent up till now, entered the conversation. "But leave poor Ellen alone. She didn't come here to be pumped about her love life, or about this Travis guy. Let's talk of pleasanter things. How's that new display going? I was very impressed, and Jenny's enjoying the book she bought."

Ellen threw Mike a relieved look, and the rest of the evening passed without incident. It wasn't till she was driving home that the whole conversation came back to haunt her. What was it about Travis that his name kept coming up in conversation and his face kept appearing behind her eyelids?

Seven

The car is traveling along the highway, the radio blaring a popular song, and the boy in the back is singing along. The family is setting off on vacation, and they haven't a care in the world. The driver glances toward his wife, sitting in the passenger seat, and a warm glow suffuses him. They waited so long for this child, they give thanks every day for their good fortune, and just to hear his happy, carefree voice is a delight to them. The school holidays have only just begun, and they've planned to spend two full weeks together. The passenger reaches over to place a hand on her husband's knee, and they drive on in silence, each lost in thought. They left their neighbor's party early in order to get on the road, planning to reach their destination – Petaluma – before sundown. Alcohol has been flowing at the party, held to celebrate a twenty-fifth wedding anniversary, but aware of the drive ahead, the pair have imbibed cautiously, the man having only two beers, and the woman, a couple of glasses of wine.

The road is busy this holiday weekend, and the driver is careful as other vehicles weave in and out around him. Suddenly the man sees a truck tearing towards them. It's crossed the center line and is heading straight for them. He hears his wife and son scream as he furiously turns the steering wheel in an attempt to avoid the inevitable collision. Sweat beads on his forehead, and his whole body begins to tremble. The screaming grows louder as he hears his own voice join in. The hand on his knee tightens, the nails digging into his leg through the thin material of his slacks, then slackens, and he grits his teeth with his last conscious thought before everything goes dark.

Travis awakened with a start. He unclenched his teeth and tried to slow his breathing. His body was in a cold sweat. He sat up quickly and looked around, expecting to see a crash scene, expecting to see the mangled bodies of his wife and son, but he was alone. He was alive, and they were dead. Nothing had changed. The silence of Ron's spare bedroom enveloped him, and he slumped back in the bed again. Hell! The nightmare was back!

As it was still dark, Travis checked the time on his cell phone. Only four o'clock. He knew from experience there was no use trying to get back to sleep, so he swung his legs out of the bed and sat there rubbing his head. This was the first time he'd had the nightmare since coming to Oregon. He thought he'd left it behind him, that he could start afresh here. Here, where there were no memories. What a lame hope that had been. He shook his head in disbelief. There was no escaping it. *Was this going to be his life from now on? What had he to offer a woman?* He grunted and ran his fingers through his already ragged hair, remembering why he'd taken the easy way of satisfying his sexual appetite, one night stands, easy women who expected nothing more. But now he'd met Ellen, Ron's sister. She was something else. A man could drown in her calm eyes and slake his thirst in her strong body. He rested his cheek on his thumb and rubbed his forehead with his fingers.

The sound of a car on the road outside brought Travis back from his reverie. He needed to get out of here. He stepped into the shower, and soaping himself thoroughly, turned on the cold water and stood there, the stream of water cascading over his body. He didn't know how long he stood there, letting the water wash away the memory of his dream. When he finally emerged, he pulled on a pair of jeans, tee and woollen *Pendleton* shirt, and made his way to the kitchen, the sun was already beginning to appear above the horizon. Gulping down a mug of strong coffee and sticking a piece of burnt toast between his teeth, he opened the door.

The morning air felt fresh against his face as he leapt onto his bike and set off down the highway. The breeze blasted him, dispelling any remaining cobwebs, and Travis finally began to shake his nightmare.

By the time Travis reached Florence, the sun had risen higher in the sky. It was going to be a good day, although there was still a nip in the air. Summer would be here soon, but it hadn't arrived yet. As he rode down Highway 101 through the town, Travis felt a pang of hunger and, making his way to Old Town, parked his bike by the river. He'd be sure to find a coffee shop open for breakfast. Stepping out, he walked briskly past the bookshop, giving only a passing glance to the window display of which Ellen was justly proud. The aroma of coffee and frying bacon and onions came wafting out of an open door. He walked in and, taking a seat in one of the booths, ordered his favorite breakfast of scrambled eggs with bacon, biscuits and gravy, plus a side order of onion rings.

Replete, Travis wiped his mouth with a paper napkin and drained his third coffee of the morning, reflecting that if he was becoming addicted to coffee, at least it was a healthier addiction than some he might have fallen prey to. The dunes called, and returning to his Harley, he rode south across the bridge, turning right when he came to the turnoff leading to the famous sand dunes. Once there, it took only a few minutes to park his bike and hire an ATV. These small dune buggies had become popular with tourists, and they suited Travis' mood this morning. He was the only customer, so hopped onto the vehicle and thundered off, finding forgotten delight in the miles of sand to be traversed. He steered the buggy up and down sand hills out of sight of any living creature, the sand abrading his face and the wind tearing at the tail of his shirt.

Travis rode and rode, each drop into a sand-filled hollow taking away more of his angst, till at last he returned to where he had begun, feeling spent but lighter. On his bike again, he rocketed back into Florence, and as he reached Old Town, he stopped almost opposite *The Reading Nook*. From there, Travis could just make out the figure of Ellen moving about the shop. His feet touched the road as he tried to figure out what sort of excuse he could find to walk across and enter her territory. Because that's what it was – her special domain, and one in which he hadn't been made welcome. As he watched, the female form he'd been contemplating moved towards the door, and in an instant, he powered up and was off.

*

When Ellen opened the door to set out her display board, she caught a glimpse of a silver motorbike shooting off into the distance. It looked vaguely familiar. She stood for a moment, gazing after it. Surely… no, it couldn't be. What on earth would Travis be doing down here at this time in the morning? Ellen felt a twinge of something she couldn't identify. She relegated it to the back of her mind and continued with her morning set-up. It wasn't until she was sitting in her tiny office with her daily caffeine and sugar hit – strong black accompanied by a cinnamon roll – that she took time to analyze it. She replayed the incident, closing her eyes to better see the flash of silver. Again she felt the twinge of… disappointment! Her eyes snapped open, and she reached for the coffee cup. Disappointment?

Taking a sip of the warm liquid, Ellen tried to logically examine her feelings in an attempt to determine why the sight of Travis' bike roaring off into the distance could be a cause for disappointment. She was unable to come up with any reasonable explanation. It worried her, and all day, her thoughts kept reverting to that feeling. It was like a sore tooth, one which her tongue sought out, one which caused her discomfort, but which she couldn't leave alone.

Uncharacteristically, Ellen was eager for the day to end. She longed to be able to return to her home, the little house that was hers, and hers alone. The place where she could relax, find peace again, and be done with the intrusion of thoughts of the tall fellow with the fading blonde hair.

It was a busy day. Customers followed each other with great rapidity. Closing time finally arrived, and Ellen was picking up her purse and preparing to leave, when the door burst open and Coralie's blonde head popped around it.

"Have you heard anything?" Ellen's neighbor asked, a worried look on her face, but before Ellen had time to answer, she burbled on. "One of my clients today… she said she'd heard…" Coralie paused and took a deep breath before continuing, "she'd heard the site had been sold! Oh, Ellen, what will we do?" she wailed. "What if… I can't think…"

This was the last thing Ellen needed. "Steady on," she murmured, drawing Coralie to a chair and sitting down beside her. She took both of the woman's hands in hers and patted them ineffectually. Ellen's own heart was thumping at the news. She'd put all thought of the proposed development behind her, leaving it in what she considered to be Mike's capable hands. She'd heard nothing since their dinner and had supposed that there had been no progress with the development application. Now this!

"Well, if it's been sold, there's not much we can do, but there's still the development application. Mike said we'll have the opportunity to have our say then." Ellen hoped she sounded more confident than she felt.

"Mike?" Coralie looked up, her eyes widening. "Is he...?"

"My cousin's partner. You remember... the one who came from Australia last year? She's back with Mike, and they're living up at Seal Rock."

"And he'll help us?" Coralie's voice rose, and her face lost its worried look. "What can he do?"

"Probably nothing. No," Ellen added, seeing Coralie begin to wilt again, "I don't mean he can't help. He's promised to find out what he can, but it'll be up to us – the shopkeepers – to raise our objections to the proposal." Ellen freed her hands from those of Coralie, which had been clutching hers firmly, and began to play with the end of her plait. "He said something about finding out if the site had any historical significance. Don't know how we do that. Maybe we need to have a meeting – after the festival. Some of the old-timers might be able to help. I'll probably be seeing Mike and Jenny at the weekend. I'll check with him then."

Coralie visibly brightened at Ellen's words and stood up. "Thanks, Ellen. I feel better now. Sorry to have kept you. You were about to leave?"

'Yes, it's been quite a day.' Ellen picked up her purse and ushered Coralie out. She followed, locking the door and walking to her car, which was parked in its usual spot.

When she reached home, Ellen closed the door on the outside world and began to run a bath. The room was filling nicely with steam, when the phone rang. Cursing silently, Ellen turned off the water and picked up the phone.

"Ellen, is that you?"

Ellen sighed and plopped down at the kitchen table. It had been a busy week, and she realized she hadn't made the promised call home to check on her parents. Refraining from asking who her mother thought would be in Ellen's house at this time of night, other than Ellen herself, she replied: "Hi, Mom, what's up? Dad okay?"

"Sure is. No more of that…, but that's not why I've called. It's the Rhody Festival this weekend. You haven't forgotten, have you? We… I… thought it'd be nice if you and Ron came for dinner on Sunday. The parade will be over by then. Maybe that fellow who's staying with Ron…" Her mother's voice petered away, perhaps remembering Ellen's extremely vocal antipathy to the man.

"No, I don't think so." The last thing Ellen wanted was to sit at the dinner table with Travis, and her parent's dinner table too. "I mean, yes, I do know it's the Festival this weekend. All of us in Old Town have set up special window displays, and yes, dinner would be good, Mom. I'm sure Ron would appreciate that too. I guess he'll find a way of getting down for it. He never misses the parade and all the displays. But remember, he's not driving yet." As she spoke, Ellen realized that, of course, it would make sense for Travis to be there, to give Ron a ride down and back, if for no other reason. She rubbed her forehead and spoke quickly before she had time to regret the words. "Yes, Travis would be a good idea. But you'd better talk with Ron, Mom. Was that all? I was about to get into the bath."

"Don't brush me off, girl."

Ellen smiled. There was something to be said for being called a girl in her mid-fifties.

"You'll be polite to him, won't you? I won't have rudeness…"

"Of course." Ellen gazed out at her garden where her own rhododendrons were beginning to flower, the white, pink, purple and red blending to form a colorful picture. She hadn't made time for it for weeks, and now the busy tourist season was almost upon her. She'd get the weekend over first, then do some trimming before the summer began in earnest. The coming Rhododendron Festival was a major event in the Florence calendar and had been happening for over a hundred years. Once a year Florence paid homage to the flower, which grew wild in the surrounding hills and fields, by putting on what was the second oldest flower festival in Oregon. Three days of the long weekend would be taken up by pageants, displays, and a variety of activities, beginning with the crowning of the Queen of Rhododendra on the Friday and concluding with the Grand Floral Parade on Sunday.

As she soaked in her bath with a refreshing glass of wine, her hair wound up around her head like a crown, Ellen considered the conversation with her mother. So, how would she feel if Travis *did* come to the family dinner? Surprisingly, her immediate feeling wasn't one of anger, or even irritation. The fluttering at the base of her stomach was uncomfortable. It was something she hadn't experienced for years.

Eight

Old Town was already busy when Ellen arrived on the Saturday morning of the Rhody Festival. She parked in a side street some distance from the shop and made her way down to the river. Bay Street was closed for the festival, given over to old cars, flowers and motorbikes. The road was lined with large American flags set on poles along the edge of the sidewalk, almost obliterating the beautifully restored old homes, now inhabited by shops and art galleries. The light breeze blew a few strands of Ellen's hair loose, and she could hear the shop signs creak as they became caught in a sudden gust of wind. Crowds were forming, and the street was lined on each side with motorbikes, rear end in to the curb, their owners sitting proudly astride. It was quite a sight, and she could feel the excitement of the Festival building up. Her eyes scanned those nearest as she walked quickly past, wondering if Travis was one of the bikers displaying his pride and joy. There were so many, it was difficult to make out the owners, and she wasn't familiar enough with his Harley to recognize it in the melee, but at first glance, she couldn't see either the bike or its owner. Averting her eyes, lest she seem to be too curious, she reached her doorway without incident.

The morning passed in a blur of customers. Ellen barely had time to turn around from one, before she was approached by another. It was around lunchtime before she managed to draw breath and realized that her careful display of Travers books had been sadly depleted. She was heading towards her storeroom to fetch another supply when the doorbell clanged. She looked round, expecting to see yet another customer. Instead Ron stood there, with Travis behind him.

"Yo, Ellen!" Ron waved his bandaged arm. "Do you have time for a couple of old soldiers?"

Ellen felt her gut clench, but this time it wasn't in annoyance, rather something she couldn't – or wouldn't – put a name to. "Come in. You've caught me between bouts. I was just fetching more books for the display." She pointed to the empty spots on the table.

"Popular, are they?" Travis' deep voice drawled from behind Ron. "Thought folks might have tired of them."

"Not at all. As you can see, they've been one of the main sellers this morning. The tourists are lapping them up. We've had a number of overseas folks here for the Festival and, to them, they're a bit of our heritage."

"But fictional," Travis interjected.

"With a strong factual basis," Ellen rejoined. "This guy knows what he's about. He doesn't try to caricaturize the Native American like some authors do."

"Hmm."

Ellen stared at Travis. What was it with the guy? On his last visit he'd seemed to favor the Travers books, now he was expressing doubts about them, if his expression was anything to go by.

"You can 'hmm' all you like, but they're good, and they sell. Now will you either help me with another carton or get out of my way so I can fetch them myself?"

Travis followed Ellen into her storeroom and hefted the carton in his arms. On this occasion, Ellen noted the strength of the man and the breadth of his shoulders as she walked out behind him. Chiding herself silently for this change in attitude, she spoke more sharply than she intended.

"Put it down there, beside the table. I'll get them out later. Sorry," she drew her hand across her brow. "It's been a busy morning, I do appreciate your help. I didn't mean to sound abrupt."

"No problem." Travis straightened up and held out his hands. "Anything else I can do? We wondered…"

"If you'd had any lunch," Ron concluded. "Know you'll have been busy and probably haven't taken time. How 'bout we fetch you something?"

Ellen relaxed, buoyed by the thought of someone else fetching lunch for her. She smiled at the two men. "That'd be great. I would appreciate it."

"Lots of stalls around. What takes your fancy?" Travis spoke first.

"Oh," Ellen's voice was flustered. "Anything really. I can't leave…"

"Understood. What about some clam chowder? Saw a stall down the way a bit."

"Thanks. That'd go down a treat."

Ellen gazed after the tall Californian swaggering out of the door and hid a smile. She felt a strange softening towards him.

"Good bloke, eh?"

Ellen swung around. She'd forgotten her brother was standing there watching.

"Maybe." She was giving nothing away. "Did you two come down on his bike?" she asked, to change the subject.

"Sure did! Took me back some. Might get me another bike one of these days. That Harley sure goes."

"Oh, Ron!" Ron might be her older brother, but sometimes Ellen felt he acted like he was a good ten years her junior. "A bike? What next? You already have a pickup, a boat and an ATV. How many more toys do you need?"

"I'm just a boy at heart," Ron said. "But, seriously, what d'you think of Travis?"

Ellen felt herself blushing and started to sort the oddments on the counter, looking down to avoid meeting her brother's eyes. She was startled when Ron's hand covered hers forcing her to be still. She raised her eyes. "He's okay, I suppose," she said. "Seems to be a big help to you, and that alone would put him in my good books. But… what… where…?" She waved her arms around to encompass the many questions in her mind regarding her brother's new best buddy.

"I told you. He's an old army mate… from California… had a bad scene down there, and he's come up here to start afresh. Can't blame a guy for that."

"No." The word came out slowly. "But what does he do for a living?" Ellen took a deep breath. "Is he like you? Does he get by on his Vet's pension?" There, it was out now – her key disquiet about Travis.

"You'll have to ask him." Ron was giving nothing away.

"Do you know?" Ellen's curiosity was made more so by Ron's reticence.

"As I said, it's up to him. It's not for me to say."

Ellen was stuck. She knew her brother well, and when he took this tack there was no shifting him. Blowed if she'd ask Travis what he did – that smacked of showing too much interest in the fellow. Maybe Dad would get it out of him at dinner the following evening. Dad was good at that – didn't brook no for an answer. But she wondered why it was such a secret – surely the guy didn't have criminal tendencies? She'd stay wary till she had an answer.

"Here we are!" The door was pushed open, and the object of their discussion backed in carrying three containers of soup and holding a bag of crackers under his arm. "Where shall I put them?"

"Bring them back to the office," Ellen directed, leading the two men to the back of the shop and clearing a spot on her desk. "Pull up a chair." She looked around, realizing there were only two chairs.

"It's okay. This'll do me." Travis perched on a corner of the desk, lifted the top off one of the soup containers, and put down the crackers. "So," he began, "this is where you hide out?"

Ellen suppressed the irritation that threatened to well up again. What was it about the guy? Could she really be attracted to him? She knew next to nothing about him, apart from the fact he was a friend of Ron's. And that wasn't much of a recommendation if past experience was anything to go by. No, she'd be best to steer clear of any of Ron's buddies. She sneaked a look at Travis out of the corner of her eye as she eased the lid of her own soup. He was pretty easy on the eye. Coralie was right about that. Might be around her own age – a bit younger than her brother. Her eyes swept over his broad shoulders stretching the soft suede of his fringed jacket. While he was busy drinking his soup, crunching on a cracker and jawing with Ron, her glance was drawn down to the tight jeans fitted into his long black boots, one of which was swinging from the desk. He put his drink down. Ellen quickly looked away and busied herself with her own lunch.

"It was kind of your folks to invite me to dinner tomorrow." Travis seemed determined to engage her in conversation. "I'll be giving Ron a ride again tomorrow, so…"

"Makes sense," Ron put in. "I need to get back up home after dinner, and this is still…" He held up his wounded arm.

"It's what Mom does," Ellen said, then, realizing she might sound ungracious, repeated Ron's words. "It does make sense… and you'll be made very welcome."

"By you, too, I hope?" There was a glint of something Ellen couldn't quite identify in Travis' eyes.

She smiled. "And by me too." When he smiled, his eyes crinkled up at the corners making her want to share the joke, even if it was at her expense. Ellen finished her soup and gathering up the rubbish, tossed it into the bin.

"Now, guys. I need to get back to work. Lunch is over. My customers will be pouring through the door again any minute. What do you two have planned for the rest of the day? Are you part of the biker line-up?" She raised her eyes to Travis in a challenge.

"Not me!" He managed to look sheepish. "Can't be doing with a show like that. No, me and Ron'll mosey around. Take in a few of the stalls, check out the floats readying themselves for tomorrow, watch some street performers, that sort of thing."

Ellen looked at him suspiciously. He was trying too hard to sound like the layabout she'd first taken him for. There was more to this man than first appeared. He would take a bit of getting to know. And, as the two men sauntered out the door, she wondered if getting to know him was really what she wanted. Wouldn't it be easier all round if she kept her distance? She'd managed to eschew men for long enough. Why should she allow this one get under her skin?

*

"What's with you?" Ron punched Travis on the arm with his good fist. "Thought you'd decided to leave Ellen be?"

"Just teasing her a bit. She didn't rise to the bait, though. Must be getting into her good books," he grinned and stroked his moustache. "The bad boy act gets them every time."

"Not *my* sister. If she thinks you're a clone of me, you're done. She hasn't had much time for my goings on, not since I got back from 'Nam. Thinks I'm a layabout, and anyone I hang out with must be one too. She could be right about that." He gave his companion a meaningful glance. "Maybe she needs to see your true colors. You could be a big hit then."

Travis' face closed up. In the last two years he'd become a different person, one who he wasn't sure he even liked, but one who could cope with his life as it was now. He'd donned a mask, and to take it off and show his true self, the person he'd been before it all happened, that was to court disaster, reveal his vulnerability. Flawed he might be, but the face he presented to the world was one he'd cultivated, and to remove the curtain would open up the hurt, the hurt he only suffered in the dead of night, the hurt he would never shake.

"No," he said, decidedly. "Best leave it be." Noting his mate's worried look, he tried to change the subject. "Didn't want to be part of it, but wouldn't mind having a gander at the bike festival." Looking along the road, Travis was amazed at the line-up on both sides of the road. They must have come from near and far to be part of the Florence Biker Festival. The pair wandered up and down the street, stopping every now and again to jawbone with a proud owner.

"I'm feeling thirsty. How about you?" Ron asked, as they came to the end of the display.

"Mmm, wouldn't mind something," Travis cleared his throat, realizing it needed some lubrication. There was a bite in the sun too, and he was beginning to feel hot in the jacket that had become his standard attire.

"How about here?" Ron gestured to a nearby tavern.

"Okay by me."

"Ron!" The voice stopped them in their tracks, and turning, Travis found himself face to face with a bearded man and a dark-haired woman who had come up on them from behind. He looked to Ron for guidance.

"Mike, Jenny!" Ron shook the man's hand and gave the woman an awkward hug. "Travis, this is my... our Australian cousin Jenny and Mike, her..."

"Travis." He shook Mike's hand and stretched out to do the same to Jenny, surprised when she gave him a peck on the cheek. She clearly didn't share Ellen's inhibitions abut Ron's friends.

"Been enjoying the Festival?" Jenny burbled. "I've never seen anything like it. I'm so glad we came back to Oregon in time for this. Last time I was here, Maddy was in hospital, and I missed all this. Did you see the pageant earlier? Wow, that was some show!"

"Got the calm Jenny here pretty excited," put in the man called Mike, nudging his companion, who smiled at him intimately, before turning a calculating eye on Travis.

"So you're Travis," she said, with a gleam in her eye and seemed about to say more, but Ron intervened.

"We were just going in here. Care to join us?"

Travis regarded the two newcomers. So this was Ellen's Australian cousin. The one Ron had mentioned brought his car back. His first thought was that the two women weren't at all alike. Sure, they were both tall with dark hair, but it stopped there. This woman, with her sharp features and high cheekbones had a sense of urgency about her, as if something was driving her. She didn't possess Ellen's serenity, her almost regal bearing, her innate goodness. Now where had that come from? Travis shook his head in wonder. He didn't know the woman. Had only met her a few times, and she'd been irascible, so where did this impression of tranquillity and composure come from?

While all this had been going through his mind, the others had made a decision, and Travis found himself being led into the tavern. They settled themselves into a booth by the window, and Travis and Jenny were left alone while the other two went in search of drinks.

"So," Jenny gave Travis a direct look. "What have you been doing to my cousin?"

Travis recoiled, stunned. "Your cousin? Ellen? I barely know the woman. What do you mean?" He could feel his face redden, and his feet shuffled under the table. Was she a witch?

Jenny sat back and regarded him solemnly. "You seem to have gotten under her skin. Not an easy thing to do. Ellen's usually so serene and unruffled. I don't think I've ever seen her so discomfited."

Travis saw Jenny bite her lip as if she'd said too much. She may have. Her words gave him a strange feeling – as if something was crawling under his skin. It was uncomfortable. He didn't like it. He was at a loss for words and relieved when the other two returned bearing drinks.

"Get that down you." Mike placed the inevitable Coke in front of Travis, handing a glass of wine to Jenny and taking a long draught of his own beer before sitting down beside his wife. Ron joined Travis on the other side of the table.

"Coke?" Jenny raised her eyebrows at Travis. "You don't drink beer?"

"No." Travis looked down into his glass, hoping she'd leave it at that. He'd had enough of her innuendos and didn't care to explain himself to her about his drinking habits or lack of them.

"Leave the man alone." It was Mike who came to his rescue. "Well," he took another swallow of his drink. "What did you guys get up to today?"

"We went to see The Moving Wall," Ron said quietly.

"What's that?" Jenny wrapped her hands around her glass, her eyes wide with interest. It was Travis who answered.

"It's a half-size replica of the Vietnam Veterans Memorial in Washington," he began. "Ron and I… that's where we met. Not at the memorial," he smiled deprecatingly. "In Vietnam." He paused, and Mike interrupted.

"You were both there? I was one of the lucky ones. I wasn't called." He looked down at his hands, clearly embarrassed to have escaped. "I registered, of course, but…"

"Yeah," Ron muttered.

"The Moving Wall…" Jenny prompted.

Travis continued, "It was built back in the eighties by a guy called John Devitt. Guess he wanted to share the experience of the memorial for those who couldn't make it to Washington to see the one there. Now it travels through the country. It's here this week."

"A poignant experience, I expect." Jenny's eyes softened as she spoke.

"Mmm."

"A man of few words." Jenny's smile took the sting out of her comment, and she proceeded to fill the conversational void with talk of what she and Mike had been up to: the coronation of the Rhododendron Queen and her court on Friday along with the school music program and the boat regatta and rhododendron show that morning. "And we're looking forward to the Floral Parade tomorrow," she concluded, sitting back with a sigh.

Travis was suddenly conscious of Mike's eyes on him. He finished his drink and asked if the others wanted refills. The answer was a resounding 'No' from Jenny.

"We need to be getting back to Seal Rock," she said, rising. Mike followed suit and shook hands with the men, while Jenny gave each of them a peck on the cheek. "Be sure to come visit us," were her parting words, as they headed off, leaving Ron and Travis gazing after them.

"She sure has a lot of words, your cousin," Travis said after a long pause.

"Yeah, women!" Ron agreed.

"Another?" Travis held up his empty can.

"Don't mind if I do."

*

Jenny and Mike drove up the highway in silence for a time, before Jenny turned to look at her companion. "There's something on your mind. Spit it out!" she demanded.

"Nothing really," was Mike's response. "It's just…"

"Yes?"

"Travis…"

"He's the guy who has Ellen all of a twist. Bit of a mystery, but he *is* quite a hunk!"

"No, not that… it's just… he looked vaguely familiar."

"Maybe you met him back in San Francisco?"

"Maybe… It'll come to me. Let it percolate for a bit."

Jenny knew when to stay silent. She gazed out of the window for the remainder of their trip, saving up all of her comments on the Festival and the meeting with the two men for later. But when the pickup turned up the track, they saw Maddy, her godmother, waving to them so Mike drew in and stopped. Hopping out, Jenny gave the older lady a hug, while Mike turned off the engine and stepped out on the driver's side.

"Have you time for a cuppa? Then you can tell me all about the Rhody Festival. I'd have loved to get down there, but the crowds are too much for me these days."

"Sure we do." Jenny took Maddy's arm as they walked towards the house – the house she'd come to love on her visit the previous year, the house where she'd revealed her growing affection for Mike to an understanding Maddy.

It was over an hour before the pair bade Jenny's godmother farewell and drove up the rest of the track to where their cabin stood. They could hear Ben barking before they stopped, and the black Labrador bounded to the gate to greet them, his tongue hanging out in welcome.

"Hey, old fellow. Did you think we'd abandoned you?" Mike rubbed his pet's ears, while Jenny began to unload the tray of the pickup. "Let me do that, honey." He relieved Jenny of the two rhododendron plants she was struggling with. "Where would you like them?"

"Do you think we have time to plant them before dark? I'd kind of like to get them in and watered before sundown. Don't want them to dry out any."

"Sure thing. Show me the spots you have in mind, and I'll get the holes dug, if you can feed Ben." Hearing his name combined with the word 'feed' Ben began frolicking around their feet, getting in the way and causing the pair to laugh.

"He's making up for us leaving him alone all day. Come, Ben," Jenny directed, making her way into the house and heading for the kitchen. She made sure his water bowl was full, then instructed the dog. "Now wait here, I won't be a minute." Hurrying outside, Jenny indicated to Mike the places she'd set aside for the bushes, returned to fill Ben's food bowl, then out again to retrieve a few packages from the pickup. She'd loved the various craft and food stalls and, as the day progressed, had managed to collect several bits and pieces which she now carried into the kitchen.

All thoughts of Travis and Ellen had been relegated to the back of her mind, so she was surprised when, after dinner, Mike broke off their conversation about the following day's activities to pickup a book which had been lying on a side table. He fell silent as he examined the back cover. Then he took off his glasses and pointed to the photo of the author.

"That's it!" he exclaimed. "It's in the eyes. You can grow a beard and change the hairstyle, but you can't change the eyes."

"What are you talking about?" Jenny was puzzled.

"This guy, Peter Travers. The guy who wrote this book you bought. He and Travis – they're one and the same!"

Nine

"What!" Mike had Jenny's full attention. "You mean…?"

"I do," Mike handed the book to Jenny. "If you hide the chin and hair… see the eyes? The eyes don't change. He and Travis – they're one and the same," he repeated.

"No." Jenny held the book this way and that. "I can't see it, but I believe you. So this means…"

"He's not the layabout he pretends to be. He's a famous author. The very one Ellen is promoting in her display. But he's here incognito."

"I wonder if Ron knows." Jenny took a closer look at the picture, before putting the book down. "He does look very different. Do you think Ellen…?"

"No. I'd lay bets Ellen doesn't know. But Ron? Maybe. The two were together in Vietnam all those years ago. It would make sense if he'd confided in him." Mike pulled on his beard, a habit he had when thinking.

"D'you think…?"

"No!" Mike forestalled his wife, clearly aware of what she was about to suggest. "I don't think you should say anything. It's up to Travis or Peter – whatever the guy's name is – if he wants anyone to know. None of our business."

"But…"

"No, Jenny." Mike's voice was gentle. "I know Ellen's your cousin, and I know you'd like to do something for her – help her the way you feel she helped you last year. But this is something else. Travis – as he wants to be called – must have his own reason for keeping his identity a secret. We should respect that."

"I guess so." Jenny realized her husband was right. It *was* none of their business if Travis wanted to remain silent about his writing. She picked up the book again, suddenly seeing it in a different light. "Ellen said the author wasn't available," she mused. "I wonder what happened to make him hide out up here, to pretend to be someone else."

"Maybe nothing." Mike appeared to be growing tired of the conversation. "Lots of authors write under a pen name. Peter Travers is probably just that. And as for why he's up here. The poor guy might just want a break. We all need that from time to time."

"Mmm." Jenny gazed into space, remembering she had come here for exactly that reason just over a year ago. And how her life had changed as a result. She looked fondly at Mike. To think she had considered herself finished with men and love, had believed she'd never dance with a man again, when this gentle man was waiting in her future, waiting here at Seal Rock. She sighed and reached out to touch the back of her husband's hand. He turned his over to curl his fingers around hers.

"I hope he tells Ellen," she said at last. "They'd be perfect together."

"That's not what you thought earlier," Mike reproached her. "Does his being a famous author really make all that difference?"

"Well," Jenny squirmed in her seat, realizing her husband had a point. "It's just that, Ellen owning a bookshop, and Travis writing books… it all seems to fit together rather nicely." With that, they put all thoughts of Ellen and Travis aside and concentrated on each other.

*

When she awoke on Sunday, Ellen had a strong sensation of something momentous about to happen. But whereas her instinct usually indicated to her the nature of her premonition – good or bad – this time the vision was cloudy. Rising slowly, she pinned up her hair and, turning the tap to cold, entered the shower with a shudder. A cold shower was what she needed. Well, cool, she decided, shivering under the icy blast and turning the dial towards warm. Her waking thoughts washed away with the soap suds, and by the time she was dry and dressed, Ellen felt invigorated.

This promised to be another busy day. The grand Floral Parade at noon would bring the tourists flocking to Old Town again and should be good for business. Ellen wanted to reach the shop early to be prepared for the early birds, who were sure to be wandering around seeking breakfast. Her own breakfast was on the run – a couple of slices of toast with peanut butter eaten in the car on the short trip. She'd find a coffee later. Maybe Ron and Travis would turn up again, or Jenny and Mike. They'd promised to drop in sometime over the weekend and hadn't made it the day before.

Then there was dinner at the parents in the evening, with Travis as part of the family, or as a hanger-on, she reminded herself. The thought of seeing him on her home turf was something she didn't want to contemplate. Seeing him in *The Reading Nook* was one thing, but in her parents' house where she'd grown up? She pushed that thought to the back of her mind and tried to settle on what needed to be done before opening.

It was almost time for the parade when the sound of the shop bell was followed by the familiar "Hello," and Jenny burst into the shop with Mike tagging along behind her.

Ellen's face brightened. "Hi there. Thought you'd be here around now. Down for the parade?"

"We sure are." Jenny kissed Ellen on the cheek, while Mike looked on, then patted her on the shoulder. "It's like a circus out there. Came in for a rest." With that, she sat down on the nearest chair and fanned herself with her hand.

"Come off it. It's not that bad, though it *is* nice to be out of the crush for a bit." Mike strolled over to Ellen's display table. "Selling many of these?"

Jenny seemed to be about to say something, but Mike forestalled her. "Been reading the copy Jenny bought last week. A good read, and pretty accurate, I'd say. Knows what he's talking about." He threw his wife a look, which puzzled Ellen.

"He's good," she said after a pause, looking from one to the other in surprise. There was something going on here. It wasn't like this pair to be secretive. She sighed. Maybe that was what marriage was all about – having secret looks. But it was a touch annoying. "What is it with you two? Anything I should know?"

Again Jenny seemed about to speak, and again Mike anticipated her. "Private joke," Mike brushed it off. "Sorry. Bit rude of us. Won't happen again. Now Ellen, are you going to get out to see the parade or will you be stuck in here?"

"Oh, I'll be out there. There won't be any customers while it's on, so I'll close up and open again when I see the tail end pass. Wouldn't miss it. I've heard there are some pretty spectacular floats this year, and I always love the marching bands."

"They seem so American to me," Jenny said, joining Mike at the display table and hugging his arm. She checked her watch. "It's close to noon now. Should we be making tracks?"

"Yes, you're right." Ellen was picking up her keys as she spoke. "They'll be here soon. Listen!"

Sure enough the sound of distant marching music was beginning to filter through the closed door. The three made their way out to the street, which had already filled with onlookers jostling for a spot. They pushed their way closer to the curb, heedless of disapproving looks.

"This should do," Ellen said at last, as they took up position not too far from the edge of the sidewalk. "Not long to wait now."

"Have you any plans for later?" Jenny asked, stretching her neck to peer into the distance, as if hoping for a first glimpse of the parade.

"Family dinner," Ellen replied. "Travis is invited too," she added.

"Travis?" Jenny's voice held a note of something Ellen couldn't quite identify. It was just like in the shop, she thought, Jenny was keeping something from her.

"So? He's bringing Ron down, so Mom thought it only right to invite him," she offered by way of explanation.

"Hmm. Might be a way of getting to know him better," suggested Jenny, but any reply was drowned out by the clamor of the crowd beginning to cheer. The parade had begun.

By the time Ellen returned to re-open her shop, Jenny and Mike had left to wander around the plant sale and the Moving Wall, which they said Ron and Travis had mentioned and Mike was eager to check out. The early afternoon proved to be as busy as Ellen had expected, and it was with a sigh of relief that she closed up and counted her day's takings, before making her way over to her parents' home for dinner.

*

"Where's your dad?" Rita was taking the roast out of the oven. "He's done it again! He promised he'd be back in time for dinner."

"Calm down, Mom." Ellen put the finishing touches to the salad as she spoke. "He'll be back. He always is." Ellen spoke with authority. Her dad had a habit of wandering off on his own, had done for as long as she could remember. But today, he was cutting it a bit fine.

"Dad not back?" Ron appeared in the kitchen doorway, a beer in his hand. "Want me to go look for him?"

"Fat lot of good you'd be on foot. He's taken the pickup and trailer. Goodness knows where he went off to. And what's happened to your friend? Thought he was coming to dinner?"

"He is. He should be here soon, too. He snuck off this afternoon, after the parade. Didn't want to outstay his welcome. I said to come around six."

"Well, it's ten to six now." Rita's face was turning red. "The dinner will spoil if they're both not here soon."

"Let's go through to the lounge and have a glass of wine," Ellen tried to ameliorate the situation. "We can't do much more in here now, and you need something to calm your nerves."

"I don't think… well, maybe a small sherry," Ellen's mother said, as she allowed herself to be shepherded through the house and settled in her favorite armchair. She sighed as she sat back to accept her drink. "I don't know. I should be used to your father by now. It's just that…"

When Dick didn't return in time for dinner, and there was no sign of Travis either, Rita began to wring her hands.

"It's okay, Mom. Travis has probably forgotten," Ellen tried to reassure her mother, while mentally castigating the man and reverting to her original opinion of him. "And Dad, well, you know Dad."

"But it'll be dark soon," Rita wailed. "Ron…"

"Don't look at me. Ellen, maybe you should go out and look for him. I know I offered earlier but…" Ron's voice died away.

"I know, I know. You can't drive. I think we should sit down and have dinner. Mum's put a lot of work into this meal. We shouldn't waste it. Then, if Dad's still not home, maybe we should…"

"Call the police," Ron finished for her.

"I couldn't eat a thing. Oh, you don't think he's had …?" Rita seemed to be having trouble finding the words as she twisted the edge of her apron between her fingers.

"One of his turns," Ellen filled in for her mother.

"What turns?" Ron looked from one woman to the other in surprise. "Dad's been having turns, and you both knew about it? Well!" He sat down with a thump. "This puts a different complexion on things." He rose and started pacing up and down. "We should be out there. Where the shit is Travis? He should be here. He could help us."

"He's *your* friend." Ellen's voice was acerbic. "But we can't do anything right now. We don't know where Dad's gone, and the police won't be interested in an old man who hasn't come home to dinner. The food's on the table." She led the way to the dining room and started dishing out the roast beef and vegetables onto three plates, after closing the window to keep out the smell of a distant forest fire. "Knew it would come to this after the heat today," she said.

The meal progressed without much conversation, the three eating little and pushing the food around their plates. Finally Ellen began to clear the table, more food finding its way into the garbage than had been eaten.

Ron followed Ellen and her mother into the kitchen and placed his good hand on the bench, palm down. "Dad should be back by now. He must have…" Ron cleared his throat. "Something must have happened to him."

"I agree." Ellen finished loading the dishwasher and straightened up. She had a strong sense of disaster and remembered her morning's forewarning of such an event. If only…, but it was too late to think of that now. And how could she have prevented her father from leaving, even if she'd been here?

"What if…?" Rita began to sob. "What if he's had one of his turns… out there… and the fire…"

Ellen reached for her mother's hands and held them tightly. "We'll…" But no one heard what she was about to suggest, as she was interrupted by the ringing of the phone.

*

When he dropped Ron off at his parents' home, Travis wasn't sure how he'd spend the rest of the afternoon. It was getting late. The stalls were all beginning to pack up, and he'd seen enough of the festival anyway. Parking back at Old Town he found himself standing outside *The Reading Nook* staring into the vacant shop at Ellen's book display, which was again looking sad and empty. He stood for a few minutes reflecting how his fans would be disappointed there would be no more Peter Travers books, at least not the kind he'd written before... before everything went belly up for him. His agent and publisher too, he guessed. He'd been ignoring their letters, emails and phone calls. He sighed. Maybe it was time to emerge from the cocoon in which he'd encased himself. But he'd emerge a different person. The writing he'd been doing up at Yachats was much darker. It had been cathartic – getting it all out of his system. But he wasn't sure anyone would want to read it.

He turned away, hands in his pockets and sauntered across the road and along the river, eyes down, kicking a few small stones in his path. He checked his watch, only four o'clock. Two hours to kill before he felt he could turn up at the Williams home. The thought of a home-cooked dinner made his mouth water. He and Ron hadn't bothered with much fancy stuff. Except for the odd meal out, they'd made do with tinned and frozen meals, the occasional takeaway from a local fast food outlet providing variety in their diet.

Returning to his bike, he sat straddling the machine for a few minutes, stroking his beard, lost in thought. Maybe tonight, he could get to know Ellen a bit better, maybe they could talk, maybe he could even..., but he wasn't ready to go down that path. Firing up the bike, he rode out to the dunes, remembering the freedom of riding across the sand, the smoothness of the powdery substance beneath him and the freshness of the air.

It was exactly as he remembered. There'd been a car parked at the hire shop, but once out on the dunes, it was as if he had the place to himself. Astride the ATV, Travis rode up sand hills and down into the hollows, taking an inordinate pleasure in the sense of freedom it gave him, traveling across the shifting and rolling sand dunes with not another soul in sight. He was just reveling in what he was beginning to think of as his very own kingdom, when he saw something in the distance. It looked like a dark shadow. His first instinct was to ignore it, but common sense prevailed. He rode toward the shape, slowing down as he drew nearer, and the shadow began to take substance.

As he came closer, Travis was shocked to see an overturned ATV with the figure of a man lying motionless beside it. Stopping the bike and dismounting, he walked carefully over, his feet sinking into the soft sand with every step, making it a longer process than he'd anticipated.

When he reached the scene, Travis saw that the body had been thrown some way from the overturned vehicle and lay in the sand at an awkward angle. Moving as quickly as he could, Travis reached the inert form. He bent down to determine the man was elderly and, more importantly, was still alive and conscious, though clearly in pain.

"What happened?" Travis' voice was soft, almost a whisper, as if to mirror the gravity of the situation. He bent down and put his ear close to the man's mouth in an attempt to hear what the stranger had to say, but the only response was a deep groan. Travis straightened up. He looked around. There was nothing and no one in sight. He brushed his hands on his butt as he pondered what to do. Obviously he needed to go for help, but he didn't want to leave the man unattended. He took his cell phone from his pocket and examined it dubiously. Would there be a signal out here? He could try. But the message *no signal* appeared, no matter how often he tried. He looked around again. Then, bending down closer to the figure on the ground, spoke quietly, "I need to go for help, bud. I'll be back." Again the only response was a groan. With a last look at the recumbent figure and the overturned ATV, Travis mounted his quad and headed back to the rental center.

"Look as if you've seen a ghost, man," greeted the owner, dressed in typical Oregon fashion, jeans and checked flannel shirt, his large belly hanging over a thick leather belt and his beard making Travis' own look like an effete fuzz.

"There's someone out there," Travis gestured the way he'd come. "He's come off his ATV. It's overturned, not on him, thank God, but he's hurt real bad. We need to get him back here… an ambulance…" He ran out of breath and dragged his fingers through his hair.

"Come off his ATV, you say? That'll be him that came earlier." The man pointed to the pickup sitting by the shop, and this time Travis noticed the trailer hitched behind it. "Brought his own. Been out there some time." As he was speaking, the man was moving towards a larger vehicle. It was what they called a king-sized buggy – used for taking groups of people out on the dunes. "I'll go out and see."

"But…" Travis couldn't' see the point of this. "Surely an ambulance?"

"Wouldn't make it out there. Wrong sort of wheels. Hop on. You can show me where he is, and we'll see what we can do. Used to be a paramedic in the city, before I opted out of the rat race and came here." He loaded a first aid kit and a stretcher into the back and gestured to Travis to join him. "Call on that." He passed his cell phone to Travis before they took off.

To Travis' surprise, the phone connected him to emergency services, but the news wasn't good. A traffic accident – a multiple vehicle pile-up – had taken place on the road out to Eugene. It seemed all the local ambulances and emergency vehicles had headed out that way, and the traffic was gridlocked with the flow from the Festival. They weren't going to see one here anytime soon.

They reached the vehicle and its owner sooner than Travis had anticipated, and Travis watched while his companion, Big Ben as he'd asked to be called, examined the injured man.

"He seems concussed," Big Ben reported, "and probably something broken, but we need to move him. Can you bring over the stretcher? I'll explain how you can help me move him without damaging him anymore than he is already."

By the time they'd loaded the now comatose man onto the back of the large vehicle, the day was sinking into darkness. Travis wondered what their next move would be, once they returned to the rental center. If the ambulances were still all busy, how were they to get him to hospital? When they got back, Travis found out.

"You can take him in my station wagon," Big Ben instructed. "I need to stop here, but you can drive him."

Travis broke out in a cold sweat. His legs began to tremble, and he felt physically sick. He couldn't drive. He hadn't driven since… Shit, this was a real fuck up!

"That'll be right, won't it?" The other man didn't wait for an answer. "I'll see if he has some ID in his pickup," he said, walking over to the other vehicle and returning with a wallet. "Here it is. Dick Williams. That'll be him."

Ten

"Dick Williams?" Travis repeated the name, his tongue curling around the words. It couldn't be. Surely not? Williams was Ron and Ellen's family name. But he was due to be there for dinner, so surely their dad would be at home right now, not lying on the sand dunes like some derelict with no home to go to?

"You right, mate?"

Travis gave himself a shake. "Sure, so that's the guy's name. You got his wallet there?"

"In the glove box. There's a number here. I'll call his folks if you…"

Travis began to tremble, a sinking sensation in his stomach. Big Ben couldn't be expecting him to… No, it was out of the question.

"Ambulance?" he stuttered.

"No chance. They're all at that pile up. Will be there for hours, it sounded like. No, we need to get this guy to hospital on our own. I can't leave here, but you can take my station wagon. There's room for him to lie out in the back if we put the seats down. Are you sure you're all right? You look a bit strange."

Travis realized he'd gone white at the thought of driving. He couldn't. He hadn't even been in a car since… But he was stuck in this situation. A man could die if… "Can't you go?" he asked weakly. "Maybe I could stay here?"

"No, no. Can't do that. Here." Ben threw the keys at Travis, whose hands automatically rose to catch them. "You open it up, and I'll get him ready. I've some blankets in the shed. And we need something to stabilize him. Seems to have done a bit of damage."

Travis wanted to ask Ben why he couldn't go himself, but the other man didn't give him the opportunity, disappearing into his office. He sighed, drew a deep breath and looked up to the heavens, praying he could do this.

As he opened up the station wagon and lowered the back seats, Travis found himself repeating the positive affirmations his counsellor had tried to teach him two years earlier. He'd decried them at the time, but they'd been stuck there in his subconscious waiting for this moment. Shit, who'd have thought it? He'd vowed never to drive, never to enter a car again, and here he was preparing to be the Good Samaritan to a stranger. Maybe it was fate, kismet or whatever people called it. He sighed heavily. A bit of good cheer would go down well, help his nerves, but he'd sworn off that too.

"Coffee, buddy? Look like you could do with one." Big Ben was carrying a swag of blankets over one arm and a mug of coffee in his other hand. "Get yourself around that, while I set these in the back."

Coffee – a life saver. Travis sipped the hot liquid greedily, feeling its warmth trickle right down to his toes.

"Ready?"

The question came all too soon. Travis gulped, wiped his mouth with the back of his hand, and put down the empty mug. "Ready as I'll ever be," he replied, moving to help load their patient into the back of the vehicle.

"I've called the hospital. They're expecting you. You should make it ahead of the road accident, though they'll most likely be taking their folk to Eugene. Out-of-towner are you? Know the way?"

"Yeah, took my mate a week or so ago," Travis replied.

"Good stuff. You can bring the car back…" But his final words were lost as Travis maneuvered the vehicle down the track and out onto the road.

The journey was a nightmare, made more so by the thought of the injured man lying behind him. Travis was sweating profusely by the time he drew into the courtyard of the hospital emergency entrance. As Ben had predicted, he was expected, and a couple of staff, waiting with a stretcher, were soon wheeling this Williams guy away.

"Do you want to stay with your friend?" A smiling nurse had

appeared as if from nowhere and was gazing up at Travis.

"He's not," Travis began, then hesitated. "I'll park this somewhere and…"

"Good. The doctor will need to see him right away, but you can sit in the waiting room. There's coffee…" She smiled again and was off.

Travis took his seat in the empty room, grabbing a Coke from a machine strategically placed on one wall. He sat, eyes downcast, holding the can, both hands between his knees. He'd done it! He'd not only been in a car – he'd driven it. Maybe saved a guy's life, too. That should count for something in the book of rules, if there was such a thing. But it didn't make up for… Nothing could do that. He crushed the now empty can in one hand and looked around for a bin. He checked his watch – way past half six. What would Ellen and Ron be thinking? He pulled out his cell phone to call, then put it away again, seeing the sign forbidding cell calls. Interfered with the equipment or some damn thing, though what equipment there was in this sterile waiting room, he was blowed if he could see. Should have called from Ben's, but he'd been in too much of a lather thinking about the drive ahead of him. He rose to find a pay phone, then sat down again. He'd screwed up again. Best to let it be. Ron would understand, his folks probably wouldn't care – just another of Ron's no-good friends. And Ellen? She was better off without him. He'd known that from the first, but… He dragged his fingers through his hair, folded his arms and sat back for a long wait.

*

"Hello, is that you, Dad?" Ellen's voice shook. There was silence on the other end, then an unfamiliar voice answered.

"Who am I speaking to? Is this Mrs Williams?"

"No, it's Ellen. I'm her daughter. Who's this?"

There was a deep sigh at the other end of the phone. "It's Ben Kovak from the ATV hire out on the dunes. It's about Dick Williams… your dad?"

"Yes." Ellen's body began to tremble. She gripped the telephone tightly.

"What's the matter? Who is it?" Rita's face paled, and she made a move toward the phone. Ellen held up her hand to ward her mother off.

"Wait," she mouthed. The voice on the other end of the phone continued.

"He was here," Ben coughed. "We...ell, there's been an accident. ATV went over. Not on him, though." He coughed again and cleared his throat. "Taken to hospital. Umm, maybe you should..."

Ellen didn't wait to hear any more. She replaced the phone and turned to the others.

"Dad's had an accident. We'd better get to the hospital."

"What...?" Rita picked up the edge of her apron and began twisting it in her hands. "Is...? How..."

"Sit down, Mom, and let Ellen tell us what she knows." Ron shepherded his mother to the sofa and sat down beside her. 'What's up, sis?'

"I don't know much more. Someone called Ben from the ATV hire place. Dad was evidently out on the dunes, and there was an accident."

"Oh no!" Rita began to wail. "I didn't know he'd taken that damn thing. I told him to get rid of it. You men!" she rounded on her son. "You're all alike with your boats and bikes and ATVs."

"Now Mom," Ron remonstrated, and was clearly getting set to defend his father and himself when Ellen intervened.

"That doesn't help now. He's alive. It didn't fall on him. For that we can be thankful, but he's been taken to hospital, and that's where we should be going now. We can go in my car. Ron, can you help Mom fetch her coat while I get it started?"

There wasn't much conversation on the way to the hospital, all three too shocked to speak. When they drew in and parked, Ellen turned to her mother in the back seat. "Now don't be too upset, Mom. Dad'll probably look pretty awful, and he won't want to see you in tears," she added, seeing her mother's eyes begin to well up.

The trio hurried into the building, Ron ahead of Ellen, who was holding her mother by the arm. She could feel the older woman quivering as they headed toward the reception desk.

"You must be Dick's family," the nurse greeted them. "He was brought in by his friend." She nodded to a figure on the other side of the room.

"His friend?" Ellen looked over. At first, she was only aware of the back of a tall man standing at the soft drink machine. Then she took a closer look. There was something familiar about the broad shoulders and the beige jacket, the way the long lean legs were splayed out to maintain balance. It couldn't be… her stomach churned and her heart pounded in recognition.

"Hey, buddy. What are you doing here?" Ron greeted the man, who hearing Ron's voice, turned to greet them, Coke in his hand.

"You… you…," Ellen spluttered. "What… how…" Her throat constricted, her tongue sticking to the roof of her mouth. She tried to swallow.

Rita looked at the stranger, then her gaze moved from Ron to Ellen and back again. "Who's this? A friend of your father's? I don't think…"

"It's Travis. Ron's friend. The one who was supposed to come to dinner," Ellen said wearily, adding in an undertone, "and I've no idea what he's doing here."

"Ron. Ellen. And you must be Mrs Williams." Travis nodded to the three. "So Dick Williams *is* your dad. I wondered. It's a common name…" His voice petered away, as if realizing this was no time for small talk.

"You'll be able to see him soon," the nurse spoke again. "Doctor's with him right now. If you take a seat…"

Rita sat down heavily, twisting her hands in her lap.

"How long…?" Ellen began, but the nurse had returned to her paperwork, head down to preclude any further questions.

"Guess we'll have to wait," Ron said, joining his mother on the hard plastic chairs, and leaving Ellen standing staring at Travis.

"Want one?" Travis offered his Coke to Ellen.

"No." She was still trying to work out why he was here, and how it came about that he'd brought her dad to hospital. "How did you meet Dad?" she asked at last.

"I didn't. At least, not till after…" Travis opened the can and took a long swallow.

"Then how…? Did you go in the ambulance?"

"No ambulance. Brought him in Big Ben's station wagon."

"You what?" The words shot out. Ellen was about to castigate him for his carelessness in risking her injured father in a station wagon, when another thought crossed her mind. "But you don't drive," she accused.

"Do now… or did tonight," his voice was terse. "First time in years… not something you forget. Like riding a bike, as they say." He twirled the can in his hands.

She was about to question him further, when she heard Ron cough behind her. Turning round, she saw a doctor walk in. She moved to join the other two just as he began to speak, and gripped her mother's hand.

"Is he?" Rita's voice trembled as she asked the unmentionable. Ellen's hold tightened.

"He'll live." The doctor put their fears to rest, and the hand in Ellen's slackened. "He's pretty shaken up, a few broken ribs and some concussion. Won't know how bad that is till after a few weeks. We need to get him into surgery now, but you can see him briefly before he goes. He won't know you," he warned, adding. "It's thanks to this guy here he's alive. Could have lain out there all night, and ambulances all tied up in a traffic accident on the 126. He rubbed his forehead, before pointing to the far corner. "Over here."

He led the way, Ellen and her family following, as she took a backward look at Travis, now standing with his arms hanging by his sides, looking lost. Ellen felt ashamed at her initial annoyance and gave him a brief smile as they left, vowing to find out more after they'd seen her dad.

*

Well, this was a turn up for the books. Travis watched the three Williams leave with the doctor. Of all the guys in Florence, he'd managed to rescue Ellen and Ron's dad. He drew a deep breath and sank down into a chair. Two cans of Coke in such a short time had elevated his sugar level to such an extent he could barely keep still. Realizing he hadn't eaten since lunch and that had been a hot dog from one of the stalls, he looked around, but the drinks machine and another one serving chips and chocolates seemed to be the only form of sustenance available.

He could leave, he supposed. He had to return Ben's car and fetch the bike. But Travis was reluctant to leave just yet, before he knew the outcome of Dick's condition. And there was Ellen. He'd caught her fleeting smile as she turned to go. Maybe bringing her dad here had won him some brownie points after all. It would be worth waiting to see her again. He crossed his legs and clasped his hands behind his head. Closing his eyes, he pictured her as she'd stood there, before she realized how he'd helped. Boy, she sure got riled up easy. Sign of a passionate nature? He chuckled, then mentally rebuked himself for the thought.

Travis opened his eyes again. Nothing had changed. The nurse was working in the shadow of a desk lamp. No one had entered or left. The only sound was the hum of the vending machines and the tick of the wall clock. A man could go mad here. He stood up and began to pace around the room. The nurse looked up disapprovingly, then returned to her task. Travis sat down again. The events of the day began to replay in his mind. Suddenly he sat up straight. He'd driven a car! He'd driven all the way in from the Dunes. And he'd promised to drive back again. He rubbed his eyes and tugged on his beard, then folded his arms. Shit! Maybe he was cured, cured of this aversion to anything that reminded him of that night. No, cured was putting it too strongly. He'd never be cured of what ailed him, but this was a step forward, a sign he could begin again. Well, wasn't that why he'd left California? Why he was here in small town Oregon?

His eyes closed again, this time of their own accord. He must have dozed off because the next thing he knew, Ron was shaking him by the shoulder.

"They say it's best we go home. We can't do anything here. Dad's being x-rayed and won't be compos mentis for hours yet. Best we get a good night's sleep and come back in the morning."

"I know I won't sleep a wink," Rita complained.

But Ellen took her by the arm and, ignoring Travis, began to lead her to the door. "You'll take one of those sleeping pills the doctor gave you, and it'll be morning before you know it." Then, as if suddenly remembering him, she turned to face Travis. "What about you? Can you still drive?"

Travis stifled a grin at her sudden concern. "Guess I'll have to," he replied, yawning.

"What about Dad's car?" Rita looked around as if to see it sitting there. "It must still be out there at the dunes. We can't leave it there. We should…" Her voice died away as if unsure of the rights of the matter.

"I can bring it back for you," Travis found himself offering. "If it's not too late." He checked the wall clock, surprised to see it was close to eleven. "Or maybe…"

"Oh, would you?" Rita almost whispered the words.

"Surely," Travis replied, not at all sure what he was agreeing to. "I can drop it off…" Then he hesitated. If he returned Dick's car, then how was he to get home himself? "I brought Ron down," he started.

"I'll stay with Mom tonight," Ron said. "You could too, but…" He looked at his mother and sister.

"There's no room," Ellen said. "When I moved out, Mom and Dad turned my room into a sun room with plants and stuff. No room to swing a cat." She appeared to think for a moment, then spoke quickly. "You can stay at my place for tonight. I'll ferry you over to pick up your bike before we come back in the morning. That'll be right, won't it? You won't mind an early start?"

She didn't wait for a reply, but quickly jotted down her address on a piece of paper. "I'll stay up till you get there, but don't be too late," she adjured, before heading out into the darkness after her mother and brother.

*

Ellen's eyes snapped open, her stomach churning. She sat straight up, gulping for breath, her hands gripping her sheet tightly to her neck. She was in her own bedroom, and it was still dark. She turned on the bedside lamp, wide awake. It was the same dream as before, but this time it had been clearer, much clearer. She had seen the two people in the front seat so distinctly, she could have been seated right behind them. No, that wasn't right. It had been as if she was above and behind them. Then there had been a bang and bright lights, so bright she'd had to shield her eyes, then… She shook her head in a fruitless attempt to dismiss the sights and sounds. But the squealing tires, the low thud of the impact, the screech of metal meeting metal, the shattering of glass, the almost inhuman screams, the emergency vehicles and crew, the mangled pile of cars and the hovering helicopter were all too real.

Knowing she'd not get back to sleep in a hurry, she slipped out of bed and, pulling on her old blue candlewick robe, headed to the kitchen. At the doorway, she stopped. The light was on. Sitting at the table with his back to her, was a man with blonde hair. The hair was longer, but she recognized the shape of his head and the way it was tilted to one side. With the light shining on it, it was all too familiar. He was the man from her dream.

Ellen's right hand rose in an involuntary movement to clutch the collar of her robe and pull it up tight to her neck. The other felt for the surface of her dresser as she tried to make sense of what she was seeing. The figure turned, and Ellen gazed into a pair of striking pale blue eyes set in a familiar face, bordered with faded blonde hair and beard. She blinked, then remembered. Travis. He'd come to sleep in her spare room. She'd offered him a bed for the night without too much thought. Had shown him in there herself, just before going to bed around – she checked the clock on the oven – four hours ago. Now here he was, sitting in her kitchen as if he belonged there.

"Couldn't sleep?" His lazy voice was real. This was no dream. "I made myself some coffee. Hope that was okay. Like some?"

"Coffee… that would be good." Ellen sensed her voice was coming from a long way away, as if her head was stuffed with cotton. "I had a bad dream," she said by way of explanation.

"Me too. Here, get that down you." Travis poured her a strong black coffee.

Ellen sipped the liquid, the hot caffeine bringing her fully awake.

"So," Travis began. "What's your dream about? May help to share it some."

"I don't…" Ellen took another sip of her coffee, then placed her mug carefully on the table. Would it hurt to share with him? "I can't," she said, finally. "I… I… sometimes I receive messages, see what's going to happen." She stole a look at Travis, prepared for his ridicule. Heaven knows, she'd been subjected to lots of that. But, instead of looking sceptical, he leant forward, interested.

"Really? I'd heard that some Native Americans had the sight – isn't that what it's called? A gift, isn't it?"

"Not always." Ellen picked up her mug again and wrapped her hands around it. She gazed at Travis. It had been him in her dream, hadn't it? But the child? The car? She shook her head. It didn't make sense.

They sat in silence. Then, "Do you have a child?" Ellen asked abruptly.

"No!" Travis sounded stung, as if her words had opened an angry wound, one which had only been papered over, ready to erupt at any time.

Ellen ran her fingers through her night-time hair, the long thick strands lying across her shoulders like a curtain. 'Then it couldn't have been…' She lifted the mug to her mouth and took a gulp of the hot liquid. "Forget I said anything. Sorry."

"No," Travis' eyes bored into hers, "Tell me!"

"It's this dream I keep having – a premonition, I imagine. There's a car with a couple and a young boy. Then an accident – lots of noise, people, shouting, blackness…" Her voice died away at the expression on her companion's face.

Travis appeared stunned. "But that's my dream!"

A shiver ran down Ellen's spine. She was chilled, as if a window was open allowing an icy blast to blow in, causing the back of her head to freeze. But all the windows were closed. This was weird, unlike anything she'd known before. It was beyond belief. How could it be?

"*Your* dream?" her voice was ragged. Her eyes widened in shock. "It can't… how…?"

Travis reached across the table to cover Ellen's hands which were still wrapped around her coffee mug. "Ellen, it's already happened. It was two years ago."

Distraught, Ellen pulled away from his grasp. "But it can't have! I mean…," she paused, "I always… I've always seen events before they happened. This…" She waved her hands in the air. "This doesn't make sense."

Eleven

Travis didn't say anything for a few moments, then made up his mind. He pushed his chair back and met Ellen's wild eyes. "I'd like to tell you a story. How long have we got?"

"Until I need to drive you back to the hire place – a couple of hours at least. I don't think either of us will be getting any more sleep tonight."

The pair sat in silence, then Travis began to speak.

"Well, it goes back a long way, back to when I set foot on Vietnam soil, I guess." Travis fingered his beard and gazed into space. He was seeing himself, a raw nineteen year-old, fresh out of high school, landing in this foreign place along with a horde of other young Americans.

"That would have been?"

"Nineteen-seventy. The war had been going for some years by then, and there were mass protests back home." He shook his head. "Never thought I'd be one of those to go, but as soon as I left school…" Travis cleared his throat, the memory of receiving his letter as fresh as on the day it arrived. "As soon as I saw the word 'Greetings', I knew what it meant – every man and boy in the States knew what that sort of letter meant – I'd been drafted."

"Ron got one too," Ellen said quietly. "It nearly broke Mom's heart. But he was keen to get out there, do his bit. What about you?"

"I wasn't really sure. I hadn't a clear idea of what I wanted to do with my life, so it delayed the inevitable search for a job. Didn't think I wanted to go to college or university, not then. Didn't want to go to war either. Thought of trying to dodge the draft – go up to Canada or get busted for smoking pot. Smoked it anyway. I guess we all did back then." He rubbed his eyes and dragged his fingers through his hair. "We were among the last to go," he said wearily. He picked up his mug, put it down again.

"Well, when we got there, it wasn't what I'd expected. Don't really know what I'd expected. Something like *Mash*, I suppose, though the show hadn't come out then." He laughed, a haunted laugh. "Thought maybe I could make a difference, that it was a patriotic war. I couldn't have been more wrong. 'Kill anything that moves' seemed to be the slogan. But I'm getting ahead of myself. They sent me to training at Fort Knox – among the gold!" Travis smiled grimly. "That's where I met Ron. We went out at the same time, two grunts together – that was us."

He dropped his eyes. "The destruction, the carnage – it was like nothing you could imagine. Helicopters swooping to fire on farmers in rice paddies, people salvaging household items from homes we'd set on fire, millions of innocent civilians killed and wounded."

Travis passed his hand across his eyes, remembering. "There was little regard for the Vietnamese people. Our guys shot early and often – they didn't seem to care who'd become trapped in the war zone. It was a nightmare." He closed his eyes, seeing a Vietnamese corpse with the Ace of Spades – the death card – in its mouth, and shook his head again. "It haunts me still – always will."

Ellen gasped, her hand coming up to cover her mouth. "Ron never talked about it," she said weakly. "I didn't…"

"Nor did I. When I killed my first child – saw him fall from a bullet from *my* gun…" Travis heard Ellen's quick intake of breath. "I didn't think I could go on. That's why…" He covered his face with his hands, then sat upright again and met Ellen's eyes. "That's why, when I came back, I knew I had to do something, knew if I was to live with this guilt, I had to make some sort of recompense. I wasn't like those guys who wanted to stay – stay to make some form of atonement. No," he sighed. "I wasn't brave enough for that. I came back."

"So?"

"I went to college, studied teaching. Decided to try to help young people that way." Travis twisted his fingers together, gazing at them as if they held the answer to the meaning of life. "Found I had a knack for it, could relate to the kids. Started researching my family tree, too. That's when I found…" He looked at Ellen through half closed eyes. "That's when I discovered my Native American Heritage. It's on my mother's side – both lines. Cherokee."

"Hmm, so you said. You didn't know before that?"

"Well, there were rumors, you know. But nothing definite. Anyway, I got caught up in the whole family tree thing, started to research it. Then, when I finished my degree, I sought out an Indian school and taught there." Travis stole a glance at Ellen and noted he'd piqued her interest. She hadn't been expecting anything like this.

Ellen's eyes lit up. She pushed her hair back over her shoulder. Such beautiful hair, thought Travis. How he'd love to run his fingers through it.

"You? You taught in an Indian school?"

"Sure did. That's where I met my wife, Allie." Travis' eyes began to sting, and he closed them for an instant to hold back the incipient tears.

"Was she a Native American?"

"No." Travis opened his eyes again and regarded Ellen, who was now observing him with interest.

"So you're married?"

"No." Realizing his answers might sound blunt, he spread his hands on the table, palms down. "Let me finish, and you'll see where I'm coming from, and how it all leads to my dream."

"Sure, your dream." Ellen sat back, mug still held in both hands. "Go on."

"We married, and as we both loved children, we wanted to start a family right away." Travis fingered his beard again. "I wanted to have my own child… saw it as way of giving back the life I'd taken, if that makes any sense." He met Ellen's eyes and saw only compassion there.

"Anyway it wasn't to be… not for years anyway. Then, just as we'd given up hope, along came Ricky – our own little boy."

Gazing across the table, Travis could see comprehension dawning in Ellen's eyes.

"Then…?" Her voice was subdued.

"Yes. That's what you saw – what I see when I close my eyes." There was a long pause. "I killed *him* too." Travis swept his hand over his eyes to hide the moisture beginning to form in the corners of his eyes. He blinked, as if returning from a daze and saw the sympathy in Ellen's expression. "So now you have my story."

"Oh, you poor man. I can't imagine how that must have been. But you didn't kill him. It was an accident. I saw it. There was nothing you could have done. The truck was careering out of control. The lights were blinding. But…" Ellen began, speaking slowly. "It's not the whole story, is it?"

Ellen was becoming too curious. There were still some things Travis wanted to keep to himself. He ostentatiously looked at the clock. "Shouldn't we be making tracks? When did you say you wanted to be at the hospital?"

Ellen followed his glance. "You're right," she sighed and stretched her arms above her head. "Time to shower and dress. Breakfast?"

"I'll grab something on the way back. You?"

"Coffee'll see me through for now. I'll drink it while I dress."

Half an hour later the pair were heading out to the dunes to retrieve Travis' bike. It was a damp, misty morning, which didn't encourage conversation. Travis was glad. He'd talked enough to last him for some time. Used up all his words and revealed more of himself than he cared. What was it about this woman that encouraged confidences?

When they reached the dunes, he hopped out. It was only when he began to close the car door that a thought occurred to him. "What'll you do about the bookshop today, if you're caught up at the hospital?"

"It'll have to stay closed. Pity, as there'll still be a host of tourists around, but it can't be helped. I'll call Coralie from next door to put up a sign. I think you met her."

Travis essayed a smile. "The blonde bombshell? I remember. But say, maybe I could help out, could keep it open for you. Don't have anything else on my agenda today."

Ellen appeared to think for a moment before replying: "Are you sure? I wouldn't like to impose, but…," she paused. "It would be real good of you. Here are the keys." She rifled in her purse before handing him a keyring. "Should be back later. You'll find the cashbox in the back office – the key with the green tag. Thanks." She smiled, a smile that lit up her face. "I don't know why you're doing this for me. I haven't been…"

Travis held out his hand for the keys, his fingers meeting hers. He felt a distinct tingle as flesh touched flesh, before Ellen drew away as if stung. She drove off in a flurry of dust, Travis gazing after her in disbelief. So, the implacable Ellen could be moved. He turned to his trusty Harley, none the worse for its night in the fresh air. There was no sign of Big Ben this morning. Whatever had kept him here last night had ensured he didn't make an early start this morning. Travis smiled, and scribbling a note on the back of an old envelope, found in his pocket, he slipped it under the office door and set off back to Old Town.

*

"Well, I think we should tell her," Jenny said vehemently, while Mike turned the car into a parking spot. "It's not right that he's hiding his other identity from her, whatever the reason."

"Let the man be. I'm sure he'll tell her in his own good time. And it's not the end of the world if he doesn't. Ellen'll have enough to worry about when I give her my news."

"You're right. Fancy that bastard making his announcement this weekend, when he knew all the papers would be full of the Rhody Festival."

"Probably why. Timed it so it'd be lost at the foot of the back page or somewhere equally difficult to find."

"It's not too late, is it? To do something about it, I mean."

"Never too late – not until they start bulldozing the place down," Mike replied grimly, turning off the engine. "Let's go in and give Ellen the news, then we can work out a plan of action."

"Hello!" Jenny's greeting echoed through the shop. "Ellen!" she called out loudly, when her cousin didn't immediately appear.

"Ellen's not here." The figure which emerged from the back office was certainly not the one Jenny expected to see.

"Travis, what are you doing here?" Mike was first to recover from his surprise. "Where's' Ellen?"

"At the hospital." Travis laid down the pile of books he had been carrying and put his hands on his hips.

Jenny thought again what a fine figure of a man he was – the perfect match for her cousin – but was puzzled at his presence here, especially without Ellen. "But you…" she tried to find the right words – words which wouldn't let him know of Ellen's apparent aversion to him.

"Is she hurt?" Mike saved her by asking the obvious question.

"Not her, her dad."

"Uncle Dick?" Jenny's tongue twisted awkwardly around the words. A year ago she hadn't even known of this uncle's existence. "What happened? You were all having dinner last night…"

"Didn't transpire," Travis spoke brusquely. "Her dad had an accident out on the dunes, ATV turned over. Happened to be there and brought him into the hospital."

"*You* did?" Jenny couldn't believe her ears.

"Long story. He was unconscious last night, and the family are going back this morning. Ellen was on her way there when she dropped me off." Travis bit his lip. Too much information. He saw Jenny's eyes widen as she put two and two together and made at least five. He was about to attempt to clarify, when Mike forestalled him.

"She'll be back later, then? There's been some news on the development front. Wanted to have a chat about it. You knew about that?" Mike raised his eyebrows and tugged on his beard.

"Yeah, some. Ron mentioned something about it, and I was here when the little lady from next door was haranguing on about it. A big developer, isn't it?"

"Balcombs."

Travis whistled between his teeth. "Balcombs. Shit! Came across them few years ago down home. They play dirty. What exactly are they up to here?"

Mike hesitated before replying. "It seems they've their sights set on this block of shops. They've registered a development application and an offer to purchase, conditional on the approval. It'd be a disaster, not just for Ellen and the other shopkeepers, for the whole neighborhood. It's a historic site…"

"Are you sure?"

"What?"

"About it being a historic site."

"It was just a figure of speech. I don't really know. You mean…?"

"If we could prove it was really a historic site of some sort. That would put a spanner in their works. I remember..." But what he remembered was lost as the door swung open and Coralie burst in. Today she was expertly coiffed, her blonde hair piled in curls on top of her head and sporting what could only be described as fuchsia highlights, her bosom overflowing from a low cut black tee shirt. All three blinked.

"And you are?" Jenny was first to regain her equilibrium, the men apparently stunned by this vision of feminine excess.

"I'm Coralie... from next door. I came in to... Where *is* Ellen?" Coralie looked around the shop, as if realizing for the first time that Ellen was absent.

"At the hospital," Jenny and Travis spoke at once.

"Her dad's been taken ill," Jenny explained. "She'll be back later. Can we help?"

"No." Coralie turned her attention from Jenny to the two men and seemed to draw herself up, bosom heaving. "Well, it's you again," she addressed Travis, moving towards him coyly. Travis backed away, almost toppling the pile of books he'd laid on a table. Ignoring his retreat, Coralie began to follow him with a smile. "Now what...?"

But by this time, Mike had recovered from his surprise and deflected her attention.

"Travis is minding the shop for Ellen for a while, and we're here now too. We haven't met. Mike." He held out his hand. "And Jenny, Ellen's cousin." He nodded in Jenny's direction. "Have you two met?"

Coralie accepted the proffered hand and turned to look at Jenny. "No. So you're her cousin from Australia. Heard about you, of course, but I was away when you were here last year." She was clearly about to make some additional remark and had half turned towards Travis again, when Mike intervened.

"Well, you can see Ellen later. As you can probably appreciate, we're a bit tied up here at the moment and..."

"I can tell when I'm not wanted. I'll catch up with Ellen when she gets back." And with a backward glance at Travis, Coralie flounced out, the door slamming behind her.

The three looked at each other and began to laugh.

"Got me out of a tight corner there," Travis exclaimed. He raised his eyebrows and blew air through his lips. "Thanks, pal. Now where were we?"

"You were remembering," Mike prompted, "about Balcombs and a historic site."

"Yeah," he leant back against the table, ankles crossed and arms folded. "Was about ten years ago, as I recollect. Same company, most like. Tried to rush things through," Travis stroked his nose. "Locals protested. Didn't do any good, till someone came up with the evidence."

"Evidence?" Jenny appeared puzzled.

"Evidence of the history of the site. Put paid to their redevelopment plans, and everyone was happy."

"Everyone except Balcombs," Mike suggested.

"Except them." One corner of Travis' mouth turned up in slow smile.

"So all we need to do…"

"Is find some evidence to prove it's a historical site," finished Travis for him.

"But how do we do that?" Jenny was still puzzled.

"You have an expert historical researcher standing right beside you," Travis reminded her, nodding towards Mike.

"And…" Jenny picked up a book from the display and turned to the back cover. "This *is* you, isn't it?"

"Jenny," Mike warned.

"It's okay," Travis drawled. "Guess I knew it wouldn't stay secret for long. So you found me out – saw through the disguise." He stroked his beard. "Have you told Ellen? She didn't…"

"Not yet," Jenny replied.

"And not ever," Mike added. "It's your life, buddy, and up to you to let people know."

"If you guys have worked it out, it'll be all over soon enough. But I'd like to tell Ellen myself, if it's okay by you. I was about to earlier, but…"

"Yes, and I'd like to know about earlier." But Jenny spoke in such a low tone that neither of the men heard her. Just as well, she decided, determining to get to the bottom of the matter next time she spoke with her cousin. There was something here she didn't understand. How had Ellen come to leave Travis in charge of her baby when she couldn't stand the man?

*

"You're here already!" Ellen rushed into the hospital, out of breath, only stopping when she saw her mother and Ron seated in the waiting area.

"What kept you?" Rita fussed, standing up to give her daughter a hug. As Ellen's arms wrapped around her mom's trembling body, she realized for the first time, how vulnerable the older woman was. Rita had always been the rock for the whole family. Right now, that rock was beginning to crumble.

"I'm here now." Ellen tossed her heavy plait over her shoulder and helped her mother sit down again. "Is there any news?"

"They say we should be able to see him soon." Ron stood up and began pacing up and down in front of the two women. "I'd…" but a glance from his mother silenced him.

"Do sit down," Ellen entreated her brother, finding his movement disturbing in the otherwise quiet room. They were the only ones there.

Ron sat, dropping his hands between his knees and staring at the floor. "What possessed him?" he said finally looking up at the two women. "There was no need…"

"Your dad has always had a mind of his own," his mother replied, her voice gaining strength as she denounced her husband. "Always," she repeated. "Why, I remember…" But what she remembered was going to have to wait till another time, as just at that moment, a figure, dressed in hospital white, emerged from the door at the far side of the room. All three rose as one.

"Is he…"

"Can we…"

Ellen and her mother spoke together, holding hands as if to ward off any bad news.

"You can see Dick now," the doctor smiled. "He's a little brighter this morning. He'll know you. But he's not out of the woods yet. He took a heavy fall. We've strapped up his ribs, and he's looking better. But the concussion will mean he's a bit fuzzy. He's on painkillers to reduce the pain."

Ellen felt her mother's hand loosen in hers, as the doctor's calming words flowed over them.

"You can go up now."

The two women headed to the elevator, but Ron hung back.

"Are you coming?" Ellen asked her brother.

"Be with you in a sec. You go on up." And he turned towards the doctor, as they entered the elevator.

"Do you think?" Rita's voice was loaded with concern, and the color drained from her face as they neared Dick's ward.

"You heard the doctor, Mom. Dad won't be himself. But I bet he'll be pleased to see us." Ellen tried to hide her own concern, taking her mom's arm as they entered the small private room, where Dick Williams was lying, his face almost as white as the hospital blanket which covered him.

"Hello, Dad," she said, moving towards the bed. "You don't need to speak. Mom and I are here." She moved forward and followed Rita to the bedside. She gave an involuntary gasp, quickly stifled, as she took in the still, fragile shape in the bed. How could this corpselike figure be the same man who had ranted at his family only a few days ago – the head of the family, who challenged anyone who dared oppose him? How quickly he'd lost his commanding presence and turned into a weak old man.

"Dick!" Ellen heard her mother's shocked cry and turned towards her. "He's… he's not…" Rita whispered.

"No, Mom… He's just fallen asleep," she soothed, anticipating her mother's next words and suppressing her own worst fears in an attempt to steady her mom. "It'll give Dad's body time to recover." Ellen tried to speak calmly, but she, too, was shocked by her father's appearance.

Only Ron, who'd just stepped in, seemed to take it in his stride. "Seen a few like that. Better than being awake and suffering. You're right, Ellen. Sleep'll help the recovery process." Ron shook his head. "Saw too many like that in 'Nam."

Ellen turned her head sharply to meet her brother's eyes. This was the first time she could remember Ron referring to his war experience. What had brought it up now? He must have had some inkling of her thoughts, as he slowly tried to explain.

"Seeing Dad lying there… so soon after we visited the Moving Wall… and Travis… it brought it all back." He put his hand over his eyes. "Sorry, sis. Didn't mean to upset you. Thought I'd put it all behind me, then it comes out again – just like that."

Ellen looked askance at her brother. This, coming so quickly after Travis' disclosures of the morning. It was too much. She returned her attention to her parents. Her mother was going to need support in order to cope.

Rita sat down quickly, her head in her hands, and began to rock back and forth, wailing loudly.

"Mom," Ellen put her arms around the older woman. "Mom," she repeated. "This won't do Dad any good."

"I thought you said he was asleep – he can't hear us." Rita lifted her reddened eyes to meet Ellen's. She grabbed her daughter's hand and held on tightly. "What are we going to do?" she sobbed, the tears running down her cheeks unchecked.

"Well, we can't do anything for Dad here," Ellen attempted to sound unruffled, but was only just managing to hold back her own tears. "Why don't we get a cup of something and have a chat to the doctor again?"

"I'll do that," Ron offered, seemingly relieved to take on this task. "You fetch Mom some coffee. There's a machine out there."

The trio made their way out of the ward again and traveled down in the elevator together. Then Ron went off to locate the doctor, while Ellen settled her mother in a seat and addressed the challenge of getting coffee from the vending machine.

*

It was lunchtime when Ellen pushed opened the door to *The Reading Nook* and heard the bell's familiar sound.

"You're back!" Travis looked up from the display table where he seemed to be packing up the current display. "Thought it might be time for a change," he said with a guilty look, like a small boy caught with his hand in the cookie jar.

"Hmm." Ellen considered his words. "Maybe, but it's a pity..." She picked up one of the books. "He writes well and the kids love his books. I don't understand..."

Travis cleared his throat. "There's... I..." But Ellen didn't find out what he was going to say, because, at that moment, the door behind her opened again to admit Jenny and Mike.

"Hoped you'd be back by now," Jenny exclaimed. "How's your dad?" Without waiting for a reply, she threw her arms round Ellen and hugged her tightly. "We came in earlier, and Travis said you were at the hospital. Is Uncle Dick okay?"

"He will be." Ellen untangled herself. "He was asleep when we arrived, but the doctor's happy with him. A couple of broken ribs and some concussion. We're lucky it wasn't any worse. They've strapped up the ribs and apparently it's only a matter of time for them to heal, a few weeks, the doctor said. He can come home tomorrow. Evidently he may be a bit fuzzy from the concussion for a bit, and he'll be on painkillers for a time. They x-rayed him last night, and there's nothing major." She pulled on her plait. "He was getting fuzzy enough without this happening," she said sorrowfully. "He looked so old and weak, lying there. I didn't…" she began, then stopped. Her face brightened.

"What brings you two down here again so soon? Not becoming bored with each other's company already?"

Mike coughed. "No… we… Have you seen the paper?"

"Paper? I haven't had time to turn around," Ellen replied. "What's the paper got to do with anything?"

"Look, guys," Travis said. "We're not busy right now. What say we all go out to lunch and Mike can fill you in, Ellen?"

Ellen gazed around in surprise. This sounded serious. What else could happen? She'd had these premonitions, yes, but now that she'd discounted Travis, surely it was her dad's accident she'd foreseen? "Okay," she agreed and joined the others as they headed outside, only stopping to lock the shop door behind her.

"Now, what do you have to tell me?" All four were seated on benches around a wooden table looking out at the river with large bowls of clam chowder and garlic cheese bread, thickly spread with butter, sitting in front of them.

"Well, it's like this," Mike began, only to be interrupted by Jenny.

"The development – it's in today's paper."

Ellen slumped in her seat. "Oh!" The word escaped with a flow of breath. "I'd forgotten all about that… there's been so much…" She drew herself up straight, head erect. "Right, tell me the worst. Where is it up to?"

"The development company have put up their proposal, but their purchase is dependent on approval of their plans, so…" Mike placed his hands on the table, palms down. "We still have time."

"Time for what?" Ellen was bewildered. So much had happened today. First Travis' revelations, then seeing her dad lying there, helpless. Now this, with Travis sitting beside her, his thigh almost touching hers under the table producing a tingling that she'd never expected to feel again. She attempted to dismiss the sensation and concentrate on what Mike was saying. "You mean…?"

"Yes," Mike sounded eager now. "We have time to organize a protest, time to find evidence."

"Evidence?"

"That's what I wanted to know," Jenny said. "Seems we need to find some historical stuff. Travis…"

Ellen turned to look at Travis. So he was becoming involved in this too.

He smiled deprecatingly and lifted his hands. "Came across these guys in California. Know what they did there. Maybe I can help. Mike and I…"

Ellen looked back at Mike. She was puzzled. "But what…?"

"Travis and I…" Mike cleared his throat and pulled on his beard.

"Yes?" Ellen squirmed with impatience, wishing the two of them would get on with it.

"We can do some research," he looked across at Travis as he spoke. "See what we can find," he finished.

"You and Travis?" Ellen wondered if she was hearing correctly. What could Travis contribute? Even though, after this morning's revelations, she was beginning to view him in a different light, she couldn't see where Mike was coming from.

"Travis…" Jenny began, her eyes moving between the two men, while Ellen looked on helplessly.

"I think…" Mike spoke hesitatingly.

"I think I need to say something, Ellen," Travis' deep voice resonated beside her.

Ellen's eyes widened as she knew deep down that what Travis was about to say could change her opinion of him. Whether for better or worse, she wasn't sure. She began to tremble. This morning she'd seen a Travis she hadn't known existed – a gentler, more vulnerable person. He'd pulled back the curtain he kept around himself and revealed a man haunted by his past, a man desperate to make atonement for earlier actions. Was he going to destroy this new vision she held of him?

"This morning…" he paused, and Ellen could see him biting his lip. "There wasn't time to tell you the full story."

A shiver ran down Ellen's back. What more could there be? Had he deliberately caused the accident? No, she couldn't believe that. She twisted her hands together under the table and waited for him to continue speaking.

"When Ricky was born, I wanted him to understand his Native American heritage. I didn't want him to grow up like me – ignorant of his roots. I told you I'd researched my past. What I didn't say was that I became so involved, I began to research the Native American way." He gave Mike an apologetic look. "That's where I came across Mike's work and heard him speak at a conference. Anyway, when Rick was little, I began to tell him stories about the Native Americans, then I began to write these stories down. I didn't want to use my own name so…"

Suddenly Ellen saw it all. Travis Petersen – Peter Travers. "You're…" she exclaimed. "You're Peter Travers! And all this time I've been raving on about him and how he's gone AWOL; you've been right there all the time."

Twelve

"Guilty." Travis had the grace to look sheepish. It seemed to Ellen that Jenny and Mike heaved a sigh of relief.

"So... why keep it secret all this time?" Ellen was bewildered. Her head felt as if it was full of cotton wool. The room began to tilt, then righted itself.

"Are you all right?" Jenny's voice came from a long way away. Ellen put her hand out to steady herself and encountered Travis' firm warm thigh. She drew it back quickly, as if burnt.

"I need some fresh air." She rose, standing still for a moment as the room seemed to swirl again, then walked unsteadily to the door. Once outside she inhaled a deep breath of the cool air and took in the peaceful scene. The river flowed smoothly along, a few birds taking the opportunity to swoop down on a piece of flotsam. She gripped the white metal handrail and breathed in again, letting her breath flow out slowly.

Travis Petersen, she thought, and Peter Travis. How could she have been so blind? Why, the names were almost the same. What a fool she'd been. And how long had the others known? She was the one with the ability to see things that weren't there. Why was she so blind when it came to this man? Well, not exactly, she reminded herself. There was the dream. It was weird. She'd never known anything like that before. Never before seen an event which had already happened… and to someone she'd yet to meet. She shivered and wrapped her arms around her body. There was something strange going on here, something she'd no control over. Funny, her dreams and premonitions had never troubled her before. She'd accepted them, taken them for granted. Even felt privileged to have been given this gift, to be able to help and comfort others. But this strange link to Travis… it was beyond her understanding.

She became aware of a shadow stretching across the boardwalk. There was someone standing right behind her.

"Are you all right?" Travis' Californian drawl broke into her thoughts. She turned to face him, her eyes raking the high cheek bones, the blonde beard, now neatly trimmed, before meeting the steely blue eyes, which were full of concern. "I'm sorry if I gave you a turn. I wanted to tell you earlier, but…"

"No." Ellen put up her hand to ward off something she couldn't see. "I'll be fine. It was a shock." As she spoke, she realized how lame her words were. Why had the revelation of his author identity come as such a shock? Why had it affected her in this way? She had no answers, and she was one who always had answers. Travis was speaking again.

"After the accident…" He looked at his feet. "I couldn't write." He met her eyes again. "I wrote for Ricky, you see. Of course, I was pleased my books sold, sold pretty well." Travis gave a weak laugh. "But they were always for Ricky. Even when he became older… He was fourteen when…" His voice broke, then he continued. "With him gone, there was no reason." He dropped his eyes again. Ellen's dropped too, and she saw his feet move restlessly, making patterns on the dusty wood. "It was as if I'd dried up inside, with Ricky and Allie gone. I packed a bag and left. It's been just me and the bike since. Been a bit of a nomad, always moving, never making friends. Then I came across Ron on the internet. Thought I'd try catch up. And here I am."

"Yes, here you are," Ellen said. *And here I am, here we both are. Why?* In Ellen's world, everything happened for a reason. There was a rhythm to life. But she had yet to work out why Travis had appeared in her life like this. She tried to subdue the fluttering his nearness caused her, to ignore the attraction she felt for this man, who was no longer a stranger.

There was an awkward silence.

"I guess we should go back in." Ellen pulled on the end of her plait, and with a noticeable distance between them, the two walked back to the restaurant, still in silence.

"There you are," Jenny looked from Ellen to Travis and back again. "Did…"

"Jenny," Mike warned.

"Sorry about that. I had to…" Ellen's hands waved in the air in an attempt to explain her sudden exit. "I'm fine now."

"Coffee anyone?" Mike said, trying to make a return to normal.

"Please. Black." Ellen slid into her place, relieved to be rid of the anxiety which had possessed her earlier.

"Me too."

"Make that three," Travis slid in beside Ellen, who noticed he was taking care not to touch her. A tiny part of her, quickly supressed, wondered if he felt it too – the almost animal attraction which she'd have been quick to deny, had anyone asked. But no one did, though Jenny did give her cousin a knowing look.

*

Back at the shop there was a flurry of customers. When they'd left, Ellen looked around with pleasure, tinged with something she identified as sadness. She'd hate to see it all go, destroyed under a developer's hammer. For a moment she envisaged what her life would be like without her haven of books to come to every day. Then, giving herself a shake, she set to work.

Now she knew there would be no more Peter Travers books, Ellen decided to finish what Travis had started and take down the display. Pity, she thought, studying his photo on the back cover and seeing, for the first time, the likeness to the man she'd taken to be one of Ron's hangers-on. She shook her head at her own foolishness. There it was, right there in front of her – those eyes. Those steely blue eyes that had met hers so frequently over the past week. Those eyes, even more insistent in real life than they could ever be on the printed page.

She'd almost finished and was contemplating her next display, when she heard the door open. Turning, she was confronted with the object of her thoughts.

"Hi!" Travis sauntered in, hands in his pockets. "I… I thought I owed you an apology… more than an apology."

Ellen waited, her hands holding the last of his books. She looked down at it, the back of the book with his photo, then up at the man himself. She shivered, her stomach doing summersaults. Her breath caught in her throat.

"Yes." Ellen waited.

"Umm. Dinner?" Travis raised one eyebrow.

"Dinner? You're inviting me to dinner?" Ellen couldn't believe her ears. She took a deep breath.

"Yeah. Heard *Driftwood Shores* isn't too shabby."

"Not too shabby at all." Ellen's lips twitched into a smile.

Seemingly heartened by her smile, Travis found more words. "Down by the ocean, isn't it? That big hotel? When are you free? How about later in the week? Or will you be visiting your dad?"

"No, Dad should be home by then, and he won't want me fussing around all the time. Mom'll do enough of that for all of us. Friday would be good." She put down the book which she'd been gripping tightly all of this time.

"Okay then." Travis looked nervously over his shoulder, then back to Ellen. "Pick you up here? Around, um… seven? Is that okay?"

Ellen almost laughed at Travis' hesitation. The poor guy was making it hard for himself. Maybe he was as out-of-practice with dinner dates as she was, because that's what this was, wasn't it? A date?

*

Ellen was still smiling an hour later when she got into her car to go home. Checking her watch, she decided to have a quick bite before visiting the hospital. Her mom and Ron would have been there most of the day, and she was completely drained after everything that had happened. The early start had caught up with her too. Her eyes burnt, her back hurt, and her head ached. She needed a long hot shower, a strong coffee, and something in her stomach. But, despite this, there was a lightness in her step that hadn't been there for some time. Ellen was humming to herself as she let herself into her small house.

She walked through the airy living room, glad she'd knocked down the dividing wall when she'd bought the place all those years ago. Now the large area opened up into a small kitchen and the sliding glass door which led to her garden. Ellen filled the coffee pot and set it on the stove, taking a minute to open the windows and breathe in the fresh evening air, before heading for the shower. This was her sanctuary; the place where she could forget her troubles and enjoy the peaceful surroundings – untroubled this time by Travis' presence. Though she did feel he'd left a trace of himself behind. It was imperceptible, but there, nonetheless.

As she stood under the blast of hot water, the specter of the development proposal loomed large in her thoughts. Ellen sighed, as she held her face up to the cascading stream of water. In the tumult of Travis' presence and the worry about her dad, the threat of the development had become lost at the back of her mind. Now, after Mike's news at lunchtime, it was back at the forefront. Tomorrow, she resolved as she rinsed off the remains of the soap and stepped out of the shower, wishing she could wash away all of her worries as easily. A meeting of those involved might be a good place to start. She'd contact the other shopkeepers and go from there. She wasn't sure where Mike and Travis were going with the historical angle. Surely, she thought, brushing her hair thoroughly before re-plaiting it, all that would have been gone into before the existing properties were built?

Ellen was about to leave when her phone rang. Tempted to ignore it, she took a quick look, and seeing it was Jenny, she decided to accept the call.

"Glad I caught you. Just a quick call. Wanted to check how your dad is."

"I'm on my way to the hospital now. You just caught me going out the door." Ellen juggled her purse and keys as she spoke, hoping that this would indeed be a short call.

"Oh, sorry. Thought you'd have been by now." Jenny sounded surprised.

"No, came home first. I was exhausted and needed a shower and some food. Is that all you wanted? I can call you back later." Ellen was eager to leave and…

"Well…" Jenny's voice was hesitant. "What's with you and Travis? I mean…" she blustered.

"What do you mean? There's nothing…" Ellen cursed her cousin's perceptiveness. She remembered Jenny's look when she and Travis had re-entered the restaurant. She should have known Jenny wouldn't let it go.

"Really?"

"Really. Well, he's invited me to dinner… as an apology," she explained, anxious to get off the phone.

"Right. And this dinner is when?"

"Friday. Look, I really have to go. Can I call you when I get back?"

"Better yet. Why don't I drop down tomorrow? You can tell me everything then, and I can catch up with your folks too."

Aware she wasn't going to get out of this easily, Ellen agreed and concluded the conversation, but it had unsettled her. It was one thing to have arranged to go to dinner with Travis, but it was quite another thing to have her friends and family speculating on their relationship, one which didn't – and probably never would – exist.

*

Ellen had such a busy morning dealing with customers and setting up a new display of books, she'd almost forgotten Jenny's promise to drop in. She was making a list of her neighboring shopkeepers, when the doorbell jangled and her cousin was standing there, an enigmatic smile on her face.

"Mike's in the library," she said, explaining away his absence. "He's doing some research on the shops – searching out old plans or some such thing. He and Travis had a long chat on the phone this morning, and they seem to have divvied up the work."

"What work?" Mystified, Ellen put her pen down, a curl of concern wrapping itself around her gut. *What was Travis up to now?*

"Oh, you know," Jenny waved her hands in the air. "They're trying to find the evidence you need, the historical stuff. At least that's what Mike's doing. I think Travis is looking into the development guys. See if he can find any dirt on them."

"Dirt?" Ellen wasn't sure she approved. "I hope…" But she wasn't sure what she hoped either.

"Seems he wants to help if he can. I think he rather likes you, Ellen." Jenny cocked her head to one side. "What about this dinner date you mentioned?"

"It's not really a date," Ellen demurred, forgetting she'd called it exactly that to herself. "It's an apology." Even as she spoke, she realized how weak her words sounded. "And I do think I deserve one," she continued in her own defence. "To think he stood in here on several occasions and let me think… Why, he even talked about his own books as if…" She shook her head in mock disbelief.

"Well, whatever it is, you're having dinner together. What are you going to wear?" Jenny's eyes raked Ellen up and down. "You can't go like that."

Ellen looked down at her normal work-a-day outfit of jeans topped by a checked flannelette shirt. Her only variation was a long skirt, usually on days when she'd run out of clean jeans. Clothes had never been important to her. Comfort was her main concern. Taller than most women, she'd learned early in life that frills and furbelows weren't for her, and while in her teens she'd tried to be fashionable like other girls, she'd soon settled for the sort of clothes she now wore like a uniform.

"What's wrong…?"

"I mean…" Jenny smiled gently. "You look great, but maybe… You do have other outfits?"

"Mmm." Ellen mentally reviewed her wardrobe. It had been some time since she'd dressed up. Her date with Paul last year hadn't called for anything out of the ordinary – and just as well too, she thought, remembering that disastrous evening. Well, at least Travis hadn't suggested taking her to the casino for dinner.

"Well?" Jenny was becoming impatient. "A dress? Something elegant?"

"I don't do elegant. Look at me!"

"I'm looking. And I see a tall elegant woman, or one who could be, given…"

"Tosh! I'll find something," Ellen brushed off her cousin's words. "You've never criticized my clothes before."

"I'm not criticizing. You always look great. I'm just saying… If Travis is going to the trouble of taking you out, maybe you should make an effort."

"I will. Now is that all?"

"How's Uncle Dick? Did he get home today?"

Ellen breathed a sigh of relief that Jenny had changed the subject. "He did. Mom and Ron fetched him in a taxi this morning. I spoke with Mom a few minutes ago, and he's looking a lot better, still in bed, but home. He'll need to rest for a time to let things heal. I'm heading over there shortly. Why don't you come with me? Or will Mike…?" Ellen's eyes turned toward the door, wondering if he was about to appear.

"No, he's good for a couple of hours yet. The library doesn't close till eight, and once he gets his teeth into a bit of research, he's lost to the world. I'll send him a text to let him know where I'm going and he can pick me up there."

*

"That Travis seems a nice chap," Rita said, handing Jenny a steaming mug of coffee. "Dick wouldn't be here if it wasn't for him." Her hand shook a little as she appeared to contemplate the alternative.

"Yes, Mom." Ellen sipped her coffee and picked up a macadamia nut cookie. She never bought them for herself, but her mom always had a packet, and they were too good to refuse. She hoped her mom wasn't going to try to match-make here. Jenny was bad enough. Maybe she shouldn't have agreed to dinner, but it would have been churlish to have refused, and deep down, Ellen did want to go. It would give her the opportunity to get to know Travis better – to know the real Travis, the one behind the façade. He'd pulled back the curtain a little by telling her about his dream and revealing his alter ego, but Ellen was sure there was a lot more to this man. And she intended to find out.

Ellen wrapped both hands around her mug and inhaled the coffee aroma, while she pictured the tall lean body of her dad's saviour. He was quite an enigma. It appeared he'd led a pretty normal, even exemplary, life up to the accident, but what then? The past two years were unaccounted for. What had…?

"What?" Ellen was dragged out of her musings by her mom's voice repeating her name.

"Where were you? Jenny was telling me you're going to dinner with him."

"Who?"

"Travis. That's who we were talking about." Rita set her mug down on the table. "Sometimes I wonder what I spawned. Between you and Ron…" She stood up. "I'll just see if your dad wants anything else."

Ellen and Jenny met each other's eyes and laughed. "I thought she'd given up on us long ago," Ellen said. "She's not going to get the grandchildren she hoped for, so I thought her match-making days were over." She sighed, but was unable to repress a tinge of pleasure that her mother still thought she had a chance in the marriage stakes. Then she pulled herself together. Who was she kidding? Marriage wasn't for her. What had put even the thought of it into her head?

Ellen took a long swallow of the hot drink. "And I do have a decent outfit," she told Jenny, harking back to their previous conversation. "You don't need to worry about me on that score."

Thirteen

Everything was quiet. Breathing in, Ellen sniffed the familiar aroma, a blend of books, print and her scented candle. Today the scent was a mixture of lemon and cedarwood. She'd selected this one specially to have a calming influence, but the butterflies in her stomach were evidence she was far from calm. She stroked the soft material of the golden-colored caftan she'd chosen to wear tonight and wondered if Jenny would approve of her choice. Ellen hadn't seen either Jenny or Mike since the beginning of the week. She'd tried to ring them today without success.

Ellen picked up the sheet of paper from the counter and re-read it. It made no more sense now than it had when it arrived with the mail that morning. She folded it and slipped it into her purse, promising herself to forget it until tomorrow. Tonight was about Travis, her and Travis. A shadow passed the window and the door opened, the familiar sound of the bell startling her.

"Howdy!" The Travis who stood before Ellen made her heart beat faster. He'd brushed up well. Still in the ubiquitous beige fringed jacket, his shirt was a crisp white, and instead of the turquoise jewelry, tonight he sported a simple string tie. He was gazing at her intently, making her wonder if she had a smudge on her nose, or if she was looking strange.

"Hello," Ellen managed to get the word out, her throat constricted by excitement and something akin to terror. She didn't do terror, Ellen reminded herself, shaking.

"Ready?"

"Sure."

The pair left the shop, Ellen delaying only to lock the door behind them, automatically checking the handle as she always did. Travis looked at her, then at the bike sitting by the curb. He didn't say a word, but she could tell he'd intended to take her to the restaurant on the back of his Harley.

She smiled and shook her head. "I don't think so." She gestured to her long garment. "My car is around the corner. We can go in that if…" She paused, remembering Travis' challenge with cars.

"Surely. I seem to have gotten over my aversion to them." He stroked his beard. "Lead on."

At the restaurant, a neatly dressed waiter showed them to a window table, and Ellen took her seat with relief. Conversation had been sticky in the car. With each of them on their best behavior and trying to be polite, the words had dried up. She looked around. Being a Friday night, the room was busy with a mixture of locals and tourists, mostly the latter she guessed, since she didn't recognize anyone. Many of the tables held family groups, some still in their casual daytime attire. There was an air of festivity about the place, with lots of chatting and laughter.

"Nice spot," Travis picked up the menu. "Come here a lot?"

"No, not much. A bit rich for my usual haunt." Ellen looked out at the deserted beach and remembered her last visit. She and Jenny had come here for dinner the previous year. As her eyes grew accustomed to the darkness outside, she recalled the tender scene they'd seen right outside on the beach. A young couple in the throes of first love – a proposal, no less. She turned back to the man opposite her. Last time she'd been counseling Jenny and hinting that there was going to be more in her life than her proposed bookshop. Ellen had predicted a happy relationship for her cousin, and now she was settled with her Mike.

Tonight Ellen was sitting opposite a man herself. A man who moved her as she hadn't been moved since Will. Even before Will, back when… What did it mean? Did it mean anything at all? Ellen was perplexed. Her gift always failed her when it came to her own future. She was able to help others, but had to muddle along with her own life. It had always been this way. She realized Travis was speaking to her.

"Sorry, I was miles away. I…" She was about to tell him of the young couple, then thought better of it. As a man, he wouldn't be interested in such things. Why, he might even… Ellen blushed. "What did you say?"

Travis' lips twisted up in his enigmatic smile. "I was asking if you'd decided." He nodded towards the menu Ellen was holding.

"Oh… not yet." Ellen looked at the menu for the first time and studied the offerings. The waiter placed a glass of red wine in front of her and a glass of some clear liquid with a slice of lemon in front of Travis.

"I ordered wine when you were lost in thought," Travis explained. "Hope you like red."

"Yes, fine." Ellen picked up the glass and took a sip, keeping her eyes lowered. What a fool he must think her. Not a good start to the evening. "None for you?" she asked, pointing to his glass. "What's…?"

"I don't," Travis replied shortly. "Lemon, lime and bitters," he held up the glass. "My poison for tonight. What about the Friday special?" he suggested. "Haven't had a good prime rib for ages."

"No, I guess you and Ron aren't up to much as cooks." Ellen bit her lip to hide her amusement.

"I can cook," Travis protested. "But not lately," his voice dropped, and Ellen wished she could take back her words. The last thing she'd wanted to do was remind him of his past, even though it was a past which piqued her curiosity.

She looked at the menu again. "I think I'll go for the salmon – the Pacific Northwest Wild Caught Salmon with the maple glaze, lemon basmati rice, green beans and bacon," she read from the menu. "I'm not a big fan of red meat," she apologized.

"Mmm. Well you can't go wrong with salmon. Catch it around here, don't they?"

Travis seemed to be as ill at ease as she was. What were they going to talk about? Was this evening going to be as much of a disaster as her last foray into dating with Ron's other mate? No, Travis was no Paul. For one thing he was more intelligent, and he… Ellen tried to find the correct word. He stirred her to her very core – what an old-fashioned phrase, but it described perfectly the way he made her feel.

The wine seemed to remove her inhibition. "This is nice." Ellen met Travis' eyes and smiled. "It was good of you to suggest it. Quite the place here in Florence." She stroked the tablecloth, so unlike the bare wooden tables of most local eateries.

Travis visibly relaxed, leaning back in his chair and picking up his glass. "Been doing a bit of research," he said. "This company, Balcombs," he paused. "They're bad news." He swirled his glass around as if wondering how much to say, then added, "Seems they have a history of intimidation."

"Sir, madam." The waiter placed two brimming plates before them. *Driftwood Shores* was certainly living up to its reputation for good food and plenty of it.

"Let's eat first and not spoil this fine fare with talk of those bastards," Travis said, leaving Ellen to curb her curiosity.

When they finally laid down their cutlery, Ellen's plate was still partly full. They both sighed with pleasure.

"That sure was a fine meal," Travis wiped his mouth with the napkin and gripped the edge of the table as the waiter removed both plates. "Dessert or...?"

"Coffee'll be fine, thanks." Ellen couldn't eat another bite. She was glad she'd worn the caftan and didn't have a tight waistband to worry about. "That was delicious. Now, what were you about to tell me before our meals arrived?"

"Right." Travis leaned forward. "As I said, I looked into Balcombs and their dealings. I thought I remembered them from down in California and I was right. They appear to keep within the law, but only just, and some of their actions have been very suspicious."

"You mentioned intimidation. What...?"

"Yes," Travis continued. "Seems there were some mysterious accidents, and at least one fire."

Ellen began to tremble and slid the letter out of her purse, her hand shaking. She hadn't envisaged anything like this.

"What do you have there?"

"It... it arrived this morning." She handed it across the table just as their coffees arrived.

Travis took the folded paper. "Can I read it?"

"Of course. Please do, and tell me what you think." Ellen picked up her coffee and tried to relax, but her whole body felt strained.

*

Travis gave Ellen a worried look, his brow furrowing as he unfolded the letter and began to read:

Dear Ms Williams,

As you may be aware, our company, Balcombs, has submitted a development application for the block which includes your shop, The Reading Nook. It is not our intention to inconvenience any of the existing tenants, however, some re-structure will be necessary in order for our plans to come to fruition. Our proposed development structure can be viewed in the foyer of your local library, and we are sure you will immediately see the benefits to the whole community of the project we have in mind. We do intend for our purchase and the development to go ahead and will brook no opposition.

Please be mindful of the fact that it would be unwise to attempt to mount any campaign or other type of objection to the proposal, as it could only cause hurt and damage to existing structures and connections.

Yours faithfully,

Stephen Wright on behalf of Balcombs

"Well!" Travis finished reading and dropped the paper as if it had stung him. "That makes their intentions clear."

"It does? It seemed gobbledygook to me. Do you think…?"

"I do. They're warning you off." He raised his eyes. "Have your neighbors received similar letters?"

Ellen's eyes widened. "I don't know. I haven't… Coralie didn't… But she wasn't in today, so she may… Sorry, I'm babbling." Ellen pulled on her plait, something Travis had noticed she did when worried or upset. He thought it cute in a woman of her years, even though he hated to see her so distressed.

"I was intending to call a meeting – of those affected. Do you think I should?"

Travis could see Ellen's usual self-confidence had left her, and while pleased she was asking his advice, he was concerned to see how much the letter had affected her.

He studied for a few minutes before replying. "Yes, I think you should. Would you like me to be there?"

"Please." Ellen reached across the table to pick up the letter, and Travis couldn't resist the temptation to cover her hand with his for a moment. She withdrew hers quickly. "This is it, then."

"It?" He had no idea to what she was referring. The letter? His hand? Has he been too precipitate?

"What I saw. That day you came into the shop. The first time. When Ron had injured himself. That morning, I had a premonition. It was a portent of some disaster, but I couldn't determine what it might be. I can't always be clear," she explained, pulling on her hair again. "At first I thought it was a warning about you." Ellen tried to laugh, but didn't succeed.

"So that's why…"

"Yes. Sorry I was so boorish when we first met. I thought you were just another of Ron's old army mates. I know you are, but… Anyway, that was my first thought, then there was Dad's accident. But this is worse, much worse."

Travis could see her tremble and this time he caught both of her hands in his and held them tightly. They sat like that for a few moments, during which he could see fear and determination war with one another in her expression.

"Drink your coffee," he said, letting go and picking up his own cup. "It'll help calm you. These premonitions, omens, whatever you call them. Do they always herald disasters?"

"No." Ellen seemed to be recovering. "They often foretell happy events. For example – with Jenny – when she was here last year. I could see great happiness for her. There were challenges to overcome, but joy was there too. But this…"

"So, can you see to the end of this business?" Travis was curious. Despite his long association with Native American people, he'd never come across one with this sort of gift before. Gift or curse – he wasn't sure which.

"No." Ellen rubbed her forehead. "I can't usually see things for myself, that's the odd thing. Why I didn't immediately link the two – the development and the presentiment of evil I experienced. Maybe it's because there will be others involved," she spoke as if she were thinking aloud. "That might be why."

"When do you intend to hold this meeting?" Travis tried to envisage what he might have to contribute, and if he'd have time to do more research into this company, Balcombs.

"It'll have to be next week. We'll all be busy on the weekend. It hasn't let up since the Festival, and Memorial Day is coming up. I think some of the tourists have decided to take a longer break and stay over."

"Hmm, Memorial Day," Travis shuddered as if someone had walked over his grave. "Try to avoid that one. All that glorification of the fallen, decoration of cemeteries and war graves. Leaves me cold. Ron and I were there. Saw enough dead soldiers to last a lifetime."

"Mmm." Ellen paused, visibly shaken by the reminder of the horror Travis had experienced. "Well, I can contact everyone on Monday, so how about I try to set something up for next Wednesday evening. There should be around eight of us. We can all fit into the shop. That'd be best, don't you think?"

Travis agreed. He'd have four days to get in touch with his contacts down in California. So far, he'd done his searching on the Internet, but now he had some facts – dates and locations – he could ring some old mates down there and see what they could turn up.

"Why are you doing this?" Ellen's voice broke into his thoughts. "I mean, it's not your problem." She hesitated, as if unsure how to continue. "Are you…do you… don't you feel the need to start writing again?"

Damn the woman. It was as if she could see right into him. He cleared his throat. He hadn't intended to tell anyone. It was tempting fate to reveal too much too soon. What if…?

"I… the point is…"

"You have. I knew it." Ellen sounded almost gleeful, the concern which had clouded her face only a few minutes earlier had vanished. It was as if the sun had come out after a rain shower.

The woman really was a witch. How could she know? He'd barely admitted to himself that he had started again.

Ellen leant on the table, arms folded. "What are you writing about now? You said there was no more Peter Travers, So?"

"No more of the stuff Peter Travers wrote, no, you're right there.

That man has gone for good." Travis gazed up at the ceiling before continuing, his fingers drawing lines on the tablecloth. "It's darker, much darker." He met Ellen's eyes. "I'm writing about my experiences – how they've affected me. It's not a memoir – a fictional character. But he has a lot of my angst."

"A cathartic experience, then?" The look in Ellen's eyes was too much. Travis couldn't meet them.

"Maybe," was all he would admit. "Might include a corrupt developer or two," he tried to jest. "Shall we go?"

The return trip was more comfortable than the drive to the restaurant. It was as if both Travis and Ellen had settled something. Travis knew he wanted to see more of this woman and had an inkling she might feel the same way about him. She'd pulled her hand away from his the first time he'd attempted to cover it, but had allowed both of his to grip hers the second time. Her hands had felt soft in his; they were large for a woman but small compared to his own.

Arriving at *The Reading Nook*, Travis turned to Ellen before getting out. "Well…"

"Thanks for a lovely evening. I'm sorry we ended up talking so much about my troubles," she apologized, her face gleaming in the streetlight. Travis thought he hadn't seen such an honest face in a long time – a far cry from the women he'd met in recent years.

"No problem. I enjoyed it." He knew his voice sounded gruff, but this woman moved him in a way he didn't entirely understand. "Maybe we can do it again?"

"Why not."

He stood on the sidewalk and watched her drive away, before walking to his bike. Ron's little sister had cast a spell on him. Maybe Ellen's magic wasn't only her ability to see things, maybe there was something else, something that had enslaved him.

*

There was a smile on Ellen's face as she drove off. The evening hadn't gone quite the way she'd expected. She'd hoped to learn more about Travis, but instead, they'd ended up talking mostly about this damned development stuff. Strange, now she'd shared it with Travis, she felt more confident they'd find a solution. It might be difficult, but they'd win out in the end.

It wasn't till she was home and getting ready for bed that she took time to consider what Travis had revealed about his writing. The man had been through some difficult times. She might never know the full story. But it did make him vulnerable – a far cry from the outcast and layabout she'd first imagined him to be. As she closed her eyes, her last waking thought was of Travis riding off on his Harley, even though she'd not seen him do it that night. She thought of the stories of King Arthur and his Knights of the Round Table, books she'd loved as a child. Travis reminded her of those knights.

Fourteen

Ellen's dream of Travis as one of the Knights of the Round Table seemed fanciful in the clear light of day, as she prepared for work. She chastised herself for such foolish thoughts and geared up for a busy Saturday, a spring in her step as she recalled the previous evening and the promise of another.

Leaving home earlier than necessary, she detoured via her parents' home to check up on her dad. She'd been ringing her mom each day, but hadn't made it home since Wednesday. As far as she knew, Ron was still there, so she hadn't been overly worried, but it was time she showed her face.

"Anyone home?" Ellen's voice echoed through the house, as she pushed open the door and headed for the kitchen.

"Ellen." Rita Williams turned around from the stove and greeted her daughter with a warm hug. "Oh, it's so good to see you." She was almost in tears.

"Mom. What's up?" *What could be wrong now?* Ellen didn't know if she could take any more bad news. "Is Dad...?"

"Oh, he's recovering from the accident. It's like the doctor said – lots of rest. But you know your dad. He's the devil to keep in bed and..." She wiped her eyes. "He can't eat. We have to feed him liquids. He wants soup all the time – pea soup – Andersen's pea soup. He loved it as a child, and nothing else will please him. And he has these turns. He forgets. He keeps going on about someone beating him up. As if... Then there's his ATV. He wants to check that it's in the garage. And of course it isn't. It's at the wreckers, and I won't care if I never see one of them again." Ellen's mother finished her tirade and slumped down into a chair.

Ellen's earlier joy drained away as soon as her mother began talking. This was why she stayed away from home. It had all become too hard.

"What about Ron? Can't he help?" Ellen looked around, but her brother was nowhere to be seen.

"Still in bed," Rita said. "But he's no help. He tries, but Dick's taken against him too. Blames him for something – we can't figure out what. But that temper of your dad's really gets up when he sees Ron, so he's been keeping out of Dick's way. It's easier."

"Oh, Mom," Ellen wrapped her arms around Rita. "I didn't know. Is there anything I can do?"

"I don't rightly know." Rita got up and went over to the stove again. She stirred a pot from which arose the aroma of pea and ham soup. "Yes," she met Ellen's eyes. "I'm making his soup for him, but the store didn't have Andersen's yesterday, so this'll have to do." She gave it a fierce stir. "But he can't live on that, no one can. The doctor said to try for variety – a balanced diet of sorts. Though how he can have a balanced diet on liquids I'm blessed if I know."

Ellen hesitated, moving from one foot to the other. She felt guilty having to leave. "I have to go to the shop. It's Saturday. I can't close it. It's my busiest day. Maybe…"

"You go on. Don't listen to an old woman's complaints. I feel better already having gotten it out of my system."

"Mom, these turns you say Dad has. Is it like before? When you said he seemed to lose himself for a few minutes then come back?"

"Sometimes," Rita said, reflectively. "And he seems to have forgotten going out on the dunes too… and Travis…"

Ellen felt her face redden at the sound of Travis' name. She hadn't spoken to her mother about their dinner date, and didn't intend to. Hopefully Rita had forgotten Jenny's reference to it. "Might that be from the concussion?" she asked. "Don't they say…?"

"Yes, the doctor did say that," Rita agreed. "But it doesn't help, when I don't know what's due to the blow on the head, and what's due to something else. But away with you. You have a shop to open. And don't spend your day worrying about me. We'll be fine, Ron and I."

"If you're sure." Ellen wasn't sure herself, but did need to go. "How about I call in when I close up?"

"That'd be grand."

Ellen gave her mom a kiss and left, but all the way to the shop her mom's words were going around and around in her head. It was only in the past year that Ellen had been conscious of her parents' mortality, really only in the past few weeks. It had come as a shock when her mother had confided her worries about her dad, then that had been overshadowed by his accident. The frail body in the hospital bed hadn't seemed like her dad at all, more like a sick old man. Which he was. Both her parents were in their eighties, but she'd tended to ignore that when they were both fit and well, and in her dad's case, bullying everyone. It sounded as if he was back to his old self, at least where Ron was concerned – the two had never got on. But she was the favorite, the one who could do no wrong – except for the fact she'd never married, she grimaced. Mom and Dad were at one on that front. A good reason to keep her growing friendship with Travis under wraps.

Friendship, she mused. Was that what it was? A grin replaced the grimace as she recalled how her whole body had shuddered when his hands gripped hers on the table. She hoped he hadn't noticed. It was embarrassing to feel that way. At her age – she should know better, be more self-contained. Then she remembered her counsel to Jenny, only a year ago, and Maddy's words. She remembered them exactly. *"You think if she can find love a second time, there may be hope for you too?"* Was this really what she was thinking? Could she find the love which had eluded her? Could she find it with Travis?

Ellen reached her shop before she could come to any conclusion. Just as well, she decided, parking round the corner. She barely had the key in the door before a blonde whirlwind rushed up behind her.

"Did you get one too?" Coralie waved a sheet of paper in Ellen's face. She recognized it – it was identical to the one she'd received. So Travis was right. Ellen hadn't been singled out for attention. If both she and Coralie had received a letter, then so would all the other shopkeepers in the block.

"You'd better come in." Ellen finished opening the door, as Coralie pushed her way through and stood, arms akimbo and eyes blazing, waiting for her attention. "Let me put my purse down and my signs out, then I'll be with you." As Ellen performed these tasks, she tried to work out how much to tell Coralie, who was not noted to be one to keep a secret. *Though what was there to be secretive about? Was there really a threat to the group if they decided to take action? How could they just sit still and see their livelihoods disappear?*

"Well?" Coralie's patience was seemingly at an end.

"To answer your question, yes I received one too. I guess everyone did."

"Well, what are we going to do about it?" Coralie's voice rose.

Ellen took a quick look around to check there were no customers. "Calm down. Yes, we need to do something, but now's not the time. I was planning to arrange a meeting on Wednesday, after we close."

"Not till then?" Coralie's voice rose even higher as she … "We…"

"They're not going to knock us down before Wednesday." Ellen's calm voice seemed to have an effect as Coralie dropped her arms, and her next words were spoken in a normal tone.

"No, I guess not. But what do they mean by this last bit?" She pushed the letter into Ellen's face, her finger pointing to the words which had concerned both Ellen and Travis. "It could only cause hurt and damage to existing structures and connections," she read. "Sounds a bit…" Her eyes widened as if in fear. "Does that mean…? Should we…?"

"We can't sit back and do nothing," Ellen repeated the words she had spoken to herself earlier. "Travis is going to…"

"Travis? Isn't that the guy…? What's he got to do with this?" Coralie looked around the shop as if she expected Travis to appear.

"Nothing really, but he's offered to help, find out what he can about this company – Balcombs – and their dealings in other places." Ellen stopped, wondering if she'd said too much. But Coralie was off on another tack now.

"He's a bit of a spunk, isn't he? Are you and he…? Didn't make much impression there, but he's not really my type." She affected to study her nails. "Well, Wednesday, you say. I'll remember that." And with these words, she swept out again.

Ellen gazed after her in amazement. She'd only known the other woman for a short time, and didn't really know much about her, but she did seem to come on strong whenever there was a member of the opposite sex around. Jenny had reported that both Mike and Travis had trouble keeping a straight face last time she'd appeared. She could be attractive if she didn't dress so… Ellen couldn't think of a word that wasn't an insult, so decided to focus her attention on something else.

The empty display table was beckoning for her attention. She stood looking at it for a moment, then made a decision. Memorial Day was on Monday, and despite Travis' comments, she knew that a lot of her customers valued the contribution made by the armed forces over the years. Yes, a display featuring war memoirs would prove popular, and she thought she had a couple of old GI Joe dolls tucked away somewhere. They'd be just the ticket. She could set up the window for Memorial Day too, with flags and pictures of soldiers, going back to the Civil War. There would be extra visitors in town for the ceremony at the Veterans' Memorial Park. It would certainly appeal to them.

The day passed quickly, as Ellen set up her display and catered to an ongoing flow of customers, many of whom commented on her new presentation of memorabilia. Closing time brought a final bustle of tourists looking for Native American tales, and she had to unearth the Peter Travers books she'd recently stacked in her office. Travis' fans wouldn't disappear just because he'd decided to stop writing these books. As she ushered out the last customers and locked the door behind them, Ellen wondered if Travis' new writing would prove to be as popular. Darker, he'd said, and clearly for an adult audience. She wasn't sure exactly what he meant. Perhaps his writing was a way to exorcise his memories, but that wasn't something she could ask him about. He would have to tell her in his own time.

*

It was almost seven o'clock when Ellen's car drew into her parents' driveway, and she immediately noticed her brother standing on the porch.

"Waiting for me?" Ellen meant this as a joke, but it seemed all too real as Ron walked toward the car.

"Actually, yes." He leant down to speak through the open door.

"Can't you wait till I get out?" Ellen picked her purse up from the floor of the car and tried to move, stymied by her brother's shoulders in the doorframe. "Ron!" Her voice held all the pent-up exasperation of a busy day on her feet.

"Don't want Mom to hear me," he said, almost in a whisper. "It's Dad."

"What's he been up to now?"

"He's driving Mom mad. Expecting her to be at his beck and call all day. And he won't let me help. He lies up there and pounds on the floor with his stick. He keeps on till she goes up. She's going to get sick too, if it doesn't stop soon. She's too old to be continually going up and down stairs."

"Can't you just go up in her place?" Ellen couldn't see what the problem was. She was keen to finish this conversation, so she could get out of the car. And she was hungry, having skipped lunch.

"Tried that, and he threatened me with the stick. He's a sick man, but he's still the old bully he always was." Having said his piece, Ron finally moved away from the car door to allow Ellen to alight.

"Ellen, Ron. Where did you get to?" Rita sounded flustered as she greeted the pair.

"He came out to meet me," Ellen's voice held a trace of the relief she felt, seeing her mother looking exactly as always. She gave Ron a quick glance in an attempt to gage his feelings, but he was gazing up at the ceiling from where there came a loud pounding.

"That's your dad." Rita started towards the stairs.

"No, Mom. I'll go." Ellen dropped her purse on the sofa and headed upstairs.

"Ellen. You're a sight for sore eyes. So you've finally come to visit your old dad, have you?" The gruff voice was at odds with the frail man lying against the frilled white pillowcase.

Ellen was shocked to see how her dad appeared to have shrunk in the past two weeks. He was no longer the commanding presence who had enjoyed the role of head of the family, the tyrant who'd refused to accept Jenny as his niece only a year ago. This was a sick old man. Swallowing her apprehension, she managed to find a cheerful tone.

"You old fraud," she accused him. "What are you doing up here banging on the floor with that cane? Do you think Mom has nothing else to do but run up and down the stairs all day? And I was here only a few days ago, so what are you grumbling about?"

"Ah, my little Ellen." Dick took Ellen's hands in his gnarled ones. "I can't stand it up here – away from everything. I need to know what's going on, and Rita… your mom…"

Ellen felt the tears well up, recognizing that her dad was lonely, sick and lonely, stuck up here away from the heart of the house. She was just beginning to feel sorry for him when he continued, "And that brother of yours. No good, never was. Time he got himself a proper job."

"There's not much wrong with you, Dad." Ellen was about to continue when she noticed a vacant look in her father's eyes. It lasted for well over a minute, before his eyes met hers again.

"What was that you said?" his voice now that of a querulous old man. "I'm not deaf, you know."

"Of course not." Ellen withdrew her hands gently. "I'm going back downstairs now. Mom's preparing dinner. I'll bring yours up, shall I?"

"Dinner! Some damn fool liquid nonsense. Wouldn't feed it to a cat." Ellen bit her lip to hide a smile – her dad couldn't stand cats.

Ellen's mind was working overtime as she made her way back down the stairs.

"How did you find him, love?" Rita sounded tired, as well she might, Ellen thought.

"He's not himself," Ellen replied. "But it must be lonely for him, stuck up there. And it's not easy for you either, with him expecting you to run up and down, fetching and carrying all day. We don't want you to get sick too." She smiled at her mother and threw a warning glance at Ron, who was leaning against the table, a frown on his face. "I wonder…"

"Beware a sister who wonders," Ron threw in with a grin, reminding Ellen of many of their childhood squabbles, when he asserted his older status.

"What is it, dear?" Rita stopped in the midst of setting the table to hear what Ellen was saying.

"I wonder if we could bring Dad down here. There's the big old recliner in his study. Maybe we could move it into the living room. Then he could see what was going on, watch a bit of television. He'd feel part of the family again – and it would save your legs, Mom."

"Oh, I don't..." Rita began, but Ron interrupted.

"Good idea, sis. I need to be getting back up home anyway. Can't be leaving Travis on his own up there. Who knows what sort of mischief he'll be up to."

Ellen felt the heat suffuse her body, as she tried to avoid Ron's eyes, but he wasn't looking at her. He was focussing on his mother.

"Should be getting this arm back in the next week or so. Can get back to normal then." Ron tried ineffectually to swing his arm around.

"How do you plan to get home?" The three were eating dinner and had all but demolished Rita's famous meatloaf dish.

"Mmm," Ron wiped up the last of his gravy with a piece of bread. "I don't suppose you...?" He cocked his head towards Ellen. "No, I guess not," he said, as she shook her head. "Well, maybe Travis. I'll call..."

"He'll be down in Florence on Wednesday," Ellen said, without thinking.

"He will?" Ron swivelled around to face her. "What has my little sister been up to?"

"Nothing," she denied, hoping her face didn't give her away. "But Travis and Mike – they're helping research the development thing." Ellen shook her head slightly to indicate to her brother that she didn't want her mother worried about this. "Anyway, Travis is coming to a meeting on Wednesday. He could take you back up then, if you can stick it out for another couple of days," she joked.

"Maybe," Ron drawled. "I can help move Dad downstairs and get him settled. If he'll permit me."

"He will. I'll see to it." Ellen rose. "I'll tell him right now."

"That's my girl. Dad always did listen to you."

When Ellen came back downstairs some time later, she was smiling. "It's fixed," she said. "Dad's agreed Ron can help move him down tomorrow, after you get the recliner set up in front of the television. He seems brighter at the idea of being in the center of things again. Can I help with the dishes before I go?' she asked, seeing the table was already cleared.

"Bless you, no," Rita replied. "The dishwasher will see to that, and Ron's been real good at loading it for me."

"That's something I can do with one arm," Ron laughed. "I'll see you out."

"Are you sure Travis is only coming down here for this meeting of yours?" Ron asked, as Ellen opened her car door and prepared to slide into the driver's seat.

"I'm sure," Ellen replied firmly. But as she drove off, she admitted she wasn't sure at all. In fact, a not so small part of her hoped the meeting wasn't the only thing that was bringing him down here mid-week.

Fifteen

Wednesday came around almost too soon and Ellen began to set out some chairs in a semi-circle in the middle of the shop. There would be around eight of them, she guessed. All but one of her neighbors had agreed to attend, only Bert from the tobacconists telling her he was about to retire anyway and "didn't want a bar of any danged protest movement."

She couldn't subdue the bubble of excitement at the thought of Travis' participation in the evening. She hadn't heard from him since Friday, but had no reason to think he'd changed his mind. Ellen stood, looking at the chairs, wondering if there were enough. What if Mike decided to come too? Jenny had called yesterday to say he was getting stuck into his part of the research, and Ellen had mentioned the meeting and that Travis was coming. That may have been a mistake, as her cousin had started to ask some awkward questions. Might have been best to have kept her mouth shut. Ellen bit her lip. She wasn't accustomed to being secretive. Honest and open – that was her. This Travis thing had brought out a whole new side of her, one she wasn't sure she was comfortable with. Why the need for secrecy anyway? She wasn't entirely certain. She only knew she didn't want anyone speculating about their friendship, relationship, or whatever.

Ellen was still carrying on this conversation with herself, when there was a knock at the locked door behind her. She frowned and checked her watch. She wasn't expecting anyone this early, planning to have a bite to eat and freshen up first. Turning, she could make out a male figure peering through the darkened window. Oh, hell. It wasn't Travis, was it? Ellen patted her hair and walked over to open the door.

"Ron! What are you doing here? Travis hasn't arrived yet, and we won't be finished till…"

"Hold your hush. Can I at least come in?"

"Sorry." She stood aside to let him enter.

"Just dropped by to say, tell Travis not to worry. Old Barry came by, and we're going for a drink, then he'll drive me back up home. He's waiting for me in the car." Ron gestured out into the dark evening.

"Right. Will do. Now you're here, tell me. How's Dad settling in downstairs? Is it working out for him, and is Mom finding things a bit easier?"

Ron swung a chair around with his good arm and sat in it, legs astride and arms leaning on the chair back. "Seems to be working just fine. Dad can drift in and out of sleep day and night – suits him down to the ground. Though the television does get a bit loud sometimes with his addiction to old movies late at night and in the early morning. But Mom seems to cope with it, and having him down there does save her legs."

"I guess her hearing isn't as acute as yours," Ellen suggested with a smile.

"You could be right. Didn't think of that. Hello, who's this?"

Ellen's eyes moved to the still unlocked door where Coralie was standing backlit by the street light. Tonight she'd gone all out and was wearing a pair of slinky black pants, topped with a bright pink fitted angora top. She teetered in on dangerously high heels and stood, silent for once, eyeing Ron.

"I don't think we've met," she said quietly, patting her carefully coiffed topknot and holding out her hand.

Ellen goggled. Where was her usually blatant come-hither neighbor – the woman who made up to every man in sight?

"Ron." Ron stood up and took her hand. "Ellen's brother."

"My," Coralie simpered and turned to face Ellen. "You didn't tell me about him." Her voice was subdued – quite unlike her usual self.

"He's just going, aren't you, Ron?"

Ron appeared not to have heard Ellen speak. He was still gazing at Coralie, who had turned her eyes back to Ellen.

"I thought I'd just pop in early in case there was anything I could do to help." She looked at the circle of chairs. "Were you intending to offer coffee?"

"I'll be off, then." Ron seemed to collect himself and headed for the door.

"Right. I'll be sure to tell Travis," Ellen called after him. "Catch you later."

"Coffee?" Coralie repeated.

"That would be great. I bought some instant, and you'll find sugar and milk in the bottom cupboard. I need to do a couple of things before the others arrive, but if you could put on the jug and set out a few mugs – I think I should have enough."

Snacking on a sandwich while she re-plaited her hair, Ellen reviewed what had just happened. Not only had Coralie become a different person, but her brother had noticed a woman for the first time Ellen could remember. This required some thinking about. It certainly took her mind off Travis.

"Your brother," Coralie began, when Ellen emerged from the office. "Married is he?"

"No – never seemed interested that way."

"Oh."

Ellen wondered if she'd given Coralie the wrong impression. It wasn't that Ron didn't like women. He was just as heterosexual as any other guy. But, since returning from Vietnam all those years ago, it had seemed he'd lost interest in that side of his life, being content with his mates and his boat.

But she didn't have time to worry about Coralie and her brother, because the others started to arrive, and although there was still no sign of Travis, Ellen decided to start the meeting.

"If everyone has coffee, let's sit down," she said, her words followed by jostling and murmuring as everyone took their seats.

"Now, we've all received one of these." She held up the ubiquitous letter to a murmur of assent. "I asked you all here tonight so we could discuss what we're going to do – form a plan of action." She was about to continue when Coralie spoke up, her voice rising to a squeak.

"But what about that last sentence? What do they mean by 'hurt and danger'?"

There was a muttering of agreement.

"Sounds like they're trying to intimidate us."

Several others nodded.

Ellen felt her body deflate, like a burst balloon. Were they all going to cave in to the developer's demands? She thought there would have been more of an outcry against the proposal.

"So are we going to let them?" There was a tightness in her chest as she waited for a response.

"We…ell," Tony, who leased the toy shop two doors down from *The Reading Nook* began, "seems to me…" But before he could finish, the door opened, and a tall figure hurried in, bringing a rush of cold air with him.

"Howdy, folks. Sorry I'm late." He took a seat amidst some puzzled looks.

"This is Travis Petersen," Ellen announced. "He's a friend, and he's promised to try to help us. He's from California, and he's been doing some research on Balcombs. Now, what were you going to say, Tony?"

But Tony seemed to have lost track of what he was about to say. "Let's hear it from the newcomer," he said.

"Coffee?" Coralie offered, rising and smiling at Travis, but tonight her usual flirtatiousness was missing.

"Please." He blinked and glanced at Ellen as if for guidance, while Coralie disappeared into the back of the shop.

"Right then," Travis began. "I'll start at the beginning." He looked around the group. "When I heard about the proposed development, the name Balcombs rang a few bells for me. I thought it might be the same company that tried to screw with a friend of mine down in California."

Ellen saw a few nods and noticed Tony and Jackie lean forward as if to hear better.

"I promised Ellen I'd check them out. Thanks," he nodded to Coralie, who'd returned with a mug of coffee and handed it to him. "Well, I was right. They did the same thing – submitted a development proposal, acted as if it was a *fait accompli,* and arranged for purchase based on the approval going through. The point was, Balcombs hadn't outlaid any money for the buildings. It was all just a proposal."

"You mean…?" Tony spoke for the group.

"Yeah. Same thing here. The purchase is dependent on the development going through."

"But what about the letter?" Coralie had her copy right there in her hand. "They say…"

"I know what they say. Ellen showed me hers." Travis smiled warmly at Ellen triggering a trembling in her whole body, as she remembered his hands holding hers over dinner. "They tried that tactic down there too. Intimidation, not to put too fine a point on it."

"So what did he do, this friend of yours?" Bob, who had kept quiet up till now, suddenly spoke up. "We don't want no trouble." He looked at the others, as if seeking their agreement. "We're a peaceful lot up here."

Peaceful? Ellen could bet each and every one of them had at least one gun at home. They might only use them for hunting, but if their lives or the lives of their family members were threatened, she wouldn't care to think what they might do.

Travis took a sip of coffee. "First thing to do is to check out what they're proposing. Has anyone been to the library to look at the plans?"

There was a general shaking of heads, and Ellen realized that she, too, had been too busy to do this simple task.

"Right, well you need to do that. In order to fight, you need to know exactly what you're fighting. Know your enemy. Next, they got up a petition."

"A petition? Phooey. What good will that do? There are only a few of us."

"Only a few of you shopkeepers affected, yes. But if it goes ahead, how many others will also be affected? Think!" Travis pointed towards the door. "If these shops go, how might that affect the other shops around?"

"And our customers," Ellen put in, now aware of the wide impact of the whole project. Whereas before, she'd only been thinking of herself and others like her, she could now see the greater ramifications.

"And…" Ellen prompted him, but Jackie spoke at the same time.

"This friend of yours – in California – what happened? Did the developers win?"

"Yeah," Bob said, folding his arms defensively. "It's a lot of work. Can we guarantee a result?"

Travis stroked his beard. "Well, nothing's guaranteed. Life's not like that. But to answer your question," he nodded towards Jackie. "The developers backed down. Had to. You see, the group my friend was part of – they discovered that the block in question had been built on an old graveyard. Probably should never have been built in the first place. Anyway, they managed to convince the powers that be that any demolition and further building would disturb the place too much. The whole thing went belly up."

Ellen saw a few grins around the group, but there were also several who shook their heads. Bob spoke for them. "Not likely to find that here, are we?"

"Maybe not a graveyard, but there might be something… something that would call a definite halt to the whole thing."

Ellen decided it was time for her to intervene, "Another friend of mine – Mike – is a historical researcher," she explained. "He's looking into that side of things. Been in the library checking out old documents and stuff. I bet he's checked out the plans too." She fell silent, realizing Mike probably knew a lot more about the proposed development than any of those present.

"Why's he not here, then?" It was Bob again.

"I'm not sure. I didn't… I guess he hasn't come up with anything as yet."

"And what if he doesn't?" Coralie's voice was dejected.

"Let's be positive. Mike's a good bloke. I'm sure he'll find something. In the meantime, how about we get this petition organized." She looked toward Travis for guidance.

"Anyone done anything like this before?" Travis asked, while Ellen scanned the group seeing everyone shaking their heads.

"Right. Well, how about Ellen and I put something together? We'll get it out to you all for your input, then we're off."

There were murmurings of agreement, with Coralie the only one still asking the "what if" questions.

The group left in ones and twos, till only Ellen and Travis remained.

"I'll give you a hand with these chairs." Travis began picking them up. "Where would you like them," he enquired. "Is there a special spot?"

"Just place the soft ones around the shop," Ellen said, pointing vaguely into the corners. "And the hard ones can be stacked. I'll put them in the storeroom later. Phew, I'm exhausted." She dropped down into one of the remaining chairs, her head drooping, and sat like that for a few moments before raising it again. "Thanks for coming tonight. I really don't know what I'd have done without you. They listened to you. It wouldn't have been the same if I'd tried to tell them. The men probably wouldn't have listened to me, and Coralie would have panicked. She was about to when you arrived."

"Yeah. Noticed she was a tad subdued tonight – not her usual boisterous self."

"No. Sorry, I seem to have run out of steam. Now, this petition. What do you...?"

"Why don't we work on that together? Two heads are always better than one."

"Would have to be after I close up."

"Sure, I can do that. Here?"

Ellen looked around and was about to agree, then changed her mind. "Why not come to my place? We can have a bite to eat and work at the same time."

"Sure thing."

Ellen stood up and repositioned the chair in which she'd been sitting. "How about Friday? I can be home by five-thirty."

"That works." Travis stood there, arms dangling, shuffling his feet awkwardly. "Well, I'd better be off. Sure you'll be all right to lock up on your own?"

"I'll be fine," Ellen replied, amused and flattered he thought she might need taken care of. "Friday, then?"

"Friday," he confirmed, as he headed for the door.

Ellen watched the door close behind him. What had she just done? Her hands made an involuntary movement to cover her cheeks. She'd invited Travis back into her home ostensibly to put together a petition – something that could easily have been done here, or in a coffee shop. Why on earth had she done it? She was regretting it already.

Sixteen

Ellen rushed into the house at twenty-five past five on Friday. A couple of late shoppers had meant she didn't leave as early as she'd intended. They were regular customers and, hearing rumors of the development proposal, wanted to offer their support. Travis was right. There were many locals who'd hate to see any changes.

But the delay meant she had no time to prepare for Travis' arrival. Well, he'd have to take her as she was. She looked down at her work uniform of comfortable blue jeans and loose checked shirt and grimaced. Jenny certainly wouldn't approve. Glad she'd had the foresight to stock up on salad and cold cuts, Ellen quickly set up the table in the kitchen and removed a bottle of wine from the rack. She was about to pick up two glasses, when she remembered. Travis didn't drink. She replaced the wine, though she would dearly have loved a glass to give her courage. "Courage for what?" a tiny voice in the back of her head asked. Ellen ignored it.

A loud rapping at the door signalled Travis' arrival, and taking a deep breath to calm the butterflies, now turning cartwheels in her stomach, Ellen answered the door. Travis stood there, his broad shoulders filling the doorway, his silver Harley shining in the roadway outside.

"All set?" he asked, following her into the house. "Wow, a veritable feast," he exclaimed, his eyes alighting on the spread on the table.

"It's not much," Ellen felt obliged to say. "A working meal. I just got home."

"I know. Saw you still beavering away when I came through town."

"You…"

"Came down earlier and detoured past the library. Looked at the plans the bastards have on display there. Have to admit they've made a good fist of it. If you didn't know there was a plan to demolish all you good folk, you might think they were doing the town a favor. Seen it yet?"

"No, not yet. I haven't…" Ellen pulled on the end of her hair. "I will."

"Course you will." Travis didn't seem troubled by her delaying what was, for her, a dreaded task. The last thing she wanted to do was to see what they planned to do with her special part of the street. But she remembered what Travis had said at the meeting – know your enemy.

"I'll go tomorrow," she promised. "After I close."

Travis smiled, a smile that lit up his whole face. "No rush. I know it's hard for you, but if you're opposing it, you need to know…"

"I know – what I'm opposing," Ellen sighed and her fingers reached up to hold her eyelids closed for a moment, then she opened her eyes again. "Better now. How about we eat first and work later?"

"Fine by me. Okay if I sit here?"

"Juice for you?" Ellen held up an orange juice container. "Sorry I don't have Coke."

"Juice is good."

Hell, Ellen thought, *we're back to words of one syllable. How on earth are we going to get through the evening – and put together a petition?*

"Wow, this is good." Travis forked up Ellen's special salad mix with relish. "Sure beats Ron's attempts."

"How's his arm doing?"

"Seems to be managing all right. Think he said he'd to go back to hospital after the weekend. Might get the bandages off then."

"He'll be pleased about that."

The conversation stalled.

Shit!

"Do you think you'll stay up here? After Ron's arm's right I mean? You must be missing California." *There, that should get some more out of him.*

"Well, it's pretty good here. Quiet. I like that. There's nothing to take me back down there now. Haven't been back since…"

Ellen bit her tongue. She'd said the wrong thing again, but Travis clearly noticed her discomfort.

"Look, don't be afraid to mention it. Now you know what happened. No sense avoiding it like the plague. There was an accident. My wife and son were killed. I blamed myself. I'd been drinking, not much, but..." He dragged his fingers through his hair. "They said it wasn't my fault – *you* said it wasn't my fault. But *I* was driving. I don't drink – haven't touched a drop since." He gave a wry smile. "Didn't drive either – seem to be cured of that, thanks to your dad. Besides, can't show my face down in the old place – too many memories. Spent the past two years floating around. Not proud of a lot of things. That's it in a nutshell. Now what is it about you that draws it all out of me, when I haven't been able to talk about it since?"

Ellen's heart contracted. While Travis had been talking, she'd been feeling increasingly sorry for this man who seemed to have erupted into her life from nowhere. Now she couldn't help herself. She stretched her hand across the table to cover his in silent compassion, her eyes misting at the thought of what he had gone through, what he was still going through. She wanted to take away his guilt, smooth his troubled brow. But that was out of the question and would be an unwelcome intrusion, she was sure. So instead, she remained silent and directed sympathetic thoughts his way.

They finished eating in a companionable silence. Travis' outpourings seemed to have helped them revert to their previous comfortable friendship.

"Coffee?" Ellen asked when they'd both eaten their fill. "If you go through to the living area, I'll bring it in. My laptop's on the coffee table there, and we can work on that."

"Coffee would be good. Sure I can't help?"

"No, I'll be right with you." Ellen needed some time alone before she sat down with Travis again, though the house was so small that 'alone' was the wrong word, as the kitchen opened out of the living area. Breathing space was a more appropriate term. She busied herself stacking the dishwasher while the coffee brewed and was soon carrying the two coffee mugs through.

"Neat system you have here," Travis said, inspecting Ellen's laptop. "Pretty sophisticated."

"Thanks. I often have to bring stuff home, so decided I needed a high-end machine here too." Ellen carefully placed the mugs on the table and sat down beside Travis. "Now, where do we start?"

An hour later, Ellen stretched her arms above her head. "Well, that's done, thanks." She was surprised how quickly they'd managed to put together the wording for a petition which would work for everyone – shopkeepers and customers, plus any other locals or tourists they could persuade to sign. "I'll show it to everyone tomorrow, then once they agree, we can get it out there."

"We make a good team." Travis' words came as a surprise, but Ellen had to agree. They'd worked well together. Their thoughts on this aligned – they were on the same page, as some might say.

"I'll print it up tomorrow," Ellen said, closing down her computer and feeling a trifle sorry that their evening together was at an end. It had been both better and worse than she'd anticipated. Better in that they'd eventually found it easy to talk with each other – Travis was good company when he was relaxed. And worse in that… Ellen wasn't sure what she'd expected, but had a slight sense of disappointment.

"It's still light," Travis stood up and walked across to the glass sliding doors of the kitchen. Turning back towards Ellen, he grinned. "How about a spin?"

"A…" Ellen gulped, and the butterflies returned. "A spin? On the Harley?"

"The only bike I've got." Travis' voice was amused.

Ellen felt she was caught between a rock and a hard place. On the one hand she'd vowed never to get on one of these things again – especially that one. On the other, she really wasn't ready for this evening to end. Her dilemma was resolved by Travis taking her hand and pulling her to her feet. "You'll love it – the wind on your face. All your troubles seem to melt away, and it seems you have a few of those right now."

The offer, combined with Travis' cajoling tone, was enough to dispel any residual concerns Ellen might harbor, and she found herself straddling the powerful machine, her arms tightly wrapped around Travis' waist, as they took off into the fading evening light.

It was fun! Ellen was surprised how much she enjoyed the sensation. Her arms encircling Travis' strong torso, her own body pressed tightly against his causing tremors which had nothing to do with the shuddering of the bike between her legs. As Travis had promised, the wind against her face and in her hair was exhilarating. It left no space for anything else. Thoughts of her dad's sickness, her mother's concerns, the development – all flew out of her mind as if blown away on the breeze. Ellen gave herself up to the sensation. Why had she been so determined never to ride? Why had she been so obdurate when others – including her brother many years ago – had encouraged her to ride pillion with them? This was wonderful. She was a free spirit, flying through the night into the encroaching dusk.

All too soon, it seemed, they were back. Parked in front of Ellen's house. "Wow," was all she could say, her breath coming in gasps.

"Worth it?" Travis chuckled, his mouth turning up at the side.

"It certainly was." Ellen loosened her arms, which were still wrapped round Travis' waist, feeling the loss of warmth as she did so. She stepped off the bike. "Thanks." She stood on the curb, uneasy and unsure what to do next. Should she turn and go into the house? Stand around and try to make conversation? What was the etiquette for such a situation?

"Thanks," she said again, only to have Travis' arm encircle her waist and pull her down so his lips could touch her cheek gently, before he revved up again and with a, "Be in touch," he was off.

Ellen stared after him with a sense of *déjà vu*. Her hand rose to the spot where his lips had touched and against which his beard had brushed. It tingled. She made her way inside with an inner glow and a sense of recognition. This was what had been missing earlier.

*

Travis was jubilant as he rode up the highway. He realized he was beginning to have feelings for Ellen – real feelings. Not the casual lust he'd felt for all those others in the past two years – and there had been a lot. He'd been no angel. He'd tried to lose himself in the sex. It hadn't worked. Afterwards everything was still there – the accident, his remorse, and added to it was guilt. Every time, he felt he was being unfaithful to Allie. It didn't matter that she was dead; the guilt was still there.

When he drew up at Ron's, he cut out the engine. The gentle sea breeze ruffled his hair, the only sounds the roaring of the waves and the distant sound of cars on the highway. There was a light on, so Ron was most likely watching television, but with the volume turned down, as the noise didn't carry out here. It was peaceful, as if the rest of the world had disappeared, and there was only him, his bike and the ocean.

Sighing, Travis dismounted and, energised, bounded up the steps to the front door. "Hey!" he called out, as he pulled the door closed behind him. "What's up?" He parked himself in an armchair opposite Ron and out of view of the television, which as he'd predicted, was muted.

"Hi there." Ron placed the beer he'd been drinking on the floor. "Want a Coke?" Without waiting for a reply he continued, "How'd it go with my little sister? Hope she wasn't too rough with you."

"She was fine. Got the petition done," Travis muttered, deciding to keep details of the rest of the evening to himself.

"Hmm. She might not be too bad for you," Ron pointed a wavering finger at Travis. "What you need is a good woman."

"How many of these have you had?" Travis walked over to pick up the now empty beer bottle, one of several lying on the floor. Ron had clearly been drinking all evening. "And what brought this on?"

"A good woman," Ron repeated. "And Coralie, another good woman – she's..." his voice petered out and his eyes closed.

Coralie? What was Ron talking about? She was the last person Travis was interested in, with her blatant flirting and come-hither eyes. Surely Ron had gotten confused between Ellen and that bimbo? He laughed as he helped his old buddy out of the chair and led the mumbling figure to bed, where he dumped him on top of the covers. Let him sleep it off. He'd make more sense in the morning when he'd most likely have no recollection of their conversation.

Ron might be in a drunken stupor, but Travis was wide awake. The ride had energized him. The sensation of Ellen's arms tight around his waist had aroused him, and he needed to work it off. In his room, he opened the window to better hear the roar of the ocean, the crash of the waves against the shore and the battering of the beach by the chunks of driftwood that regularly made their way up the coast. It was wild up here. He leaned out of the window imagining he could see the light of the Heceta Head lighthouse illuminating a path between him and Ellen. Oregon was famous for its lighthouses, and Heceta Head, situated midway between Florence and Yachats, was deemed one of the most beautiful, not only in Oregon, or in the United States, but in the world. But the topography and distance were such that he could neither see the lighthouse nor its beam.

Travis looked up at the stars instead. Those were the same stars shining on him and Ellen. Travis closed the window. Where had such fanciful thoughts come from? Ellen was the one who was fey, not him. Opening up his laptop, he immersed himself in his writing. This was the work that was beginning to help bury the past and give him hope that there was a future; that he could write again and find happiness. As Ellen's image tried to force itself into his consciousness, he dismissed it to concentrate on his dark hero.

Seventeen

Ellen couldn't understand why Ron was visiting her in the shop so often. He'd called in from time to time before, but had never been a frequent visitor. Books just weren't his thing. Now – in the past few days, since he had the full use of his arm back and was driving again – he was hanging around like a bad smell.

"Oh, for goodness' sake," she finally said to him. "Why don't you go do something? Go get your hair cut if you've nothing better to do than get in my way." *Now why did I say that?* she wondered, as Ron walked off in disgust. *I didn't mean to. The words came out of their own accord, with no intention on my part. It's as if someone else – someone I have no control over – put the words into my mouth.*

No one was more surprised than Ellen when Ron returned, having taken the advice she'd involuntarily given. She examined him, stunned. "You've… you've had your hair cut," she exclaimed, seeing a new version of her brother: one without the lank ponytail he'd sported for the past forty years. "It looks… very smart." She hid a smile. Smart! Her brother was transformed. He looked years younger with his short silver-streaked locks.

"You were the one who told me to do it," Ron said defensively, turning around to give Ellen a view of his now naked neck and sleek haircut. "You didn't tell me…"

"Wait a mo'," Ellen said, as a customer approached holding a couple of books. "Let me attend to this lady first." She managed to make small talk while she handled the transaction, then as her customer left, turned back to Ron. "I didn't tell you what?" She was mystified. What on earth was her brother on about?

"You didn't tell me Coralie was the hairdresser."

"What…" Ellen gave her brother a bewildered look. Then she remembered his obvious interest in her neighbor before the meeting. "Oh, you met?"

"Sure did." Ron appeared to have developed a swagger along with his new hairstyle. This was a side to her brother she'd forgotten. It reminded her of their teenage years, when he'd been a smooth operator, the idol of all of her friends. It gladdened her heart to see a return of the old Ron, but Coralie? Still, her neighbor had been more subdued of late. Since she'd met Ron, Ellen realized. Maybe they'd be good for each other. It would certainly give her mom something else to focus on, besides Ellen's own non-existent love-life.

"Did she do this… this transformation?" Ellen chuckled.

"Sure did," Ron repeated, looking a tad sheepish. "What do you think? 'Time I got rid of that old tail,' she said. This look is more stylish." He preened.

Ellen almost choked. What had got into her brother? How on earth had Coralie managed to effect this change in one haircut, which had only lasted – she checked her watch – around half an hour.

"Do you… is she…?" Ron dropped his eyes and began to study the floor as if the answer to the meaning of life was written there – or at least the answer to his questions about Coralie.

"She's not married, if that's what you want to know," Ellen replied. "Other than that, I don't know much about her. We're neighbors, not friends. Are you…?" Ellen wasn't sure what she wanted to ask, or if she really wanted to know anything about her brother's intentions, so she didn't finish her question.

"And what about you – you and Travis?" Ron was quick to turn Ellen's question back on her. "Something going on there?"

"No! What's he said?" Ellen's heart rushed up into her throat, beating rapidly at the thought she might have been the subject of discussion between Travis and her brother.

"Nothing. Do you think us guys have nothing better to do than gossip about you?"

Her heart slowed to a more normal pace. "Well, since neither of you talk very much at the best of times, I guess not. So what are you up to now, now that you're all gussied up?"

"Might head home to check up on Dad. Mom says he's beginning to get more irritable – a sure sign he's improving."

"He's eating better. I called in last night. He'll be pleased to see you, even though he may not show it. I think he's getting stir crazy, stuck in the house. But he's not able to go out yet, and Mom needs to be there with him. Just because he's feeling better, doesn't mean he's ready for business as usual. Make sure he doesn't try to do too much. You could give Mom a break. That'd be good."

"See what I can do."

Ron left, and Ellen breathed a sigh of relief. Now she could get back to work. She'd been checking on the list of people who'd taken copies of the petition and was amazed at the strength of the support their project was achieving. She leafed through the returned pile. A few more to go and they'd be ready to submit something to the council. Mike still hadn't come up with anything that could be counted as evidence for a historical basis to their claim, so the petition was all they had.

The ringing of the shop phone interrupted her. An unexplained shiver ran down her spine as she was picking up the receiver. She almost dropped it.

"Hello, *The Reading Nook*. How might I help you?" Ellen tried to inject some of her usual enthusiasm into her voice, failing dismally.

"Are you Ellen Williams?" a cultivated voice enquired.

"That's me." This time she was able to add a more cheerful tone.

"A word of warning. Don't meddle in things that don't concern you. You're on dangerous ground. Take care."

"What?"

But the caller had rung off. She checked for caller ID, but it was a withheld number. Putting the phone down, Ellen stood motionless. The room swirled around her. This was trouble, trouble with a capital T. She was still reeling from the call when the sound of the doorbell startled her. Travis walked in. She was so pleased to see him, she almost threw her arms around him, but stopped herself just in time. They weren't on those sort of terms.

"You're as white as a sheet. What's happened?"

Ellen pointed to the phone, but couldn't find any words. Her throat constricted. Her tongue stuck to the roof of her mouth.

"Here," Travis was standing in front of her with a glass of water, before she realized he'd moved. He led her to a chair.

"Now, for God's sake tell me what happened."

Ellen regained her breath and her voice, but felt as if something was stuck in her throat. "I took a call." She pointed to the phone on the counter. "A man's voice, educated, maybe Californian." She tried to recall exactly what she had heard. "A warning."

"What sort of warning?" Travis crouched down beside her. "Was he specific?"

"No, he only said…" She put her hand to her forehead to better recall. "He said to take care – to stop meddling." Ellen opened her eyes and raised her head to meet Travis' eyes. "But I'm only one of the shopkeepers around here. How did he know I was organizing things?"

"You're the leader," Travis said bluntly. "Anyone can see that. You're the one the others look to for help and advice. Look how they all agreed with you at your meeting."

"With your help."

Travis brushed this off. "Well, I have some news," he said. "Heard from my mate in California."

"The one who had dealings with Balcombs?" Ellen brushed a stray hair back from her forehead. She was beginning to feel better.

"The very one. Seems there was a court case down there. The owners were accused of corrupt dealings – bribes, intimidation, the works. Result was they've been banned from building in the whole state of California. Their license was revoked."

"So they've come up here," Ellen said slowly. "And…"

"And they're doing exactly the same thing here." Travis finished for her.

"But how does that help us?"

"Not sure that it does, really," Travis seemed to lose his confidence. "But maybe we… you, can use it with council. At the very least it might delay approval – give us more time to come up with something."

"Well, they're not going to win here either," Ellen declared, as she stood up, raising her head proudly. "We'll show them who they're dealing with. I got a shock, that's all. I'm over it now," she said, suppressing the memory of the shiver which had told her all was not well. She'd had sensations like that before, and they almost always heralded disaster. She was in no doubt now. This development had to be the catastrophe she'd foreseen, and the best way through was to follow her instincts. They told her to be careful, but to keep going and she'd win in the end.

"You should call the police."

Ellen considered his words. It seemed like the obvious thing to do, but something stopped her.

"No, I don't think so. What could the police do? Where's the evidence? A phone call… from a withheld number? They'd laugh at us." She bit her lip at the realization she'd said 'us' not 'me', and gave Travis a sidelong glance, but he didn't appear to have noticed her slip of the tongue.

"What else has been happening?" Travis wanted to know. "What about those petitions?"

"Going great. I was just checking them off when the call came in," Ellen threw a quick glance at the phone, daring it to ring again. It remained mute. She changed the subject. "Have you seen Ron?"

"Saw him this morning." Travis appeared puzzled. "Now he's mobile again, we lead our separate lives. He's not dependent on me to get around. What's up?"

Ellen began to laugh. "You won't recognize him. He's had a haircut. I sent him off – not sure why – and Coralie got her hands on him."

Travis chortled. "Coralie? When he got drunk one night he was trying to… well, maybe not." Travis stopped as if remembering something he was reluctant to share. "Glad she didn't manage to get her hands on me."

"I think he likes her. It's odd. He doesn't usually notice women, but Coralie seems to have made an impression."

"She seems to try it on with every man she meets. But you say Ron's fallen for it?"

"His taste in women always did run towards the…" she hesitated, "the exotic. When he was younger, that is – before he went to Vietnam. Since then, he hasn't seemed interested. Not till now," she said, a trace of wonder in her voice.

"Took some that way," Travis responded.

"Mmm. Didn't affect you, though."

"Not me."

They stood facing each other, but avoiding making eye contact. Seconds passed. The shop was silent. A few cars passed in the street outside. A dog barked in the distance. A querulous child cried as its mother wheeled it past the door. They were enclosed in a time capsule as surely as if there was a physical barrier built around them.

"Was there anything else?" Ellen broke through the silence.

"Yeah. Dinner… you agreed to have dinner with me again."

Ellen's stomach swirled. She hadn't been wrong about Travis' interest, then. First time, an apology dinner – yes. Second time, the petition had to be constructed. She was ignoring the bike ride, but that had been… what exactly? She chose not to go there. This… this was definitely a date.

"Thought maybe a picnic. I can pick you up on the bike after work, get one of those hamper things they put up at that Wine Gallery place, and we can take it up to the lighthouse. What d'you say?"

Ellen's heart thumped at the thought of another bike ride. She remembered sitting behind Travis, the closeness of his broad shoulders, the softness of his jacket against her face as she leant against him, the smell of his hair in her nostrils, the intimacy of the whole experience. She, who had always hated bikes and the guys who rode them. Dismissed them as deadbeats, not to be trusted and certainly not to keep company with. She couldn't believe how eager she was to repeat that experience.

"Yes, please," she said, quivering in excitement.

"Tomorrow? Can you get closed by five-thirty?"

So soon?

"I'll try – as long as there are no last minute customers."

"See you then." As Travis brushed past Ellen on his way out, he paused to lay a hand on her shoulder, seemingly about to say more. The heat from his body permeated her very core. He hesitated, then, "Cheers." He left.

Ellen put her hand on her stomach as if by holding it there, she could quell the build-up of elation. Unbidden, a smile lit up her face. Despite the ominous phone call and threat to the shops, she felt like dancing around the store, but of course she couldn't do that – not at her age. She felt like a girl again. Such was the effect this man had on her.

*

Travis was walking on air. He'd equivocated for the last few days, wondering if it was the right thing to do. Not completely sure of his own feelings, how could he even imagine Ellen's? He couldn't forget that she was Ron's sister – his little sister. They might both be grown up and middle-aged, but family was still family and Ron seemed to look out for her, try to steer her in the right direction. He laughed to himself, imagining anyone trying to steer Ellen in any direction she didn't want to go. She was a strong woman. That was part of the attraction for him. They could meet as equals.

She'd agreed, agreed to see him – not as an apology, not for work, purely for pleasure. And he intended to make sure it was a pleasurable evening for her – for them both. Travis whistled as he walked along the street, too full of energy to ride just yet. He walked the length of the street, finishing up on the boardwalk. Leaning his arms on the white metal railing, he stared out at the Siuslaw River, flowing sluggishly this morning. He gazed up at the arches of the bridge, a fine example of that two-tied arch design. He'd heard it was also a drawbridge, but had never seen it open. His eyes were drawn to the seagulls perching on the old pylons, their wild high-pitched cries disturbing the calm of the day.

His thoughts turned to Allie. He could see her narrow face, her glossy black hair with the grey strands which she attempted to hide, and about which he'd often teased her. For a moment he was swamped with grief, the view of the river blurring. Then he pictured the round beaming face of Ellen as she'd been when he left her. Allie would have liked Ellen. He was sure of that. They had a lot in common – not in looks, but both were strong determined, independent women. Yes, they would have been good friends, he thought, realizing how ridiculous that notion was.

Travis checked his watch. Time to get back. He'd set himself a writing deadline. Knew he had to keep to it if he wanted to make a fist of this book. He needed the discipline writing gave him – a discipline that had been sorely lacking from his life for some time. He set off back with a smile on his face and a spring in his step

Eighteen

It had been a busy morning, preventing Ellen from too much contemplation of the evening to come. However, around lunchtime the custom began to taper off, and her attention wandered to the guy who had triggered a few sleepless nights. At least she hadn't had that frightening nightmare lately – not since she and Travis had shared their dream experiences. Thinking of Travis made her remember her promise to him – the promise that she'd visit the library to view Balcombs' plans.

Popping her 'closed for now – back soon' sign on the door, Ellen hopped into her car and drove the short distance to the Siuslaw Library. There in the foyer, exactly as she'd been told, were large boards showing the proposed development. There were photos showing the artist's impression of the finished project and, in a glass case, a three dimensional model. They certainly hadn't spared any expense. All this for a proposal which had still to receive the green light – and which wouldn't see the light of day if Ellen and her colleagues had anything to do with it.

On the face of it, everything looked good. A white glass-fronted building rose up from a landscaped courtyard. There were even little figures of people going about their business. All very modern – clean cut lines and geometric proportions. It was only when you considered the destruction which would have to take place before this edifice was built, that the travesty sunk home. Ellen turned away, shuddering, apprehensive it might actually come to fruition. She couldn't bear to contemplate it.

"Examining the new buildings? What do you think?" Ellen turned to identify the speaker as a member of the City Council.

"I can't say I like it. In fact," Ellen's voice gained traction, "it's the most pernicious piece of architecture I've seen in a long time. Maybe in a city, it might blend in. But how could anyone imagine it would fit into Old Town? Why…" Ellen ran out of steam and waved her hands in the air.

"So what are you going to do about it?"

Ellen looked askance at the lady standing in front of her, a light suddenly going on in her head. Council members – why had no one thought of approaching them. Of course some might be in favor of the proposal, but here was one who certainly did not seem to be.

"Umm. Working on a few things." Ellen wasn't eager to give too much away, in case she was mistaken.

"Well, see you do." Ellen's companion swept off leaving her surprised.

Driving back to the shop, Ellen tried to dismiss the plans she'd seen. Reaching her beloved store, she acknowledged the building did look old. But surely that was part of its charm? Maybe Mike would come up trumps. It still seemed to her the historical angle was the best one. Petitions and council members were fine in their way, but if they had real evidence – historical evidence – that would sway any committee and stand up in court.

*

Ellen swept back a stray lock of hair and tossed her plait back over her shoulder. It had been a hectic afternoon, with the shop scarcely empty for more than ten minutes at a time. Checking her watch, she noted she had just time to freshen up before Travis was due to arrive. She locked the door and placed the *closed* sign on it, before closeting herself in the office. She tidied her hair, removed the grime of the day from her face and hands, and changed into the outfit she'd packed this morning. All too soon, it seemed, there was a peremptory knocking at the door, and glancing in that direction, she could distinguish Travis' tall silhouette against the clouded glass panel.

"I'm coming," she yelled, even though she knew he couldn't possibly hear her, as she hurried to open it for him.

"Hi." An unusually subdued Travis stood there, dressed this evening in pressed blue denims topped with a pale blue open-necked shirt under the usual suede jacket. Ellen could tell he'd made an effort and was glad she'd taken time to change herself. She looked down at her own pressed jeans fitted neatly into the calf-length black cowboy boots and pulled on the edge of her new pink and white checked shirt. The outfit had looked all right when she left home this morning, but now she wondered if…

"You look good," Travis smiled, that smile of his which lit up his whole face, his lips curling up on one side.

Ellen's stomach turned over and her legs trembled. Hell, this wouldn't do. She took a deep breath. "You look pretty smart, yourself," she said. "Shall we go?" She needed to sit down and would welcome the leather seat on Travis' Harley as an opportunity to calm her ragged nerves.

"I packed the hamper stuff into the saddlebags," Travis explained, as they stood on the sidewalk, the large silver beast looking as if it was straining to be on its way.

"Right," Ellen replied, mounting the bike behind him, her hands stretching around his waist as if she did this every day. It was everything she remembered: the wind in her hair, the smell, a mixture of sea and oil, the familiarity of the man sitting in front of her. She gave herself up to the pleasure, the pure sensation, as they sped up the highway through the lines of trees on one side, the land falling away to the ocean on the other. This part of the coast had a wildness about it that matched her companion.

"Here we are," Travis wheeled the bike into the parking lot. "It sure is impressive," he exclaimed looking up at the tall white edifice sitting high on the headland. "What is it about Oregon and lighthouses? They're everywhere – on souvenirs, even tea towels."

"Oh, we're very proud of them," said Ellen, pleased to engage in normal conversation after the wild ride. Her legs were still weak, whether from the bumpy ride or from Travis' nearness, she wasn't sure. "There are eleven along the coast, and this one was recently restored. We think it's the most beautiful of all." Ellen gazed up at the familiar building, its white sides glowing in the afternoon sunlight. "They say it's the most visited of all of them," she stated proudly.

"I suppose you've been here a lot?"

"Not really – not since I was younger. These days it's a place that attracts tourists, and I don't have much time for that."

"Mmm. Well, I hear there's a beach with picnic tables. Think I'm a bit long in the tooth for the blanket on the sand business these days." Travis hefted the two saddlebags off the bike. "Down here is it?" he asked, nodding in the direction of a pathway.

"Yes. I'm right behind you," Ellen hid a smile at the picture Travis' words presented. While sitting on a beach blanket with a fire burning on the sand sounded romantic, and had been fun in her younger – much younger – days, now picnic tables fitted the bill much better.

*

The light was beginning to fade by the time the pair had demolished all the food. Ellen was surprised how quickly time had gone. Conversation had never flagged and had covered books, music, travel – keeping well away from the personal issues they'd shared earlier and the present challenges both were facing. It had been comfortable, without any of the awkward silences they'd experienced on previous occasions.

"I guess we should be getting back," Ellen said, stretching her arms above her head.

"I guess," Travis replied but made no move to leave.

"The light will be starting soon. It has a really strong beam, the brightest on the coast." As she spoke, both turned their eyes toward the lighthouse where, sure enough, the wide beam began to light up the sky.

"It's magical," Travis' hand reached over to cover Ellen's, the first time they'd touched since dismounting from the bike.

They sat in silence admiring the magnificent spectacle.

*

The trip home was over all too soon. This time Ellen had made a decision. To dispel any awkwardness in parting, as soon as she slipped her legs off the bike, she spoke.

"Would you like a coffee… or a hot chocolate?" she asked tentatively, a wide smile on her face.

"Love to. Hot chocolate sounds just the thing," Travis turned off the engine which was still running, and stepping off the bike, followed Ellen into the house.

"You cut some," Travis indicated the bowl of rhododendrons sitting in the middle of the table, the mix of pinks and reds making a splash of color on the otherwise dull surface.

"Yes, don't usually. I like to see them still on the bushes, but I felt the place needed something to brighten it up."

"You brighten it up all by yourself," said Travis gallantly.

Conscious of her heart beginning to race and a blush rising to her cheeks, Ellen wasn't sure she was ready for this side of Travis. The evening had gone well so far, mostly because they'd kept away from anything personal. Maybe this invitation to a late drink had been a mistake?

She busied herself with heating milk and fetching the chocolate out of the cupboard to hide the growing red of her face, while conscious of Travis prowling around the room behind her.

Gradually her heart resumed its normal beat, and Ellen was brave enough to turn to face him again. Holding a cake tin in one hand she asked, "Cake too – or have you eaten enough for today? That was an amazing feast you provided."

"Don't thank me – I only bought the stuff. It was good, wasn't it? But a piece of cake would go down a treat. Make it yourself?"

"I wish," Ellen replied. "Mom made it. She still sends me home with a parcel of goodies. Thinks I don't look after myself properly. Anyway, it provides her with a purpose, besides looking after Dad. Guess I'm still a little girl to her," she grimaced.

"And how is your dad?"

"Improving slowly. The danger now seems to be that he'll feel well, so try to do more, and that could lead to a blood clot or something," Ellen sighed. "It's taking all Mom's will to keep him under the thumb. He's not an easy patient, but then, he's never been easy to live with, and his current condition has only served to exacerbate his stubbornness."

Ellen set the two hot drinks and a plate of cake on a tray. "Let's go through here," she said, carrying it into the living room and placing it on the coffee table. She settled on the sofa with Travis beside her. As she picked up her mug, Ellen noticed Travis was sitting closer tonight than he had on the previous occasion, when they'd been putting together the petition. It would only take a small movement on her part for their legs to touch. She was suddenly very aware of that space between them and felt an uncanny urge to minimize it. Her heart had resumed its frantic beating. She took a sip of the chocolate.

"Mmm, this is good," said Travis, gulping his own and taking a bite of cake.

Ellen silently chastised herself for her sentiments. Travis was probably completely unaware of the effect his closeness had on her. She took another sip and tried to think of something innocuous to say. It had been so easy on the beach – none of the awkwardness she was now experiencing. She felt like a silly teenager again. She took a deep breath and replaced her mug on the table, only to find Travis' hand on her thigh, its warmth burning through her jeans.

"Ellen," Travis' voice was thick.

Ellen turned to face him. He was closer than she'd anticipated. She could feel his breath fan her face as he gazed into her eyes. She had no words.

They sat immobile for what seemed like minutes, but was only a few seconds, then Travis moved. His lips met Ellen's. Her body trembled and weakened as she experienced the softness of those lips surrounded with the soft facial hair. She'd never imagined a beard could feel so soft. It was almost like silk, brushing against her face. She wanted to rub her nose in it – to inhale the essence his masculinity. There was a familiar ache in her gut, the sort of ache she'd almost forgotten.

"Not here," she muttered weakly, but his lips persisted in their pressure, and his tongue worked its way into her welcoming mouth.

Eventually they made their way into the bedroom, with Travis half carrying the fully aroused Ellen and laying her gently on the white candlewick bedspread. Her newly sensitive body felt every one of the raised ribs on the bedspread's design through a haze of desire.

"Why do you hide the fact you're a woman – a beautiful woman?" Travis asked, raining kisses on her upturned face.

Ellen opened her mouth to deny it, but the words died on her lips. She reflected hazily on her usual daily garb. She was a big woman, not fat, big bones her mother used to say – and she did tend to hide her curves in oversized garments.

"You're so…womanly," he murmured, as he prized open the buttons on her shirt. "Why do you hide behind these ridiculous garments?"

Ellen shuddered and moaned as his mouth found her nipple. A great longing surged up in her. She became aware of the cool air on her now naked body as Travis moved to remove his own garments, then he lowered himself slowly, his skin meeting hers, and she sighed in satisfaction. This was what she wanted – this man moving inside her. Ellen felt herself drown in ecstasy as they culminated their union. She floated in a frenzy of rapture, only coming down to earth again when Travis began to stroke her back sending shivers of pleasure through her whole body.

"Ah," she exclaimed. "How do you…?" Her words were cut off by his nimble fingers finding sensitive spots she hadn't known existed. She gave herself up to the sensation, and it was some time later, before she found her voice again.

They lay on their backs, spent, hands clasped. Ellen smiled lazily and turned to her companion to see a similar expression on his face.

"Well," he said, tightening his hand in hers.

"Well, yourself," Ellen was filled with happiness. How could she have doubted this man? How could she have doubted her own feelings? Then a little stirring of misgiving crept into the back of her mind. What if…

She pushed herself upright. "I think…" she began, only to have Travis gently push her down and close her lips with yet another kiss.

"Not now," he murmured, his lips leaving hers for a moment before resuming their caress, this time moving from her lips, to her shoulder, then the hollow below her collarbone.

"Mmm." It would be so easy to lose herself again, to give in to the temptation and revel in the sensations and emotions aroused by his touch. "No." Ellen tried to rise again, this time managing to pull the edge of the bedspread over herself in an attempt to hide her nakedness. Now that their lovemaking was over, she was aware of her ungainly body. She vaguely remembered Travis referring to it as womanly and beautiful, but that had been in the heat of his desire. She was sure it would appear different to him in the cold light of its aftermath.

"No?" Travis appeared perplexed. "What do you mean by that? Didn't you… weren't you…?"

"Yes and yes. But we… Ron…"

Travis sat up and gazed into space. "Yes, Ron. You're still Ron's sister. What was I thinking of? You must be joking, Ellen. What has Ron got to do with this… with what we feel for each other?" His voice had lost its earlier warmth and now sounded almost cold.

"Feel…? Then…?"

Travis dragged his fingers through his hair. "You don't think… my God, you do, don't you? You think it was just sex for me?"

Ellen dropped her eyes, still clinging to the coverlet with both hands, her eyes wide with dismay. Had she messed up this relationship even before it began?

Travis leaned toward Ellen and gently stroked her shoulder, then her head. He began to undo her long plait, running his fingers through the thick tresses as he did so. "I've wanted to do this, ever since we sat in your kitchen. You have beautiful hair – beautiful woman, beautiful hair." He buried his nose in the long strands, letting it run through his fingers. Ellen shivered with renewed desire. Maybe, just maybe, she could believe him. Maybe this *could* be for real. A sense of calm pervaded her whole being. She closed her eyes and submitted her body to his will.

Nineteen

"Breakfast?" Ellen asked with a smile.

Travis watched her elegant body move around the kitchen, her luxurious hair lying on her shoulders like a shiny cape. He admired the way she held herself, regal and proud – like some of the Native American female warriors he'd written about in a previous life. She truly was a magnificent woman – magnificent in all respects, he thought, remembering the night they'd spent together. Neither of them had gotten much sleep last night, yet here she was, looking as fresh as if she'd had her full eight hours. He was so lost in thought, Ellen had to repeat her question.

"Breakfast?"

"Oh." Travis returned to the present. "Yes, please. But don't go to any trouble. I need to get back." As he spoke, he realized Ron might be wondering what had happened to his erstwhile housemate. Although they led their separate lives, Travis thought he'd made some remark about a picnic, though couldn't recall if Ellen's name had been mentioned. What was he going to tell Ron, who was so protective of his little sister?

"You won't tell Ron, will you?"

It was as if Ellen had read his thoughts. Was she a mind reader as well as a goddess?

"I mean," she twisted her long hair in her fingers, making him want to take her all over again, right there and then. He crossed his legs to disguise his rising desire. "It's my family," Ellen continued, clearly unaware of the effect she was having on him as she swirled around the kitchen in her long robe. "For years, they've been trying to marry me off. No," she laughed. "I'm not imagining anything of that nature, but…" she rolled her eyes and laughed again.

Travis thought he'd never heard anything as bewitching as Ellen's tinkling laugh. It made him want to smile, to lift her up and twirl her around till they were both dizzy, then to carry her off to bed again.

While she'd been talking, Ellen had been cutting up fruit, preparing toast and fetching jars of peanut butter, jam and honey from the pantry. She placed all of these on the table along with two mugs of strong black coffee.

"Don't know about you, but I'm going to need this if I'm going to stay awake all day," she said, taking a long drink. "Mmm, that's better. How are you this morning?" she asked

"Pretty fair."

"Only pretty fair?" she laughed again, and Travis reached across the table to take her hand. He picked it up and began to nibble gently on her fingers, finally turning it over to plant a kiss on the palm.

"Is that better?" With his lips still near her palm, he raised his eyes to meet hers which were twinkling with amusement.

"Oh, I could get used to this, but…" She drew her hand away. "I have a shop to open. We don't all make our own schedule. What do you have on today?"

Travis tugged his beard. "Well, first I guess I'd better head up to Seal Rock. Check in with your brother. Make up some story about where I've been all night."

"Oh, I didn't mean… I don't want you to lie on my behalf." Ellen sounded concerned.

"No problem. I'll fudge something. I guess we guys aren't so fussed about these things."

"I guess not. Well, I'd better get changed and ready for work."

Travis rose, and walking around the table, caught Ellen in his arms. "I haven't hugged you this morning. Did I tell you how gorgeous you look with your hair like this?" He lifted the heavy locks and placed a kiss on the nape of Ellen's neck, feeling her shudder under his touch.

"I must…," she slipped from his grasp.

"I'll be off." Travis picked up his jacket from the back of the chair.

"I may drop in on you later," he said, as he headed for the door, his last glimpse of Ellen a swirl of material and hair as she drifted out of the kitchen.

It wasn't till he was halfway back to Seal Rock that the significance of what he'd done sunk in. He'd bedded Ellen – his best bro's sister. He shook his head to clear the doubts that began to fill it. Yes, she was beautiful, all he'd ever wanted in a woman, but… Who was he to foist himself on a decent woman? It was okay to do women like those he'd met in the past two years. They didn't expect anything permanent. But Ellen? She was a whole different ball game. He'd bet she played for keeps. Shit! Why hadn't he kept it in his pants? But she was just too damn tempting. Now he had to go home and face her brother. What the hell! But it had been pretty bloody fantastic. Maybe he could risk another dinner. He began to sing with the wind in his hair.

*

Ellen had a busy morning unpacking a delivery of new books and checking them into her inventory, so it was almost lunchtime before she had a chance to consider the implications of the previous evening. Despite this, a warm glow had suffused her the entire morning, making what would otherwise have been a boring task, become a piece of cake. She was in her office, reliving those amazing moments with Travis, when the doorbell followed by Jenny's familiar voice interrupted her train of thought. Ellen hurried out to greet her cousin with a warm hug.

"You're looking very chipper this morning." Jenny held Ellen at arm's length and examined her. "If I didn't know any better I'd say…"

But Ellen didn't find out what Jenny would say, as just at that moment, her mobile chirped with a text message. She took a quick glance. *Tonight? Dinner? T*

Ellen couldn't hide the smile which tweaked her lips, or the red blush which suffused her face and neck.

"What… who…? It's Travis isn't it?" Jenny whooped. "I knew it! Tell me!" she demanded.

"Nothing to tell," Ellen lied, then aware Jenny wasn't going to be fobbed off so easily, added, "He's asked me to dinner," dropping her eyes to hide her delight.

"Dinner! A proper date, then. Now we really do have to find you something special to wear. You can't go looking like that."

Remembering Travis' comments about her outfit last night, this time Ellen was in the frame of mind to accept Jenny's advice. "What do you think, then?" she asked, tentatively.

"Well," Jenny appeared to appraise her tall companion. "Something elegant, not too fussy. Classical lines, I think. Something to show off your great figure instead of hiding it under all those layers."

Ellen winced to hear Travis' words echoed by Jenny. Maybe she *had* been trying to hide from the world. "But I don't have time," she remonstrated. "I can't leave."

"Course you can. You've done it before. Just pop up your little sign, and we can check out the boutique on the corner. They're sure to have something."

"You've sure become bossy in the past year." Ellen pretended to object, but followed Jenny's advice, and the pair set off.

*

All afternoon, Ellen kept throwing glances toward her office, where the new outfit hung in all its glory. She'd managed to eschew what she considered to be the ultra-feminine garb, and had settled on a pair of long pants teamed with a knee-length tunic split to the thigh, both in a vivid shade of royal blue. Jenny had considered her usual boots too heavy for the new gear, so they'd also managed to pick up a pair of matching blue pumps. Ellen worried she'd gone too far – spending all this money on an outfit on the basis of one night of passion. She wasn't accustomed to making rash purchases, especially when it came to clothes. *What would Travis think? He'd know full well that she'd bought the outfit especially for him. Did she want him to know how she felt? How did she feel?* She spent the afternoon in such a dither, she was glad it was relatively customer-free.

By the time Ellen was dressed and had her hair in place – on Jenny's advice she'd twisted her plait into a coil on top of her head and felt as if she had a sack of corn sitting up there – she was beginning to wonder if it had all been a mistake, if she was too old for this sort of thing. Ellen reminded herself she was younger than Jenny, now happily settled with Mike. She heard the roar of the Harley. It stopped outside, and she moved to the door as if propelled by an invisible force.

As soon as Ellen saw Travis her worry disappeared, and she was back in the cocoon of warmth his presence induced. She looked down at her outfit and assessed the bike, and her ability to ride it, dressed as she was. *Could she? Probably. Did she want to? Probably not.*

"Wow! New outfit?"

God, was it so obvious?

"Yes," Ellen smiled at Travis' evident approval. She moved into his outstretched arms as if it was the most natural thing in the world, careless of any passers-by who might be watching. Her mouth opened beneath his, and his kiss transported her to another world, one in which nothing and no one existed except the two of them. When Travis finally released her, Ellen's breath was ragged.

"Let me see you properly," Travis led Ellen back into the shop. "Love the outfit. Good colour. But you've done something else too." He eyed her from head to foot. "Your hair…" He twirled his hand to indicate the corn sack on top of Ellen's head.

"Is it too much? It was Jenny's idea… I…"

"I like it best around your shoulders, but it looks okay. Sort of regal, like you."

"Oh." Ellen recalled those times when Travis had seen her hair loose – that very morning when he had buried his face in it. She could see the memory in his eyes too and had a strong feeling that if they didn't leave now they'd… They'd what? She didn't answer herself, instead asking, "What did you have planned?"

"We…ell," Travis seemed to hesitate. "I did plan on booking *Driftwood Shores* again, but Ron…"

"Ron?" Ellen was astounded. "Ron's going to *Driftwood Shores*? It's hardly his style." She had a sudden thought. "Who? He's not…?"

"Yeah," Travis seemed amused by her surprise. "He's asked Coralie to dinner, and that's where he's taking her."

Ellen had to sit down. Her brother taking a woman out to dinner. And not just any woman – Coralie! "Well!"

"So I guess we don't want to go there too and cramp his style?"

"No...oo," Once she'd recovered from the surprise, Ellen was disappointed. She'd been looking forward to this evening so much, and had pictured them back at *Driftwood Shores*. Back at the window table, but this time having a more romantic meal.

"So, where shall we eat?" Travis was jangling the keys in his pocket and shuffling his feet. He looked so much like a disappointed little boy that Ellen forgot her own upset, her only desire being to comfort him.

"Anywhere with you would be just grand," she spoke without thinking, then wondered if she had been too forward, relieved when Travis' face lit up.

"How about that *Bridgewater* place? It's just along the way?"

"Perfect, we can even walk there. It's a lovely evening."

As they walked along the road, Ellen couldn't help musing over her brother's transformation. Ron and Coralie – she'd never have predicted that. So much for her so-called second sight. It had really let her down there. But what could she have done even if she had been able to foretell their getting together? Nothing. She decided to forget them and concentrate on her own evening, on the man who was holding her hand and walking along beside her, the warmth from their touching shoulders causing ripples of excitement to surge though her.

They stood outside the restaurant's glass façade, the soft tones of the piano wafting out into the street. Like most of the buildings here in Old Town, it had an olde worlde feel to it. This particular building had been built in 1901 and was deemed to be the most historically significant building in the area, still in virtually its original form – a classic example of the false-fronted general stores built in the early pioneering days.

"There's so much history here," Ellen sighed, thinking of her own store, even though it was built much later, after the Second World War. These days, the formerly working class neighborhood of mills and warehouses had been transformed into a tourist paradise, although many of the original landmarks such as the ferry wharf were still in use.

"Shall we go in?" Travis had his foot on the first step and appeared perplexed by Ellen's hesitation.

"Of course." She emerged from her daydream and followed him

into the bustling restaurant. Without a booking, they had a short wait, allowing them time to peruse the menu. They sat shoulder-to-shoulder on a zebra-patterned sofa in the lounge with the early evening sun pouring in through the glass doorways, before being shown to a table right next to the piano. They settled into the high-backed rattan chairs and accepted the drinks they'd ordered earlier. Surrounded by the hum of conversation, they were also being serenaded by the mellow tones of tunes such as *New York, New York* and *If You Wish Upon a Star*. It was an evening made for romance.

*

After another night of glorious passion, Ellen was more confident of her feelings for Travis, and of his for her. This time, as they lay spent in the aftermath of their love-making, they talked. They talked about their childhoods, early hopes and dreams. As they lay entwined, Travis' strong arms wrapped around Ellen's shoulders, their faces almost touching, Ellen learned of Travis' past two years – the devastation which had led him into some very strange places. But it wasn't all one-sided. Ellen herself found the courage to reveal secrets of her own: her long-term relationship with a married man, finishing only when his wife and son had visited. *The Reading Nook*; her more recent liaison with Will and his departure for Canada.

By the time the sun started to peek through the curtains, they were both exhausted, but Ellen sensed a strong connection to Travis, one that she'd never experienced before. She stretched out, luxuriating in his nearness, unwilling to leave the cosy nest.

"Morning," the voice in her ear was accompanied by a beard grazing her cheek, a kiss on the cheek and a warm hand stroking her thigh.

Ellen turned into Travis' arms, revelling in the sensation of his skin on hers, its soft and silky texture. Reluctantly, she slid out of bed, heedless of the octopus-like arms which tried to hold her there.

"Where are you going?" Travis' voice was still heavy with sleep.

"Work morning for me, honey. Do you want some breakfast?" Ellen stepped into the shower without waiting for an answer. The vigorous flow of water soon dissolved the remnants of sleep, leaving her wide awake. A mug of strong black coffee and she'd be ready to face the day.

Ellen had already finished breakfast and was preparing to leave, when Travis finally made an appearance in the kitchen. His rumpled morning appearance brought a smile to her face, as she raised it for his kiss.

"You need a twenty second hug," Travis told her and proceeded to make good his words, leaving Ellen gasping for breath.

"Maybe ten, next time," she laughed. "Twenty is a long time. Look, I need to get going. Can you find your own way out and lock up behind you? There's breakfast…" she pointed to the table on which was a bowl of chopped fruit, cereal and a plate of toast, "and plenty of coffee in the pot."

"Tonight?"

Ellen paused, "I don't think…" She was torn. Part of her wanted to agree – to spend as much time as she could with this lovely man who was turning out to be such an amazing, generous, beautiful, funny, engaging and special person. But another part – the sane, sensible part – knew that her body needed rest. She was in dire need of a good night's sleep and was only going to get that if she slept alone.

"No," she repeated. "Not tonight. I think we both need a rest."

"We can rest together." Travis moved to take Ellen in his arms again, but she adroitly slid away.

"No, really," she chuckled. "Anyway," she added, on a more serious note, "it's time I called in on Mom and Dad. Been a few days since I saw them." She tried to look apologetic, but she knew her face held more of a yearning look than anything else.

"You win," Travis held up his arms in mock surrender. "But I'm not done with you. You know that, don't you?"

"Yes, likewise," Ellen's voice was soft as she let herself out the door.

*

Travis sat there, arms folded behind his head. His gaze took in the well-worn wooden furniture, the Native American wall hangings and the old pendulum clock on the far wall. He remembered his surprise at the sight of the blue dreamcatcher which hung directly over her bed.

There was so much about this woman he still had to learn.

His mind roved over the previous evening and night. So much for his earlier misgivings. This was real. Ellen wasn't one of the women he could treat to his old slam-bam-thank-you-ma'am routine. He leant forward and rubbed his chin. He was falling for her. He recognised the tenderness in the way he'd touched her, the way his gut had reacted to her quickly suppressed whimpers of delight when they made love. And that's exactly what it had been. They'd made love. It was more than just sex, much more. Hell, what was he going to do? Could he trust himself to form another relationship? He hadn't done too well with his first one, or since. Maybe Ellen deserved better.

*

As soon as Ellen entered her office, her eyes fell on the pile of petitions. She needed to put them into some sort of order then deliver them to City Hall. Hoping the morning wouldn't be too busy with customers, Ellen set to this task, finally finishing around lunchtime. Deciding not to waste any more time, she closed for lunch and, grabbing a sandwich on the way, drove around to City Hall to deliver her now large package of papers.

It was with a sense of relief that Ellen returned to the store for the afternoon. The petitions would do their work. Now it was time to look at other avenues through which their opinions could be heard. Recalling her meeting with the council member at the library, she decided to talk with some friends in the Native American community about that possibility. But she put it aside to take care of another day. She needed to visit her parents, check on Dad and find out how Mom was coping. Then an early night was called for. As the afternoon wore on, Ellen began to wilt, the lack of sleep for the past two nights was catching up with her. *Not as young as I used to be. Was a time when I could stay up all night and be full of beans the following day,* she thought. She considered putting her head down on the desk for a moment, but was afraid of falling asleep.

If she and Travis were to continue to see each other, Ellen would need to work something out whereby she could have a decent sleep.

She simply couldn't be falling asleep here in the shop on a regular basis. Her lips curled up into an involuntary smile as she contemplated the prospect. Was she really envisaging a future which included Travis – all on the basis of two nights together? Ellen felt the smile widen to become a beam. She was, she really was. She, Ellen, the woman who'd defined herself as 'always the bridesmaid, never the bride' actually believed she'd found her soul mate. And it felt so good.

Twenty

"You've been poring over these old documents for ages. Haven't you come up with anything yet?" Jenny leaned over Mike's shoulder, his beard tickling her cheek. "Mmm," she murmured, "feels nice."

Mike reached back to stroke her arm before replying, "It's not so easy. I've been trying to get back to the original plans of the land – the first owners and uses of the place." He scratched his head, pulling on his beard. "There are so many gaps. Back then, people weren't so diligent about keeping records. I need to go down to the library again – check out the old papers. It's painstaking work."

"Don't I know it!" Mention of old papers reminded Jenny of her quest the previous year, when she'd been seeking the truth about her birth. It was there, in the Florence library, she'd found references to the mother and father she'd never known, leading her to the truth about them. And to the discovery of her cousin Ellen, and her own Native American heritage.

"I should go visit the graves again," she said, almost to herself.

Mike rose and hugged her. "It still bothers you, doesn't it?"

Jenny's eyes misted remembering the tale of the two young star-crossed lovers who'd been her parents, killed in a car accident just as she was about to be born. "I wish… I wish I'd been able to do more."

"You did what you could," Mike reminded her. "Their motto on the gravestones was your contribution – a fitting one too."

"Together forever," Jenny repeated their mantra. "But they aren't – they're in separate graves, in separate cemeteries." She wiped away an incipient tear.

"We'll go this afternoon. Then I'll go to the library, and you can visit with Ellen or go see Uncle Dick," he suggested.

"I don't think Uncle Dick would want to see me, sick though he is. He still hasn't fully accepted that I'm Jed's daughter." Jenny brightened. "But Ellen, yes. I can call in there. She's seeing Travis and has been very quiet on the subject since I helped her choose a new outfit. It's time we had a chat."

"That's settled, then." Mike returned to his computer, and Jenny soon found herself ignored again as he became lost in his research.

"I'm popping down to see Maddy," Jenny called, going out the door. "And I'm taking Ben with me," she added, as the black Labrador followed her out.

Jenny and the dog made their way down the path to Jenny's godmother's house, the only other dwelling on that track. The door opened just as they arrived, and Maddy came out to greet them.

"Well, you two are a sight for sore eyes," she said, "Come on in. You'll be ready for coffee, I'm sure."

Jenny followed her godmother into the house, breathing in the atmosphere of the familiar place, while Ben padded about sniffing the furniture for a bit, before settling down at Jenny's feet, his head on his paws. As she accepted a coffee from the pot, which seemed to be always ready on the stove, and bit into one of Maddy's favorite macadamia cookies, Jenny sighed.

"What's up?" Maddy took a seat opposite and picked up her mug.

"Feeling a bit down," Jenny replied. "All this searching for the history of Ellen's shop. It's…"

"Bringing it all back," Maddy finished for her.

"How did you know?" Jenny's eyes widened as she wrapped her hands around her mug, the warm liquid comforting her.

"I know my Jenny Wren," Maddy replied. "I guess you'll be going to visit?"

"You're a mind reader – just like Ellen."

"And how *is* Ellen?" Maddy settled back for a long chat. "What about that friend of her brother you were trying to persuade her about?"

"I was doing nothing of the sort," Jenny objected. "If I recall correctly, you were the one in matchmaking mode."

"And didn't she rise to the bait?" the older woman chuckled. "Did anything come of it?"

"Might have," Jenny winked. "They've been out to dinner. Oh," she added, seeing Maddy about to speak, "she assured me it was an apology dinner."

"Apology dinner – what's that when it's at home?"

"Seems he wanted to apologize for deceiving her. Turns out he's actually a famous author – Peter Travers. Ellen has had a display of his books up for ages, and he pretended to know nothing about them."

"Peter Travers," Maddy gazed up at the ceiling as if thinking hard. "Think I've heard of him. Doesn't he write those books based on Native American folklore? Sorry, I'm interrupting you."

"That's okay. Yes, that's him. Anyway they had this apology dinner. Took her to *Driftwood Shores*."

"Very nice place for an apology!" Maddy smiled.

"And here's the thing. He asked her out again. Last night. And this time she didn't even try to pretend it wasn't a date. In fact, she agreed I could go with her to choose an outfit."

"Oh, I'm so glad," Maddy's face was wreathed in smiles. "She deserves someone nice. Not to be left on the shelf like me. That's what they called it in my day, you know. As if women were merchandise, waiting for a man to come along and pluck them off the shelf."

Jenny burst out laughing at the thought of anyone plucking Maddy off a shelf at any time.

"But you've been happy, haven't you?"

"I most certainly have. But that's not to say if the right man had come along…" She threw a glance at the picture of the soldier on the wall. "When my Rick was killed I doubted I'd find another to match him – and I didn't. But that doesn't mean I sat around twiddling my thumbs. No, there were a few…" Maddy gazed into space again, before continuing. "Sorry, I'm getting away from Ellen again. So, a new outfit, eh? That says something."

"It surprised me too – that she agreed, I mean."

"And?"

"We haven't spoken since. Mike's suggested we go down to Florence today. We can visit the graves together, take some flowers, then I can visit with Ellen while he goes to the library."

"That sounds like a good plan, dear. Have you been to the cemeteries since you and Mike got back?"

Jenny shook her head, lowered her eyes, and blinked. "No. Haven't had the courage. Not sure why." She raised her eyes, and shook her head to dismiss her sadness.

Maddy reached over and Jenny felt the wrinkled hand pat hers. The warmth of the gesture made her want to cry. She sniffed. "I'm fine." She sniffed again. "Don't know why it's so hard. I didn't even know them."

"That's probably why. If you'd grown up with them, known them all your life, you'd have had time to love them and grieve properly. But finding out like you did, last year… nearly sixty years later." She shook her head. "And last year you had a lot of other things happening too. Now you're back – you and Mike – and you're feeling it. It's only natural."

Jenny retrieved her hand and wiped her eyes. "I suppose so. Oh, Maddy, I'm sorry. I didn't come down here to cry on your shoulder."

"My shoulder's plenty big enough for that." She paused. "Now finish that coffee before it gets cold."

Jenny gulped down the remainder of her coffee and finished off the cookie. "I have to go now," she said. "We'll need to leave soon. Oh, Maddy," she hugged her godmother. "You always make me feel restored. It's as if this house…," she waved her arms around. "I don't know… It's as if it holds some magic potion. I always leave feeling better than when I arrived."

"Does me good to hear that. It certainly did the trick for you last year, anyway. Though maybe a certain gentleman helped in that too, and possibly a magical old sand dollar." The pair were silent remembering Jenny's visit, and the challenges she'd faced and the old sand dollar that had brought them back together.

"Well it all turned out for the best," Jenny said at last, giving Maddy a final hug. "I'm really off now. Come, Ben." The dog rose, stretched, and followed her out.

Walking up the track again, Jenny was filled with gratitude for her life. Just over a year ago, she'd arrived here facing an unexpected redundancy only to discover she'd been adopted at birth. Now, here she was – with her own bookshop back in Australia, with a man she had never dreamed of meeting, and a life which spanned two continents.

"What are you smiling about?" Mike greeted her as she opened the door. He planted a kiss on the top of Jenny's head.

"Maddy," Jenny replied. The one word said it all.

"Worked her magic, did she?"

"You know, I really feel blessed. Between Maddy and Ellen, it's as if I'm cocooned in a magic circle." She stretched her arms above her head. "What did I do to deserve all this?"

*

Jenny bent down to trace the words on the gravestone.

Thea Miller
1930-1950
Beloved daughter and sister
Together Forever

"And mother," she said quietly. Rising, and brushing the grass from her knees, she walked across the path to join Mike who'd allowed her this moment to herself. "Ready now," she said brightly. "Thanks," she stretched up to kiss him on the cheek and was rewarded with a warm hug. "That's both done now."

"Better?"

"Much," Jenny tucked her hand into Mike's as they returned to the car together. "Okay if I leave you at the library and take the car?"

"Surely. Take as much time with Ellen as you need."

Jenny smiled fondly knowing that, as soon as she left Mike, he'd become lost in his old documents and wouldn't notice time passing. "I'll text you when I'm on my way," she said.

After dropping Mike off, Jenny made her way down to Old Town. As she reached Ellen's shop, she thought how dreadful it would be if all of this disappeared under the developer's hammer. She was muttering to herself as she pushed open the door, pausing only to admire the new window display.

"Summertime, eh," she said to Ellen, pointing to the array of books featuring sun and sand, with a layer of sand on the bottom of the window, and a couple of sand dollars taking pride of place.

"Made a mess setting it all up, but I think it's working." Ellen stood examining it for a moment. "Come on in."

Jenny threw a lingering glance at the sand dollars before following her friend into the shop and through to her little office.

"Take a seat," Ellen lifted a pile of books from a chair and took the other herself. "It does my heart good to see you. You resolved something today?"

"You *are* a witch!" Jenny smiled.

"Sometimes," Ellen grinned. "You're feeling better too. I can tell that just by looking at you. Your body language says it all."

"Right. Well, I didn't come here to talk about me." Jenny gave her cousin a meaningful look. "How did it go?" She was delighted to see Ellen blush, the coloring rising beautifully up her neck and face.

"What?" Ellen started to tidy the files on her desk, avoiding Jenny's eyes.

"Don't be difficult. Your date. With Travis." She sat back and waited.

Finally Ellen looked up. "It went well."

Jenny fidgeted with impatience. "Well? What sort of a word is that? More information," she demanded.

"Not much to tell. We went to the *Bridgewater* to avoid Ron."

"What's Ron got to do with it?"

"Seems he took Coralie to *Driftwood Shores*."

"Coralie? The…"

"The very one – my neighbor Coralie," Ellen chuckled.

"You've changed the subject. We were talking about you – you and Travis."

"Were we?" Ellen started to fiddle with a couple of paperclips, while Jenny stifled the impulse to take them from her. Eventually Ellen met her cousin's eyes. "It's all so difficult," she admitted. "I mean, I like him – a lot – but… I don't know…"

"It's not like you to be so indecisive."

"I'm not usually like this. If I could just…"

"You could see my future happiness, but you can't see your own – is that it?"

Ellen seemed relieved. "In a nutshell."

"If you enjoyed the evening, maybe he did too." Jenny was trying to find out more about the date, but was wary of being too intrusive. While she wanted to ask if they'd slept together, she respected the other's privacy and didn't want to step too far. "Did…" she began, unsure how to continue.

"He stayed over – if that's what you're trying to ask," Ellen stated bluntly. "That's part of my problem." She began to twist her hands, looking agitated. "I… I don't know. He's… these last few years have been tough for him." She appeared to be having difficulty in getting the words out – not her usual calm, confident self. "That's why… I wonder if it was too soon," she finished.

Jenny bit her lip. How could she provide assistance on this? But Ellen had been so helpful and supportive of her last year, she felt it incumbent on her to offer some sort of advice. She thought carefully before replying.

"Maybe, he's feeling just as tentative as you are," she said at last. "When you're older – like us." She shot a glance across the room, remembering Ellen was quite a few years her junior. "These things sometimes move more quickly. Sometimes more quickly than we're ready for. When that happens, it may be that we need to take a step back, regroup as it were."

"You make it sound like a military campaign," Ellen laughed.

Glad to hear her cousin sounding more cheerful, Jenny ploughed on. "With Mike and me, for example," she hesitated, wondering if she really wanted to share this confidence. "We… when we went to Crater Lake, we…" She took a deep breath. "We sort of fell into bed together, then," she hurried on, "I got cold feet."

"So?" Ellen began to look interested.

"So we decided to take it more slowly. I don't think either of us was ready," she said reflectively. "Worked for us." Jenny smiled.

"Don't think we have the same problem." Ellen frowned, then her mouth twisted into a smile as if reminiscing. "We were both ready. That's probably the problem." She pulled on the end of her plait and straightened her back, her head rising regally. "But it's our problem, and we'll work it out. Now where *is* the lovely Mike?"

A little flustered by the quick change in subject, Jenny took a few seconds before replying, "He's in the library – more research for you.

He's convinced he can find some evidence to top the development, that it's only a matter of time, meanwhile…"

"He's so good. I delivered all the petitions, and I'm trying to arrange a meeting with some of the councillors. Don't know what more we can do, other than stage a protest outside City Hall," she joked.

"Or outside the developer's office. Where is that anyway?"

Jenny saw Ellen's face cloud over.

"I'm not sure. According to Travis they've been drummed out of California – that's where he'd heard of them."

"That sounds serious."

"Nefarious dealings," Ellen's voice quavered a little.

"But… not here?"

"Well, I did have a phone call."

Jenny's eyes widened with alarm.

"Oh, nothing to worry about. I admit it shook me at the time, but we continued with our plans, and there's been nothing since. They may have learnt their lesson down south and be willing to play fair here."

"I wouldn't be too sure." Jenny shuddered. "Don't take any risks," she advised. "What does Travis have to say about it?"

"Same as you. But we need to go on – it's the only thing to do, and I do have a good feeling about it… in the end," she said, her voice dropping on the last words.

Jenny picked up on them immediately. "What do you mean by 'in the end'? Is there going to be trouble before then?"

"Maybe," Ellen's tone was non-committal, but Jenny identified a touch of bravado in her voice.

"You see something, don't you?" she accused.

"Listen to you. Do you think I can predict every little thing that's going to a happen in life? How boring that would be! There'd be nothing to look forward to."

"Or to be afraid of. Well, you were spot on with me and Mike."

"That was pretty general. I couldn't predict the specifics, but I got a notion there was a link between the two of you."

"And can you identify that link between you and Travis?" Jenny couldn't resist returning to the topic at the forefront of her mind.

"There's something," Ellen hesitated, as if trying to decide how much to say. She dropped her eyes and appeared to make a study of the desk, then raised them to look at the dreamcatcher on the wall. "Those dreams…"

"Oh, my God, I'd forgotten all about them. Are you still having them?" Jenny's jaw dropped. How could she have been so callous as to have forgotten Ellen's nightmares?

"That's the weird thing. My dreams – they were Travis' dreams too. They'd already happened. It was *his* accident I saw. And no, I don't have them anymore. Not since we discovered…" Her voice faded away. "I'm the one who should be trying to tell you what it all means," she said, with an attempt at a smile.

"Oh, Ellen, you need a hug," Jenny said, and put her words into action.

"Thanks," Ellen returned the hug. "Now enough about me. What have you been up to at Seal Rock and what did you have to do today?"

Jenny recounted her recent activities culminating with the visit to her mother's grave. "And that's where I was just before I came here," she finished.

"Thought so." Ellen nodded.

"And now," Jenny checked her watch, "I'd better pick up that man of mine and see what he's managed to uncover. I'll just text him to let him know I'm on my way."

As Jenny bade farewell and drove off, she wished she could wave a magic wand for her cousin to make sure everything worked out well. She sighed, in the belief that Ellen still had a few bridges to cross before she found her own happy ending.

Twenty-one

Ellen watched Jenny leave with mixed feelings. While it had been good to share her misgivings, she wondered if she'd said too much. A solitary person, in the short time she'd known Jenny, Ellen had come to love her Australian cousin and to rely on her as a friend. Who else could she talk to? Who would understand how she felt? Out of the blue, a warm, comforting presence rose up in her mind's eye – another wise woman – Maddy, Jenny's godmother. Of course. Why hadn't she considered her before? Maddy had lived long enough to have seen all sorts of people and events, things those of younger years could only imagine. She'd make time to visit her up at Seal Rock.

Just as Ellen had made the decision, a customer entered. He was dressed more smartly than her usual clients, in a business suit with crisp white shirt and a rather violent red tie. He appeared very self-confident as he perused the shelves, unlike the usual browser. He picked up one book after another and replaced them with such lack of interest, Ellen chose not to disturb him. She was sure he'd come her way when he was ready, either to make a purchase or ask a question.

Finally he approached her. "Ms Williams?"

"That's me," Ellen replied, surprised he knew her name and addressed her so formally.

The man leant back on his heels and picked up a pottery owl which was sitting on the counter, turning it round and round in his hands. "Lovely shop you have here. I have to congratulate you. You've put a lot of work into it." His eyes roamed around the shop. "But you didn't listen," he said, his eyes narrowing. He dropped the owl, letting it smash on the floor.

Ellen stood stock still, her gaze riveted on the smashed knick-knack. Her breath quickened in consternation. Her heart began to pound. She looked up to meet his eyes. They were cold.

"Lots of books. What good are they? Can you eat them? Can you build with them? You were told, but you went ahead with your silly petition." He picked up a book from the display table and deliberately dropped it on the floor too, then another, then another.

Ellen watched the books hit the floor, their spines cracking and their pages tearing and was galvanized into action. Anger replaced fear as she saw her precious books being damaged. She rushed at the man like a whirlwind and began to pound him with her fists, making no impact on his solid body. He brushed her off as if she were flecks of dust, turned and left.

Ellen crumpled. She knelt down to pick up the damaged articles. She hugged them to her, sobbing, the teardrops cascading down her cheeks. She licked the salt from her lips and wiped away the tears, recouping her anger. How dare he! How dare he come into her shop and cause such wanton destruction! She sat back on her heels and recaptured the event. It was his calm demeanor that had been so menacing. He'd been so polite, charming even, but his actions had belied his words.

Sweeping up the shards of pottery, Ellen carried them and the damaged books back to the office. Suddenly, shock hit and she sat down, shaking. She dropped her head into her hands as she realized how vulnerable she was, a woman alone in her shop. She'd never felt this way before, and was quick to dismiss the tinge of anxiety. That's what he wants, she told herself. His type play on the fears of vulnerable women. Ellen picked up the phone to call the police, then laid it down again. She'd cleared up the mess, got rid of the evidence. It would only be her word, and she didn't know who the man was anyway. She didn't want to be considered a silly woman. That wasn't her style at all. Ellen stood and drew herself up to her full height. Vulnerable she was not. Afraid she was not. She'd show them. How, she wasn't sure yet, but show them she would. She wouldn't let this attempt at intimidation scare her.

Before she left work, Ellen made a call to Maddy arranging to see her next day. Having done that, she felt more settled, convinced that a chat with the older woman would put an end to her worries – to those concerning Travis at least. She wasn't sure how Maddy could help with this other stuff.

*

"Come on in. Coffee pot's on the stove." Maddy's warm greeting was balm to Ellen's troubled soul. She stepped into the house, feeling it close comfortingly around her. *This is what soothed Jenny all last year*, she thought. *I was right to come here.* She sank down into a deep armchair, feeling guilty at allowing Maddy to wait on her.

"Looks like you're in need of this," Maddy gave Ellen a mug of steaming coffee and offered her a plate of chocolate chip cookies. "I find there's nothing quite like chocolate to take away all life's woes." She sat down opposite. "Now what's troubling you?"

"How did you know?"

"I have my ways," Maddy's eyes twinkled. "But a little bird told me that you and this… Travis, isn't it?"

Ellen nodded, unable to do anything else. She was the one who was supposed to have second sight.

"So I guess that's why you're here. You want some advice from someone who's been there – many times," she chortled. "Tell me about him."

Ellen ran her fingers around the warm mug and gazed into the black coffee, before raising her eyes to meet Maddy's. "He's kind, gentle, vulnerable, and there's this connection I don't understand – it's weird, bizarre even."

"Well you should be used to that – with your gift."

"Gift, huh! But it's not my usual thing. I seem to be linked to his past in some curious way – a way I can't understand."

"Do you need to understand it?" Maddy's voice was gentle.

"Maybe not." As she spoke, a weight fell from Ellen's shoulders. She realized she'd been puzzling over the weirdness of their common dreams, trying to make sense of it for days. Not consciously, but it had been there, simmering away in her subconscious. Now, talking with Maddy, she began to understand it didn't matter. It had happened. It was over. And she had to live with that.

"So he's a kind, gentle guy. What's so wrong about that?"

"Nothing. But… he's been through a lot. His wife and son were killed in an accident two years ago." Ellen's voice broke as she recounted the incident.

"Oh, the poor man. And you? How do you feel about him?"

"I don't know…" Ellen put her mug down and pulled on her hair, tidying a few stray hairs behind her ears. "It's different to the other men I've been involved with. It's all happened so quickly."

"Tell me about the others."

Ellen gazed at Maddy in surprise. What did the others matter? But she proceeded to comply with the older woman's request. "My most serious relationship was with a married man – Jackson. I'm not proud of it, and it lasted for years. He kept promising we'd be together, and I kept hoping and believing him. The way he'd painted his wife to me, I didn't feel any guilt, only a sort of sadness that she couldn't make him happy."

"And what happened?"

"It wasn't till one day – oh, I still cringe when I think of it – one of my regular customers was in the store with her boy. I didn't have the book he wanted, so needed to take their details so that I could order it in. She gave me her name and address, and suddenly I knew. I couldn't take my eyes off the boy. This was Jackson's son, a boy who needed to have his father there when he was growing up. After that, I couldn't go on. It broke my heart."

Ellen saw Maddy nod as if she understood. "After that I eschewed men for a while, then I met Will. He had a son too, one he was fond of. He was divorced, so no guilt feelings. We had some fun times. It wasn't earth shattering, but…"

"It didn't last either?" Maddy prompted.

"He moved to Canada. His ex and son were there, and the distance got to him. He asked me to go too, but…"

"There wasn't a strong enough connection?"

"I guess not. I had my shop. There were my parents… and Ron, I suppose."

"None of which would have stopped you if he'd been the big love of your life."

"No." Ellen moved restlessly.

"So now we come to Travis. How does he compare? How do you feel about him?"

Ellen shifted in her seat. She'd come here for advice, so why did she find Maddy's questions so intrusive? Why did she feel so uneasy?

"You're uncomfortable?"

Maddy's questions pulled Ellen out of her reverie. "I… I… Travis… it's something else." Ellen knew she wasn't making much sense. "I like him… a lot. But I'm not sure of him." The words began to pour forth in a rush. "At first I took him to be one of Ron's hangers-on – a loser, so I guess I tried to ignore him. Then he saved Dad, and I found out a bit more about his past, but he was still pretty much an unknown quantity. Then this business about him being the author Peter Travers. That really annoyed me at first, but I got over that. Now it's… I don't know if can trust him. When he's not annoying the hell out of me, we get on pretty well."

"That's men for you."

"Thing is," Ellen confided. "He's suggested we go on a trip. How could I possibly? I have a shop to run."

"Do you want to go?"

"That's not the point. I can't go. There's the shop… Mom and Dad… No it's impossible."

"What does your heart tell you? That's the only thing that matters."

Ellen closed her eyes and looked deep inside herself. She saw Travis, his high cheekbones, his blue eyes, his teasing grin. She experienced a warm sensation. She opened her eyes. "My heart says to trust him, to say yes."

"There, that wasn't so hard, was it?"

"But… what if… by his own admission, he's behaved pretty wildly over the past two years. What if I'm just another in the string of women he's…"

Maddy gave Ellen a stern look. "Do you really think that? I've never met the guy – though I hope one day I might – but from what I've heard, he's not the sort to play fast and loose with the sister of a friend. And didn't you say you'd found him to be honest and gentle?"

"Eventually, yes," Ellen smiled at the memory of their last time together, then her smile faded. "But that doesn't take care of the shop."

"Listen to yourself. You're putting up all the obstacles you can think of to stop you moving this relationship forward. There's someone who can look after the shop for you, not a million miles from here. Your cousin. Jenny would lend a hand in an instant."

Ellen looked up at the ceiling, where dried flowers hung from several high beams. Jenny, of course. Why hadn't she thought of her? A small voice at the back of her mind told her she hadn't considered Jenny, because she… Did she really want an excuse?

"And Mom and Dad?" she asked, still vacillating.

"You have a brother," Maddy sounded a tad tetchy. "Ellen, my dear, you have to let go sometime – put yourself first. One of your great strengths is your concern for others, but it can also become your downfall, if you let it rule your life."

Ellen's jaw dropped. In her down-to-earth way, Maddy had hit the nail on the head.

"But…" she tried to object.

"Follow your heart," the older woman repeated. "There may be a future for Travis and you, there may not. Time will tell. But it would be foolish to turn down this opportunity to find out."

Ellen digested this last piece of advice. She wanted to refute what Maddy was saying, but her instinct told her it was all true. And why had she sought the older woman's counsel if she hadn't intended to follow it?

"Mmm, you could be right," she said at last.

"I haven't lived this long without learning a thing or two about the human psyche. We all think we know ourselves pretty well, but it's often the case we only see what we want to see." Maddy appeared to take a deep breath before continuing. "You, for instance. You've become Ellen, the dedicated shopkeeper, the devoted daughter, the caring sister, the community leader. Where, in all this, is Ellen, the woman? You've subsumed your own life to be all things to all people. Maybe it's time to take stock. Do something for yourself."

Ellen could barely believe what she was hearing. It was as if her own words were coming back to haunt her. Wasn't this exactly the sort of advice she'd often given others. Now it was being dished out to her, and she wasn't sure how she liked it. In her heart of hearts, she knew the truth of Maddy's words… but to put them into practice? Could she really do it?

"I…" she began.

"Why don't you call her right now? Or, better still, go right on up the track. I know Jenny and Mike are home. Saw the pickup drive up before you arrived."

"Umm," Ellen hesitated. It wasn't like her to be so indecisive. Maddy had put her on the spot, the clever lady that she was, given her an option which brooked no excuses.

"I'll go now," she decided, surprised to see Maddy beam and to find she'd said the words aloud. "I'd better drive. It's light now, but it'll probably be dark by the time I leave, and I don't relish walking down this track in the dark."

*

Driving up the track to Mike and Jenny's home, Ellen reflected how she'd been backed into a corner. She'd come here to ask for advice, and now she had it, she felt duty bound to accept it, even if it meant going against her own instincts – or did it? Had Maddy only told her what she really wanted to hear? What she'd known all along? Ellen's head hurt trying to work out what had come from Maddy, and what had been in her own mind. She was glad when she saw the cabin appear ahead.

"You made it!" The door opened to reveal Jenny's cheerful face. "Maddy said you were on your way. I think she was worried you'd change your mind and go back the other way. What's up?"

"Didn't she say?" Ellen was slightly perturbed Maddy had felt it necessary to herald her imminent arrival.

"No, only that you'd had a good chat and you had a favor to ask me. Come on in. Won't you join me in a glass of wine?"

"A small one then."

"Hi, Ellen," Mike called, before returning to his computer.

"Wonderful company, isn't he?" Jenny said fondly, clearly quite happy to have him spend time lost in his work.

"Now, what's this all about?" The two were seated on a sofa, their wine sitting on the coffee table, along with a hastily prepared plate of biscuits and cheese. "What's the favor you need?"

Ellen twisted her fingers, wondering if she was ready to confide in Jenny, then remembering Maddy's wise counsel, she began. "How would you like to… I mean, would you be willing to look after *The Reading Nook* for a few days?" Hearing Jenny's gasp of surprise, she quickly made an attempt to back off. "Okay, I knew it was a crazy idea. Of course you wouldn't…"

"No, I was just taken aback. Would you really entrust your baby to me?"

"You mean you would?" Ellen sighed with relief. "It was Maddy's idea. She thought you would, but I…"

"Of course I will. But why? I mean… where will you be?"

Ellen swallowed, her tongue sticking to the roof of her mouth. "I… Travis… that is… he's asked me to go off with him on a trip. Only for a few days," she hurried to add, seeing Jenny's grin.

Jenny clasped her cousin to her. "I'm so glad. So you… the two of you… it's…"

"It's nothing yet, not really. But Travis seems to think it would be a good idea to get away from here for a bit – together. Too many busybodies around Florence, not to mention Seal Rock and Yachats," she added with a twinkle in her eye.

"I have to agree with him. It wasn't till Mike and I got away from here that…" Jenny threw a tender glance at her partner, now engrossed in his task and unaware of the conversation between the two women. "It was at Crater Lake," she reminisced. "But you don't want to hear about that again. Though I do recommend it as a romantic spot. Where are you going on this trip of yours?"

"I'm not sure. I haven't even agreed to go yet. There seemed to be all sorts of reasons not to go, but your godmother managed to demolish them one by one."

"She's good at that. So, you'll tell Travis now?"

"Guess so."

"When?"

"Boy, you sure don't let go."

"Do it now. I'll get another glass of wine."

"Not for me. I have to drive down the highway. So, I'll call later, when I'm home."

"Well, be sure you do. No excuses."

Twenty-two

Ellen couldn't wait till she reached home. She stopped the car at the end of the track and took out her cell phone. For a few minutes she sat, looking at it, a fluttering in the pit of her stomach. Did she really want to do this? Brushing away her doubts, she scrolled down to Travis' number and pressed.

"Yo, Ellen," Travis' deep voice echoed in her ear. Ellen's nervousness made the phone slippery in her fingers. She almost dropped it.

"I... I'd like to accept your invitation... for the trip." There was silence. Shit, had he forgotten? Had he changed his mind? She almost ended the call in embarrassment. Then she heard him whooping.

"Really? That's grand. You've sorted everything out? You can get away?"

"Jenny's going to look after the shop for me. As for the parents, Ron will have to..."

"I'll brief him on that."

Ellen smiled into the phone. Trust Travis to take it on himself to sort out her recalcitrant brother. "You do that," she laughed, all her fears dismissed and a tremor of excitement pulsating at the edge of her being.

"How about this weekend?" Travis continued.

"So soon?" Ellen felt weak at the thought of all she would have to do before she was ready to leave.

"Where are you now?" Travis asked.

"At the end of the track – up here at Seal Rock. I just spoke with

Jenny and wanted to…" Ellen's voice died away as it occurred to her that she'd pass Ron's house – and Travis – on her way home.

It appeared he had the same thought. "Why not drop by?"

"I don't think…"

"Ron's not home. Down in Florence again, I suspect. Do come."

Ellen dithered. It was getting late, and she had an hour's drive ahead of her. If she detoured in Yachats, spent time with Travis, when would she reach home? On the other hand, it was tempting to see him tonight, unexpected. He was right there on the other end of the phone, waiting for her reply. And Ron was out. Although she hated this secrecy, Ellen was still not ready for her family to know she was seeing Travis. She didn't want to raise their hopes only to have them squashed again. She made an instant decision.

"Right. I'll see you in …"

Darkness began to fall as Ellen headed southwards on the highway. Now that she had made her decision, she was eager to see Travis again. Her body remembered the sensation of his skin against hers, and she trembled in anticipation of a repeat of their previous encounter. It's Ron's house, she reminded herself. He could arrive home at any time, so there'll be no passion tonight. But even as her inner voice prompted her, she imagined the feel of his lips on hers, the softness of his beard against her neck.

When she finally parked outside the beachside home, Ellen was in a state of nerves. She sat still, taking a few deep breaths. Cool, calm and collected, she told herself. That's how she'd be. She'd have a coffee and chat, and leave. Her best intentions fled, however, as soon as Travis opened the door and wrapped her in his arms. She became a quivering jelly. The sheer size and strength of the man made her feel as light as a feather – she, who'd been a big girl all her life, was nothing in his arms.

"Mmm," Travis nuzzled her neck, sending shivers down her spine. Ellen gave herself up to the sensation, then struggled free.

"Wow, that's a welcome!" she managed to say, catching her breath. The pair stood beaming at each other.

"I guess you'd like coffee?" Travis dragged his hands through his hair, then stuck them in his pockets, leaning back on his heels and making no attempt to move.

"That would be nice." Ellen slid past him into the room.

"Right." Galvanized into action, Travis headed for the kitchen. "Black do? Don't think we've any milk. Might be some cookies somewhere."

"Black's fine." Ellen could hear him rustling about in the cupboards, but didn't make any attempt to assist. Two men living up here alone – she could just imagine what the kitchen looked like. She knew her brother's habits and made the assumption Travis was of the same ilk where housekeeping was concerned.

She was gazing out the window at the stars, when Travis returned.

"Here you are," he handed her a giant-sized mug of coffee and slung an arm around her shoulders. "They're bright tonight. Shine on us both." He turned Ellen to face him, planting a kiss on her forehead. "I often look at them and think of you."

Ellen reached up with her free hand to stroke Travis' eyebrows, moustache, finally threading her fingers through his beard and rubbing her nose in it, revelling in his manly smell. She allowed herself to enjoy the sensation for a few seconds, then she pushed on his chest. "Let's drink our coffee." She led him to the sofa and plopped herself down.

"So, our trip," Travis moved closer till their thighs touched, providing Ellen with a titillating warmth.

"Jenny suggested Crater Lake," she said, hoping a return to normal conversation would still the pounding of her heart.

"Lovely spot," Travis' voice faltered. "Maybe a bit too close to…" he hesitated. "I was thinking of riding north. How does Canada sound? Vancouver Island? Victoria?"

"Sounds lovely," Ellen curled her legs up under her, grasping her ankle with one hand. 'I've never been there, but I've heard good things about it. Isn't that where the Butchart Gardens are?"

"Yeah, built in an old quarry. We can go there too."

Ellen only partly heard Travis' words, one of the words from his earlier conversation sticking in her mind. "Did you say ride? You mean for us to… on that… that…"

"The Harley, yes. There's nothing like a long bike ride. If you loved the short ones we've had down here, you'll thrill to the wind in your hair on the open road – the sense of freedom it gives you," Travis enthused.

Ellen's heart tightened. Yes, she'd loved the rides they'd taken together – the wind in her hair, Travis' body close to hers. But to ride all the way to Canada – that was something else. Something she wasn't sure she wanted to do. She pressed her lips together, wondering what to say. It was difficult to refuse Travis when he was so fervent, and she knew he'd only recently been able to ride in a car again. Maybe the distance was too great for him to be cooped up in a car? It was a quandary, but one which she didn't have to deal with right now. No need to spoil the mood.

"Mmm, maybe," she muttered, planning to return to the topic later. "Tell me about Vancouver Island."

Travis spoke, while Ellen listened, her eyes rarely leaving his animated face as he described the beauties of the island and its main town. This was a Travis she hadn't known existed. She'd seen glimpses of it during their special times together, but never this wholehearted eagerness. He was like a young boy, and Ellen had a hint of what he'd been like before the accident, before he became so tortured and broken. She didn't want to spoil the mood, but a glance at her watch told her it was time to go.

Ellen put down her coffee mug and stretched her arms above her head, uncurling her legs as she did so. "Ow," she said, "I've been sitting like this for too long. Your descriptions were so fantastic – it was as if I was there. I can't wait to see it in the flesh, as it were."

"Do you have to go?" Travis rose with her, and before she knew it, she was clasped in his arms, her knees weak and her control fast going the same way.

"Ron," she uttered her brother's name in an attempt to evade what seemed to be the inevitable.

"Probably won't be back," Travis said, when they heard a sound at the door. They sprang apart just in time, and were standing side by side, when Ron entered, whistling.

"Ellen," his voice held surprise. "What are you doing here?" He looked from one to the other summing up what they might have been up to.

Ellen thought quickly. "I was up at Seal Rock visiting Jenny and Mike – Maddy too – and thought I'd drop in on you, see how you're doing. Travis made me coffee." She picked up the mug and held it towards her brother. Even to Ellen, the words sounded pretty lame, but Ron didn't seem to notice.

"I was down in Florence," he said, and Ellen saw her opportunity to put the onus back on him.

"I heard you were seeing Coralie," she spoke unthinkingly, and was surprised by her brother's reaction.

He shuffled his feet, dropped his eyes, and muttered something indistinct.

"What did you say?"

"Coralie – she's a nice girl. We talk."

Ellen looked across at Travis and raised her eyebrows. Talk – with that bimbo? Travis raised his open arms behind Ron's back. Clearly this was something for them to discuss later.

She returned her attention to Ron. "I'm sorry I missed you. I'm about to go, but it seems you've made a good recovery. Did you see Mom and Dad when you were down there?" she asked without much hope. But again Ron surprised her.

"Sure did. Mom's finding it hard. The old bugger's decided he needs his stick for walking – not sure how true that is, but he takes it everywhere with him and uses it." Ron reflectively rubbed the back of his leg.

"He didn't…"

"Caught the edge of it." Ron grinned. "I was quicker than he was. I don't think he'd use it on Mom," he added, becoming more serious.

"I should hope not."

"But you were leaving?"

"Yes." Ellen was torn. She wanted to get on the road, but was anxious to hear more about what was going on at home.

Appearing to appreciate her dilemma, Ron patted her on the shoulder. "I'll call you tomorrow, sis. You should be going before it gets any later."

Ellen nodded and looked toward Travis. Surely he wasn't going to let her get away so easily. He wasn't.

"There's coffee in the pot, Ron. Look like you need one. I'll see Ellen out."

"That was neat," Ellen congratulated Travis as they stood by her car. "I couldn't think how to give Ron the slip."

"You're talking to the master of such maneuvers," he replied, holding her again. "So… this weekend?"

"I'll have to check a few things," Ellen avoided giving him a straight answer. "I need to make sure Jenny is available – we didn't talk times – and the parents. After what Ron's just said, I need to check on them."

"Always the little helper, aren't you?" But there was no malice in Travis' words, and he kissed her soundly before helping her into her car. "I'll call you tomorrow too," he added, as she put the car in gear and drove off.

Driving back, Ellen's mind was working overtime. Uppermost in her mind was the proposed bike ride to Canada. She needed to discuss this with Travis as she wasn't sure she could cope with sitting on a bike for the time it took to get there and back – at least four days on the back of the Harley. It all came down to how much she was prepared to do for him. A lot, she decided, but four days on a Harley, that might be stretching the friendship.

Then there were her parents. She didn't like what she'd heard from Ron. It sounded as if Dad was becoming uncontrollable. The knock on the head – or whatever had been happening prior to that, seemed to be having an effect on his mental state. How long could Mom put up with him like that? And how could she convince Mom she couldn't go on?

By the time Ellen reached home, she'd remembered Maddy's wise words about doing something for herself. It had never occurred to her that she spent her life taking care of others. She wondered if it had always been the case, but didn't think so. Somewhere along the line, this gift she had of being able to see the future had morphed into something else entirely. She had begun to work with others to ensure that the good things happened, and the bad were ameliorated.

It wasn't such a bad thing, being the good Samaritan, the one who could always be relied on to be there – to offer a helping hand. However, as Maddy said, it had meant that she, Ellen, always came last. But she began to argue with her own reasoning, surely her instinct to help was a blessing not a curse? She'd been given this gift of seeing. Had she not been also given the next step of caring? But did caring for others mean she had to put herself last? This was the crux of the matter.

Ellen entered her little home, still wide awake. She pottered around for a time, then sat down at the computer, an idea forming in her mind. She'd completely forgotten the power of the media. The local paper was a prime avenue for their protest. She dithered between writing a letter to the editor and a media release – either would be an opportunity to make their point. She wouldn't write from the point of view of the small shopkeepers, but from the view of the line of shops to the wider community.

Contented once more, she began to compose – first a letter, then a media release. She'd decide which to send in the morning. It was sufficient for now to get her thoughts down. It was late by the time she'd finished, making sure she presented her case in the best possible light. She re-read the documents. Yes, they'd do. Her eyes were beginning to close, so it was time to finish and go to bed. Time enough to worry about Travis and the Harley in the morning – and she'd call in on her folks then too.

Twenty-three

The sound of birdsong wakened Ellen from a deep sleep. She lay still for a moment, then leapt up remembering all the things she had planned for the day, starting with a visit to the parents. She grabbed a quick breakfast of toast and fruit, and as she munched on that and drank her first cup of coffee of the day, she thought about what Ron had told her the night before.

It sounded as if Dad was going downhill. He still appeared to be physically strong – too strong, if Ron was to be believed. The pair had always been at loggerheads, ever since Ron was a teenager – but to take a stick to him? Maybe her brother had been exaggerating, but he'd sounded pretty believable. She needed to sort it out. She certainly couldn't go off for the weekend leaving her mother alone with Dad if he was prone to violence. She put her cup down with a thump. Wasn't this exactly what Maddy had been talking about? Well, she thought as she dumped her dirty dishes in the sink, she'd go over and see how the land lay before making any decisions.

"You're an early bird," Rita greeted her daughter, when Ellen popped her head around the door. "I was just making your dad some breakfast. Would you like some?"

The delicious aroma of scrambled eggs met Ellen's nostrils. "I've had…" she began.

"There's plenty, and I bet you didn't have a proper cooked breakfast, did you?" Rita didn't wait for a reply. "Sit yourself down and help yourself to coffee from the pot while I take Dad's through."

Ellen did as she was bid, thinking how comforting it sometimes was to be treated as a child. How easy it would be to dismiss all of her woes and give in to this sort of treatment.

"Now then, what brings you here so early? Shouldn't you be opening up around now?" Rita placed a steaming plate of eggs in front of Ellen and settled herself comfortably as she refilled her mug.

Ellen spluttered. "You're the one who has me sitting here eating a second breakfast," she accused. "I only dropped by to see how things were." She took a mouthful. "These are yum. You haven't lost your touch," she congratulated her mother. "Ron said…"

"Oh, your brother! He's been round here bothering your dad. You know what he's like," she sighed.

"Who? Ron or Dad?"

"Both of them. They're a right pair. What I'd give to see the two of them shut up together – see who came out best." Rita smoothed the tablecloth as if it might smooth away their differences. "But Ron's been good. I'll say that for him. Since your dad's accident he's been here regular, especially recently. Makes me wonder if there's something else bringing him down to Florence." She raised her eyebrows enquiringly.

Ellen was in two minds. Should she reveal what she knew of Ron's attraction to Coralie, or would that leave the door open to discussion of her own relationship? "Maybe," she said carefully, but Rita wasn't really expecting an answer.

"It's your dad," she began, her eyes filling with tears. "I don't know what to do with him these days. One minute he's full of life and ranting on about how he's going to change things and how Ron's never been any good. The next he's gazing into space – lost to the world."

Stunned, Ellen covered her mother's hand with hers, the soft wrinkled skin reminding her of her mother's eighty-odd years. Her own eyes began to glisten.

"He's still active," Rita continued. "If you can count going out to the mailbox ten times a day and ranting at the inefficiency of the mail service. But he's no company." She wiped her eyes. "Sorry, my dear. That's not what you came to hear."

"Yes it is," Ellen bit her lip. That settled it. She couldn't leave town with her mother in this state. "What can I do to help?" she asked.

"I don't rightly know," Rita replied sadly. "Probably nothing. You're a good girl. You've always been there for us – looking after Dad and me. But you have your own life too. There's your books and your shop. Our lives are almost over – you still have a lot of yours ahead of you. There's still time…"

"Mom!" Ellen couldn't believe what she was hearing.

"Tush, I know it's too late for any grandchildren – unless Ron gets his act together and finds some spry young thing. Though what spry young thing would have him?" she asked, almost to herself. "But it would do my heart good to see you settled before our time's up."

"Don't talk like that, Mom. You – and Dad – have a good few years left in you. It's not like you to talk that way."

"It's this accident… your dad… made me think. We'll not be here forever, and before we go…" She held up a hand to prevent Ellen interrupting, "I'd dearly like to see you settled," she repeated. "You need to stop thinking of us. It's time you put yourself first. There I've had my say."

"Maddy said that too," Ellen said quietly.

"Maddy?"

"Jenny's godmother – up at Seal Rock. I spoke with her last night – went up to see Jenny and Mike," Ellen said.

"And she said what?"

"That I should look out for myself instead of considering others all the time. She didn't mean you and Dad," Ellen added quickly, hoping her mother hadn't taken her words the wrong way.

"And what were you discussing for Maddy to give you this advice?"

Damn! Ellen had forgotten how astute her mother could be. She'd put two and two together and made five.

"Umm… we were just talking about the possibility of my taking a few days off. She suggested Jenny could mind the store and…"

"Best thing for you," Rita surprised Ellen with the power behind her words. "This stuff has been tough on you too. And the worry about your shop on top of everything. A few days away would do you the wonder of good. Where were you thinking of going?"

"Well… maybe north… Canada," Ellen's voice grew stronger. "Vancouver Island sounds interesting… and the Butchart Gardens are there."

A smile spread over Rita's face, and her eyes took on a faraway look.

"Victoria. Vancouver Island. Takes me back. Your dad and I went there for our honeymoon. What a wonderful time we had. We walked for miles, took tea in little English-style tea shops, ate the delicious local salmon. I remember the flowers everywhere – even on the lampposts. It's a beautiful place – very different from here. And the gardens… well, they're something else. You'll love it. Will you be going alone? Won't it be a bit lonely?"

Ellen hesitated. She didn't want to give too much away. "I'd be going with a friend," she said at last, then in an attempt to allay any further questions, added, "but I can't go just yet, not with Dad the way he is."

"Stuff and nonsense. Of course you can. As I told you, Ron's been popping in regular."

"But you said…"

"I said a lot of things. Doesn't matter about your dad's attitude to your brother. That'll never change. Ron's been a big help to me. He's turned into quite the handyman, now your dad's not able to do things around the house the way he used to."

"Ron, a handyman?" Ellen had received yet another surprise about her brother. "But he's never…"

"Maybe he never had the chance. But he does now, and let me tell you he's pretty good at it. Guess he's been watching your dad all these years. You know Dad would never brook any help, so there was no call for Ron to do anything before, but now… well, he's risen to the occasion. Quite a turn up for the books. So you can go off on your little jaunt without worrying about us," she concluded.

"Well, guess I should go now. I'll take all of that on board," Ellen assured her mother as she took her leave.

She certainly had a lot to think about as she drove down to Old Town. She was a bit irked to learn her parents didn't need her quite as much as she'd imagined. Here she'd been, picturing herself – if she had ever thought about it – as the mainstay of the family, and now it seemed her role had been usurped by Ron. Ron, her no-good brother, had suddenly come up trumps. But that left her free to go off with Travis. Now the only discussion she needed to have was about the bike, and she wasn't so sure she'd win that one.

*

Ellen spent most of the morning expecting the promised calls from Ron and Travis, but it was almost lunchtime before her cell phone rang and Ron's smiling face appeared on the screen. "I called in on the folks this morning," she said, even before her brother had time to greet her. "You were right. Mom's not too good, though she's putting a brave face on it. She says you've been a big help. What else can we do?"

"Give a guy time to speak," Ron's slow voice sounded happier than usual. "I'm doing what I can, but I think Dad needs more than we can do."

"What do you mean?" But even as she spoke, Ellen knew. She knew Dad wasn't the man he'd been. His health was on a downward spiral, and the accident may only have accelerated the process.

"He's going to be too much for Mom to cope with before long," Ron replied, his voice tinged with sadness. "I know he and I haven't always seen eye to eye, but it's hard to see this happening to him. We need to…"

"No!" Ellen's every instinct was to deny what she knew to be true. While physically strong, their dad was slipping away from them.

"Mom says these *spells*, as she calls them, are becoming more frequent. They scare her."

"They do? She didn't say." Ellen sat down in a nearby chair and gripped her phone hard. Had she spent too much time talking about herself, and failed to take into account how her mom was feeling? Surely not? Ron's next words shocked her.

"I saw Mom this morning too. She worries about you. Said she'd given you a heart-to-heart and told you to think more of yourself and less of others. She's concerned you're getting too involved in opposing this development, too. Mentioned you're thinking of taking some time off. Travis said something about that too, this morning. Canada, I believe?" Ron chuckled.

"Really?" Ellen attempted to buy time as she tried to work out what to say. How much did Ron know?

"All is revealed, little sister. You've enslaved my old buddy. He's asked my permission," Ron chortled.

"For what?" Ellen grew cold at the idea of Travis and her brother discussing her. She didn't want to even imagine it.

"Keep your shirt on. Very correct, he was. Quite the gentleman if a tad old-fashioned. Appreciated I'd worry about you – knowing how he's spent the last couple of years. Wanted to make sure I knew he was on the level. Nothing underhand there. Have to respect him for that."

Ellen listened open-mouthed, her anger boiling up like an erupting volcano. But Ron hadn't finished.

"Told me he'd asked you to ride up north with him – some mention of gardens or some such," Ron dismissed the iconic Butchart Gardens in a word. "Anyway, bottom line is I said it was okay with me, if you agreed, that is."

"Are you finished?" Ellen could barely control her indignation. "How dare the two of you discuss me as if I were a piece of meat? It's none of your business who I do or don't go to Canada with – or do anything else for that matter," her voice became louder as the thought of the two of them discussing her fuelled her anger.

Ignoring Ellen's annoyance, Ron continued, "So, I can continue to call in on the olds while you're gone. You can rely on me. I'll check with Mom every day – make sure she's okay. You can go off with a clear conscience."

"I'm glad one of us can have that," Ellen snapped into the phone before cutting Ron off.

She was still fuming when she answered a call from Jenny only a few minutes later.

"And, can you imagine," Ellen concluded, "Travis actually had the nerve to ask Ron's permission to… to court me?"

"I think that's sweet."

"Sweet? What's sweet about it?" but Jenny's words had extinguished Ellen's anger. She began to laugh. "You're right, of course, but…"

"I know. It's difficult for you to be treated as a woman, for someone else to be looking out for you, rather than you being the strong one. As my children would say, you need to chill."

Ellen giggled at the term, which sounded strange coming from the formerly uptight Jenny. "You know you're the third person to tell me that in the past couple of days – not in exactly those words, though. Mom and Maddy have both had a go at me, telling me to look out more for myself – to chill, I guess," she laughed again. "Maybe there's some truth in it."

"There certainly is. Now, when do you want me down there? Have you spoken to Travis?"

"Last night. I called in."

"And?"

"He suggested this coming weekend, but it's too soon. I can't expect you to be ready by then."

"What's to get ready? It's only me you need down there, not a circus. The weekend is fine with me. Take a couple extra days too, if you want. Anything special I need to know? How about I pop down tomorrow so you can give me a tour?"

"You seem to spend your time on the highway. Haven't you anything better to do?"

"Not at all. Mike enjoys getting down to the library, and I think Maddy would appreciate a trip down too. Maybe we can all have afternoon tea together?"

"It's a date." Ellen rang off in a much better frame of mind. Talking with Jenny was like a dose of good medicine.

One more call to go. Ellen was on tenterhooks waiting for Travis. By the time he did ring, in the late afternoon, she'd gone through all sorts of possibilities, including that he'd changed his mind and the trip was off. Her stomach was doing somersaults every time the phone rang, turning her into a nervous wreck. She was so relieved to hear his voice that she would have agreed to anything. As it was, she found herself agreeing to ride the Harley to Vancouver Island the coming weekend. When the call ended, she stared at her phone in amazement. *What had she just agreed to? What had happened to her resolve not to ride up there on the bike? What was it about this man that had her in such a turmoil she ended up agreeing to everything he said?*

Still smiling to herself at her lack of willpower, but excited at the thought of the trip ahead, Ellen settled into her office to check what she'd written the night before. In the cold light of day, the media release seemed to her to be a little too moderate in its tone, so she modified the content, giving greater emphasis to the damaging effect of a new development in this area, and itemizing the disadvantages to the community as a whole. Finally, satisfied that she'd struck the right note, she emailed it to the paper.

*

Looking at her watch, Ellen was about to check her day's takings, when a thought struck her. Coralie! Could she really be interested in Ron? Ellen hadn't known him to take notice of a woman in years, and now it seemed that Coralie had him in her sights. Coralie, who made up to every man she met. Coralie, who…

Without taking time to consider her actions, Ellen popped her *back soon* notice on the door and stepped outside. Peering through her neighbor's window she could see that Coralie's client was about to leave. She waited till the woman closed the door behind her, nodded and smiled, then entered the hairdresser's.

"Ellen. What are you doing here? Don't tell me you want a haircut too? Your brother…"

"No." Ellen fingered her plait. This was the first time she'd been in a hairdressing establishment in as long as she could remember. "Not me. You made a good job of Ron's, though. It's him I've come to…" she hesitated, unsure how to broach the subject.

"You want to know my intentions?" Coralie came forward laughing. "I know, I know. I have such a reputation. You want to make sure I'm not just toying with Ron. Sit down."

Ellen sat, wondering what she was about to hear.

"It's all an act, you know. I'm really pretty shy, especially where men are concerned, and the only way I know is to act like I have all the confidence in the world. I know I'm sometimes a bit over-the-top, but it works for me. Keeps them at arms' length.' She chuckled, then her voice became more serious. "But not Ron. Your brother is something else. He makes me feel safe, makes me want to take care of him. I'm not playing around, Ellen. I really care for him. I'm hoping that, maybe…" Coralie twisted her fingers together and dropped her gaze. When she raised her eyes again, Ellen could see them filled with unshed tears. "Do you think…? Could he…?"

Bemused, and not a little amazed at this revelation, Ellen smiled. "Well, you're the first woman he's looked at for years, so I think you're in with a chance," she said, mentally berating herself for not having realized Coralie's behavior was covering up a sense of insecurity and hoping she'd spoken the truth. Ellen would hate for Ron to be let down. "I'd better go now." She left and walked back next door slowly, pondering this new side of Coralie.

Twenty-four

Next morning Ellen busied herself making lists. She knew Jenny ran her own bookshop, but that was in Australia, and she was sure things were done differently there. Saturday would be here all too soon, and she'd be leaving her baby in Jenny's tender care. Worried as she was, she couldn't suppress a thrill of excitement at the thought of spending several days alone with Travis. It was something she'd never done before – gone away with a man. Her previous relationships had been very much fly-by-night, except for Will and Jackson, and well… Jackson had been married, so there'd been no question of sneaking a few days together, and Will… she didn't know why, but it had never come up. This was a first.

Ellen thought back to Maddy's words – was it only a few weeks ago? She'd told Ellen she'd know when real love came along. Ellen shivered in anticipation. Was this it? Was this the love she hadn't even known was waiting for her? She gave herself a shake and dedicated herself to business as the shop began to fill with customers. By the time Jenny popped her head through the door, the weekend was the furthest thing from her mind.

"Okay, then. Lead me to it," Jenny greeted her. "But how about a coffee first? I picked these up across the road." She handed Ellen a large takeaway coffee and took a paper bag out of her purse. "Have a cinnamon roll too," she offered. "I don't know why I don't get fat when I come here. Everything is so yummy – and so sweet."

"I expect you use it all up, the way you and Mike run around."

"Mmm there is that," Jenny bit into the sweet bun. "Now, tell me what I need to know."

For the next half hour, Ellen instructed Jenny in her system and routines. "But it'll only be for a few days," she said at last. "I expect we'll be leaving Saturday and back Monday."

"Don't rush back on my account," Jenny looked around the shop with pleasure. "You do know I based my shop on this one. I love the ambiance you've created here. It's a peaceful haven, the most restful shop I know. I may not have quite managed to replicate it, but I've had a good try."

"And this friend of yours, she's managing it while you're gone?"

"Rosa, yes. She takes care of all the financial stuff. She's good at that. I prefer the day-to-day bits and selecting the books. Love the aroma of a good bookshop. I see you still have your candle there," Jenny pointed to the candle behind the counter, which today gave off a geranium fragrance.

"Always. I hope you'll keep that up when I'm away."

"Sure will. It's part and parcel of this place."

"Well, that's about it," Ellen concluded. "Hope you don't have any unwanted visitors."

"What do you mean?"

"It's probably nothing to get het up about, but on Monday… there was this man came in. Seemed like a regular customer at first, browsing the shelves. Though I did think it odd he didn't seem to be taking much interest in any of the books."

"So?"

"He warned me off – told me I hadn't listened." Ellen paused, remembering. "Then he dropped my ceramic owl – the one I used to keep right here," she laid her hand on the counter. "Then some books… It was frightening at the time, but I don't think he'll be back. Anyway," she grinned at her cousin. "It's me he's after, not you."

"Sure thing. I'll let Mike know. He may join me. He'll come down to Florence with me each day, for sure."

"It's a fair way to come every day. Would you like to stay at my place? You'd be most welcome."

"Thanks, but probably not. Mike likes his own bed, and there's Ben. He's just become used to having us back again. It's really no distance at all. You'd know all about distance if you lived in Australia. Look, I don't have to pick up Mike for a bit yet. Why don't I get my hand in? You hide yourself in the office and do what you need to there. I'll mind the shop. And you can tell me if I balls up," she laughed.

From her retreat at the back of the store, Ellen heard a continual stream of customers being served by her cousin's dulcet Australian tones. She relaxed, confident she'd be leaving the place in good hands – and it was only for a few days. What was she worried about? But there was a nagging somewhere at the back of her mind. She brushed it away. Her mind was full of doubts and misgivings these days. She was taking off. She was going to enjoy herself and forget about the shop, forget about the developers, forget about her parents, forget about Ron. She was going to focus on Travis, being with Travis, and the warm glow she felt at the very thought of him.

Ellen was just picturing Travis and reliving the sensation of his lips on hers, his warm arms around her, when she heard his voice. Had she summoned him with her thoughts? What an idea! But it stuck with her as she walked out to greet him.

"Morning," she said, feeling a little shy in Jenny's presence.

"Morning to you both," Travis included Jenny in his greeting and stood in the middle of the shop, hands on hips, legs splayed, taking up more space than anyone ought.

"So this is the new shopkeeper," he joked, then on a more serious note. "We're real glad you agreed to help out. Ellen and me." Travis glanced in Ellen's direction. He shuffled his feet, "Hmm," he nodded in the direction of Ellen's office.

Jenny was quick on the uptake. "You need some private time. Be my guest. I've been filling in here anyway."

Ellen led the way back to her office and closed the door. "That was a bit rude," she began, only to be closeted in a pair of strong arms and to feel Travis' soft lips on hers – exactly as she'd been imagining only moments earlier. Had she really called him into existence? Was this the real Travis or a clone she'd conjured up? She castigated herself for having such ridiculous thoughts. He was real, all right – no figment of her tortured imagination.

"Put me down, you great hulk," she said, but her tone belied the harsh words.

With a final kiss, Travis released her. "So you're all set?"

Ellen nodded.

"For tomorrow?"

"Tomorrow? I thought…"

"Don't think, just do. Now you have Jenny all clued up, what's to stop us taking off tomorrow? Ron's taking care of the folks, isn't he? He might even introduce them to Coralie."

"He… oh, you're teasing," Ellen said with relief. Her parents weren't ready for that shock yet. Though it might not be a bad idea. It would certainly give her mom something positive to think about.

"So… tomorrow?" Travis repeated.

"Tomorrow," Ellen agreed trying to suppress a bubble of excitement. "But we should check with Jenny first." She opened the door to find Jenny standing behind the counter of an empty shop.

"Jenny."

Ellen's cousin looked up from having seemingly been engrossed in a book. "What's up, guys?"

"Would you… how about if…"

Travis broke in, "What Ellen's trying to say is, would it be okay with you and Mike if we took off tomorrow? With the Fourth of July coming up next weekend, might be best if we avoid all the traffic leading up to it."

"Of course. I'd forgotten about the holiday. Life seems to be one big holiday here. But that's fine by me. I think I have the hang of things by now, haven't made too many blues."

"Blues?" Travis was mystified.

"Mistakes. Sorry, my Aussie terms pop out from time to time. Mike teases me about them." Jenny's laughter filled the shop.

"You've been wonderful," Ellen said gratefully. "I have every confidence in you. I've never left the shop with anyone before and…"

"Understood. I'll treat it as I would my own – better even. I know I'll have both of you to answer to if anything goes wrong."

"And you'll keep a look out for any strange men?"

"Sure will."

With that, Ellen had to be satisfied. Travis and Jenny left together, the latter intending to meet with Mike at the library. The proposed afternoon tea had fallen by the board when Ellen realized she was to be off next day, and Maddy hadn't come down anyway. She had a few loose ends to take care of, and wanted to check that the *Siuslaw News* had received her media release and to enquire if there was a chance it would be printed.

*

When she arrived home that night, Ellen couldn't settle. She moved from one room to the next, from one activity to another, till she finally forced herself to sit down in the kitchen. She took a deep breath. She was behaving like a crazy woman. She needed to put her thoughts in order and get everything done in a timely fashion. After all, there wasn't too much to do – pack, call Mom. That was it. So why was she running around like a mad woman?

She picked up the phone – call Mom first to check on Dad and let her know when she planned to leave. Travis had said he'd pick her up early – around eight – but maybe they could stop off on the way? That would work, she decided, forgetting it would also give away the fact she was going away with Travis, and raise her mother's hopes.

"Hello dear," Rita sounded more chipper today.

"How're things? How's Dad?"

"We've had a better day." Ellen could hear the relief in her mother's voice. "Went for a short walk down the street, talked to a few neighbors. Your dad liked that. Didn't have any blank moments either. How about you? You *are* taking that trip you mentioned, aren't you?"

Before Ellen could reply, Rita added, "And don't worry about us. Ron's promised to look in even more often. He might as well be living here."

"You're sure?" Ellen had a sudden qualm, wondering if she was being selfish.

"Quite sure. Now, when are you off? Remember next weekend's the holiday."

"Yes, Mom," Ellen couldn't contain a smile at her mother's usual habit of organizing everyone around her. "We're actually going this coming weekend, tomorrow to be precise. I'm leaving early so thought…"

Again her mother was two steps ahead of Ellen's thinking. "Now don't you be thinking of coming round here on your way out. You'll want to have an early start before the roads are too busy."

"Yes, Mom," Ellen repeated. "So, I'll keep in touch. You can call me on my cell if you need me… I'll see you when I get back."

"You enjoy yourself now and don't be worrying about us. We'll manage fine."

As she hung up, Ellen realized she had no idea when they'd be back. Travis had mentioned a few days. That could mean two days to a week. No, he couldn't mean a week. That would take them into the holiday weekend. She had to be back before then. She couldn't expect Jenny to… Blast, all this thinking was giving her a headache. She brewed a cup of herbal tea and forced herself to sip it slowly, while deciding what to pack.

She wouldn't need much for a few days. It was summer, so a few light shirts with some jeans should see her through, plus maybe a sweater for the evening. It could probably get quite cool up there at night. There wouldn't be much room on the bike, either, so Travis couldn't expect her to take anything dressy. As she began to pile some garments together, however, a thin turquoise dress made its way into the pile. She'd bought it years ago – when she was seeing Will – but there'd never been the occasion to wear it. She'd completely forgotten about it on the shopping spree with Jenny and didn't imagine there'd be an occasion on this trip, but, she reasoned, it wouldn't take up much space.

When she was finally ready, Ellen made one last list. She'd slip it under the shop door as they left town. The person she'd spoken to at the paper had promised her article would appear this weekend and she wanted to ensure Jenny bought a copy. The *Siuslaw News* was a local paper. It wouldn't be available where they were going, and she didn't want to miss it.

*

Next morning Ellen was up at dawn. She bounced out of bed, full of energy and the anticipation of the next few days. She sang to herself as she showered and dressed, this morning in a pair of tight jeans and figure hugging pink shirt. She'd show Travis she could dress in gear that didn't hide her figure. A pair of long boots and a short denim jacket completed her outfit and should be suitable for the back of the bike. She was ready and waiting when she heard the Harley pull up outside. With a tremor in her gut and a smile on her face, Ellen picked up her bag and walked outside.

Three hours and some 150 miles later, Ellen's rear end was beginning to feel numb, and she was bitterly regretting having given in to Travis' desire to travel this way. Sure, the wind in her hair was great – to start with. But after the first hour it was more like a roaring torrent in her ears, and the sensation of Travis' body against hers had long ceased to provide her with any sensory pleasure. She longed for the comfort of a car, the ability to leisurely examine the road map and comment on the various places through which they were passing. Instead, everything swept past in a blur.

Travis must have sensed her discomfort, because she was aware of the bike slowing, and they turned into a roadside diner.

"Thought we could do with a bite to eat," he said, in answer to her unspoken question. "Maybe a rest stop, too?" He chuckled to see her dismount stiffly. "Has it been too much for you?"

"No," Ellen was unwilling to admit defeat. "I'll be fine. Just need a stretch. And she proceeded to do just that, stretching first one leg, then the other and raising her arms high above her head. To her surprise, it did make her feel better, and now she had time to consider it, she *was* hungry. "Food would be good too."

"It's all the fresh air," Travis inhaled vigorously. "Gives you an appetite. You're enjoying the trip, aren't you?" he asked anxiously, as Ellen continued to bend and stretch in an attempt to regain some feeling in her extremities.

"It's an experience," Ellen replied. She might think it a mistake, but she sure as hell wasn't going to admit it. She'd soldier on and enjoy it if it killed her. And it might just do that. How much farther did they have to go? They couldn't have reached the halfway mark yet. Then there'd be the trip home. But there *would* be the part in-between. She'd concentrate on thinking about that – about a nice soft bed, cuddling up to Travis for… Damn, she still didn't know how long he intended this trip to last. She knew she should have asked before now. How could it have slipped her mind?

"I'll just..." Ellen pointed to the restrooms and headed in that direction, leaving Travis to make his own way into the diner. By the time she joined him in a booth, he already had two mugs of steaming coffee sitting there.

"Look as if you need that," he nodded towards them.

"I sure do," Ellen picked hers up and took a gulp. Boy, it felt good. The warm liquid seemed to go right down to her toes. She wiggled them inside her boots.

"What would you like to eat?" Travis handed her a menu. Ellen scanned the offerings, selecting a soup and salad option – pumpkin soup with a Caesar salad to follow – while Travis chose a Reuben sandwich with fries. "Can't tempt you?" he asked when his large platter arrived with an overgenerous serving of fries.

Ellen shook her head, tucking into her healthier choice.

By the time they finished, and had two mugs of coffee under their belts, Travis looked at his watch. "Ready to move on? I'd like to get up there tonight. The last ferry is at nine-thirty, but I'd like to make an earlier one if possible. Takes almost two hours across. I've booked us into the *Victoria Harbourside Hotel and Marina*. It's a bit of a mouthful, but I hear it's pretty nice."

"Ready as I'll ever be," Ellen replied, but she was certainly feeling better, and the notion of getting back on the bike didn't seem as daunting as she'd expected. "Umm, how many nights have you booked?"

"Didn't I say? I've booked through to Tuesday. I thought..." Travis' voice faded away as he seemed to grasp the fact they hadn't discussed a timeframe for the trip. "That's okay by you, isn't it?"

Ellen nodded. At least three full days. She hugged herself at the thought and determined not to spend one minute of them worrying about what might be happening back home.

As she settled onto the back of the Harley, ready for the next phase of their journey, Ellen's mind was filled with the thought of the hotel Travis had taken the trouble to book. It sounded quite plush. Maybe there *would* be the opportunity to wear the dress she'd packed so casually. Her arms encircled his waist as if they belonged there and gripped tightly.

Travis turned to smile at her. "All set?"

She nodded, and they were off.

*

"Wow, this is nice!" Ellen gazed round the room in delight, going immediately to the large window, attracted by the view of a wide stretch of water.

"It's what they call the Inner Harbor," Travis came up behind and wrapped his arms around her.

Ellen leant back, feeling his strong body against her. She turned into his arms. Travis nuzzled her neck.

"Not too exhausted? How about we go downstairs for a meal?"

"In…?"

"In the restaurant we saw on the way in – the Blue Crab Bar and Grill."

"Oh, it looked wonderful," Ellen couldn't contain her joy. The trials of the trip – all the stiffness, aches and pains – were forgotten. "Do I have time to change?" She thought of the dress packed for just such an occasion.

"Not now," Travis laughed. "We'll do the dress-up thing another night – maybe tomorrow. Right now we should get downstairs before they close." He took her hand, and they went down in the elevator, holding hands like a couple of teenagers.

By the time they were seated, it was clear that most of the other diners had almost finished their meals. "Are you sure…?" Ellen asked.

"Checked before we went upstairs," Travis responded. "Only problem is there might be a reduced menu."

"Sir, madam," a waiter approached them and set napkins on their laps with a flourish. "I'm sorry, sir," he addressed Travis, "the kitchen is about to close. I'm afraid we can only offer the salmon…" He looked at both in enquiry.

"Perfect," Ellen was quick to respond. "Canadian salmon for our first meal in Canada. What could be better?"

The meal, when it arrived, lived up to her expectations, and although she was sure he'd have preferred a well done steak, Travis appeared to enjoy his too. They washed the meal down with a glass of white wine for her and a long glass of some non-alcoholic concoction for him and, after perusing the dessert menu, decided to wait till another evening before savouring its tempting delights.

"Coffee?" asked Travis.

"No, I think…"

"Ready for bed?"

Ellen blushed.

"I've been watching your eyes almost closing. Thought you might fall into your dinner. Think we both need a good rest if we're going to be any good tomorrow."

Ellen allowed Travis to help her up, and they traveled up in the elevator, her head on his shoulder. "Sorry, I almost fell asleep," she said, embarrassed, raising her head as they reached their floor.

"*No problemo.* Just the long ride catching up with you. A hot shower and bed for you, my lady – no argument."

Ellen was too tired to argue, though it did cross her mind that this wasn't how she'd intended to spend their first night in a hotel together. As she snuggled up behind Travis, her arms around him, her last thought was one of contentment before she fell asleep.

*

Ellen awoke to bright sunlight streaming through the uncurtained window. She put up her hand to shade her eyes from its brilliance.

"You're awake."

The voice came from the pillow next to her, and turning, Ellen's eyes devoured the man lying beside her.

"Good morning."

"Good morning to you. Sleep well?"

"Mmm." Ellen stretched, her legs encountering Travis'. She made an attempt to draw them back, but found herself caught in a scissor hold. His lips met hers, and she breathed in his morning smell, her arms automatically moving to caress him as his fingers sought out her secret places and began to pleasure her. Ellen moaned and wriggled closer, her body arching as she gave in to sensation. Travis pulled her on top of him, his fingers on her nipples sending thrills of ecstasy through her entire body as he finally entered her. Unbeknown to her, this was what she had been searching for all her life – this feeling of completeness, of being at one with another human being. Then all thought disappeared. She was lost in the moment.

By the time they both returned to full consciousness, their watches showed it was almost nine o'clock.

"We should get up," Ellen murmured.

"We should?"

"Yes." She sat up, her unplaited hair falling about her shoulders.

"I do love it like this," Travis threaded his fingers through the long tresses, twisting them around to bring Ellen's face closer to his. His lips met hers again, and she was silenced by his kisses.

"So what are we going to do today?" Ellen had finally extricated herself from Travis' clutches and sat on the edge of the bed, just out of reach of his big arms.

Travis rolled over to face her. "What about those gardens you were keen to see? Butchart. Wasn't that it? If you can bear to get back on the bike today."

"Think I can manage it." Ellen laughed, as she eluded his grasp and slipped into the shower. She sang as she stood under the streaming jet of water, happy to be alive. She hadn't known what was missing in her life till now. All her doubts and fears had vanished. She was sure Travis was the right man for her – a true companion, a kindred spirit. Maddy had been right. She'd followed her heart, and here she was in this glorious place with this wonderful man.

When they'd enjoyed a leisurely brunch of omelettes with jumbo shrimp, crab, caramelized onions, arugula, goat cheese, and potatoes, plus lots of toast and lashings of coffee, they were ready for the road. Although it was close to the end of June, there was a nip in the air, so Ellen was glad of her jacket as she once again took her place behind Travis, her arms automatically reaching around his waist. Today he covered them with his, and held them tight before revving up the bike.

After the good night's sleep, Ellen felt refreshed and enjoyed the ride more than on the previous day, when the scenery had flashed by in a blur. Today, she took time to examine the route. As soon as they left the hotel, she could see why the region was named British Columbia.

Everywhere were signs of what she took to be a British, even English influence, from the horse-drawn carriages, to the signs advertising high teas, and the plethora of flowers in their hanging baskets which provided a colorful adornment to the streets. By the time they reached the gardens themselves, Ellen was enthralled by the picturesque scenes as they rode towards the west coast of the island.

"Well, here we are," Travis wheeled the bike into a parking spot and stepped off, holding out his hand to assist Ellen.

"I'm not so stiff today," she laughed, but she still enjoyed his gallantry, continually amazed how feminine and dainty he made her feel. Tossing back her plait, she shrugged the strap of her purse over her shoulders. "Where now?" but before Travis could answer, she spied the model of a large boar in the courtyard. "Look at that," she cried, almost skipping over to examine the sculpture. She watched, as other visitors to the gardens rubbed the boar's nose, which appeared to be shiny. Probably from much rubbing, Ellen guessed, reaching up to rub it herself and closing her eyes as she made a wish.

"What did you wish for?" Travis was standing behind her.

Ellen turned with a start. "That would be telling. What have you there?" she asked pointing to the paper in his hand.

"A map of the gardens. Seems to me we could easily get lost here. Did you know there are fifty acres of them?"

"Really? All I knew was it was built in an old quarry. Mom and Dad came here on their honeymoon, so the gardens have been here a long time. Older than you and me. A map's a good idea. Let me see."

The pair pored over the map for a few minutes, then Ellen folded it up. "Let's just wander," she said. "We can check it as we go if we need to identify anything. I want to revel in the experience. I love my garden at home, but it's nothing like this. I've never visited anything on quite this scale before."

Holding hands they strolled along the paths, enjoying the brilliantly colored displays of flowers everywhere they looked, and the many different gardens. Travis was particularly interested in the water features – the Fountain of Three Sturgeons, the Goddess Fish and the Ross Fountains from which high streams of water spurted up before cascading down again into the Star Pond.

"To think this was once a quarry," Ellen exclaimed, as they stood looking down on a sunken garden, "and it was all conceived by one woman."

"She did most of the early work herself too," Travis read from the guide book he'd picked up along with the map, "Jenny Butchart. She must have been quite a woman."

"Another Jenny." Ellen hadn't given a thought to what she had left behind at home since she'd put her leg over Travis' Harley the day before. Now, however, she had a sensation of unease, and her hand reached into her purse for her cell phone. Maybe she should check that all was well.

She had just taken it out when Travis' large hand stretched over hers. "No," he said, as if reading her mind, "this is time for us. Everything will be fine back there. You'd hear otherwise. Trust Jenny. Let's just enjoy ourselves."

With a doubtful glance at her companion, Ellen dropped the phone back in her purse. He was right, of course. It was what she'd decided – a few days completely free of worry or concern.

The rest of the afternoon passed pleasantly as they ambled around, stopping from time to time to admire a particularly vivid flowering plant or a unique sculpture and the totem poles, which were a surprise to Ellen. Travis read from the guide book, enlightening Ellen to the finer points of the gardens and their formation and upkeep. Finally, they'd both had a surfeit of flowers and color.

"Did I see there was a restaurant somewhere?" Ellen asked.

"Tired or hungry?"

"Both. It might be nice to eat here rather than go straight back to the hotel, don't you think?"

Travis studied his guide book. "There are a few places to eat," he said. "But it seems a long time since we've eaten, so let's have the full dining room experience."

"Are we dressed…?" Ellen began, but Travis laughed away her concern.

"Look around," he said, and sure enough everyone in sight was dressed just as casually as they were.

"Okay," Ellen agreed, and they made their way back through the rose garden to the restaurant.

Unlike their experience when they arrived at the hotel, here there was a full menu to choose from. Deciding to forego an appetizer, Travis chose the roast half rack of lamb, while Ellen selected the west coast halibut fillet. This time she refused wine, instead joining Travis in a sparkling mineral water. As they ate, they chatted comfortably about their day, in an unspoken agreement to avoid touching on any painful subjects. It was as if they were cocooned in a bubble of happiness. After sharing a dessert plate of chocolate torte with toasted almonds and rose sorbet, Travis took out his guide book again.

"What now?" Ellen teased. "Haven't we finished for the day?"

"Yes and no. What would you say to some entertainment? It says here they have entertainment on the concert lawn on summer evenings. And tonight…" he turned a page, "we have some Dixieland jazz."

"Oh, that does sound fun. Let's go."

"Better have some coffee first," Travis decided, signalling the waiter.

An hour later, they strolled across the lawn to where rows of chairs were set up. Looking around, Ellen noticed that many of the other people had come prepared with warm rugs and flasks of hot drinks.

"Looks like we may have forgotten something," she whispered. "Must get cold here in the evenings."

"I'll keep you warm," Travis responded, suiting action to words by wrapping his arms around her.

"Mmm," Ellen murmured, snuggling up to him. She could get used to this.

Once it began, the music was wonderful, and they both enjoyed the foot-tapping rhythm of the New Orleans-style band. They barely noticed the darkness falling and the cold beginning to nip at their faces and fingers, until the band took a break.

"Time to go?" Travis removed his arm from around Ellen's shoulders and began to rub his hands together. Ellen did the same.

"Guess so."

They stood up and left the lawn as the band was starting up again. The music followed them, almost to the parking lot, and they bounced around in tune to keep warm. They were suddenly aware of the difference in evening temperature here from at home.

"We *are* in Canada," Ellen said, grinning as she joined Travis on the back of the Harley once more. She was becoming pretty used to this perch by now and wondered why she'd ever been so reluctant to ride on the silver bird, as she now viewed it. It was exactly like a silver winged creature that carried Travis and her around, setting them down in exotic locations. Ellen smiled and chided herself for being so fanciful. This was a different Ellen from the one who worried over her parents, took responsibility for her errant brother, even from the one who ran the bookstore. This Ellen was carefree and in love – there, she'd said it, albeit silently.

Twenty-five

Next morning, the pealing of church bells reminded them it was Sunday. Ellen lazily rolled over to observe the man beside her. His morning face was rumpled, his hair awry and she could see the golden-white hairs on his beard shining in the morning sunlight. She sighed, reflecting that this was a first for her – someone of her own, someone with whom she belonged. Memories of her previous relationships flashed through her mind. With Will, they had been two lonely people – though she had never admitted to being lonely – who'd found comfort in each other. Jack had never been hers. No, this was something different entirely.

"Penny for them?" Travis' voice broke into her musings.

"Not worth it," Ellen shook her head, strands of her long hair falling over her face, only to be gently stroked away as Travis kissed her gently then buried his face in her hair.

Travis' hands moved to encircle Ellen's face. "Glad you came?" he asked, stroking her brow, nose and lips before claiming her mouth once again. Her answer was to move even closer to him as a surge of longing flooded through her, and her body dissolved under his caresses.

It was some time later before Ellen was able to give a verbal response to his enquiry, by which time her body had provided an answer for her. "I think you know I am," she finally said, shaking her hair free from his hands.

She was combing out her hair and beginning to plait it, when Travis emerged from the shower, beads of water still clinging to his hair and beard. "Shall we stay around town today?" he asked. "Wouldn't mind doing that harbor-side walk we saw in one of those guidebooks."

"Sounds good to me," Ellen turned to greet him, "and I'd like to check out any local bookshops."

"Thought we'd left the bookshop lady back in Florence," Travis jested.

"We did, but…" Ellen said wistfully.

"Only joking. Of course we can. Be interested to see them myself."

"We may see Peter Travers featured," Ellen couldn't resist needling him. "What name are you going to write under now?" she asked, curious about his new writing persona.

"Hadn't thought. Maybe it's time for Travis Petersen to come out of the closet. See what my agent thinks."

"What has he said about your new book?" she asked, surprised to see him redden. "You haven't told him, have you?"

"I'm not very far into it yet," Travis neatly dodged the question. "Still not too clear how it's going to turn out."

"Can I read it?"

"Whoa!" Travis was clearly taken aback. "That's enough about my writing. I've left it back there with all the other contentious issues. Now, let's get breakfast over and out into the fresh air."

Ellen knew when to shut up. She'd gone too far, but she was interested to know about his current work. Even as an adult, she'd enjoyed all of the Peter Travers books and was keen to see how his style might have changed with a different genre. There was also a small part of her which wanted to see how much of Travis Petersen, the man, was in this new book.

*

"There are at least ten of them." Ellen pointed to a list of bookshops in the brochure she'd picked up before leaving the hotel. They'd spent the morning walking along the harbor, taking in the water views on one side and the many gardens and large homes on the other. After a satisfying ploughman's lunch in a waterside tavern, they were finishing off the day in downtown Victoria.

"We can't do all of them, so let's see which ones we come to first."

"Works for me."

They managed to find three shops in fairly close proximity to each other, and Ellen embarrassed a stunned Travis by asking if they stocked any Peter Travers books. One did, one looked blank, while the third offered to order one in for her.

"Satisfied now?" Travis asked, as they left the third shop after politely declining their kind offer.

"Mmm. I was actually more interested to see how they were set out, their window displays – things like that. Seems Peter Travers isn't quite so popular up here." She dodged as Travis aimed a mock punch in her direction.

"Now, how about we head back? There's time for a rest before dinner," Travis said, but by the twinkle in his eye, Ellen knew that a rest wasn't exactly what he had in mind and shivered in anticipation – a late afternoon of intimacy wouldn't go astray.

Arriving back in their room, Ellen saw her turquoise dress hanging up where she'd left it, ready to wear to dinner this evening – the romantic dinner Travis had promised that first night. This was going to be the culmination of their visit. They'd decided to leave next day and take the return trip more slowly, maybe stopping off in Seattle to visit the Space Needle and allow Ellen to rest her aching joints.

She threw her purse down on the bed and turned into Travis' arms with a provocative smile. He was just teasing open the buttons on her shirt when a ringing came from the side of the bed. "Damn! I suppose I should answer that. Must have left my cell here all day." Ellen twisted out of Travis' arms and picked up the phone. "Hello, Ellen here – what!"

The words echoed in her ear, "There's been a fire."

"A fire? Where? When?" Ellen looked around wildly and caught Travis by the arm, as she slumped down on the bed. Her eyes grew bigger, and her whole body began to shake. She gripped the phone tightly, trying to make sense of what her cousin was telling her. "Slow down, Jenny. Were you there? In the shop? When it…"

Jenny's tremulous voice was breaking as she answered, "It happened overnight. I… the candle… I don't know how it could have…"

Ellen heard Jenny take a deep breath, and felt her whole body grow cold. Her head was spinning. It felt as if it was going to burst. Her shop! Her baby! Had it all gone? Jenny was still talking, but Ellen's brain had ceased to function. She didn't hear what her cousin was saying. All she could see in her mind's eye was her bookshop, her pride and joy. She could see the flames, the blackened building, the destruction. She could almost smell the burning. She closed her eyes as if to shut out the images, but they were still there, imprinted behind her eyelids. Clearly seeing her distress, Travis took the phone from her.

"Travis here. Ellen's a wreck. What's happened?" He sat down beside Ellen keeping his free arm around her as he spoke. Ellen continued to sob uncontrollably.

Travis hung up at last. "There's been a fire at the shop."

"I got that much," Ellen wiped her eyes ineffectually with her hand and tried to stifle her sobs. "Had Jenny…?"

"She's been trying to get you all day, but…"

"The damn cell's been sitting here all day." Ellen looked reproachfully at the metal object as if it had chosen to stay behind in the hotel room, while its owner was out enjoying the day. "What did Jenny say?"

Travis handed her a tissue, and she used it to rub her eyes, making them redder than ever.

"Seems it happened last night — or sometime during the night. Jenny's beside herself, thinking she may have left the candle burning. With the late start on Sunday…" Travis spread his hands.

"We'd already left the hotel when they discovered it," Ellen concluded for him. "Did they call…?"

"The fire brigade and the police, yes. Seems the sprinklers came on and put out the fire, but there's water damage."

"Oh, shit! What a mess."

"You're insured?"

"Yes, but what good's that? How could Jenny…?"

"If that's what it was." Travis looked grim. "Seems to me a little candle wouldn't do much damage. You keep it in a special burner, don't you?"

"Ye…es." Ellen pictured the candle in its burner which always sat behind the counter. "You mean…?"

"I mean Jenny may have had nothing to do with it."

Ellen pushed herself up. "I need to get back." She looked around, unsure what to do first. "We must…" She sat down again, covering her face with her hands. "What am I going to do?"

"You're not on your own. I'm here." Travis wrapped her in his arms, his chin on top of her head. His assurance was of some comfort to Ellen, but didn't still the drumming in her ears. "We can leave right now if you want, but do you really want to ride all through the night? Wouldn't it be better to wait till morning? We can leave early and go straight through. There's nothing you can do back there anyway."

"I can…" Ellen began, but his words sank through her distress, and she agreed to go along with his suggestion. She looked longingly at the dress hanging in solitary state. There would be no romantic dinner that night.

Travis' eyes followed hers. "We can order room service and have an early night, though I don't expect either of us will get much sleep."

Ellen lay down, her eyes wet with tears.

"Drink this – you've had a shock."

Ellen propped herself up, looking blearily at the cup in Travis' hand. "What is it?"

"Hot, sweet tea. Best thing I know for shock. Drink it up. Unless you'd rather have something stronger. I could…"

"No, this is fine." Ellen held the cup in both hands and gulped down the sweet liquid. She screwed up her face. "How much sugar did you put in it?"

"Six spoons – too much?"

"Ugh. I think I'd like a shower."

"You do that, and I'll order something. A sandwich all right?"

"I don't think I could eat anything right now…, but maybe later…" Ellen swallowed a few times in an attempt to get rid of the dryness in her mouth. She was having trouble moving – stuck to the spot. She knew she wanted a shower, but the effort of getting there seemed beyond her. Eventually she made her way into the bathroom, walking as slowly as an old woman. She peeled off her clothes and stood under the water, the tears running down her cheeks again. Her shop – *The Reading Nook* – her special place, her haven – ruined! She couldn't imagine what she'd find when she returned to Florence. She dreaded seeing what damage the fire and water had done. Ellen let the water run, pouring over her, till her tears were dry, then she lifted her head.

She wouldn't be beaten. She'd go back, inspect the damage and work out what needed to be done. She recalled Travis' words. Maybe it hadn't been Jenny's fault. If that were the case, then…

"Travis…," Ellen wrapped a towel around her and walked back into the room. "If it wasn't the candle, then what…?"

*

Travis was ordering a couple of sandwiches and salads, when Ellen walked out of the bathroom dressed in only a towel. She looked so forlorn, he wanted to pick her up in his arms and carry her away. Instead, he tried to give her an honest answer without worrying her unduly. "Might be the Balcombs thing," he muttered. "Could know you're away and took the opportunity… Just meant to scare you, and it got out of hand."

"Out of hand? The whole place could have burned down, the shops on either side too. Maybe that's what they wanted," she said bitterly. "Would save them a whole lot of trouble if there was nothing left to demolish."

"Steady on. We don't know that for sure. I only said…"

"But it makes sense."

Travis was pleased to see a vestige of the old Ellen returning.

A knock at the door interrupted the conversation, and a smartly dressed waiter wheeled in a trolley containing a platter of sandwiches and two bowls of salad. "Will that be all, sir?"

"Thanks," Travis reached into his pocket for a tip, and the waiter left.

"Try to eat something," Travis cajoled, once Ellen was snuggled up in bed. He sat beside her and stroked her forehead, brushing back some stray tendrils of hair which had escaped.

"Maybe just a bite."

Travis was shocked to see how badly affected Ellen had been by the news. He was at a loss as to what else to say.

"Thanks," Ellen caught his hand.

"For what?" Travis was mystified. He'd done nothing – bar ordering food she didn't want.

"For being here. This is too much to take in… if I'd been alone… Having you here makes all the difference." She smiled – a smile that lit up her face before it disappeared again.

If we weren't here, Travis thought. If I hadn't been around to take Ellen away, she might have been in the shop when… His skin grew cold at the thought. He'd told Ellen they'd probably only meant to scare her, but that's not what he really thought. Jenny had handed the phone to Mike, and like Travis, Mike had taken a dimmer view of the fire. It was highly unlikely it had been caused by the candle. Whoever set the fire had meant business. What they hadn't counted on were the automatic sprinklers. Sure the place was a mess, but if it hadn't been for those sprinklers, the whole row of shops could have gone up. Ellen was right about that.

There was no question of lovemaking that night. Travis gathered the distraught Ellen to him, and wrapped in each other's arms, they both endured a fitful sleep, till the early sunlight began to stream in soon after five.

"Time to get up, sweetie," Travis gently stroked Ellen's cheek, seeing her morning smile fade as she remembered.

She sat up with a start. "The fire… oh my… when can we leave?"

"As soon as you can be ready. The ferries start in just over an hour, but we should have something to eat first."

"I think it would choke me. Maybe a coffee, then we can stop somewhere?"

"Sure thing," Travis agreed, resolving to grab a sweet roll along with a coffee on the way out. He'd noticed them in the foyer the day before. That should last him for a bit, because Ellen was in no mood to delay.

As they rode south, Travis could feel Ellen's arms gripping his waist as if holding on to a life raft. There was an urgency about her clasp that hadn't been there on the trip north. He wanted to cover her hands with his, to comfort her, tell her everything would be fine, but he couldn't do any of those things. The bike needed his full attention, and he wasn't at all sure everything *would* be all right, far from it. His face became grim as he recalled all he'd heard about Balcombs. They were a corrupt outfit who'd stop at nothing to get their way – and Ellen stood in their way.

It was late afternoon when the Harley turned into Old Town.

They'd made good time with only a few stops. They drew to a halt outside *The Reading Nook* – or what had been *The Reading Nook*. As Travis helped Ellen dismount, her hands flew to her face. He held her back as she tried to run into the shop.

"Steady on. We need to go carefully." Travis pointed to the police tape and the figures moving about inside the shop.

"What… who…?" Ellen sounded hysterical, quite unlike her usual calm self.

"Wait here, Ellen. I'll check." Walking up to the tape, Travis called, "Hey there. I have the owner with me. Can we come in?"

"Sorry, sir," the man who appeared was wearing the yellow uniform of the local fire department. "Siuslaw Fire and Rescue. We can't permit you to come inside."

"I need to see the damage," Ellen appeared at Travis' shoulder and grabbed hold of his arm. He tried to shield her from the sight of devastation through the broken window, but was too late.

"Oh, my God, my shop!" Ellen wailed, and would have fallen to her knees if Travis hadn't taken her in a firm hold.

"We can't do anything here. Would you like to go home?" Travis steered Ellen back to the bike and enveloped her in a tight hug.

"Bastards," she yelled, her anger spilling over, distress seemingly forgotten.

"So, home?" Travis repeated.

Ellen climbed onto the bike, her movements jerky, almost robotic. Taking this for agreement, Travis headed to Ellen's house.

*

Ellen gazed around the room as if she was seeing it for the first time. The room was the same; it was Ellen herself who was different. This Ellen was a different person from the one who had left it so joyfully only three days ago. Then, she'd been full of anticipation of a weekend with Travis, sure she could beat the bastards who wanted to see her shop, and others like it, gone for good. Now, she didn't know what to think. Anger was her dominant feeling. How dare they treat her baby this way? But underlying the anger was a sense of desolation. All those years of work – gone in a flash.

"Are you okay?"

Ellen turned. For a moment she'd forgotten the man beside her. She'd been too consumed by the disaster to her shop, and therefore to herself, and so accustomed to managing alone. She reached out her hand, then let it fall again. What could Travis do? What could anyone do? She had to handle this herself. She just needed time – time to think, to work out a plan.

"You don't have to deal with this on your own, you know."

Ellen stared at him. It was as if he'd read her mind.

"What do you mean? It's my shop. I need to…"

"I'm here. I can help. And there's Mike and Jenny, Ron too…"

As if in response to the sound of their names, there was a knock at the door and a loud "Hello, anyone here?" Mike and Jenny burst in, Jenny immediately rushing to hug Ellen, who stood stiffly in her arms.

"I'm so sorry," Jenny whispered, her eyes full of tears. "That this should happen on my watch. At first I…"

"Jenny blames herself," Mike's voice interrupted. "But now, the firemen seem to think it's arson."

At the word 'arson' Ellen came alive. "The bastards," she shrilled. "If they think they've won, they're mistaken."

"I think we all need a strong cup of coffee." Travis said. "I'll…" He moved to the kitchen where Mike joined him, leaving the two women still hugging.

"I'm so sorry," Jenny repeated. "I can't…"

"Stop it," Ellen said, "It wasn't your fault. It would have happened anyway. If anyone's at fault, it's me for leaving you at risk. What I can't understand is what prompted them to act when they did."

"I can tell you that," Mike said, walking back into the room. "Look at this." He held up the Saturday paper, open at Ellen's media release. Local Shopkeepers Protest Development said a large headline across the page. Underneath was a photo of *The Reading Nook*, and one of Ellen.

"Oh, they published it, then." Ellen gazed in fascination at the article.

"That's probably what set them off," Travis returned and handed everyone a coffee. "Hope black's okay. Doesn't seem to be any milk.

Your photo's there too, Ellen. They'll know who you are."

"They already did. That man… in the shop… do you think…?"

"Sure do."

The four talked through the situation while drinking coffee, but a couple of hours later they hadn't reached a conclusion.

"We'd better go," Mike said at last. "The police will want to see you." He looked at Ellen.

"I'll take her in tomorrow," Travis said.

"I can…" Ellen began, before realizing she'd be grateful for Travis' support. "Okay, thanks. I'm feeling pretty useless at the moment. I'm not sure where to start."

"We'll start with a visit to the police and take it from there." Travis was taking charge, and Ellen was amazed to think she was permitting him to do so. She walked with him to the door to farewell Jenny and Mike, then stood looking at him, expecting him to follow them.

"We need to talk." Travis closed the door and pulled her down on the sofa.

What was this about? What more was there to say? The four of them had thrashed it out, considered all possibilities and failed to come up with a plausible answer.

"I'm worried about you," Travis began, taking Ellen's hands in his. His hands were warm and firm, a bit like the man himself. She found herself relaxing for the first time that day. There was something comforting about his concern. It would be easy to fall into the temptation of relying on him. But Ellen had always been self-reliant, proving resilient to whatever life threw at her. This was going to be no different. While grateful for his concern, she was about to dismiss it when he continued, "You can't stay here on your own. It's not safe. Not now that…"

"I can take care of myself," Ellen pulled her hands away and twisted them in her lap, then pulled on her plait.

"Stop it, woman!" Travis stood up and began pacing up and down. "Listen to me. Just for once, will you let go – allow someone to take care of you?"

"But…"

"No buts. Until this thing's settled you can't be here alone. And if you won't move out, then… maybe I need to move in."

"Here?" Ellen's voice rose. "You want to move in here?"

"That would seem to be the best plan. If you don't find the idea too repellent."

Ellen's hands stilled. She felt a strange sense of release. "You mean you would…?"

"Of course I would. What do you say?"

"Okay, then… just till…"

"We get this all sorted out," he concluded.

Why did she feel a rising disappointment at his words?

"That would be good," Ellen looked down at her hands, unwilling to meet Travis' eyes. This was the man with whom she had shared such passion only a few nights ago. He was suggesting moving in with her, and all she could say was 'That would be good'? But it was the circumstances, she argued silently; it wasn't as if he'd made the suggestion out of love or even lust. It was to be purely an arrangement of convenience – for her protection. Could she live with that?

"Then it's settled. I'll need to go up to Ron's to pick up some stuff, my laptop and such, but I'll be back later tonight. Will you be okay till I get back or…?"

"Of course I will," Ellen roused herself and took a few deep breaths. "There, better now. You get on. I'll unpack here and have something in the oven forwhen you return."

He kissed her cheek. "You don't need to…"

"Don't tell me what to do. You're not moving in here if you intend to boss me around. Just remember it's *my* home."

"Yes, ma'am," Travis kissed her again and gave her a mock salute as he left.

*

Now what had he done? Travis wondered as he started the bike and headed up the highway. Everything had been going well – he and Ellen slowly building a relationship, beginning to relax with each other – when this had to happen. It was a shit thing to happen to her, and he'd felt he had to move in – not out of any obligation, but to ensure her safety. He cared too much to risk anything happening to her and he didn't trust that development mob an inch. But that was the only reason. He'd been clear about that, hadn't he? He didn't want it to be a precursor to anything more permanent. Time enough for that when... well, time enough, anyway. All thought of anything more had to be in the future, the distant future. At a time when he felt he'd finally put his demons to rest.

Twenty-six

Left alone, Ellen wandered from room to room, loath to start on anything, but finally she began unpacking. She sighed as she took out the turquoise dress and shook it out, regretting the lost opportunity to wear it. Why hadn't she worn it for Travis before, she wondered? Well, no matter, she hung it back in the wardrobe. Maybe another time – when this was all over. Right now, she couldn't imagine wanting to dress up and go out ever again. It was as if a blanket of mist had fallen over her, obscuring everything.

By the time Travis returned, Ellen had managed to defrost a lasagne dish she'd cooked a couple of weeks earlier and had thrown together a salad from some remnants of lettuce, tomatoes and bell peppers. That would have to do. Luckily she always kept a good supply of mineral water in the garage. She'd need to shop next day, although the notion of doing anything as ordinary as shopping for food caused her insides to churn. She looked at the carefully set table with distaste. Her stomach still rebelled at the thought of eating.

"Wow, this looks good," Travis' bulky frame seemed to fill the kitchen. In the short time he'd been gone, she'd forgotten how very masculine he was. "You'll have some too, won't you?" he asked, as Ellen made no effort to serve herself.

"I don't…" she began.

"Need to eat something, keep up your strength. You can't fight the bastards on an empty stomach." Travis' tone was gentler than his words, indicating his real concern.

Ellen picked up the serving spoon and dished up a small helping of lasagne onto her plate, followed by a couple of lettuce leaves and half a tomato. She forked them around the plate in an effort to please him.

"Won't you try?"

She took a long drink of mineral water in an attempt to lubricate her still dry throat. It helped. She picked up some food and tentatively placed it in her mouth, chewed carefully and swallowed. She didn't choke. Another drink, another mouthful, and soon she had eaten all the food on her plate. To her surprise, she felt better.

"Better?" asked Travis, as if reading her mind. "You're still in shock. Do you have any liquor in the house?"

"You don't drink," Ellen was shaken out of her trance by his unusual request.

"It's not for me. I think you need something to help you sleep tonight – unless you have sleeping pills."

"No pills," Ellen stated decisively, "but I think there may be some Jack Daniels Mike brought over one night."

"That'll do the trick." Travis waited patiently while Ellen ferreted around in the pantry, finally emerging with a bottle three quarters full. He poured a healthy measure. "Now get that down you," he instructed, and watched while she screwed up her face and drank it down.

Ellen shuddered as the fiery liquid rushed through her, but she did feel some improvement.

"Now, bed."

Castigating herself for her weakness, Ellen followed Travis' directions and was soon tucked up in bed, Travis' large body close to hers. She fell asleep with his protective arms wrapped tightly around her.

*

"When can I …?" Ellen gazed up at the cop's impassive face. She was losing patience. They'd been here for the past hour and were no further forward. The grey-haired man opposite had taken down all their details and appeared to listen as she described the proposed development and the threats she'd received. Why were they still sitting here? Why wasn't he on the phone arranging to have someone go arrest the guys at Balcombs? That's what they did on the television shows – at least on the few she'd watched.

"That'll be all for now, ma'am," he said, putting down his pen and closing the notebook in which he'd been assiduously making notes. "My men – and the firefighters – have finished for now. You can go back in. As I said, we've identified it was arson, but there's no evidence as to who was behind it. Might have been some kids out for kicks. But the investigation will be ongoing."

"Ongoing?" Ellen felt Travis' firm hand on her shoulder, preventing the outpouring of rage that was boiling up in her. "Right, we're out of here." She picked up her purse and followed Travis out of the room, and into the street where she began to vent.

"What the hell do they think they're doing? Young kids, my ass! It's obvious to anyone with any sense, who's behind this," she fumed. "And they're going to let them get away with it. Just like they've done before. I… I…" She looked around for something to punch, but Travis was the nearest object, and he didn't deserve her anger. It subsided as quickly as it had erupted, and she slumped against her car. "What are we going to do?"

"First we're going to check out the damage. He said we can go in, but be prepared for a shock. Then we're going to have lunch to talk about it. You barely had any breakfast, and I need you firing on all cylinders today."

Ellen regarded Travis with something akin to respect. Here was someone who was on her side, who cared what happened to her and her shop. And he was right – she did need to keep her strength up. She'd be no good to man or beast if she became sick from lack of nourishment. And, she was beginning to feel some hunger pangs.

"Right," Ellen agreed, seeing a surprised look on Travis' face. "But don't think I'm always going to give in so easily."

They drove over to the shop to find the tape gone and the window boarded up. The place had a bedraggled air about it, like a crumpled old man.

"My poor shop," Ellen sat in the car, unable to move, then something seemed to snap inside her. She leapt out. "Let's do this."

Travis followed, a few paces behind, a solid presence, should Ellen find the sight that awaited her too much to cope with. She was grateful to him for being there for her, grateful she wasn't facing this alone. She pushed the door open and tentatively stepped inside.

It was a mess. Ellen walked carefully, stepping over damp ashes and sodden books, holding her hand over her nose to mask the acrid smell biting at her nostrils. Her eyes stung and began to water, whether from the smell or tears, she wasn't sure. Probably both. She heard Travis' indrawn breath immediately behind her and turned.

"Pretty awful, isn't it?" She moved on, heading for her office at the rear of the shop, stepping over puddles and piles of paper, touching the soaked, and half burnt objects that used to be comfortable armchairs. But as she moved farther in, she discovered the damage became less.

"Look, Travis," Ellen picked a couple of books from a shelf. "These have only a little smoke damage," her voice began to sound more hopeful. "And these…" she moved closer to the back of the shop, "these have hardly any damage at all." She turned to her companion with a teary smile. "It could have been worse."

Travis nodded. "Your office seems to have survived untouched."

"Pretty much." Ellen picked up a sheaf of papers which had fallen to the floor and turned on the computer, watching with relief as it booted up as usual. "First, lunch as you suggested, then we need to get this place cleaned up and tidied."

"Today?" Travis seemed surprised by her urgency. "I thought…"

"What? That I was going to sit around feeling sorry for myself?" She shut down the computer, stepped out of the office and stood, arms on her hips, her eyes roaming around the room. "With a bit of help, we can get the worst of it done in a few days – get rid of the mess and mop up the water. Then we'll need to get rid of the smell." Ellen covered her nose. "But, after that, it'll be a matter of fixing up the ceiling, painting and restocking. It can be done."

Travis gazed at this re-energized Ellen, his eyes reflecting the amazement he clearly felt at her fast rebound from the disaster. "I'll help, of course, but who…?"

"Jenny and Mike said they'd pitch in, and we may be able to talk Ron into helping too, given that Coralie is right next door," she said slyly. "Talk of the devil…"

At that moment Coralie herself pushed open the door, almost gagging at the smell. "Yuk, what a shambles!" She stepped gingerly across the floor to join Ellen and Travis. "So this is what we can expect? I guess we don't have an option. We'll have to give in."

"Not on your life," Ellen was galvanized into responding. "I'm not beaten, and I hope you're not either. I'll be up and running again before you know it."

"You will?" Coralie looked around with a pained grimace, as if trying to imagine the shop restored to its former glory and failing miserably.

Ellen turned to Travis. "One more thing before we leave. I'll call to arrange for the window to be replaced. I expect it'll take ages for the insurance to come through, but I need my shopfront. I'll aim to have a fire sale on the weekend. Some of the books aren't too badly damaged. They can be sold at reduced prices, and it'll show everyone I'm still in business."

"But the shop…" Travis gazed around once again as if trying to picture how it might look by the weekend.

"Not in the shop. No, we'll hold the sale on the sidewalk – a sidewalk sale, that's what I'll have. As soon as the new window goes in I'll put up a sign." Satisfied with her decision, Ellen nodded. "Now, I'm starving, let's get some lunch."

*

"That was Ellen." Jenny put down the phone.

"How is she today? She was pretty spaced-out yesterday." Mike lowered the paper he'd been reading.

"Surprisingly good. She and Travis have been to the shop, and she's planning to start the clean-up soonest, even to be back in business by the weekend with a sale."

"She's a strong woman, but can she be serious? The place must be in a terrible state."

"Seems to be. I said we'd go down and help. We did offer yesterday, remember?"

"Sure, but hadn't envisioned it would be quite so soon. The police are okay with it?"

"Must be if they let her back in. She said the damage could be worse. Sounded like the old Ellen. She and Travis have just had lunch and are heading back there when they've been home to pick up some stuff. She seems pretty organized – she's arranged for the window to be replaced and rented a trash dumpster, whatever that is."

Mike laughed. "I think you'd call it a rubbish skip. I came across that term back in Oz. I had to ask what it was."

"Right, and they say we all speak English. Well, I said we'd join them and be available for as long as needed. That okay by you?"

Mike looked longingly through the study door at his computer, sitting there waiting for his return. "Sure. We can't let the two of them do it on their own. I can be ready in five."

"Make it ten. I need to change first." Jenny looked down at her neatly pressed jeans and fresh pink striped shirt. "Old clothes are the order of the day if we're going to be splashing around in ash and muddy water."

"Might be useful to pack a few face masks too. Bet the stench is pretty high."

"Good thinking."

It was half an hour before the pair set out for Florence. They'd packed a couple of buckets and scrubbing brushes along with some rubber gloves, and Mike had found some facemasks left over from a painting job.

"What do you think about Travis and Ellen?" Jenny asked as they drove down the highway.

"I don't... think of them, that is," was Mike's reply.

"Oh, men! I think it's nice she's found someone – someone like her, I mean. He was very attentive yesterday. It's what Ellen's been needing," she smiled smugly.

"Now you've highjacked me, you want everyone to pair up. It won't work. Not everyone is as easy game as I was."

Jenny punched Mike gently on the arm. "Easy game? That'll be right. We circled each other like a pair of angry dogs for a while," she sighed as he took her hand, remembering how it had been her godmother's accident which had brought them together initially. Then the search for her birth mother. She smiled fondly at her companion. "I've been lucky. I'd like Ellen to find what I have."

"Hmph." Mike drove on in silence.

*

Ellen and Travis stood at the open door, wondering where to begin. The stench was unbearable. Travis couldn't believe Ellen wanted to start on this today. Her recovery this morning had been nothing short of a miracle – the despairing and grief-stricken woman of the previous night, who'd cuddled up to him for comfort, had turned into a dynamo of action. He wasn't sure how they were to get any work done, and was questioning the wisdom of Ellen's decision, when a car drew up behind them.

"Hi there," Jenny called. "Need some help? The reinforcements are here."

Ellen's eyes lit up when she saw the facemasks Jenny and Mike were unpacking. "Why didn't we think of that?" she exclaimed, fitting one around her mouth. "This is good," her voice came out strangely muffled. "We can get on now."

"Thanks, guys." Travis was grateful for their arrival. Two extra pairs of hands would certainly make things go faster, and the facemasks were a godsend. It would have been impossible to stay inside for long without them. Hearing a loud roar behind them, Travis turned round. The roll-off dumpster had arrived. Wow, that was quick! Ellen really knew how to get things moving – the right people to call.

"Heard about your fire," the man unloading the metal container shook Travis' hand. "Hell of a thing to happen. Did they find out who did it?"

"Not yet," Travis' lips tightened, then relaxed into a grim smile. "But they will. I'm sure about that," he lied.

"No luck, then?" Mike came closer and spoke quietly in Travis' ear.

"None," Travis' voice was just as low. "No evidence, they say. But we know the culprits, though there's no way of proving it. They're a wily bunch. Are you any closer to finding any historical evidence?"

"Not yet, but I haven't given up. Neither has Ellen, it seems," he nodded to the shop where the two women, facemasks in place, scarves tied around their hair and wearing rubber gloves, had begun shovelling up piles of burned offerings.

"No." Travis scratched his head. "I thought the fire had finished her, but here she is, planning a fire sale on the weekend, and determined that *The Reading Nook* will rise again – a phoenix from the ashes."

"Hey, what's keeping you two? Are we going to have to do all the work?" a voice echoed out from the shop, followed by Jenny with a load of sodden paper. She deposited it in the dumpster and disappeared back inside.

"Better join them, pal. Show them what a real worker can do," Travis said, and the two men walked into the shop.

*

"Phew. Well, we've made a good start," Ellen wiped her brow and examined the state of the floor.

"Here, you're covered in ash," Travis dampened the corner of a rag and wiped it off her face. "I think we've done enough for today. Thanks for all your help," he directed his words to Jenny and Mike, who were standing beside two empty pails. They'd been refilling them with clean water all afternoon as the water in them quickly became black from dirt and ash.

"No worries," Jenny waved her hand in the air. "Sorry, you don't say that here, do you? No problems, then. Guess you want us back tomorrow?"

"Please," Ellen said. She looked at Travis. "I need to get out of these clothes and do some shopping if we're going to eat for the next few days." Seeing Jenny's surprised expression, she added, "Travis offered to keep me company in case they come sniffing around home – purely a precautionary measure." She tried to avoid Travis' eyes, which she was sure were twinkling.

Mike coughed and threw a glance at Jenny.

"It's not what you think," Ellen remonstrated tensing, then ran out of words and looked beseechingly at Travis for help. To her annoyance, he threw an arm around her shoulders and tugged on the end of her plait.

"My new housemate," he declared. "A sight better looking than her brother, don't you think?" At his words Ellen's tension evaporated, and they all began to laugh.

"Where *is* Ron?" Jenny asked. "Thought he might be helping too."

"He's promised to come tomorrow. Had to do something for Mom and Dad today, he said. I should give them a call."

"Later." Travis steered her outside with Jenny and Mike. "You've done enough. Let's get home and settled before you call. You'll sound fresher then. You don't want to speak with your mom when you're tired out."

"You're right, of course. She'll only worry – and she has enough to worry her these days, without my adding to it." Ellen looked serious for a moment, then smiled as Jenny hugged her and Mike gave her a peck on the cheek, before they left.

"They're good people," Travis reflected, while Ellen locked up, glad her door had survived the flames.

After a quiet dinner, Travis pulled Ellen down on the sofa, where she lay with her head on his lap. He slowly undid her plait and, wrapping his fingers in her hair, began to massage her head. Ellen relaxed, luxuriating in the feel of his fingers kneading away the pressures of the day. She recognized she'd been operating on overdrive all day, ever since the visit to the police station. It was so soothing to be comforted in this way. She murmured her pleasure and was reaching up to clasp Travis' hand when there was a loud rapping at the door.

"What?" Ellen sat up, her hair going every which way. She smoothed it back and checked her watch, wondering who could be disturbing their peace at this hour.

As the door opened, Ron rushed in, his face white. "It's Dad," he dropped down into a chair. "I've been there all day. Mom's at her wit's end. Oh, Ellen, we have to do something about Dad."

Twenty-seven

"Steady on, pal," Travis patted Ron's arm. "Sounds like you need a coffee. I'll make some while you talk with your sister." He squeezed Ellen's shoulder on the way past.

Left alone, the brother and sister were silent. Ellen looked at her brother with widening eyes. "What's wrong with Dad? Has he had a relapse?" Her heart was thumping rapidly and her mouth drying up again. Surely enough had happened already? Dad was getting better, wasn't he?

"Dad's fine physically – almost too fine."

"What do you mean?"

"He's regained his strength all right. Fit as a fiddle, it seems. But his mind… these lapses Mom told us about…"

"I know," Ellen interrupted. "I've seen one of them. He just seems to lose it for a moment, then he's back again, as if he'd never been gone."

"That's it. Well, Mom says it's gotten worse. He's gone for longer, and even when he's back, she says he's a different person – more violent, more… more sexual," Ron reddened, having to talk like this about his father. "Mom didn't want to tell me, but I caught her crying and made her explain." Ron cleared his throat. "Ellen, Mom's scared to be alone with Dad."

Ellen felt the blood draining from her head. She turned cold and started to shiver. Not this – on top of everything else.

"Coffee up," Travis returned bearing three mugs of coffee. "Shit, what's up? What have you been saying to her?" He faced Ron, his voice filled with anger. "Hasn't Ellen had enough to deal with without your adding to it?"

"Leave him alone, Travis please. He's had a shock too. Tell him, Ron."

Travis sat silently while Ron repeated what he had told Ellen, concluding with, "We need to do something. We can't allow Mom to continue like this. Who knows what might happen if…"

"It's too much," Ellen groaned. "How can we… is Mom…?" She made to rise, but Travis put out a restraining hand.

"Let Ron talk, and drink your coffee. You're suffering from shock again."

"I'm going back there," Ron continued. "I only left to come here and tell you. Dad was asleep when I left, but he hasn't been sleeping too well nights. Tends to fall asleep in the afternoon – in front of his favorite TV show," he gave a grim smile. "Then he's awake when *we* want to sleep. He's been keeping Mom awake too, which is why I want to be there. She needs her rest. She's worn out with worry."

"Hell," Travis raked a hand through his hair. "Is there anything we can do?"

Ellen threw him a grateful glance. He'd been a mountain of strength to her over the fire, and now he was offering to help with their parents' troubles, but it wasn't his problem. "Thanks, Travis but it's down to Ron and me. They're our parents."

Ellen knew she was shutting Travis out, but, despite – maybe even because of – their new closeness she wasn't ready to have their relationship subjected to her mom's scrutiny just yet, especially when Dad was like this. She noticed his grim look and slipped her hand into his, hoping the gesture would soothe him. She turned to face her brother.

"Ron?"

"We…el," Ron hesitated. "I think the time has come…" He gave Ellen a sad look. "I know it's hard, sis, but I think we need to find somewhere else for Dad to live."

"You mean?"

"A nursing home – one where they can cope with people like him."

"People like him? It's our dad you're talking about. He's had his faults, no question, but…" she began to sob.

"Get it all out," Travis took Ellen in his arms, regardless of Ron's presence and cradled her. Ellen heard Ron rise to go.

"No need to see me out. I'll…"

Ellen heard the door close, but it was some time before she raised her head.

"You okay, babe?"

Ellen smiled through her tears at the old-fashioned term. She'd always believed men couldn't handle tears, and as someone who prided herself on maintaining a positive outlook, she'd dissolved into weeping in his presence too many times recently.

"I will be." She sat up and tried to wipe her eyes with her hand.

"Need a tissue?" Travis looked around aimlessly as if expecting a box of tissues to somehow appear.

"I'll be fine. It was just… on top of everything else. I sensed this was going to happen to Dad, but he could have picked a better time," she said, finally. "How can I do it all?"

"There's no need for you to do it all," Travis reminded her. "You're not on your own here."

"No," Ellen took the hand Travis held out. He squeezed hers, then held it to his mouth and kissed it. "I have you – and Jenny and Mike. I have a lot to be grateful for. But I'll need to go over there tomorrow, and there's the shop, the window…"

"No need to worry. You do what you have to. I can deal with the glaziers, and the three of us will do fine without you there." He squeezed her hand in both of his.

"Thanks." Despite all that was happening around her, Ellen felt a warm glow suffuse her body. Everything was going to work out. It might not happen immediately. She sensed there were going to be more hurdles to cross before the end, but work out it would.

*

After another restless night, Ellen was up at the crack of dawn. Breakfast over, she prepared to drive to her parents' home. "You're sure you'll be all right?" she fussed, picking up her purse.

"I'm sure," Travis gave her a long hug, then held her away from him. "You're looking great, babe. You blow my socks off!"

Ellen inspected the clothes she'd thrown on in her rush to get ready, realizing she'd automatically dressed in the tight jeans and one of the figure-hugging shirts she'd taken north with her. "The new me," she said hurriedly. "I'm off. I'll see you…" She reached up to give Travis a peck on the cheek only to be caught up in his arms again.

"It'll be fine, and we'll be working away. Take as much time as you need."

He patted her butt as she left, leaving the warm imprint of his hand. She'd need all the warmth she could get, to help her face what awaited her.

On the drive over, Ellen mentally prepared herself. It was all very well for Travis to remind her she wasn't alone, but as far as her parents were concerned, she'd always been the one they relied on. Correction, the one Mom relied on. Dad hadn't depended on anyone. He'd never admitted to needing help. Thank goodness, Ron seemed to have turned over a new leaf lately. Maybe Coralie was a good influence. But she couldn't think about that now. She started to itemize things to do – check with the doctor, talk with Mom, and Dad too, she expected, though that could prove difficult if Dad was being as obdurate as Ron intimated. Then they'd need to check out nursing homes. She grew cold at the thought. She'd always despised people who took what she'd always imagined was the easy way out and incarcerated their olds in these places. Maybe she'd been too hasty in her judgment. She sighed.

Ellen was no further forward in her thinking when she parked in her parent's driveway, and spied Ron standing outside with a cigarette in his hand. "Thought you'd stopped," she greeted him.

"I have," he threw it on the ground and stamped on it. "Waiting for you – and the doctor. Mom finally agreed to ring him, and they promised he'd make this his first call."

"Mom didn't want…?"

"It's not Mom, it's Dad. He makes such a fuss. Says he doesn't want any of these foreign doctors who don't know what they're doing treating him."

"He hasn't lost his bigotry, then?"

"No way, still the same old Dad in lots of ways. Glad you're here, sis.

You could always get around him. Dad's little girl."

"Not so little these days," Ellen laughed grimly. "Well, let's go in."

*

"Ellen!" Rita turned from the sink and dried her hands before hugging her daughter. "Ron said you were dropping by."

Ellen raised her eyebrows at Ron behind her mother's back. So she was supposed to be just 'dropping by'? Ron had given her the impression Mom had been fully aware of the import of her visit. Maybe the new leaf was only half turned, after all. She decided to play it cool.

"Ron tells me you've called the doctor. How's Dad?"

"Not so good," Rita began to twist the corner of her apron, then sat down and started to smooth the already pristine tablecloth. "He's… he's…oh, Ellen, I'm at my wits' end." Her eyes began to mist up. "He's not himself… no, not at all." She shook her head.

Ellen patted her mom ineffectually on the back and looked at her brother over her mom's head, mouthing, "Coffee," to the loose-limbed fellow standing on the other side of the room.

Quick on the uptake, Ron moved. "Coffee. Ellen, Mom?"

"Good idea, Ron. That would be great."

"There's some cookies…" Rita made to rise.

"Ron can find them, Mom. You sit there and let him do it. I hear he's back staying here again, too?"

"Yes. With your dad… I needed someone… Ron's been very good. And that Coralie's a lovely girl."

Ellen did a double take. Coralie? Mom had met Coralie? She was at a loss for words, but it didn't matter as Rita continued,

"She came over to see Ron the other night – brought a nice apple tart she'd baked too. None of that shop-bought stuff. Have you met her?"

Ellen swallowed. This was the last thing she'd expected. "Yes," she stuttered. "She has the shop next door, the hair salon."

"That's right. She said she was a hairdresser. Made a good job of Ron's hair, don't you think?"

Rita seemed to have forgotten her angst in her eagerness to discuss Ron's new flame. But for him to have invited her here – that was unheard of.

"Ron? I thought you were making coffee?"

"Right, I'll do that and I'll check for the doctor again," he said, sliding out of the room.

Mention of the doctor grabbed Rita's attention. "Oh, dear," she said, "I don't know what your dad's going to say when he sees him. Last time, he shouted him out of the room – said he wasn't going to have any old quack trying to tell him what to do. I'm surprised he's willing to come back after the way your dad laid into him."

"That's why you pay your insurance, Mom. Did Dad…" Ellen was interrupted by Ron's return, accompanied by a good-looking young man of Middle-Eastern appearance. So this was the old quack.

"This is our daughter, Ellen," Rita hurried forward to greet him and introduce Ellen.

"Mrs. Williams, Ellen," he greeted them politely. "The patient?"

"He's in the other room – in front of the television. That's where he spends most of his time, though he's able enough." She shook her head.

"Would you like me to come with you?" Ellen asked.

"No thanks, best I see him on my own," the doctor smiled. "You said he'd deteriorated since last time. In what way?"

Rita took hold of Ellen's arm to steady herself. "He's not there half the time, doctor, and when he is, he's not himself at all – violent, more so than usual, and… and…" Rita looked at her feet as if there were words she couldn't speak.

"Well, we'll have a look at him. Through here, you say?"

When he had left, Ellen turned to her mother. "You might have introduced us properly, Mom. What's the doctor's name? I feel a fool referring to him as 'doctor' to his face."

Rita blushed. "He has one of those foreign names – they all do these days, the doctors. I can't pronounce it so I don't try. 'Doctor' suits me fine." She took her empty mug over to the sink. "I'll just hang out the wash while he's in there."

When Rita disappeared into the laundry, Ellen turned to her brother. "What's all this with Coralie? You brought her here? What were you thinking? You know Mom…"

"Steady on, sis. Get your facts straight before you lay this on me. I didn't ask Coralie to come here. I told her I'd have to move back home so we'd have to cool it for bit, and she turned up at the door, offering in hand." He rubbed his chin. "Never seen anything like it. Charmed the pants off Mom."

"What about Dad?"

"Oh, he called her a floozy, but all women are floozies to him – except you and Mom."

"And what about you and Coralie?"

"Nothing to say."

"Nothing to say? She's the first female you've shown any interest in since forever, she turns up at your parents' with an apple tart – home-made, no less – and you think there's nothing to say? Let me tell you, bro, Coralie thinks there's something to say, or she wouldn't be chasing round here with her tarts."

Ron looked down and shuffled his feet, reaching back to tug on the ponytail that was no longer there. "We…ll, we rub along fine together. She's a good sort. And she doesn't try to turn me into something I'm not."

"Ouch. And I do, I suppose?"

"Not you, but Dad…"

"Dad's never satisfied. I hope you're not letting his opinions cloud your life. Especially now he's…" Ellen saw Ron point behind her and figured their mom was returning. He'd keep.

"Is he still in there?" Rita made a move toward the door, then paused. "Do you think?"

"Best wait here, Mom. He'll talk to us when he comes back," Ellen reassured her mother. "Why don't you sit down?"

But Rita couldn't be still, she moved backwards and forwards, wiping surfaces that didn't need wiping, reorganizing shelves, opening and closing the fridge.

It was clearly driving Ron mad. "I'll just go outside for a bit," he said, leaving.

"He's gone outside to have a cigarette," Rita said. "He'd stopped, but this business with your dad. It's set him off again. He thinks I don't know, but I can smell them on him." She wrinkled her nose.

"Mmm," Ellen agreed, unwilling to offer an opinion. Mom knew exactly how Ellen felt about smoking; she'd heard her on the subject often enough. "So you met Coralie," she said, partly to give her mom something else to think about and partly out of curiosity.

"Yes, lovely girl, I think I said. Nice Ron's found someone. It's not everyone who'd take him on."

Ellen almost choked. Mom had them walking up the aisle already. And poor Ron had no idea. Well, that settled it. She was going to keep shtum about Travis. At this stage he was recognized as a friend of Ron's – nothing else.

There was the sound of a door closing, and the doctor emerged from the other room. Rita swung around like a startled rabbit, wringing her hands.

"What…"

"Sit down, Mrs. Williams," the doctor said gently, taking a seat himself. Ellen stood anxiously behind her mother, her hand on Rita's shoulder as much for her own comfort as her mother's. As if sensing something was in the offing, Ron came back in, bringing a waft of cigarette smoke with him. Ellen waved a hand around in an attempt to dissipate the odor.

"I'm afraid he seems to be deteriorating. He can be cared for at home, of course, if that's your wish, but I'd strongly recommend a nursing home – where he can have all the care he requires." The doctor cleared his throat and eyed Ellen and her brother. "He's going to be too much for your mother, the way he's going. We may have to wait for a place, but…"

Ellen felt her mother wilt under her touch. *She* was aging rapidly too – this latest development had taken her by surprise. "It's okay, Mom. We're here for you. Ron and I will help." Ellen felt weighed down by the responsibility. Although she'd always taken charge of matters at home, this was something else. This was her parents' future. Who was she to make decisions about her father's removal to a nursing home? Was she even capable of making a wise choice? But, looking at her mother and brother, she realized it was going to be up to her. Sure, Ron would help, but he would agree with her decision rather than be part of the process. She sighed as another weight fell on her shoulders. It was all very well for Maddy and Jenny – even Travis – to tell her to look to herself. But how could she put herself first, when her parents needed her so much?

Twenty-eight

It was with a heavy heart that Ellen returned to her shop in the afternoon. Amazed at the amount of work which had been completed in her absence, she almost wept. "What would I have done without you?" she cried, looking at the overflowing dumpster on the sidewalk and the empty floor space which only yesterday had been a chaotic mess.

"That's what friends are for," a smut-covered Travis greeted her. "I won't touch you like this but consider yourself hugged," he said, pausing in the act of sweeping up some residue. "How's your dad?"

Ellen looked around for somewhere to sit. Reading her accurately, Travis led her to the office, which was still pretty much intact. She rubbed her forehead tiredly. "It's been quite a day. Dad... he's not himself. It's like Ron said. Mom's afraid to be alone with him, and the doctor recommended a nursing home, so..." her voice broke, "Ron and I have spent the past few hours visiting possible homes, checking them out to find whether they have places – and if we could bear to have Dad live there."

"And your mom? If she can't be alone with him?"

"Coralie stayed with her." Seeing the question in Travis' eyes, Ellen said, "Don't ask. Anyway we've found somewhere. It's a nice place, as these places go, and they can take him next week," she added sadly. "I just wish..." But what she wished remained unspoken when Jenny came into the office and rushed to hug her, while Travis disappeared muttering something about cleaning up.

"I've rid myself of the worst of it," she said, "and you look as if you need a hug. We're done for today." She suited her action to her words, wrapping her arms around her cousin.

"Thanks." Ellen was worn out.

"Did you see your new window? It looks great."

"No." Ellen realized she'd walked right past it. She rubbed her eyes. "Sorry, I must be more tired than I thought."

"We'll clear up here. Travis can take you home. See you tomorrow."

"You don't need…" Ellen began.

"We want to," Jenny interrupted and seemed about to continue, but Travis appeared smelling of soap.

"All ready now," he dropped a kiss on Ellen's forehead. "Now, little lady, I think you need some fresh air. How about we take a walk?"

"A walk?" Ellen asked weakly, wondering if her legs would hold her up to even walk out of the door. The trials of the day seemed to be suddenly taking their toll, and her former energy had disappeared.

"A walk," he repeated, taking her arm, "along the boardwalk, and you can tell me all about it."

Although her legs still seemed to be refusing to function properly, Ellen did relish the idea of reporting her day to Travis, so she agreed and they started off, arm-in-arm. As Travis had suggested, she found the fresh air did help, and discussing her day with its attendant challenges proved the axiom that a trouble shared is a trouble halved. By the time they stopped to lean on the white-painted metal rail, Ellen was feeling much better. "So," she concluded, "Ron will stay with Mom till next week, and we'll all go to see him settled in." She bit her lip. "It's going to be hard. I never thought… but Mom's taking it pretty well. We haven't broached the subject with Dad yet. Not sure how to do that. He won't want to go." She shook her head as if to rid herself of the image of her dad resisting the move. She gazed down into the water. "I feel we're treating him no better than an animal that's gone rogue."

Travis' arm snaked around her shoulders and squeezed. "My poor darling, you're only doing what you know you have to. You say you've found a good nursing home for him, and your mom can go each day, at least to start with, so he won't feel too isolated. There'll be others there, too, remember. People he can talk with, maybe even make friends? They'll look after him there, and if he's…" Travis hesitated as if unsure how to put it.

"He's not with it a lot of the time," Ellen finished for him. "I know, I know. But Dad was such a strong man – physically and mentally. It's so hard to see him fade away like this." She closed her eyes to dismiss the image of her dad as she'd last seen him, a sad, confused version of the man she knew. "You're right. It'll be fine, I know it will. And I have to think of Mom too. It'll be much easier for her not to have him ranting at her day in and day out, plus all the other stuff."

"Shall we go back now?" Travis suggested, and they turned as one to return to the shop, where her car and his bike were parked.

"Are you okay to drive?"

"Of course I am," Ellen's voice regained its usual strong tone. "I drove over from Mom's, didn't I?" Oh, dear, she thought, I'm talking about the house as if Dad was already gone – as if he's been rubbed out of the picture of the family home.

As they made their separate ways to Ellen's home, Ellen realized that, with all the worry over her dad, she'd completely forgotten the threat to herself and the shop. But it hadn't gone away. She had a fleeting thought that maybe they'd been too quick to replace the window – maybe Balcombs would recognize it for the defiant act it was and wreak more havoc. She found that, at this point, she didn't really care. Let them do their worst. She'd keep bouncing back, like a rubber ball. She hummed to herself, feeling unperturbed for the first time that day.

*

When they arrived home, Travis took over. He poured Ellen a glass of wine and settled her on the sofa with some soft music playing, while he prepared dinner. I could get used to this, she thought. She couldn't remember having been treated so well by a man – ever. Soon the smell of barbecued meat filtered through the house. Ellen gave a wry smile. Although not a vegetarian, she really wasn't a meat eater. Her parents had given her the barbecue one Christmas and she used it for the occasional fish dish, or maybe chicken kebabs. Travis must have sneaked out to buy the steak sometime during the day to surprise her, bless him, so she'd make an exception tonight. It would be warm enough to eat outside on the round wooden table set by the kitchen door.

The meal over, Ellen and Travis sat in the twilight, watching the setting sun.

"Thanks. That was a great meal. You're right – you *can* cook," Ellen said.

"Maybe not your usual fare," Travis apologized. "I raced out at lunchtime full of good intentions, but when I reached the store my mind went blank, so I got the old favorite."

"It was lovely, especially the salad," she complimented him, having thoroughly enjoyed the mixed leaf salad with tomatoes and croutons.

"That came ready mixed, I'm afraid. But I did want to show you I'm not a complete dud in the kitchen."

"Far from it."

They sat silently for a time, then, curious, Ellen asked, "What about *your* folks? Are you close?" From the red flush that began at Travis neck and spread upwards, Ellen could tell she'd touched a raw nerve, and immediately regretted her question.

Travis played with his knife and fork, picking them up, laying them down, then placing them carefully back on his empty plate. "Not close, no." He gazed off into space for so long she thought that was all he was going to say. Then he met her eyes and spoke again, "Not like you and your folks. We never did live in each other's pockets, but we saw each other regular – and they loved Ricky. Their grandson was the apple of their eye. We went for lunch every Sunday, regular as clockwork."

"So they're in California?"

"Sure are."

Ellen waited through another long silence.

"They took his death bad," he said at last, his voice so low Ellen had to strain to hear it. "I couldn't handle it – their grief. Broke me up, and there was nothing I could do. That's when I left."

"And you haven't…?"

"Seen them since? No. Been on the road till I came here."

"Don't you want to? To at least get in touch with them?" Now Ellen had started, she couldn't let go.

"What's the use," Travis shrugged. "Ricky's still dead. I still can't help them. Better to let be. They're better off without me."

"I don't accept that. Look what I've just been through – am still going through. What if…" A thought struck her. "Do you have any brothers or sisters?"

"Just me."

"So…?"

"Leave it, will you," his voice cracked with emotion.

Ellen was dismayed. She was sure his parents would welcome him with open arms, but knew now was not the time. He'd made progress in his time here, but wasn't ready for a reconciliation with his mom and dad. The very mention of them had the effect of pushing him into a corner – the curtain which had opened to reveal the real Travis was threatening to close.

"I'll clear. You cooked, so sit where you are. Coffee?"

There was no reply as Travis continued to gaze into space. Ellen deftly collected the plates, platter and empty salad bowl and took them into the kitchen to brew coffee, making sure she left Travis plenty of time to recover his equilibrium, before carrying out the drinks.

"Here we are." She set the mugs down and settled herself, legs curled up under her.

Travis started as if coming back from some faraway place. He appeared pleased to see her there, almost as if he'd forgotten where he was. "Mom and Dad," he said, "they'd be a bit like your folks in age, but Dad is the quiet one. Mom rules the roost."

Ellen remained silent and allowed him to talk. Now that he'd started, it was as if the cork was out of the bottle, and he couldn't stop. He reminisced about his lonely but happy childhood, his parents' despair when he was called up for Vietnam, their delight when he returned safely, then his marriage to Allie, who they loved like the daughter they never had. But, according to Travis, the icing on the cake was when Ricky was born. They had doted on their grandson, making it even more of a tragedy when, not only their daughter-in-law was taken from them, but also their pride and joy.

Somewhere, during this conversation, Ellen had moved closer to Travis, so by the time he'd stopped talking, she was curled around him, her arms around his waist and her legs wrapped around his. She stroked his forehead and leant her head to his. They sat quietly as the sun dropped below the horizon, and the evening began to cool down.

*

Next morning, after leaving Travis at the shop and accepting his warm hug of comfort, Ellen made her way again to her parents'. She spent the drive wondering how they were going to break the news to her dad, but needn't have worried. Rita had thought of a solution.

"We'll tell him we need to have some work done," she explained to Ellen as they sat at the kitchen table over their morning coffee. "He'd find it really distressing to be here when the supposed tradesmen are working, so he's to have a little vacation."

Ellen's jaw dropped. When had her mother become so calculating? "And what are you having done that's going to be so disruptive?" she asked.

"Rewiring," Rita explained smugly. "He's always been going on about it – when he was himself. It's an old house." She looked around. "So it's believable."

And not too far from the truth, Ellen thought, but kept her thoughts to herself. "So who's going to tell him?" she asked with a sinking feeling in her stomach, knowing before she spoke what the answer would be.

"Well, Ron and I," Rita began. "We thought you'd be the best person. No," she continued, obviously seeing Ellen's look of dismay, "You're his favorite. He'd take it best from you. We made the lights and the television flicker a bit last night to soften him up to the idea."

"You what?" Ellen couldn't believe her ears.

"It was Coralie's idea," Rita added. "She's good with your dad. She came up with the idea."

"So why doesn't she tell him too?" Ellen muttered under her breath.

"What, dear?"

"Nothing, Mom. I'll go through now, shall I?"

"That'd be good. He's usually more lucid in the mornings. It's later he gets…"

Ellen rose and reluctantly made her way to the living room.

"Morning, Dad."

"Is that my little Ellen?" Dick's eyes moved from the television to focus on his daughter.

"How's the program?" Ellen indicated the screen with her chin.

"Fair. They don't have the same programs these days. Not like they used to." He turned down the volume. "This game show's rubbish. Stupid compere, stupider guests."

"Same old Dad." Ellen was relieved to find her dad much as he'd been the past few months, with little sign of his current decline.

"Hear you had a few problems last night."

"Sure did. The damn service went down just as…" He was all set to bluster on, when he stopped dead, his eyes glazing over.

Ellen waited.

"Where was I? Oh, it's you, Ellen."

"You were telling me about how you lost your program last night." She crossed her fingers. "Seems that problem with the wiring – the one you've been complaining about for years – it's gotten worse. And Mom… well, she's finally decided we need to do something to fix it."

Dick looked blankly at Ellen. It was so difficult when he seemed to be quite normal, but she knew his mood could change in an instant. She ploughed on, while he was still with her.

"We don't want you to be troubled by all the noise and mess," she hesitated, then finished quickly, "so we've arranged for you to have a little vacation while it's all going on."

"Hmph." Dick turned up the volume again and spun round to face the screen completely ignoring Ellen. She stood there, helplessly for a few minutes, watching her father – the man she'd always respected and looked up to, realizing that man had gone for good. She sadly left the room.

"Well?" Rita was waiting anxiously for Ellen's return.

"I don't know, Mom. He was there, then he wasn't. When I told him, he turned the sound up again and ignored me." She pulled on her hair. "I don't know if he took it in."

"Well, you tried, honey. That's all we can do. Now will you be staying today or…?"

"I really should get to the shop. I can't leave it all to the others. It *is* my responsibility. They've been really good, but…"

"You get away. Ron's here. We'll be fine. Didn't you say you had a sale coming up on the weekend?"

"Yes." Ellen was conscious of all the things she needed to do before that. The floor had been almost done yesterday, but she still needed to sort out the remaining stock – all that hadn't been bad enough to throw out. She had to decide what could be left in stock and what was saleable on the weekend. It would take the rest of today and probably a good part of tomorrow. Then she'd need to organize for tables to set everything out on. She wondered if she was trying to do too much. No, it had to be done. It would show everyone – Balcombs included – she wasn't finished, far from it. She knew it would take longer for the shop to become functional again, but this sale would make her point.

"I'll pop back in the morning," Ellen promised, before she left.

*

Next day, after a quick visit to her parents, Ellen was back in the shop preparing for her sale. Ron had agreed to stay with their parents until their dad left, and Coralie was going to drop in each night after work. Ellen wasn't sure how she felt about that, but the family all seemed happy with it, even Dick enjoying ranting at her for being a floozy. To Ellen's amazement, Coralie seemed to be coping with this surprisingly well.

"I've come across worse in my time," was her response, followed by, "and Ron's such a sweet guy." Ellen had boggled at that. Sweet wasn't a characteristic she'd ever attributed to her brother, but there was no accounting where love was concerned. And the pair did appear to be in love.

"No Jenny and Mike today?" Travis asked as she stepped out of the car.

"I think they've done their bit," Ellen replied. "It was good of them to come down as often as they did. We're through the worst of it." She sniffed. "The smell has almost gone."

Travis stood in the middle of the floor and scanned the room. "Still a lot to do," he judged. "You'll need a complete paint job and some carpentry too, if I'm not mistaken."

"I know that," Ellen said impatiently. "I want to get this sale over first, then the tradesmen can come in and put the place to rights. Might be a good opportunity to make some improvements." Her experienced eyes considered the layout.

"You're pretty sure you're going to win?"

"Can't imagine not."

"Well, you could be right. They haven't tried anything else. But we still need to come up with something to stop them."

"I'll think about that later. First things first." Ellen looked around again. "I'll sort out the books, and I'll need a few big tables. I want to set them outside – right in front of the window. That should draw the crowds."

"How about I check around?" Travis asked.

Engrossed in sorting books into piles, Ellen barely answered him, knowing by the sound of the closing door, he'd gone off to do exactly that. By the time he returned, Ellen was kneeling on the floor, surrounded by mounds of neatly stacked books.

"I've put them into bundles," she told him, as if he'd never left. "Depending on the degree of damage and the type of book." She sat back on her heels. "How did you go?"

"Tables organized. Bob says he has a few we can use in his back shed. I'll help bring them over early so you can set up. There's not much more we can do today. I vote we call it quits."

Ellen rose stiffly. "Wow, been down there too long," she exclaimed, stretching out her arms and legs. "You're probably right. I'd have liked to stay a bit longer, but…"

"Come on, tomorrow's another day, and you have a busy weekend coming up. You need a good rest, right away from all this."

"Yes, sir," Ellen said, picking up her purse and joining him at the door. "I'll just give Mom a quick call to make sure everything's all right," she said, picking up her phone.

"Okay if I go round to check those tables Bob mentioned?"

"Good idea," Ellen waved him off and pressed her mom's number.

"Everything's fine here," Rita assured Ellen. "Coralie's just arrived, and she's helping with dinner. She's been in to see your dad and talked with him about his 'little vacation'. Says he was in a good mood – joking about taking her with him."

"That'll be the day," Ellen laughed, but she felt a tad jealous of the way Coralie seemed to be easing herself into the family. Coralie, of all people! But, she reasoned, if it was helping – and it did appear that it was. Coralie did seem to be helping both Mom and Dad cope with this unexpected turn of events. She supposed she should be grateful for that – and she was. There was just this little niggle that said she wished it had been her.

Ellen gave herself a mental shake. She had enough to do with the sale tomorrow and Sunday. She refocused on the conversation.

"And what will you be doing after the weekend? Is the place going to be able to be used as a shop again?"

"Of course it will, Mom. We'll need to do a bit of revamping, of course. But it shouldn't be too difficult. We'll show these developers they can't keep a Williams down."

"You always were the feisty one." Ellen could hear her mother's smile over the phone. "Your dad knew that. Why, when you first set up there, he said you'd make a success of it. I was surprised they ever permitted that row of shops to be built in the first place."

Ellen, who'd been paying scant attention to her mom's talk, suddenly pricked up her ears. "What do you mean?"

"Well, back then – I would just have been a girl – but there was talk of our community putting a stop to it. Culturally significant or something like that."

Twenty-nine

"Could you repeat that?" Ellen's grip on the phone tightened.

"What did I say?"

"Something about the shop site being culturally significant in the opinion of the community. Our community?"

"Well, it seems I recall there was a bit of a fuss, but it got built anyway. Why, that's old history. Surely it can't have any bearing on today?"

"Mom, it just might… it might be what we've been looking for. Is there anyone still around who was involved back then?"

"I'd have to think. We're talking about nigh on sixty-odd years ago. Do you really think…?"

"Maybe," Ellen could feel a bubble of excitement rising inside her. This could be it – what Mike had spent hours in the library searching for without success. "Can you have a think about it, Mom – please? I know you have a lot on your mind at the moment, but if you could think of someone…"

"We…ell, I'll see what I can do. Can't promise."

"Of course not. See you soon. Love you." Ellen hung up. She couldn't wait for Travis to return. This could be it – the break they'd been searching for.

"You'll never guess?"

Travis was barely in the door when Ellen grabbed him by the arms.

"Hey, steady on. I've only been gone a few minutes. What's up? Is it your dad?"

"Mom said… oh, I can't believe what she said," Ellen's face beamed with delight. "She remembers some fuss when our shops were being built. Some question of cultural significance. Don't you see? If there was controversy back then, we could have something to go on – somewhere to start." She ran out of steam and looked expectantly at Travis.

"Hmm, might be something in it. She couldn't recall the details?"

"No, she was pretty young at the time – probably had other things on her mind, but she's promised to think about it."

"Well, that's good, sweetie, but don't get your hopes up. Now, you've a big day tomorrow."

Ellen deflated like a burst balloon. Travis was right. She oughtn't to put too much store by her mom's vague recollection, but she knew… she just knew… this was their answer.

She put it to the back of her mind, and remembering where Travis had been, asked, "What about those tables? Will they do?"

"Perfect. They're a bit dusty. Been in Bob's shed for ages, but they're a good size, and he's promised to bring them over to the shop in his pickup early tomorrow."

"Goodo. We can be there at the crack of dawn. I'll need to be, to get set up." Ellen was back in business mode. The sale was her first priority. She'd worry about everything else when it was over.

"What would you like me to do?"

Ellen gazed at Travis blankly.

"Tomorrow, I mean. I know what I want to do right now. I want…" His eyes twinkled as he moved towards her, but Ellen didn't let him finish. Her mind was elsewhere – on the next two days.

"It would be great if you could help with the pricing. I'll put the books out in sections, and we can price all the ones in each section at the same. We'll have a 99c pile, one at $1.99, $2.99 and so on. Then if we're rushed, you can help take the money. You did a good job last time," she reminded him.

"Hmm. Come here you," Travis pulled Ellen towards him, his chin on top of her head. "You know I'll do anything I can to help," he murmured into her hair. "How about we send out for pizza, then have an early night so I can give you a proper cuddle?"

"Works for me," Ellen's voice was muffled, her face pressed into his firm chest.

*

The next two days passed in a blur. The sale was even more successful than Ellen had anticipated, with many of her regular customers dropping by to learn of her future plans. This, combined with a plethora of summer tourists for the July Fourth holiday weekend– many offloaded from tourist buses bound for the sea lion caves – meant that she and Travis had little time to talk. The thought of her mother's revelations stayed at the back of her mind, waiting for the proper time to surface.

However, at breakfast on Monday morning, Ellen brought it up again. "What do you think?" she asked between bites of toast. "Can Mom be right? What if…" Her eyes glazed over at the thought of having found a solution.

"Certainly worth looking into," Travis said, gulping down the last of his coffee, wiping his mouth and stroking his beard. "Want to ride by Mike and Jenny's today? Not much doing down here unless…"

"I'd like to drop in on Mom and Dad. He's due to go in to the nursing home tomorrow, and I'm not sure if he's really taken it in – that he's going. And we haven't told him he won't be coming back," she added sadly.

"Do you want me to…? No," Travis obviously saw Ellen's consternation at the idea that he'd accompany her to her parents. "Still on the secret list? You'll have to tell her sometime."

"I know, but not yet. She has enough to cope with – Dad, and Ron and Coralie…"

"You're not ashamed of me, are you?"

"Ashamed? What gave you that idea?"

"We…ll, you did take a time to come around to accepting me as a regular guy."

"You're a lot more than that – and you well know it," Ellen threw a mock punch at him. "But you don't know Mom. She'd have us married in no time. I swear she's already planning her outfit for Ron and Coralie's nuptials?"

"Ron and Coralie? They're…?"

"No – at least not that I know of. It's just her way. Give her an inch and she'd take a mile, or in this case, show her a couple, and she'll have them in bed together."

"Well, we are, aren't we?"

"Oh, you know what I mean. I'd just rather keep it under wraps until…"

"Until when?"

"At least until Dad's settled."

"So, I'll clear up here and give Mike a buzz while you do your thing, then we can take off."

Ellen was humming to herself again as she drove. It seemed strange to be free on a day when she'd normally be in the bookshop. She drove by the shop to reassure herself all was well. *The Reading Nook* looked very sad and forlorn. But it wouldn't be for long, Ellen told herself. The painters would start tomorrow, then the other tradesmen, and it would soon be as good as new – better maybe – and she'd be back in business.

"Just popping in for a minute," Ellen greeted Rita. "I won't stay, but I wanted to check in before tomorrow. Everything okay?"

"Very okay," Rita replied with a smile. "Your dad's fine. We've packed a bag for him for his 'vacation' and we're all set for the morning. Ron says they're expecting us around ten, so if you could be here…?"

"I'll come round at nine. I'll just look in on him." Ellen opened the door to her dad's room to find him gazing woodenly into the television. The sound of a cartoon program was blaring.

"Dad," Ellen called. No response. "Dad," she called again, walking up to stand in front of him. But there was still no response. Dick was lost in a world of his own. She stumbled out of the room, unable to believe that her father, the man she'd idolized as a child, the mainstay of the family, had deteriorated into this statue-like figure, oblivious to all around him. This man wasn't her father. Her father would be shouting at her, telling her about Ron's misdeeds, mocking his entanglement with Coralie. This was a mere shadow of that man. The man who was her father was gone, gone for good.

"He's…" she sobbed, falling into her mother's arms. "Is he often like this?"

"Sometimes," Ron said from his seat at the table. "Sometimes he can be as lucid as you or me. Like he was last night. Don't take on so, sis. It's going to be all right."

"I suppose," Ellen wiped her eyes. "Well, I need to get on. We're going to ride up to Seal Rock. See Jenny and Mike." She turned to her mom. "I don't suppose you've had a chance to think any more about… No, of course you haven't. Not with Dad the way he is."

"You're wrong," Rita surprised Ellen. "It's been going round and round in my head. And it seems to me that your Uncle Jed had something to do with it. It was back when your Uncle Jed was still alive. Old man Miller ran roughshod over the community and managed to get building permission. Your dad would have remembered when…"

"Uncle Jed? Jenny's father? Oh, my God! So… it died with him? There's no one else?"

"Sorry, love. That's all I can come up with."

"Okay, well thanks for that anyway. See you in the morning."

As Ellen drove back home, her thoughts went back to the previous year when she and Jenny had discovered they were related. Jenny's youthful parents had been killed in a tragic car crash just as she came into the world. The pair had been eloping to avoid the wrath of both sets of parents who disapproved of the match between the daughter of one of the town's most powerful industrialists and the Native American rabble-rouser from the other side of the tracks. How astonishing if Jed could be the answer they were looking for.

*

"So it seems your birth dad, my Uncle Jed, was involved in trying to stop the building in the first place," Ellen related to an interested Jenny and Mike.

"What a complicated series of events," Mike exclaimed. "It's fascinating stuff, but there was nothing in any of the old papers that I could see. Maybe…" Ellen could see him trying to mentally work out the ins and outs of all of this.

"I know who might be able to help," Jenny interjected. "Maddy was here at that time. Maybe she knew what was going on. Let me give her a call and invite her up for lunch. You were intending to stay, weren't you?" She looked enquiringly at Ellen and Travis, who nodded.

"We don't have any other plans."

"Good. Let's try to get to the bottom of this."

Maddy arrived in her usual graceful way, and as soon as she sat down, Jenny gave her a potted version of Ellen's tale. "You would have been there, Maddy. Did Jed really oppose these buildings? And if so, why?"

"Oh, my dear Jenny Wren. It was a long time ago, and my memory isn't what it used to be. But I do seem to recall something. Jed was always objecting to one thing or another, especially if your grandfather was involved. Not your dad, Ellen, Jenny's other grandfather – old man Miller. He had a finger in every pie back then. It wouldn't surprise me if… but I don't really know. I wonder…"

All four had been hanging on her every word, and now waited with bated breath.

"These friends of Jed and Thea, the ones you talked with last year, Jenny. They were closer to Jed than I was. They might have known and might remember."

"Anne and Bill Huggins – of course," Jenny exclaimed. "Why didn't I think of them? They were best friends with Jed and Thea, my birth parents," she explained to Travis. "They did everything together, it seems. If there's anyone still alive who knew what Jed was up to, it'd be Bill."

"Where do they live?" Ellen sat forward eagerly.

"They're still in Florence. I have their address somewhere." Jenny rose as if to look for it.

"Hon, you can't just turn up at their door and ask them about events that happened sixty-odd years ago. Have some sense." Mike patted her knee.

Jenny sunk back into her chair. "You're right, of course."

"And we have Dad going into the home tomorrow." Ellen was trying to work out the best plan of action when Jenny spoke.

"Why don't I give them a call? They know me. I can explain what we'd like to know, and maybe you and I can visit them – later in the week, once your dad's settled in? I've been meaning to visit them since we got back, anyway."

Thirty

"Are you ready?" Jenny's cheerful voice echoed through the house as Ellen and Travis were finishing breakfast.

"Come right through – we're in the kitchen." Ellen greeted her cousin, as she stacked the plates and bowls ready for the dishwasher.

"You'll be right with Jenny, honey?" Travis planted a kiss on Ellen's forehead and gave her a hug.

"What will you be up to today?"

"Thought I'd take the opportunity to get back to the old laptop. There's a tale burrowing away in here," he tapped his head. "Might be time to put some down."

"If you're sure?" Ellen hesitated, then smiled at Jenny, who'd been standing watching their interaction with a grin on her face. "We should be back by lunchtime."

"Take as long as you like. Once I get going, I'll be lost to the world for the rest of the day. Why don't you two have lunch together after your visit?"

"Good idea," Ellen beamed at Jenny. "Let's go."

As Jenny drove carefully up to the part of town where the Huggins lived, Ellen began to quiz her about the couple they were about to visit.

"Are they the ones who formed a foursome with Thea and Jed?" she asked. "The ones who told you about 'Together Forever'?"

"Yes," Jenny replied, "Anne was Thea's best friend. They're a lovely couple. Still very alert. When I called her on Monday, she was delighted to hear from me. And," she glanced over at Ellen, "she's intrigued to meet Jed's niece."

"Did you tell her what we wanted to know?"

"Only that you had some questions about Jed we thought she and Bill might be able to help us with."

"Fingers crossed," Ellen suited her actions to her words as they sped up to the cliffs.

"Come on in," greeted the cheerful plump white-haired woman. "It's been too long. You've been back in Australia all this time? And this is Ellen, Jed's niece?" Anne ran the questions all together without giving them a chance to answer.

"Welcome back, Jenny," Bill's voice boomed in their ears. "So this is Ellen? You have a look of Jed about you. My, he was a bit of a devil, but he had a serious side. Always one for the girls, too. They all loved him."

"And he chose Thea," put in Anne.

Ellen listened, entranced. When the news of the uncle she'd never heard of had broken last year, her parents refused to discuss him. Here was a couple who had actually known him. It made her feel a bit odd – as if he'd suddenly become a real person.

She saw Jenny's understanding smile, realizing for the first time how Jenny must have felt on her first visit here. It was like stepping back in time. Not only because of the furniture, which *did* look as if it was from another era. No, it was something in the way the couple seemed to take themselves back to their youth – talking about it as if it was only yesterday.

"Now, how can we help you?" Bill asked, once they were settled in the lounge room with coffee and pastries.

"It's Ellen who needs your help this time," Jenny said.

"And you two are cousins, just fancy."

"Let the girl speak, Anne."

Ellen smiled her thanks. "It's like this. I have the bookshop in Old Town, Florence – *The Reading Nook*…"

"Oh, I think we've been in there – haven't we, dear?" Anne earned a look from her husband and buttoned her lips.

"It's under threat from a group of big developers from California, and Mom…"

"That'd be Rita Williams?"

"That's right. She had some recollection of an objection to the shops being built in the first place. She thought Uncle Jed might have been involved."

"There was something – but I don't rightly recall. Do you, Bill?"

"Jed was always involved in something or other – especially if it meant needling your grandfather, Jenny. Let me think…" Bill leant back and closed his eyes, while the others watched him in silence.

He opened them again with a start and pointed into the air. "That's it. I do remember."

Ellen moved forward in anticipation.

"Jed was actively involved in the Native American community back then, and I seem to recall there was talk of some burial ground. I wasn't involved myself, you understand." He shook his head. "Never could keep up with Jed – into everything he was. But old man Miller – your grandfather, Jenny – he was on council and managed to push it through."

"So there should be records – of the objection?"

"Doubt that. The old man was a wily one. He'd have made sure there was no evidence of his machinations."

"So we're back to square one." The information which had looked so promising had suddenly blown away, like leaves in a windstorm.

"Unless…" Bill said.

Ellen raised her chin, which had fallen to her chest.

"I wonder… Anne, do you recollect who else was in council back then?"

"They'd all be long gone," Anne said drily.

"Not the councillors. I'm talking about the staff. Wasn't there that girl? She was at school with us and left to take up a junior role with council."

"What would she know?"

"Well, she was sweet on Jed."

Ellen and Jenny sat listening to their by-play, not sure where, if anywhere, it would lead. Finally Bill slapped the arm of his chair so hard they all jumped.

"I've got it! Her name was Shirley. Shirley…" he snapped his fingers, then, "Shirley Coats, don't you remember?"

"Not really. I think she was in the year below me," Anne said apologetically to Ellen. "But you'd know," she directed to Bill. "Always noticed the pretty ones," she said.

"I noticed *you*, didn't I?" he smiled tenderly at his wife of over fifty years. "But that's who she was. And I don't think she ever married."

"How would you know that?" his wife asked.

"Seem to recall something in the paper about her, not too long ago." He appeared to think for a moment, then hit the chair again. "I know. She was in that, what do you call it? The garden column – the one where they visit people's gardens and rave on about what they've done with them. Always interesting to read what some people have managed with this useless sandy soil. Anyway that's where it was."

"So she's still living in Florence?" Ellen asked.

"Sure is. May even have a copy in the shed."

"Oh, you and your shed." Anne shook her head. "He keeps all sorts out there, waiting for a use for them – old papers, boxes, containers of all kinds."

"Never know when they might come in handy," Bill retorted. "Like now." He started to rise, but Anne stopped him with a hand on his knee.

"Not now, dear. These two young things don't have all day to hang around while you dig about out there. Once you get into your rubbish, you'll be lost for hours." She turned to face Ellen and Jenny. "Can we get back to you when Bill's had a chance to have a good look for the paper?"

"Of course you can," Jenny replied. "We should be going now. Thanks so much for the coffee, and it's been so good to see you both again." She hugged Anne and was enveloped in the warm clasp of Bill's arms.

"Don't be a stranger," he said, "And lovely to meet you, Ellen. It's been good to meet another of Jed's relatives. He was a good friend."

"You must feel free to visit again too, Ellen," Anne said, giving her a hug too.

"What a lovely couple," Ellen said to Jenny as they drove off.

"They're sweet, aren't they?"

"And they may really come up with something."

"You mean this Shirley thing? Do you really think so?"

"I have a good feeling about it," Ellen smiled to herself. For the first time in this whole development mess, she saw a glimmer of light.

"Oh, you and your feelings," Jenny laughed.

Ellen laughed with her. "Well, I wasn't so far wrong about you and Mike, was I?"

"True," Jenny was forced to admit. The two drove on in silence.

*

Travis was lost in his fictional world when a loud rapping at the door broke through his concentration. His war veteran hero was caught in a tight situation and Travis was in the process of plotting his way out of it. Cursing whoever had the temerity to interrupt his muse, he strode to the door and threw it open.

"Hey there, how's it hanging?" Ellen's brother stood there with a grin on his face.

"Ron, what brings you here? Ellen's not home, but come on in." Travis opened the door wider to allow Ron through. "Can I get you a coffee?"

"That'd be grand," Ron sauntered in and right through to the kitchen where he parked himself at the table. "Nice place Ellen has here."

"Yeah, not too shabby." Travis set about brewing some coffee, realizing he wasn't going to get back to his writing anytime soon.

"Here you go," he set a mug down and took a seat opposite Ron. "So?"

"Wanted to give you this." Ron reached into his inside pocket and drew out a mail card. "Certificated mail for you at the post office box. Thought I should drop it in, while I was passing."

"Thanks," Travis fingered the card. He'd given Ron's post office box as his forwarding address. It was anonymous enough to suit him when he figured out he needed some sort of address for his bank, publisher and such. He flipped it between his fingers, then let it lie. Probably from his agent, trying to re-ignite his muse.

"So you're still with your mom?"

"Just left her off at the nursing home. She's spending most of her time there – with Dad. It's sad to see them. He's not always with it, but when he is, he wants to go home. And she wants him home – she misses him so… But what can we do? It was too difficult. She knows that." Ron shook his head at the senselessness of old age.

"It's tough," Travis agreed, wondering, for the first time in ages what was happening with his own parents. They'd been well when he last saw them, even though overwhelmed with grief at the loss of their beloved grandson. He'd left, as much to protect himself as to save them further distress. But seeing what was occurring here – how everything could change in an instant, he began to question his hasty action. The fleeting thought that he should make some contact with them was gone again before it could take root. No, he'd done the right thing – the right thing for all of them.

"So, you and Ellen? Should I be acting big brother and asking your intentions?"

Travis grew hot. This was just what he didn't want. Ron was a pal. What kind of talk was this? Could he be serious? Intentions?

"I'm here to make sure… to protect Ellen from any further attempts at intimidation. If the guys who torched the shop know where she lives…"

"Sure, buddy. Only kidding. I'm not my dad, but just the same…"

Travis picked up Ron's cigarette packet, which he'd thrown down on the table, and flung it at him, narrowly missing his coffee.

"If that's all you want, mate…" Travis was keen to get back to his manuscript, and all this talk about Ellen was giving him the jitters. He was well aware he was tangling with Ron's sister, but for God's sake, neither of them were kids. He'd gone through that with himself before he even suggested dinner in the first place. Now they had something going, something he thought was pretty damn good, something that maybe…, but he didn't want his old buddy trampling all over it. "I'll check that out," he nodded to the Post Office card lying on the table.

"I'll be off," Ron gulped the remains of his coffee. "See you soon."

Travis returned to his computer with relief, but couldn't concentrate. His mind refused to focus on the plight of his hero. His hands lay still on the keyboard as he rewound Ron's conversation. Ellen. She was special. But was he good enough for her? He'd put the past behind him, was ready to start a new life, and it seemed to him she could have a part to play in it. If she'd have him. Whoa. Moving too fast. That's what the conversation with Ron did for him. But he and Ellen rubbed along nicely. That would do for now… should do for now.

He went back to pick up the card Ron had brought. Might as well collect that now, as he didn't seem to be capable of putting down any more words. Maybe some fresh air would clear his head.

The post office was busy, and Travis had to cool his heels. He found himself tapping his feet impatiently as he waited. What the hell was he doing here? It couldn't be anything urgent. He was tired of the messages from Don, his agent down in California, wondering when he'd have a new manuscript ready, reminding him he had a public out there. This new book was taking him in a completely different direction, not one which would appeal to his existing readers. What was Don going to make of that? Travis didn't care. It was something he had to write – to get out of his head. He was about to give up and leave, when the clerk called him to the counter and had him sign for a bulky envelope.

He took it outside, turning it over in surprise. Not from Don, then. The ink was blurred making it difficult to distinguish the sender. He walked up the block to the library and, finding an empty table, opened the envelope to shake out the sheaf of papers. He was reading them for the third time when he felt a touch on his arm.

"You okay?"

Travis looked up.

"Mike!"

"I was working over there on the computer. Checking out some historical data. Saw you come in. You're as white as a sheet. Is everything okay?"

Travis stuffed the papers into his pocket.

"Fine. Just a bit of unexpected news… from down south. It'll be right."

"Jenny's with Ellen visiting these folks about the shop. Fancy a coffee? You look as if you could do with one."

"What?" Travis was distracted. "No. Thanks, but I need to be getting back."

*

Travis waited till dinner was over and Ellen had prepared two mugs of coffee. During the meal, she'd been chatting about Anne and Bill, someone called Shirley and her Uncle Jed, but it had all gone over his head. He'd tried to sound interested, but clearly hadn't succeeded.

"What's up? You've been quiet, not like yourself," Ellen said.

He reached into his inside pocket and drew out the papers. "Received these today." He took a gulp of coffee and pushed the papers toward her.

Ellen put down her cup and picked them up gingerly. "Is this what…?" She opened them and began to read, while Travis watched a variety of expressions cross her face before she finally laid the sheets down on the table and met his gaze.

"This is preposterous. They can't… Who are these people anyway?" Her eyes flashed with anger. Travis had never seen her so worked up.

"They're Allie's parents. My in-laws… ex in-laws, I suppose." He struck the table with his fist almost causing his coffee to spill over, then dragged his hand through his hair. "I can't believe they've waited all this time and…"

"But you *were* exonerated?"

Travis heard a question in Ellen's voice causing him to do a double take.

"You don't…"

"Of course not." Ellen's voice wavered.

"I was cleared of all wrongdoing. Hell I wasn't even drunk. But Allie's mom and dad… I guess they still want to blame someone, and I'm the easiest target. The truck driver died at the scene. This civil suit… they're suing me for negligence." He dragged his hand through his hair again. "I guess I *was* driving. It *was* my fault."

"No!" Ellen's voice was strident. "I saw it. You weren't to blame. There was no way you could have avoided the accident. It doesn't matter that you were the driver; the truck driver was to blame. There was no way you could have avoided it."

"But I'm alive, and they're dead. They're all dead." Travis picked up the papers and stuffed them back into his pocket.

"What are you going to do?"

Travis hesitated, and clenched his teeth. "I guess I'll have to go down there."

"I'm coming with you."
Ellen's resolute voice echoed in his head.

Thirty-one

Ellen was packing a small case when her cell phone buzzed. Tempted to let it ring, she hesitated before answering.

"Ellen, glad I caught you. About Shirley…"

"Damn," Ellen couldn't help herself. It was important for her to visit this woman – to find out what she remembered, but this business with Travis had to take priority. "Sorry, Jenny. You caught me at a bad moment. We… Travis and I… we need to go down to California. I know the timing isn't the best." Ellen's eyes swept around the bedroom, which looked as if a tornado had blown through. "I *do* need to talk with Shirley, but maybe…"

"That's just it," Jenny's voice held more than a trace of excitement. "Mike thinks he's on to something too. You can't go just yet. We need to…"

"Shit!" Ellen dropped the sweater she was holding and pulled on a stray tendril of hair. This wasn't fair. She'd been working so hard on opposing the development, and now, when there seemed to be a breakthrough, here she was preparing to leave town. She'd thought Shirley could wait till she returned, but if Mike had found something too…

"Are you still there?"

Ellen had forgotten Jenny. "Yeah, still here. Hell, what should I do?"

"This thing with Travis. Can it wait? Surely seeing Shirley and getting this all straightened out is more important?"

"It is, but…" Ellen was torn. She was stuck between a rock and a hard place. Would Travis understand if...? But she'd been so definite last night. They'd talked for ages. He'd tried to hide it, but she knew he'd been devastated by the action taken by Allie's parents, by their notification they'd started legal proceedings against him. He'd put all that behind him, had made a new start. To have it all re-emerge like this meant he'd shrunk back into his cave. He'd become a different person, one she scarcely knew. Last night in bed, when she'd tried to comfort him, he'd turned away. She bit her lip. He needed her, or did he? Was she fooling herself?

"Can I call you back?" Ellen was suddenly unsure of what to do for the best. Had she pushed herself onto Travis by insisting she accompany him? Would he prefer to be by himself? Could he cope by himself? She gave herself a shake. Cope? Of course he could cope. He was a grown man. He'd coped for the past two years. What was so different now? But it *was* different. She knew that; knew it deep inside. She sat down on the bed and gazed into space.

"What's up?'

Ellen raised her eyes to see Travis standing in the doorway.

"You've not finished packing. Changed your mind?" He sat down beside her. "I heard the phone."

"It was Jenny."

"And?"

"She wants me to go with her to see Shirley. And apparently Mike has uncovered some information too. But it can wait." She made up her mind. "I'll be finished here in a tick, and we can be off."

"Steady on," Travis took both of Ellen's hands in his. "Is this what you really want to do? I can manage on my own, you know. I don't need you to hold my hand. I'm a big boy. Not that it wouldn't be good to have you there with me, but if you need to see this Shirley person." He rubbed his thumbs over her hands. "Did you mention her last night? I was..."

"I know. You were on another planet. Bill came up with her name yesterday. She's someone who was sweet on my Uncle Jed. Bill thought she might remember something... something about why he objected to the building in the first place. But it can wait." Ellen tried to free herself, intending to continue packing.

"I don't think so." Travis looked grave. "The timing's crappy. You need me here too. But there it is. I can't put this trip off, but you can. It's my problem. Let me deal with it my way. Might be better if I'm on my own." He withdrew his hands, and Ellen could feel him withdrawing from her mentally and emotionally too. "I'll take the bike. I'll call you." With a brief peck on Ellen's forehead, he was off.

Ellen sat looking at her half-packed bag, then with a sigh, began to put everything away again. She'd call Jenny later. She couldn't rid herself of the sense of loss Travis' sudden departure had prompted. She needed coffee.

While it was brewing, Ellen went back over the conversation with Travis, trying to reassure herself all was well. It was crazy. She felt like a teenager again. Travis hadn't chosen to leave. He'd gone in response to the proposed court action, to see if he could persuade his in-laws to drop the action or, failing that, to defend himself in court. All that would take time, time which she probably didn't have.

As she filled her mug, Ellen rationalized. They were both caught up in matters over which they had minimal control. They each needed to take care of their own challenges, and whoever finished first could help the other. Put like that, it sounded simple. But it was far from simple. She could lose her livelihood if the developer won, while Travis... She wasn't sure what the outcome might be if he was found guilty of negligence in a civil suit.

Finishing her coffee, Ellen decided to take action. Her call to Jenny was quick and to the point. She arranged to meet with her the following morning to visit Shirley, and Jenny promised to bring along copies of the documents Mike had dug up.

*

Travis had been traveling for two days with little sleep when he rode into the outskirts of Carpinteria. He stopped for a coffee at a Starbucks, while he worked out a plan of action. He felt pretty rough after his trip and knew he couldn't front up to the Dodd family or a court looking like this. So, he could book into a motel or... He stroked his beard while he thought about his parents. He didn't feel comfortable turning up at their door after all this time like the prodigal son. Maybe they knew about all this. Maybe they even agreed with Allie's folks. Shit, it would have to be a motel. He could maybe call his folks from there, sound them out, see if they even wanted to see him. He'd never felt so alone, not even those two years on the road. Oregon had made him soft, brought out feelings he'd thought gone forever. He needed to harden up again, if he was to get through this.

He stopped at the *Holiday Inn* and took a room for a week. That should do it. He could always extend, he supposed. Hefting his bags inside, he looked around. Not so dusty. He sat down and sent a text to Ellen to let her know he'd arrived. He couldn't face talking to her – not yet, not after the way he'd left. He knew he'd hurt her, going suddenly like that, but he'd needed to cut her off. He'd needed to try to regain the hard outer shell he'd sloughed off since meeting her.

After a shower and a burger and chips in a nearby restaurant, Travis felt better, though it was strange to find himself back here in California, a place he'd vowed never to visit again. He knew he had to contact his parents. A phone call would be best. He had no idea how they would respond to hearing from him after all this time. After years of believing he didn't care, he was surprised how much he *did* value their good opinion. He'd left in a rush, a broken man, tired of himself and the world. What was he now? He didn't know. But knowing Ellen had changed him – given him back the self-respect he'd lost. He hoped his parents could find it in their hearts to forgive him, forgive him for the loss of their grandson, forgive him for leaving the way he did, forgive him for being out of contact for so long. That's what parents were supposed to do, wasn't it? He knew he could have forgiven Ricky for anything, if only he'd lived. Travis wiped a tear from his eye. Damn that Ellen! He hadn't shed a tear since… He was glad she'd been forced to stay back. He needed to handle this on his own.

Back in his room, Travis took out his cell phone. He took a deep breath then hit the speed dial for his parents, one he'd kept there in case… but hadn't used. As he heard it ringing, he was tempted to end the call before it had even begun, but the sound of his mother's voice stopped him.

"Travis… Travis… is that really you?" Her voice sounded tremulous, causing him a pang of remorse.

"Mom." For a moment Travis was speechless. What do you say to your mother after two years of being incommunicado? While he was trying to find the words he heard her call out, "Tom, come quick, it's Travis – our boy is on the phone."

"Mom," he said again, his voice breaking.

"Where are you? What… Why…" Travis could hear the tears in her voice.

"I'm here. In Carpinteria. I…"

"Hello, son. Your mother's just had a shock. It's wonderful to hear from you, but do you realize how much grief you've given her by dropping off the grid the way you did? You disappeared into the blue. We lost *you* too."

"I'm sorry. What can I say?" Travis was aware how lame he sounded. He felt like a little boy again, being chastised by his father. Maybe he shouldn't have called. "I… did you…?"

"We heard the Dodds were going to sue you? Is that what brought you back?"

Travis' guilt welled up. His dad was spot on. He hadn't come back out of any filial concern. Although his parents had never been far from his thoughts, they'd been associated with his past life, the life he'd been at pains to forget. No, Dad was right. He'd only come back to save his own skin. If it hadn't been for the threat of a civil suit, he still wouldn't be here.

"Your mom would like to see you. That's a reasonable request. You'd agree, wouldn't you?"

Travis could tell from his dad's tone that Mom was the only one who'd like to see him, and that, as always, Dad would agree with her wishes. He'd always had to work hard for his dad's approval, so this was nothing new.

"Maybe tomorrow?"

"Mom says to come around eleven. She'll no doubt have some of these cookies of hers in the oven. Will we see you then?"

The call over, Travis closed his eyes, picturing his parents' warm kitchen. He wished he could avoid the confrontation he was sure would be waiting for him, but it had to be done. They *were* his parents. He couldn't ignore them, and part of him *did* want to see them. But it would bring it all up again. Who was he kidding? This whole trip was about bringing it all up again. That's what this bloody suit was all about.

After a restless night Travis was anything but ready to face his parents. He dressed carefully and headed to the family home. It looked much the same as last time he'd seen it. The house set back from the road, the large avocado tree filling the front yard and Mom's geraniums providing a splash of color along the driveway. A closer look detected the grass was a tad longer than usual, and many of the fallen avocadoes had been left to rot on the ground. Some things *had* changed.

"Travis!" His mom came running out the door to embrace him, his dad walking behind more slowly. He returned his mom's warm hug, reveling in the feeling of warmth it gave him. Extricating himself he turned to his father.

"Dad."

"Son."

Travis was surprised to find his father's arms around him.

"It's been a long time. Come on in."

With those words Travis found himself forgiven and welcomed back into the bosom of his family, far from the bitter confrontation he'd anticipated. The greetings over, he examined his parents, finding they'd aged markedly in his absence and feeling some responsibility for the changes in them.

Conversation over tea and his mom's famous chocolate chip cookies covered a variety of topics, but strenuously avoided the accident which took the lives of his wife and son. Travis also avoided any mention of Ellen or his time in Oregon, referring only to catching up with 'an old army buddy' in passing. Eventually, when he could put it off no longer, he raised the subject of the civil suit the Dodds were planning to mount.

"It's a bad business," Tom said. "I'm of the opinion they should leave well alone. It won't bring back Allie and Ricky, and it'll raise a lot of old issues, bring a lot of people a lot of grief."

Travis agreed, while his mom fussed around making sure her menfolk had enough to eat and drink.

"For pity's sake sit down, woman," Tom finally said, when he could stand it no longer. "We'll burst if we have any more. Sit yourself down and enjoy the boy's company."

Travis couldn't help but smile. Now he knew he was really back home. This was the banter he'd missed without even knowing it. They were older and frailer – even in only two years – everything around the place was looking a bit shabby, but his parents were still the same two people he'd grown up with. He began to think that perhaps this trip wouldn't be so bad. Maybe he *could* work things out.

He was dragged out of his sense of security by his mom.

"So what happens next? I mean… I don't know how these things work. Will you have to go to court?"

Travis sighed, rudely brought back to the present. "I'm not sure, Mom. I plan to see a lawyer this afternoon and take it from there. Worst case scenario, they take me for negligence and slap a compensation claim on me."

"What good will that do? It won't bring their daughter back… or our grandson," she said sadly. "But it was your wife too – and your son. Can't they see that?" Her voice rose in anger and Tom patted her shoulder.

"There, there. No sense getting riled. That won't do any good either. Is there anything we can do to help, son?"

Travis was stunned by his father's attitude. Where he'd expected censure, there was sympathy and offer of help. Had it all been in his tortured imagination? He certainly hadn't been in his right mind when he'd left so hastily.

"I'll let you know, Dad. Thanks." Travis gave his dad a hug and kissed his mom warmly on the forehead. "I'll be off, now. Need to get this stuff started."

"Do you have a good lawyer?" his father called after him. Travis nodded and waved as he fired the bike up and took off.

Later that day, sitting in his hotel room. Travis mulled over his meeting with the lawyer. Bob Johnson was a guy he'd known years ago, when he lived down here. He seemed to know his stuff and was optimistic they could talk the Dodds into dropping the case. He'd lost Travis in his talk of mediation, arbitration and other terms, but it seemed the first step was for Bob to make contact with the Dodd's man, and they'd go from there. He'd made it sound simple, but Travis had a feeling it wouldn't work out quite that way.

*

Ellen felt lost. She'd come to depend on Travis' presence. Although his staying there had started out as a means to protect her, it had evolved into something much more. Now he was gone, she wandered from room to room unable to settle. The house felt sadly empty without his presence. Only the need to solve this development issue kept her from jumping in the car and following him. After all, that's why she'd stayed, wasn't it? It couldn't have been that he didn't want her with him? He'd left in such a rush, and she'd felt a distinct coldness in his farewell. Ellen shivered, although it was a warm day. Enough of feeling sorry for herself. She had things to do. She'd promised Jenny to go with her to see this Shirley woman today, then to meet with Mike afterwards. She perked up. Maybe this would bring the breakthrough they'd been looking for.

Standing at Shirley's door around an hour later, Ellen met Jenny's eyes and crossed her fingers. Were they really going to find an answer in this neat weatherboard cottage? She scanned the tidy front yard, filled with a selection of colorful flowering plants. This wasn't the home of a doddery old lady. The woman who lived here took pride in her home and most likely had a sharp brain to match.

"Come in, come in. You must be Jenny and Ellen." The owner of the voice was bent with age, but behind her spectacles her eyes were alive with interest in her visitors. They were ushered into a neat lounge room where they sat down on matching velour armchairs, Shirley making herself comfortable on what was clearly her favorite velvet recliner facing a large television.

Refusing tea or coffee, Ellen got straight to the point.

"I understand you knew my uncle Jed?"

"And you said he was your father too, dear?" Shirley turned her wrinkled face toward Jenny. "My, oh, my. At the time we heard rumors, but we didn't… oh my!" She took a tissue from the box, sitting on a side table and patted her eyes. "Jed." Her voice wavered and her eyes took on a faraway look. "He was quite a lad. So handsome. So charming. We were all crazy for him. Now, what did you want to know?"

"We spoke with Bill and Ann Huggins," Ellen said. "They remembered Uncle Jed opposing a development plan… when you worked in City Hall."

"Oh, my dear. That was a long time ago. But I do remember

something. I had a bit of a crush on him." She smiled coyly. "That's what we called it back then. He knew that and asked me to find some paperwork for him."

"And?"

"I was too junior to be allowed access to the papers he wanted. I just remember it had something to do with the original purpose of the land. And there was the tsunami issue, of course."

Ellen latched on to the first part of Shirley's answer while Jenny's breath hissed, and she whispered, "Tsunami?"

"Yes, over fifty years ago. An earthquake devastated Alaska, and the resulting tsunami swamped Oregon, many lives were lost."

"I had no idea."

"It's a fact of life around here," Ellen said, dismissively. "So Shirley do you remember anything at all about what Jed had in mind?"

"Only what he wrote down, dear."

"Wrote down?" Ellen could hear her voice rising as excitement began to bubble up inside. "He wrote something down? Something you remember?"

"I have it right there in my box," Shirley said to their surprise. "I kept everything from then. All my old school photos, cards, notes. When you get to my age, sometimes the past is more real than all that stuff on television." She reached down to the bottom shelf of her side table and pulled out an old shoebox. "It'll be in here somewhere."

Shirley began ferreting away inside the box while Ellen and Jenny curbed their impatience. Finally, just as they'd almost given up hope, Shirley produced a much folded yellowing piece of paper.

"Here it is." Shirley balanced the box on her knees while she slowly and carefully unfolded the paper. "I'm afraid the writing's a tad faded after all this time. But it's from Jed, that's for sure." She propped her glasses further up her nose and read it to herself before handing it to Ellen. "I'm not sure how it'll help."

Ellen gingerly took the sheet of paper, the blue lines of ink now so faded they were almost indistinguishable. She held it up to the light. "Do you…"

"You'll be wanting a magnifying glass," Shirley said. "Hold on." She rose and made her way slowly out of the room while Ellen and Jenny looked at each other in amazement.

Shirley returned with a basket full of magnifying glasses in various shapes and sizes, which she proffered to Ellen. Taken by surprise, Ellen picked up one at random, only to find it came equipped with a light. Holding it over the paper, she could just make out the words 'tribal' and 'termination'. It didn't make any sense to her. She held the paper this way and that but the only other words she could distinguish were 'please' and 'Jed'. She laid it down despondently.

"I'm not sure this will help," she said, "but you might want to see Jed's signature, Jenny."

Jenny took the flimsy piece of paper and pored over it. "That's all that's left of him," she said sadly at last. "Thanks, Shirley." She handed it back to the old woman.

"I'm sorry if it's been a disappointment to you," Shirley carefully returned the item to her box and tucked it back under the table. "It was a dreadful time. Jed raised a group of protesters and they marched on City Hall trying to stop the building work, but old man Miller practically ran the town in those days. Jed almost ended up in jail," she sighed. "He was such a handsome young man."

"Thanks so much for your time," Ellen rose to go. "I think you've been of some help. It was kind of you to share your memories with us."

"I was happy for the company," Shirley replied as she slowly showed them to the door. "Sometimes it's very lonely here. I might not talk to a living soul for days. Thank goodness for my cat." But she smiled as she spoke, giving the women the impression that sometimes her pet might be preferable to some humans.

Driving away, Ellen repeated the words she'd read, "Tribal... termination. Wasn't there something about a Termination Act back in the forties?"

"Don't ask me. You're the local... and the Native American. I bet Mike can fill us in. I forgot to bring his papers, but we'll be with him soon."

"Surely," Ellen replied, then became lost in thought for the remainder of the trip.

"I said one o'clock, and here we are," Jenny said as they drew into a parking spot outside *Mo's*.

"And there's Mike waiting for us," Ellen said catching sight of him standing gazing over the river.

Once inside and their orders placed for Cannonball bowls – bowls of sourdough bread filled with *Mo's* famous clam chowder – and beer, Jenny began to regale Mike with the tale of their visit to Shirley.

"So, you see," she finished. "We're really no further forward, unless…"

"But we are," Mike sounded pleased. "It ties in with what I found yesterday. Back in the period from mid-forties through the mid-sixties, there was what was called The Termination Policy."

Jenny and Ellen looked at each other, and Ellen repeated, "Termination. What does it mean?"

"It's a bit complicated, but essentially it involved trust land being removed from protected status during those years. Much was sold by individuals to non-Natives."

"So that's what Uncle Jed was protesting?" Ellen asked.

"Seems like it."

"But how does that help us now? That was a long time ago."

"That's just it," Mike's voice held a trace of excitement. "This morning I came across documents indicating there'd been a change of opinion in the seventies and eighties, and much of the earlier recommendations had been overturned. Now, this might not be tribal land *per se*, but since you're a Native American, Ellen, we should have a good case." He'd been leaning forward as he spoke and now he sat back.

"So what do we do now?" Ellen asked.

"I checked, and there's a council planning meeting at seven on Tuesday. There's the opportunity for members of the public to speak on items not on the agenda. What do you say?"

"Tuesday. That's tomorrow. I say we go."

The three spent the remainder of their lunch making plans for the upcoming council meeting, with Ellen promising to round up as many of the shop owners as possible at this short notice. When they parted on the sidewalk, Ellen had a new sense of purpose. She re-checked the text she'd received from Travis the day before. The second reading didn't provide any more information than the first. He'd arrived in Carpinteria. That was all. She turned off her cell and put it back in her pocket. No sense worrying about that now. She had other matters to take care of.

Thirty-two

Ellen clenched her hands in her pockets as she entered City Hall and walked along the corridor to the small room. It was one she'd never had cause to enter before, with high desks on the sides and a long table set out in front. She stepped inside, surprised to see how many people were present, and took a seat on one of the small blue chairs, breathing a sigh of relief when Jenny and Mike arrived and slipped in beside her.

The meeting progressed in what Ellen supposed was the usual fashion, with various council members moving and voting on agenda items. As the evening wore on, she became more and more agitated. Were they ever going to have an opportunity to put their case? However, eventually, the chairperson faced the audience and asked for any further matters of business.

Mike nudged Ellen, and she warily stood up. Once on her feet, it was easy to speak. When she referred to the development planned for the shops, Ellen was startled to hear a murmur of support and looked around in surprise. When she arrived, she'd been too engrossed in her own thoughts to notice many of her neighboring shopkeepers among the crowd. Their presence provided her with the encouragement she needed to continue to argue vociferously for a stay to the development, citing Jed's original objections as evidence there needed to be further consideration of the matter.

Ellen sat down to a round of applause, while the gentleman chairing the meeting gazed around his fellow councillors.

"I think you've given us food for thought, Ms Williams," he said.

"With my colleagues' agreement I propose to convene a special gathering of the planning sub-committee to consider what you've brought to our attention." There was a series of nods, and the meeting declared closed.

"Well done," Mike hugged Ellen as they stood to leave.

"Do you think…?"

"I do."

"You were wonderful," Jenny added. "They're going to put a stop to it, I'm sure. Did you see how the guy on the end looked at the others when you mentioned your uncle Jed? You've blinded them with history. Balcombs don't have a chance now."

"I wish I had your certainty," Ellen was doubtful. "It still has to go to the other committee. They may only have been paying lip service to my demands, given the large group supporting me," she smiled. "Wasn't it wonderful how they all turned up? At such short notice too."

"Well, you'll know in a few days. I can't see them letting it go for much longer," Mike said, as they reached their cars, supportive comments flowing around them as the others left.

"Mmm," Ellen wasn't so sure, but as she drove home her spirits lifted, and a sense of calm pervaded her. She'd done what she could. It was out of her hands. Ellen had to believe all would be well and concentrate on getting her shop up and running again. She had a meeting with a couple of tradesmen arranged for the following morning and felt a warm glow at the thought of a grand re-opening of *The Reading Nook* in the not too distant future.

Last thing before going to sleep, Ellen checked her cell phone again, hoping for another message from Travis. There was none. Should she contact him? She started to compose a message to tell him about the meeting, then deleted it. He didn't want to hear from her. Wasn't that indicated by his lack of contact?

*

Two days passed without any news, then early one morning Ellen was wakened by the ringing of her cell phone.

"Have you seen the paper?" Jenny's excited voice burst through Ellen's sleep-filled head.

"What paper?" Ellen knew she must sound dumb, but she'd been fast asleep, having stayed up late planning the shop's renovations.

"The *Siuslaw News*. Go out and pick up your copy. I'll wait."

Grumbling to herself, Ellen pulled on a robe and stepped outside to where the local paper was lying in its place below the mailbox. She opened it sleepily, standing stock still when she read the headline: *Local Shopkeeper Halts Development*. She was suddenly wide awake.

Ellen almost skipped inside to pick up her phone again. "I have it!"

"We did it! *You* did it."

"So it seems. But how… how did the paper get wind of it before us?"

"They have their contacts," Jenny replied.

"Well," Ellen curled up on the sofa ready for a lengthy chat, but Jenny was all business.

"I think you should contact the paper, give them your side of things, then… Have you been in touch with Travis?"

This wasn't what Ellen wanted to hear. She drew her fingers though her hair before answering. "No, I don't … He hasn't contacted me, Jenny. Only a brief text to say he'd arrived – and that was days ago. I've no idea what's going on down there."

"He's a man," Jenny replied, as if that said it all. "It's up to you. You do care for him, don't you?"

"Ye…es," Ellen pulled her hair over her face, nibbling the ends as she remembered Travis wrapping his hands and face in it. She shivered. "But…" she objected.

"Don't be a fool. Sometimes we need to put our pride aside and make the first move. I think *you* taught me that."

"I did?" Ellen tried to remember, but failed.

*

The meeting hadn't gone well. Travis and Bob had met with Allie's parents and their lawyer in a large glass-fronted office overlooking the beach. The setting was idyllic, but the mood inside the room was far from congenial. The couple had been distraught, barely able to speak, and Travis had experienced again all the guilt he'd been trying to overcome for the past two years. Maybe they were right. Maybe he ought to be punished.

Travis strode up and down in his hotel room, his fingers curling unto fists inside his pockets. He wanted to punch someone, but the only person he could come up with was himself. He was back in the cave he'd entered two years ago. It was a dark and dank place. A tentative knock at the door drew him out of it long enough for him to stare at the painted wooden surface as if in a trance. The knock came again, more forcefully this time. Reluctantly, Travis took his hands out of his pockets and opened the door.

"What…" he began belligerently, stopping mid-sentence when he saw his father standing there, hand raised as if to knock for a third time. "Dad?"

"Son, we were worried about you."

"No need." Travis knew his voice was bitter. He didn't want – didn't need – sympathy or help. He had to cope with this by himself, the way he had before. Ignoring the small voice telling him he hadn't coped very well then, he continued, "I'm fine, Dad. You and Mom," his voice seemed to catch, and he found himself sitting on the bed, his head in his hands. He was conscious of the door closing and felt the bed sag as the older man sat down beside him. The arm which curled around his shoulders felt strange, but the comfort it brought was oddly welcome.

"Your mom said I should come… to see how you were coping. We haven't heard from you since you arrived at our door on the weekend – that was days ago. She wanted me to make sure you weren't…" his voice died away, leaving Travis to only imagine what his mom might have been thinking.

"Have…" his father cleared his throat. "Have you seen the Dodds? Your solicitor… what does he have to say?"

"Yes," Travis sighed. "We met yesterday with our lawyers. It's not good. They want their pound of flesh – my flesh." He raised his eyes to meet his dad's. "If I could bring them back, I would. I'd give anything. It should have been me, then everyone would have been happy."

"Don't take on so. Of course everyone wouldn't have been happy. How do you think Allie would have felt with you gone? And little

Ricky, growing up without his dad? And how about Mom and me? I can see how the Dodds want to blame you – and maybe you even want to blame yourself. But it wasn't your fault, son. They said so at the time. We just have to make the Dodds see that. Nothing they do is going to bring their daughter back… or their grandson, and ours." He sighed, wiping a tear from his eye. "Now, your lawyer," he repeated, "what does he say? What's the next step?"

Travis stood up and went over to stare out the window before replying. He gazed out at the busy street, then turned abruptly.

"He's talking mediation. Seems we sit down with some other guy and try to come to some agreement or other." He grunted. "Agreement? Don't see how that can happen."

"Well, then, that's something." His dad rose. "Your mom would like you to come home. She doesn't like to think of you all alone holed up in this hotel room."

"She probably wants to feed me up," Travis tried to crack a smile. "And you, Dad. What do you want?"

"I just want this to be all over. Come home with me, Travis. You'll feel better with family around you."

"Thanks, Dad. I appreciate it. But I've got to do it my way." He stretched out his hand to shake his dad's but instead was enveloped in warm hug.

"You know where we are if you change your mind, son. We love you."

After his dad had left, Travis felt more alone than ever. He didn't deserve his parents' love and support. He should have known it would all turn to shit. He hadn't been writing since he came down here either. What was the point? He looked at his cell phone lying on the bedside table, remembering a similar phone lying on a similar bedside table in Canada. He thought of Ellen and the peace he'd found with her. She hadn't let diversity pull her down. If anything, it had made her stronger.

The urge to contact her, to hear her voice was so great, he picked up the phone. His finger was almost on the dial when it buzzed to signal an incoming text: *We won – no development. Ellen X*

A tiny surge of hope broke through Travis' self-pity. So things were turning out well up there in Florence. Good. Ellen deserved good things to happen. She was a worthy person. He drew himself up. And he wasn't? Is that what he'd been thinking? His mom and dad thought he was. Ron thought he was. Allie had thought he was. Little Ricky had loved and respected his father. Where had all this self-doubt and blame come from? Was he going to continue to allow the accident and the Dodds to ruin his life? He forced his fingers to dial Ellen's number.

*

"So I'll drive down tomorrow, right? Should be there by the weekend. It's so good to hear your voice. I thought… well, never mind what I thought. It sounds as if you could do with someone on your side in the next round of this legal stuff. You do want to see me…?" Ellen's voice tailed off. She could hear Travis coughing on the other end, and paused to allow him to speak.

"Sure. You guys did good up there. Maybe you can work some of your magic for me down here. I wouldn't have called if…"

"I'm glad you did." Ellen couldn't stop the bubble of excitement which threatened to engulf her. Travis had called. It had been a bit of a strange call, but somehow here she was arranging to drive down to be with him. Jenny had been right to encourage her to make the first contact. It had only been a short text, but his call had come almost immediately.

When she hung up, Ellen did a dance around the room, glad no one could see her. A quick call to Jenny, and she felt at a loose end. She started to pack a small bag, but couldn't work out what to take. Finally she forced herself to sit down and make a list. Then she needed to call her mom.

"I'm going way for a few days, driving down to California," Ellen bit her lip. Her parents still didn't know anything about Travis, and now wasn't the time to tell them. Maybe there was nothing to tell, never would be.

"That's nice, dear," Rita said. "Do you good to get away after all you've been through. I saw the paper… about that development being stopped. You'll be pleased about that. Have a nice little vacation and come back refreshed."

"Dad…" Ellen wasn't sure what she wanted to say.

"I'll be with Dad… as much as I can. It's not easy," Rita sighed. "But you have your own life, and I'll have Ron's company… and Coralie."

"Yes, Ron and Coralie." Ellen still couldn't get used to how her brother and Coralie had suddenly become a regular couple. It even seemed as if, with Coralie's encouragement, Ron was thinking of setting himself up to market his wood sculptures. She shook her head in disbelief.

"Well, I'll be off now, Mom. Might make a start tonight. You know how to reach me if…" She didn't envisage anything dire happening to her dad while she was gone, but one never knew.

Ellen repeated the words to herself, "Make a start tonight." She hadn't intended to leave till morning, but being summer it was light till late, and she could make a good distance before dark if she set out now. She locked up the house and, throwing her bag into the car, drove off towards Eugene and Highway Five. With a bit of luck she'd make it to the Californian border before dark. She could stop at Ashland or travel right through to Lake Shasta. Ellen couldn't wait to see Travis again, though she was aware she might have to play it cool. He was going through a difficult time and was likely to disappear into his cave at the slightest opportunity. She was going to have to put all of her own insecurities aside and support him.

Thirty-three

Ellen drew up in front of the *Holiday Inn* and gazed at the heavy columns and beams of the entrance. So this was where Travis was holed up. She was unsure what to do. It was late, and he wasn't expecting her until morning. Should she check his room or take one of her own and see him next day as arranged? Ellen was still debating the issue as she locked her car, so didn't see the figure walking towards her till she felt herself enfolded in a strong pair of arms.

"What…?" Ellen began to panic, then recognizing the distinctive scent and feel of the man holding her, relaxed into his arms. "Travis," she murmured, turning to lean into his solid chest.

"You're here!" Travis' words were unnecessary, but spoken with such heartfelt gratitude that Ellen experienced a warm glow of something she couldn't quite recognize. "I wasn't…" He released her only to hold her at arm's length and devour her with his eyes. "Oh, honey. I've missed you."

"I couldn't wait," Ellen said. "Once I knew I was coming down, it just made sense to get started. I…" She looked around.

"You must be tired. Your bag?"

"Here," she gestured to the ground.

Travis picked up Ellen's small bag. "Is this all?"

"I travel light."

My God, thought Ellen, we're back to one syllable conversation, but he did say he missed me, so it must be all right.

Once in Travis' room, Ellen looked around. Like most motel rooms, it was pretty stark. No sign of books or computer, she noticed. So he wasn't writing.

"Coffee?"

"That'd be good," Ellen suddenly realized how exhausted she was. It had been a long trip. She sank down on the king-sized bed and watched Travis make coffee. Her eyes drank in his broad shoulders, long legs and tight butt as he added boiling water to the instant coffee. God, how she'd missed him. Now she was here with him again, she could admit it to herself. In the short time she'd known him, he'd become important to her – more important than she liked. She'd vowed never to get this involved with a man again, yet here she was with one who was as – if not more – complicated than any man she'd known.

Travis joined Ellen on the bed as they drank their coffee, both swinging their legs up and leaning back on the soft pillows.

"I guess it's been tough?" Ellen said.

"Tough doesn't begin to describe it. Allie's folks are obdurate. They want someone to take the blame. The truck driver's dead, so I'm the only one left. I should have died too."

"Don't say that!" Ellen carefully placed her cup on the bedside table and turned to comfort him. As she wrapped her arms around his shoulders and nuzzled into his neck, all of the worry of the past few months seemed to pour out of her. She knew she had to be strong for Travis. She willed her strength into him and felt him gradually relax, the tension in his body seeming to seep away.

"You make me whole again," he murmured into her hair. "Can I…?" He opened the buttons of her shirt and pushed aside her bra, his head dropping to enable his lips to fasten on her nipples. A flame of desire swept through her, forcing her body closer to his. Travis removed his mouth from Ellen's breasts, and they began to tear at each other's clothes till they were both naked. They were in need – great need. It had only been a week, but both had been under such a strain, that it had seemed much longer. Ellen knew that, in Travis, she had found her soul mate, and it seemed he felt the same way about her. There was no need for words. His actions said it all, as his fingers traced her body causing her to shudder with anticipation. By the time he entered her, Ellen was shaking with an intense longing for him, a longing that could only be satisfied by his gentle touch.

When they finally drew apart, their bodies a sheen of sweat, Travis swept aside Ellen's hair, which had become disentangled from her usual plait, and cupped her face in his hands. "Oh, my darling."

Ellen felt his warm breath on her face, then his lips met hers in a long kiss. She sighed as it ended, and her eyes began to close.

*

Travis awoke to the feeling of Ellen's soft, warm body against him. His arms were around her waist, and their bodies were so tightly enmeshed, it was difficult to determine where one stopped and the other began. He lay for a moment relishing the sensation of flesh on flesh, before turning his companion around to face him.

"Good morning," he muttered into the cloud of Ellen's hair, as he breathed in her unique scent. "How are you this morning? Sleep well?"

"I sure did," Ellen murmured, stretching out her body to meet the length of his, their toes touching in a delightful movement. "You?"

"Better than I have in days," Travis admitted, realizing as he spoke that it was true. Ellen's calm had been reflected in his sleeping pattern, and he'd slept through the entire night for the first time since receiving the summons.

He drew his fingers down Ellen's back, feeling her shiver in anticipation as his hands moved lower to cup her hips. Their bodies settled into each other. It was like coming home, Travis thought. None of the frantic hunger of the previous night. That had been satisfied. This morning their loving was slower, less urgent. He moved with practiced ease, knowing exactly how to please Ellen, smiling at her moans of pleasure. Her pleasure was his pleasure. Their bodies moved in unison. They did not speak a single word.

It wasn't till they were sitting over breakfast that Ellen asked the questions Travis had been expecting.

"How did it go – the meeting with your in-laws?"

"Not good," Travis sighed heavily and laid down his mug. "We didn't make any headway. I can't say I blame them." His earlier mood forgotten, all the angst of the previous few days rose up again and threatened to overwhelm him. "I don't know…"

"It'll be all right. It *must* be." Ellen's hand covered his on the table, and her eyes met his in understanding. Then she looked down at the table and asked another question. "Your folks, they live here too, don't they? Have you…?"

"Yes and yes. I've seen them." Travis' face brightened, remembering. "Dad and Mom have been great. They wanted me to stay with them. But I couldn't inflict myself on them, not…"

Ignoring the self-loathing in Travis' voice, Ellen became more businesslike. "So, what happens next?"

"Another meeting. This time we're to be joined by someone called a mediator. It's all designed in an attempt to keep the matter out of the courts." Travis shook his head. "I can't see that happening. They're a pretty determined couple. They're consumed by grief. It's as if the grief's destroying them, and they can't let it go."

"But what good will punishing *you* do? It won't bring their daughter back." Ellen leant back as if to get a clearer picture of what Travis had told her. "When is this meeting?"

"Monday."

"Well, they're not wasting any time. Do you…? No, it wouldn't look good for me to come along."

"Definitely not. You'd be like a red rag to a bull. They'd probably try to infer I'd had you waiting in the wings," Travis said with some bitterness.

"We have the weekend. Do you want to show me around, or stay holed up here like two prisoners?"

"That's putting it a bit strong," Travis said, but he could see Ellen's point. They couldn't stay in the motel room all weekend, and his parents would expect…

"Would you like to meet Mom and Dad?" he asked suddenly.

"Wow, really?" Ellen appeared stunned. "Do they…?"

"No, I haven't mentioned you. Didn't seem right, but now you're here, I don't want to hide you." As he spoke, he realized that was exactly what Ellen had done with him, but he reasoned she had other issues to contend with back there.

"Well, if you think it'll be all right."

"I do." Travis pulled out his cell. "Mom, can I drop by this morning?

There's someone I want you and Dad to meet."

"They'll love you," Travis closed his cell and took hold of Ellen's hands again. "They want me to get on with my life, not stay lost in the past. As I have been for the past two years," he said with a sigh. "You're my future, Ellen. If..., but right now I've nothing to offer you. A man facing charges of manslaughter," he said bitterly. "I'm no good to anyone."

"Don't say that." Travis felt Ellen's hands tighten in his as she spoke. "There's always hope."

"I suppose you can see a positive resolution to all this? Isn't that how it all works for you?"

"No, not always."

Travis saw Ellen bite her lip and immediately regretted his flippant remark, but he knew he had a lot to sort out before he had anything to offer Ellen.

"Sorry, hon," Travis released one hand and placed a finger on Ellen's lips. "We'll talk about this later. Meantime, my folks are keen to meet you."

*

"This is Ellen," Travis said, as Ellen followed him through the door of his parents' house.

"Welcome," Tom Petersen came forward to greet her with a warm handshake, while Travis' mom followed more slowly, wiping her hands on her apron.

"I can't say Travis has told us all about you, because he hasn't." She favored her son with a mockingly stern glance. "But we're pleased to meet you," she added. "Travis did say you met in Oregon. You're from there?"

"Yes." Suddenly, the qualms Ellen had about this meeting fell away. She was going to like Travis' parents. "I grew up there. My family," she hesitated, the memory of her father rising up. "They all live there too."

"And Travis said you have a bookshop," his mom continued as the four moved into the kitchen, a large warm room filled with the aroma of freshly baked bread.

"There was a fire, Mom. Ellen's going to have to start from scratch."

"Not quite. It is a bit of a mess, but I'll soon have it up and running again."

"Ellen's a wonder," Travis said, his admiration mirrored in his expression. "She's also handled a huge development threat this year."

"And now you're down here supporting our boy." Tom drew out a chair and planted himself at the table. "It's been good to see him again. I suppose he's told you all about his past?"

"Maybe not all," Ellen said, feeling uncomfortable at this line of conversation. "Just the important parts."

"Leave off, Dad," Travis came to her rescue. "Ellen's had a hard time, and she's come out on top. She's a trouper. I just hope…" Ellen saw a frown appear between Travis' eyes.

"It's too bad we have to meet you under these circumstances," Edna Petersen said. "We'd hoped that Travis… We hadn't heard anything… Since Allie and Ricky passed…"

"She knows about them," Travis' voice was subdued.

"But now he's met you," Edna continued, "and you seem like a nice girl. Maybe you can help him – not forget. I guess he'll never do that, but help him make a fresh start."

"Girl!" Ellen smiled inwardly at the term, then held her breath. She could see mixed emotions flit across Travis' face, identifying guilt, sadness, embarrassment. Finally pleasure at her presence won, and he smiled across the table.

*

When he heard his mother speak, Travis felt as if a weight had been lifted from his shoulders. The guilt which had still been there, just under the surface, began to fade away. With his mother's words, the past had been relegated to exactly that. He'd been afraid his mom and dad might feel it was too soon, that he should still be grieving. But his mom's words put his mind at rest. He had her blessing. He felt free to move ahead with Ellen, to begin a new life. He just had to get over this stuff with the Dodds first. While he still had the threat of that hanging over him, he couldn't think of the future.

*

Ellen walked to the window and looked out for what must have been the hundredth time. The weekend had flown by, and now Travis was in the interview which could determine his future. She'd chosen to remain in the hotel room so as to be there when he returned or called to give her news, but now she wished she'd gone out. Driven up to Santa Barbara, visited the Mission, found a sidewalk café. Anything but being stuck here waiting.

She sighed, sat down, and looked at her cell phone yet again. No messages or emails since last time she'd looked. She checked her watch. Travis had been gone for three hours now. Surely there would be news soon? Maybe… But she didn't want to go there. He was a big guy. He could take care of himself, even if things had gone bad, really bad. But Ellen couldn't shift the memory of the presentiment of disaster she'd had outside her shop, the very morning Travis had walked into her life. A lot had happened since that she could link to the premonition, but what if the fates weren't finished with her yet? What if…?

Ellen's stomach fluttered, and her mouth suddenly became dry. She licked her parched lips and was reaching for a bottle of water, when her cell rang. She grabbed it clumsily. It almost fell as she saw Travis' smiling face and pressed to accept the call.

"We're downstairs. Get your ass down here. It's good news."

"What…" But he'd already rung off.

Grabbing her purse, Ellen locked the door behind her. He'd said, 'we'. Who were 'we'?

Ellen catapulted out of the elevator to see Travis standing there, a big smile on his face, and standing right beside him, wearing an equally large grin was his father. Travis moved to greet her with a big hug, and she held him tight, relief bringing tears to her eyes, as he rained kisses on her upturned face. Remembering his father's presence, she drew back, suddenly shy.

"Did…," she began.

"It's over. Dad turned up." Travis released his hold on Ellen to throw his arm around his father's shoulder, and Ellen could see the tears glistening in both men's eyes. "He…"

"That's enough," the older man's voice was gruff. "Now, you two will want to be alone… to celebrate. But remember, your mom wants you both to come for dinner tonight. No disappearing act back up to Oregon."

"As if…" Travis began, then seeming to remember his behavior of two years earlier, added, "We'll see you there. Tell Mom to lay on the fatted calf – and the champagne."

"Sure thing, son." He shook Travis' hand, gave Ellen a peck on the cheek and left.

"A late lunch?" Travis asked calmly, almost as if Ellen hadn't been waiting on tenterhooks all morning. "We can drive up to Santa Barbara."

"Okay, but…" Ellen was bursting with curiosity, unsure why Travis was taking so long to let her know what had happened, and curious as to why his dad had been there… then had left.

"Lots to tell you, but can it wait till we're sitting down somewhere private?" Travis said, clearly spotting Ellen's confusion.

Unclear why their motel room wouldn't have been private enough, Ellen allowed herself to be ushered out. She looked around. "Your bike?"

"Dad drove me back. I took a cab this morning. Can we take your car?"

By this time, Ellen's curiosity was well and truly aroused, though she was more than a little peeved. She wanted to know what had happened. This Travis, who wanted to take her off to 'a private spot' seemed to be a different person from the brooding man who'd left their hotel room this morning, preparing for the worst. There was a subdued excitement about him which was encouraging, albeit frustrating.

To Ellen's surprise, Travis didn't drive directly into Santa Barbara, but headed towards the foothills beyond the city, coming to a halt on a small hill opposite what looked like the Botanic Gardens. From the car Ellen could see a beautiful vista of the ocean and the islands.

Why had they stopped here?

Travis jumped out, then came round to open the passenger door to allow Ellen to alight. Still puzzled she stepped out of the car and raised her eyes to meet Travis' gaze. His eyes were twinkling, and his lips curled up at the corners in a delighted smile.

Taking both of Ellen's hands in his, Travis knelt down. If Ellen had been able to free her hand, it would have moved to cover her mouth. Her heart was thumping so hard, it threatened to break free, and if she'd thought her mouth was dry this morning, it was nothing compared to the way her throat tightened as Travis began to speak.

"I'm not one for the spoken word. Flowery speeches aren't my thing. But I wanted this to be special." His eyes moved and Ellen's followed them to encompass the dramatic view. This was a romantic location. "I wanted this to be memorable for you, something to take away the nightmares of the past weeks." He cleared his throat, while Ellen stood outwardly calm, but inwardly impatient for him to come to the point. "Now that my particular nightmare is over, I can speak freely to you. I can ask you to be my wife."

Ellen couldn't believe her ears. Something in the pit of her stomach began to flutter madly. Was Travis really proposing to her? Here? Now? Before he'd even told her what had happened that morning?

"You will, won't you?"

Her thoughts in turmoil, Ellen looked down into Travis' face, the face of the man who had come to mean so much to her, the man for whom she'd risk her life, should it come to that, the man she'd been waiting for all of her life.

"Yes," she said, trying to quell the excitement building up inside her.

Ellen had a sense of *déjà vu* when Travis picked her up, as if she were light as a feather, and swung her around and around, till her head began to spin and she pleaded for mercy.

"Lunch?" she asked breathlessly, when her feet were once more on the ground and she escaped from his warm embrace, his arms relinquishing her reluctantly.

*

They were sitting in a sidewalk restaurant, having enjoyed a pasta meal, when Travis finally opened up about the morning's mediation session. Placing her hand over his, Ellen tentatively asked how things had gone, and where his father had come in.

Slowly Travis began to speak.

"Dad was a godsend. The four of us met as planned – Allie's folks, me and the mediation guy. No lawyers this time. The guy looked more like a college professor." Travis drew a hand through his hair. "A bit like I imagine Mike in his younger days – beard, glasses, cord jacket, a bit disheveled."

Ellen nodded, eager for him to continue.

"Well, this guy – Bennett – he had each of us speak, give our side of it, how we felt, that sort of thing. It was pretty uncomfortable. Allie's mom cried, her dad didn't say much. I was almost in tears myself. This Bennett, he was just asking us what outcome we'd like to see – and I knew they'd like to see me locked up or dead – when the door opened, and who should walk in but Dad."

Ellen gasped, "So…"

"That's how he came into the picture. He knew the Dodds, of course, from back then, back when we were all a family. They were as surprised to see him as I was. He had to explain who he was to the mediator. Then he was given the opportunity to speak. Wow, I saw a side of my dad I'd never seen before. The way he stood up for me, made me feel real guilty about the years I stayed out of touch."

Ellen tightened her grip on his hand which curled to clutch hers.

"Dad asked what good punishing me would do. He reminded them the police had cleared me of all blame, of the truck driver who'd caused the accident and who'd died at the scene, along with Allie and Ricky. He reminded them he'd lost a grandson too, and a much-loved daughter-in-law. He asked them how it would help – if it would bring them back – if he lost his son too. He reminded them of the beautiful memories, memories in which I played a part. God, he was magnificent." Travis paused, clearly remembering his father's words.

"Then the mediator asked his question again, about the outcome."

"And?"

"And the Dodds surprised me. Allie's mom came round the table and hugged Dad, her dad shook Dad's hand. They thanked him. Meanwhile the mediator and I sat stunned, unsure what was going on. Anyway, the result was that we all ended up shaking hands and leaving. They agreed not to pursue the matter. I can't say they were entirely happy about it, but they accepted it was never my fault. I guess they just wanted someone to blame, and they finally realized that person was dead and that we – Dad and I – had lost Allie and Ricky too." Travis dropped his eyes and sighed heavily as if in the retelling he'd been back there, back in the scene he'd described.

When he raised his head again, he was a different person. The restored Travis of the proposal scene was back. "Now," he said, "we have a visit to make."

"We do?"

"We do."

Leading Ellen to the window of a nearby jewelry store, Travis pointed to a tray of rings. "Let's do this properly," he said. "Which one do you like?"

Ellen's gaze took in the many diamond rings glittering in the sunlight. This wasn't her scene. She wasn't into bling, as some called it. "I don't…,"she began, then her eyes caught an intricately carved gold band almost hidden at the back of the window. "Now that I could wear," she declared.

"Let's go in, then."

"Engagement, sir? This is more usually purchased as a wedding ring and sold as a pair."

Wedding?

Ellen met Travis' eyes. Her throat constricted. She swallowed hard. This was all moving too fast. Then he smiled, and it was as if the sun had come out. The tension which had been threatening suddenly dissipated. This was Travis, her soul mate, the man with whom she *wanted* to spend the rest of her life. She relaxed and smiled back, the flutter in her stomach one of absolute pleasure.

"We'll take the pair."

They remained in the shop long enough to have their fingers measured and for Travis to pocket the two ornate ring boxes. They'd discuss the wedding later. It was enough that the rings had been purchased.

"Now, I think we need to seal the deal."

As they drove back to their motel, Travis began to sing. The song was an old one – *'When somebody loves you, it's no good unless he loves you… all the way.'* Ellen joined in on the last phrase, and they continued to sing all the way down to Carpinteria.

Back in their motel room, they hugged while Travis gently caressed Ellen's face and undid her hair till it formed a cloud around her shoulders.

"No more bad dreams," he said lazily.

"Only good ones," Ellen agreed, as they dropped back onto the bed.

THE END

Thank you for purchasing this book.
If you enjoyed it, please leave a review at:

http://www.amazon.com/
http://www.goodreads.com/

Acknowledgements

This book could not have been written without the help and advice of a number of people.

Firstly, My husband Jim for listening to my plotlines without complaint, for his patience and insights as I discuss my characters and storyline with him, for confirming for me the male point of view, ensuring I had the correct American terminology, for a final proofing to ensure all was culturally correct, and for being there when I need him.

John Hudspith, editor extraordinaire for his ideas, suggestions, encouragement and attention to detail.

Jane Dixon-Smith for my beautiful cover and formatting.

My writing group, the Inkstained Groupies for their support and encouragement, my critique partner, Helen, for her continuing patience and my beta reader, Louise for her willingness to read the draft of this novel.

Annie of *Annie's books at Peregian* for her ongoing support and advice.

About the Author

After a career in education, Maggie Christensen began writing contemporary women's fiction portraying mature women facing life-changing situations. Her travels inspire her writing, be it her frequent visits to family in Oregon, USA or her home on Queensland's beautiful Sunshine Coast. Maggie writes of mature heroines coming to terms with changes in their lives and the heroes worthy of them.

From her native Glasgow, Scotland, Maggie was lured by the call 'Come and teach in the sun' to Australia, where she worked as a primary school teacher, university lecturer and in educational management. Now living with her husband of thirty years on Queensland's Sunshine Coast, she loves walking on the deserted beach in the early mornings and having coffee by the river on weekends. Her days are spent surrounded by books, either reading or writing them – her idea of heaven!

She continues her love of books as a volunteer with her local library where she chairs meetings, helps organize author talks and selects and delivers books to the housebound.

A member of Queensland Writer's Centre, RWA, ALLi, and a local critique group, Maggie enjoys meeting her readers at book signings and library talks. In 2014 she self-published *Band of Gold* and *The Sand Dollar, Book One in the Oregon Coast Series*.

The sequel to *Band of Gold*, *The Broken Thread*, will be available late 2015, and the third book in the *Oregon Coast Series* will be available in 2016.

Maggie can be found on Facebook, Twitter, Goodreads or on her website.

http://maggiechristensenauthor.com/
https://www.facebook.com/maggiechristensenauthor
https://twitter.com/MaggieChriste33
https://www.goodreads.com/author/show/8120020.Maggie_Christensen

Band of Gold

Maggie Christensen

Anna Hollis believes she has a happy marriage. A schoolteacher in Sydney, Anna juggles her busy life with a daughter in the throes of first love and increasingly demanding aging parents.

When Anna's husband of twenty-five years leaves her, on Christmas morning, without warning or explanation, her safe and secure world collapses.

Marcus King returns to Australia from the USA, leaving behind a broken marriage and a young son.

When he takes up the position of Headmaster at Anna's school, they form a fragile friendship through their mutual hurt and loneliness.

Can Anna leave the past behind and make a new life for herself, and does Marcus have a part to play in her future?

The Sand Dollar

Maggie Christensen

What if you discover everything you believed to be true about yourself has been a lie?

Stunned by news of an impending redundancy, and impelled by the magic of a long-forgotten sand dollar, Jenny retreats to her godmother in Oregon to consider her future.

What she doesn't bargain for is to uncover the secret of her adoption at birth and her Native American heritage. This revelation sees her embark on a journey of self-discovery such as she'd never envisaged.

Moving between Australia's Sunshine Coast and the Oregon Coast, *The Sand Dollar* is a story of new beginnings, of a woman whose life is suddenly turned upside down, and the reclusive man who helps her solve the puzzle of her past.

What if you discover everything you believed to be true about yourself has been a lie?

A well-kept secret and a magical sand dollar. Can Jenny unravel the secret of her past?

Read on for an excerpt from *The Sand Dollar*

Prologue

Florence Oregon, July 1950

The red Chevy convertible roars into life, breaking the silence of the early morning and throwing the young couple back in their seats. The girl turns to her companion and laughs, her long dark hair rippling on her shoulders.

"We've done it!"

"Not yet, but we'll be in Mexico tomorrow if we drive all night. We'll be safe then."

"Dad'll never think of looking for us there." She hugs herself in glee. "We couldn't have managed without help."

The boy pushes a hand through his jet black mane and looks over with a tolerant smile. "We'd have found a way. You and me, we belong together." He reaches over and grabs her hand.

"Together forever!" The girl stretches out, head back against the seat. "Faster, honey. I can't wait to get there."

The car speeds on. It's early morning and the roads are clear. All is well, till they come to a sharp corner with a rock face on one side and a steep drop on the other. The car accelerates into the bend throwing the girl hard against her companion.

"Not that fast," she laughs, then her laugh turns to a scream as the car hits the rock face and ricochets out of control. "What's the matter?" she finally manages to yell, as they sway from side to side down what is now a steep incline.

"The brakes…they won't…"

The girl screams again and her hands reach down to protect her unborn child before she is engulfed in darkness, oblivious to the crash and the continuous blare of the horn which follows.

9 780099 430951 8